CITY OF SPARROWS

CITY

OF

SPARROWS

TINA MOSS

Elderberry Press, LLC
OAKLAND

Elderberry Press, LLC

1393 Old Homestead Drive, Second floor
Oakland, Oregon 97462—9506.
http://elderberrypress.com
E-MAIL: editor@elderberrypress.com
TEL/FAX: 541.459.6043

All Elderberry books are available from your favorite bookstore, amazon.com, or from our 24 hour order line: 1.800.431.1579

Library of Congress Control Number: 2004106321
Publisher's Catalog-in-Publication Data
City Of Sparrows/Tina Moss
ISBN 1-932762-11-6
1. Children——Fiction.
2. Future——Fiction.
3. Science Fiction——Fiction.
4. City——Fiction.
5. Mystery——Fiction.
6. Suspense——Fiction.
7. Murder——Fiction.
I. Title

This book was written, printed, and bound in the United States of America.

ONE

Eyes in the alley

The streets of the old city had once run with cars and buses. People had once walked all the sidewalks and crossways. Bicycles and scooters had woven through the crowds like small, fast fish. Everywhere had been noises: people shouted and called, chatted and laughed, their many conversations blurred together in a loud buzz of voices and sounds. Policemen blowing shrill whistles had directed traffic and construction workers' tools had rumbled and whirred. The old city had been the center, a metropolis; it had been alive!

Had been, once, long ago. Before the changes. The cars of the old city had long been hushed and many lay on the roads, rotting and rusting into useless hulks. The buildings of the old city were decaying and ugly, the bricks crumbling and falling to the streets below. Broken glass from windows and street lamps littered the ground, mixed with the trash and debris of long ages of litter and carelessness.

Along what had once been a main street was an alley clogged with dirt and broken, moldy boxes and bags. The mouth of this tiny street was nearly hidden behind a rust-covered bus. Through one of the shattered and grime-covered windows a pair of plain brown eyes peered, watching the few raggedly dressed people who still lived in the old city head down the street towards the long strip of factories that had been put into production not five miles away. The eyes were furtive and narrowed, covered by a thick fringe of brown hair; they glanced back and forth at the men and women who skirted around piles of trash and puddles of brackish water. No one noticed the eyes that seemed, in turn, to notice everything.

After a few minutes another set of eyes joined the first, these ones large and bright green and framed by long, dark lashes. This new arrival peered up and down the street, frowning intently at the people.

"Anything good?" the new one whispered in a voice so soft it could scarcely be heard above the harsh whistling and clanging of the nearby factories.

The owner of the brown eyes shook her head and stepped further back into the alley, brushing her bangs back from her narrow face. "Nothing," she said petulantly, kicking at a disintegrating bag full of glass bottles. "Those people are poorer than we are!"

The other, a boy, bobbed his head knowingly. "We going back uptown?"

"Yup, come on, this was a waste of time." The girl, a tall, gangly thing of thirteen years, grabbed the boy's arm and pulled him deeper into the alley. Once they were fifty feet from the battered hulk of bus they came to a broken and rusted ladder still clinging to the crumbling side of a brick building by a few stubborn bolts. The first rung, which had once been the eighth, hung two feet above the tall girl's head. Turning back to the much smaller boy, she laced her hands together, forming a cup for him to step into, and hoisted him up until he could grab the gritty, flaking rung. Once attached to this handle, the child stepped onto the girl's shoulders and, using this extra height, wrapped his arms around the rungs higher up. Holding tightly, he dangled his legs down to the girl. She jumped and grabbed his feet—he yelped as she nearly dragged him off the ladder—then caught hold of the lowest rung.

"Okay, Squirt, go ahead!" she hissed up to the boy. He began climbing up the side of the building and the girl followed, expertly avoiding a few rungs which seemed stable, but were actually broken and would plummet anyone dumb enough to grip them back into the filthy alley. She climbed steadily for several minutes, finally reaching the roof of the building. The boy helped her climb over the short edge wall.

"We're closest to One and Five, Eryyn," the boy said, glancing at his hands, a look of disgust on his face. He rubbed his rust-stained palms on his pants. "Which?"

"Five," the girl replied, hefting a ragged bag over her shoulder. "We used One last week and Otto found us there. We can't use it anymore."

The boy scowled lightly. "What about the stuff: the radio and the light-sticks…?"

Eryyn shook her head. "We lose them. Come on, let's go."

The boy followed her across the roof, grumbling under his breath. They crossed the roof and climbed carefully over a narrow gap onto another building. In this way, they crossed the block, high above those walking the street below and safe from any too heavy to climb the rickety fire escapes. It was a trick they had mastered for the closely built buildings of the old city and had served well in the past when a fast getaway had been called for.

Eryyn led the way to the fifth of their planned hiding places and lifted the sheet of corrugated fiberglass that covered the hole in the side the abandoned truck. The inside of the carriage was dark and gloomy, but soon flickered with pale, amber illumination as Eryyn lit an inexpensive light-stick.

"Make sure you close that up tight, Sawyer," she called over her shoulder as the boy struggled to fit the heavy fiberglass back over their entrance. "We don't want anyone seeing the light from out-side."

"I'm not stupid," Sawyer retorted, then furtively shifted the sheet to the left, covering a small gap he had missed. Satisfied that they were well hidden in the truck, he turned away from the sheet, blink-ing in the low light, and flopped down on an old blanket.

"I'm hungry," he mumbled, poking at his grumbling belly.

Eryyn, who'd been pawing through her bag, glanced up and nodded. "Me too, and this stuff won't bring us squat from MJ." She dumped the bag out onto the floor and kicked at the littered con-tents.

"I don't know why you picked the Dead-End. It's no use work-ing here," Sawyer stated, leaving his blanket to sift through the items at his feet. "No one here has anything worth stealing. We should have stayed Mid-End." He held up a metal chain and frowned at the light playing off the links. "This is just plated—it's not even real gold. Master John would laugh if we brought this in."

"We'll head up to MJ's in a bit and see what we can get on the way there. If we get lucky we'll pinch something that'll buy dinner tonight."

Sawyer laughed, a bright, sweet sound that was oddly out of place in the gloomy bed of the truck. "Yeah, wouldn't it be great if one of those nice, rich Sky-Enders would actually come down here, asking to be robbed, just so we could have dinner tonight?"

"We'll hit a house then," Eryyn said simply. "Even if we just get something small, it'll be better than going hungry tonight. And from now on we'll just stay Mid-End. It's safer there anyway. Now go to sleep for a bit. We'll head out at two, before anyone starts home."

Sawyer nodded and obeyed the order, returning to his blanket and curling up in a tight ball. Eryyn sprawled out on the floor, using the empty bag as a pillow. Within moments the two young thieves were fast asleep.

• • •

True to her word, Eryyn's sharp senses woke her just before two and she shook Sawyer until he opened his green eyes and sat up. Yawning widely and stretching, he winced at a kink in his neck and rubbed at his bleary eyes.

"I was thinking that we should try one of the places on Ninth Street," Eryyn stated as she collected their bits of junk and stuffed them back in her bag. "It's lower Mid-End, but we might be able to find a house with some good enough stuff and it's not all that far from MJ's, just ten or so blocks."

Sawyer stood up, nodding, and pushed back the fiberglass door of their hideout, stepping once again onto the street. He glanced furtively up and down the lane before nodding for Eryyn to come out. Years of life on the streets and near misses from rival homeless kids had made them both cautious of their hideouts and loot. It was a well known fact among the hundreds of homeless children who populated the streets, alleys, and abandoned buildings of the city that loot belonged to no one until it was sold at one of the pawn shops. Until then anything was fair game, even in the hands of a thief. Often times, the larger and stronger thieves simply waited until they saw someone smaller with items worth taking, saving themselves the trouble of breaking into houses or working the crowds.

They met no trouble on their long walk from the truck to Ninth Street. The streets of the Mid-End were much newer and cleaner than the so called Dead-End. There were hundreds of people moving to and from work places and the air was heavy with the fumes of the nearby factories that kept the city running. Here in the Mid-End could be found small fragments of the way the original city had once been, many years ago, before the Enforcers had taken over and divided the city into its three sections: a lady walking her small dog, two co-workers meeting for lunch at a small outdoor restaurant, or group of young women waiting impatiently to cross the street.

Sawyer and Eryyn were well trained in the art of being inconspicuous. No one took notice of the two thin, scruffy children dressed in mismatched rags who wandered down the street and, by the time they reached their destination, the two had added a watch and two rings to their sack of plunder.

"This is actually enough to satisfy MJ," Eryyn said, peeking at a ring before dropping it into the sack. "It's silver, and that watch is really nice, but I think we should still bring something better. We haven't brought him anything really good for a while and he may start refusing us."

"So?" Sawyer said, leaning against a wall and scratching at an itch on his cheek. "Would that really be such a loss? There *are* other brokers…"

"None as good," Eryyn interrupted. "Master John gives the best prices."

"He's a jerk."

"It's worth dealing with him to make more money. Now stop complaining and start looking around, it's already past three." Eryyn held up the watch as proof of her statement. Sawyer, who'd never learned to tell time, squinted at the watch face, shrugged, and followed his friend down the wide lane.

Ninth Street was not a prosperous place, but it was far above the squalor of the Dead-End. The people who lived on Ninth Street worked in the factories and made enough to live comfortably, if not well. The street was lined with apartment buildings, most over five stories tall, and was kept relatively clean and free of the litter that so quickly accumulated in the lesser parts of the city. The street lamps here actually had bulbs that worked and were covered with a milky glass shield against rocks and other projectiles. A plastic wagon lay on its side in one gutter, abandoned by its owner for something more interesting and, from somewhere up ahead, a dog barked lazily, as if to warn the street's inhabitants that unworthy visitors were around.

Sawyer stopped near the wagon, looking at it curiously as Eryyn gazed around at the houses, biting her lip thoughtfully. The streets here were nearly empty of people—the adults all went to work, just to afford the rent, and the children were lucky enough to be in schools. The place was simply asking to be robbed.

Grabbing Sawyer's reaching hand and dragging him away from the wagon before he could touch it, Eryyn made her way down the sidewalk, looking carefully at each apartment house, trying to assess the worth from the way it was kept on the outside. Finally she paused in front of one building and stared for a long moment at the peeling gray paint and the neat row of flowers arranged in cheap plastic pots on the walkway. A chain link fence separated the double-decker from the street, but its gate was open, swaying and creaking gently in the late summer breeze. The windows were washed and hung with bright curtains and, from her vantage point on the street, Eryyn could see a straw welcome mat in front of one of the doors on the porch.

"I think this is the one," she muttered. "Do you think you could fit through there?" She pointed a finger to the right side of the house, at a low window just an inch or so above the ground that probably led into a basement. The glass was propped open with a small plank.

Sawyer glanced at the window and immediately nodded. Checking up and down the street, assuring himself that no one was around, he pushed through the gate and slipped into the small yard. With Eryyn at his side, he knelt down by the window and pulled it open wider. Once it was fully open the girl grasped the wooden frame and held it steady while Sawyer dropped down on his stomach and started to wriggle through the narrow opening.

Sawyer, at ten, was a small child—skinny and short—and he easily fit through the tiny window that would have trapped anyone larger. Wriggling his head and shoulders through the small opening, he looked down for someplace where he could safely drop. Eryyn, kneeling beside his legs, grew impatient with his careful prodding and gave him a hard shove. Overbalancing, Sawyer toppled into the basement with a yelp of surprise.

"*Hey...ow!*"

Eryyn winced as he thudded against the floor. Leaning forward she hissed into the window, "Keep it quiet, will you!"

"That hurt!" Sawyer's indignant voice floated up from the dark space past the window. "I landed on my head!"

"Then there was no harm done! Hurry up, you have five minutes!"

A flurry of grumbled oaths and curses answered her as Sawyer picked himself up and wandered away from the window. Eryyn settled down into a low crouch outside, glancing back to the street every few minutes just in case someone should happen to walk by and see her. Biting her lip, hating this part of the job the most, she tried to stay patient and calm while waiting for Sawyer to finish up inside the house.

Slowly the minutes slipped by and Eryyn grew more and more anxious. When she heard someone whistling a tune nearby she nearly bolted and only stayed where she was by biting her lip and pinching her arm painfully hard. Finally a small hand reached up over the edge of the windowsill, holding a small, square-shaped machine. Two oversized rings were dangling from the middle and index fingers and a necklace was wrapped around the wrist.

With a gasp of relief and delight, Eryyn reached forward and grabbed the jewelry and the small machine, stuffing them into her sack before reaching back into the basement to give Sawyer a hand out. The boy was grinning triumphantly as he presented her with a pocketful of costume jewelry and a set of bronze candlestick holders. He was wearing two new shirts—both were too large—one of which he stripped off and gave to his friend.

"There's a lot more little junk in there that they won't miss for a while. I could go back and get some," Sawyer offered as Eryyn thrust the candlestick holders into her bag. She sifted through the costume jewelry before stowing it away and shook her head.

"Five minutes in each house, that's the rule, Squirt. We don't wanna risk getting caught. Remember that house on Twelfth Street? Remember what happened when *you* decided it wouldn't hurt to stay just a *little* longer?"

Sawyer blushed deeply. "You don't have to remind me. I got away."

"Just barely. Come on, MJ's gonna like some of this stuff. You did really good. We'll be able to eat tonight."

Sawyer stood and began working the buttons on his new shirt. "Good, I'm starving. Make sure you get a good price on the silver ring—I think the purple stones are real. Don't let Master John cheat you on it."

"You're one to talk. You'd hand over everything for free if he so much as looked at you cross-eyed."

"He's creepy!" Sawyer said in his defense.

Eryyn rolled her eyes and didn't reply. Standing up, she shrugged into the new shirt and flipped the bag onto her shoulder. Brushing a few dried blades of grass off her patched and much faded jeans, she beckoned for Sawyer to follow and stepped out of the yard and back onto the street.

"Hey, you kids! What are you doing by that house! Get away from there!" An elderly man dressed in blue pants and a knitted sweater came hurrying towards them, waving a walking stick in one hand.

Sawyer immediately paused and smiled innocently, knowing that to run would be to admit their guilt. "We thought we heard a kitten, sir," he lied smoothly, using the story he and Eryyn had thought up just for this purpose. "It sounded like it fell down in that window over there. We just wanted to see it." He pointed to the yard they had just vacated and the window that they had propped open in its original spot. The man's eyes followed his gesture and he frowned.

"If there's a cat in there it probably belongs to the owner. Didn't you two think about that?" He turned back to the children and looked them over carefully, noting their dirty hair and faces and the clean, oversized shirts that were a startling contrast against their faded pants and worn shoes. "I haven't seen you two around here before. What house do you live in?"

"We live on Twelfth Street," Eryyn said promptly, "and we were just taking a little walk." She tossed her straight hair back behind her shoulders and sneered, "That's not illegal here, is it?"

The man raised his eyebrows at her heavy sarcasm. "You should learn how to respect your elders, young lady," he said, pointing a finger at her. "Anyone dressed like you has no right being smart-mouthed."

"Hey, she ain't no lady to begin with," Sawyer said flippantly, "and her clothes are none of your business. She looks a lot better than you do." Before the man could reply, the little boy grabbed Eryyn's hand and dragged her down the street, turning a corner and moving out of sight. They waited for a moment, half expecting the man to follow them, then hurriedly moved on, crossing an intersection onto Eleventh Street.

"Whew, that was too close," Eryyn mumbled once they were back on the main street. She ran her hand across her brow dramatically. "Just think of what he would have seen if I'd let you to go back into the house."

Sawyer scowled. "You're right. He would have seen me coming back out." The boy glanced over his shoulder as if still expecting to see the man coming after them. "Old jerk should learn to mind his own business."

"He's a grown-up, they never mind their own business. That's why you can't trust any of 'em. They're nothing but trouble. It's better just to avoid them."

"Master John is a grown-up," Sawyer pointed out. He hopped over a puddle that had formed in a large, broken section of the sidewalk; his heels came down just barely in the water, splashing a bit on Eryyn's shoes. She grimaced, shaking off her dirty, damp sneaker and replied, "Master John works with kids though, and still, the guy's a total sleaze. I wouldn't trust him as far as I can throw him—I just sell him stuff."

The rest of the walk to Master John's shop was done in near silence with only the occasional disdainful remark about a person walking by, or a thought on the next house they should hit. When they reached the pawnshop that would buy their stolen goods without question, there was a group of children already waiting outside.

"He won't take this many," Sawyer noted, standing on his tip-toes to see over the heads to the door. It didn't help. The majority of the kids at the front were taller than him. The smaller kids, as a rule of the pawnshop, hung out towards the rear of the line. They knew that if they moved forward they would only be shoved back by the bigger, tougher kids. It was sheer luck if Master John even noticed them and most usually ended up having to leave and find another shop. Sighing, Sawyer turned to Eryyn, his eyes slightly worried. "A lot of kids have found out about this place. There weren't this many last month."

"Yeah, but he knows which kids to take. I mean, look at some of the junk they're toting." Eryyn chuckled and shook her head amusedly.

Sawyer raised his eyebrows at his friend and said in a soft voice, "Just an hour ago *we* had nothing but that kind of junk." Eryyn scowled and refused to reply. Instead she took his hand and began winding and shoving through the crowd, heedless of the muttered curses that were thrown at her back. Finally she managed to push her way up to a spot near the door and stopped, yanking Sawyer's hand to move him up beside her.

"Hey, you little shrimp! You don't belong up here! Get lost!" An older girl, her blonde hair cut into short bristles and dyed with stripes of red and purple, reached out for the boy's arm, intent on forcing him back to where the smaller kids belonged.

Eryyn, more equal in size to the bully, snarled at the girl and held up a sharply knuckled fist.

"Don't even try it!" she growled. "He's with me, so back off!"

The blonde girl obeyed, holding up her hands in supplication. She took a few steps away from the pair, muttering curses under her breath and scowling fiercely. Eryyn grinned victoriously and patted Sawyer on the back.

"She must be new," she said, feeling smug, "or else she'd have known..."

Sawyer nodded quickly and shrugged away from her hand. He was undersized for his age, and he knew that if his partner hadn't stood up for him, he never would have had a chance of making it to the front of the line. Thinking this over bitterly, he leaned against the outer wall of the brick pawnshop and kicked his toe in the dirt while Eryyn turned to chat with another kid.

A moment later, a tall, teenage boy stepped out of the pawn-shop, carrying an empty sack. Behind him came a large, fat, balding man dressed in greasy jeans and a stained, torn T-shirt. The man rubbed at uneven beard stubble with one hand, spat out a spent cigarette, and raked his small, dark eyes over the crowd of waiting children.

"I ain't got time to deal with you all today!" he snapped angrily. "Do you want the double-damned Enforcers sniffin' around, wondering what's goin' on? Use some sense, fer cryin out loud!" Grabbing another cigarette from his pocket and lighting it, he pointed at five children, beckoning them into his shop, then gestured angrily for the others to leave.

Eryyn, one of the five chosen, grabbed Sawyer's hand and pulled him along as she wended her way through the grumbling cast-offs and slipped into the dim, smoke-filled pawnshop. Sawyer immediately began to cough and rubbed at his stinging eyes. Eryyn nudged him with her elbow as Master John turned around to face them. The broker grinned, recognizing the little boy. Here was a chance for a bit of fun. Stepping closer to the pair, he pulled the cigarette from his lips and blew a breath of foul smoke at the boy, wreathing him in a stinking, gray fog. Sawyer began to cough even harder.

"You got a problem, Squirt?" John asked, his voice harsh and dry from too much smoke and alcohol. "You sick or somethin'? Got something catching that you wanna spread around to the rest of the kids?" He laughed as Sawyer shook his head frantically and, still coughing, ducked behind Eryyn.

"He just can't stand the smell of this place, MJ," Eryyn replied, raising gasps from the four other children. "Why don't you open a window and let in some fresh air?"

"Fresh air, in this city?" Master John scoffed. "That ain't gonna happen any time soon. An' if he don't like it here, he can always get out." The broker pointed to the door, where several of the rejects were still hanging around, hoping for the slight chance of getting into the shop.

"He's fine," Eryyn answered, reaching behind her to pinch Sawyer into nodding, "and we got stuff to trade—good stuff. Would you rather we went somewhere else? I'm sure there's another dirty pig in this city who'll buy our junk. Someone who's smart enough to know how good we are at what we do."

Master John's beady eyes raked over the young girl and he cocked his head at his counter. Eryyn carried her bag over and tipped out its contents onto the chipped, stained surface.

"It's good stuff," she stated again, standing back as Master John took his place behind the counter and began inspecting their loot. He rummaged through a small pile of clothing, shaking his head and muttering about a waste of his time, then picked up the hand-sized machine that Sawyer had taken from the house on Ninth Street. His small eyes widened slightly and he pressed a button on the top end, causing a blinking line to appear on the narrow screen.

"A palm computer," he said, showing off his scarce amount of knowledge. "This'll do for some parts. Where'd you get it?"

Eryyn grabbed Sawyer's hand and pulled him from behind her, pushing him forward for the man to see. "*He* got it, from a place on Ninth Street—sneaked right in through a basement window." Eryyn's voice was proud as she pressed her hands against the boy's shoulders, not allowing him to shrink back from John's shrewd gaze.

"I should have known. What else did you get from there?" John turned back to the pile and pulled out the watch. He held it up, staring at it critically, then looked directly at Sawyer, expecting him to answer.

"N-not that," Sawyer stammered, watching the man test the casing of the timepiece, "we just 'pocketed that. I got those rings though, and that necklace, and the rest of the jewelry."

John glanced up again at Sawyer's pale face and grinned, showing gaps in his wide, yellow teeth. "You done good this time, Squirt. I keep telling you that ya gotta let me hook you up with this buddy I got—he can get you into some of the houses at the Sky-End. You'd make us all a fortune there." His gaze traveled over to Eryyn, who still stood behind the boy, gripping his shoulders. "The both of ya."

Eryyn stuck her chin in the air and shook her head, finally allowing her friend to take a step back. "Don't go trying to recruit *my* partner, MJ. He works with me, and no one else. And we ain't gonna join any stupid gang. We do fine on our own. Now, what will you give for all that?" She pointed a finger at the pile of loot on the counter. "Don't try to be cheap, I know you think it's worth something."

John grunted and spat loudly onto the floor, rubbing his hairy wrist across his mouth before mumbling his price.

"Too low!" Sawyer exclaimed, jumping forward. His terror of the man was momentarily forgotten in the face of scandal. "You've *got* to be kidding!"

"You just told us we've done good," Eryyn said angrily, "now give us what its worth, or we'll go somewhere else."

"You know there ain't anyplace better. Master John takes care of his kids."

"Cheats us is more like it," Sawyer muttered. "Tries to starve us."

John laughed loudly and swatted at the boy, who danced aside just in time, his lip curling in disgust.

"I'll give you thirty for the lot," John said, pulling a box out from under his counter.

Eryyn frowned thoughtfully as the man lifted out a thin, plastic credit tab. It was old and well used, but the last account on it had been erased. The security thumbprint glowed green, waiting to be activated by a new owner. She glanced around the shop, looking at the various items hanging on the walls and displayed in the glass counters. Her eyes came to rest on a nearly new pocketknife and widened with appreciation. It had four blades, a file, a screwdriver and a toothpick, all arranged and contained in a shiny red handle. She leaned over to get a better look at it, then asked John to take it out so she could test the sharpness of the blades.

"A kid named Rick brought that in last night. It's good," John stated. He handed it to her, then hovered close by in case she planned to filch it. Sawyer looked over her arm at the knife, his eyes wide as she pulled out each of the tools in turn, testing them against her palm. John was being truthful—it was a good blade.

"Add this in with the thirty," she said, setting it down on the counter beside the tab, "and we have a deal."

"Now *you're* kidding. That thing's worth twenty all by itself."

"So's that watch," Eryyn retorted. "Not to mention those two big rings and that computer-thingee. I'd say it's a fair trade, unless, of course, you'd rather pay more money…?"

Master John glowered at her deeply and grumbled, shaking his head. Eryyn shrugged and began stuffing her items back into her sack, heedless of the astonished looks she was receiving from the other thieves waiting for their turn at the counter. She had just turned to leave when John called her back, his voice low and angry.

"Get back here, you little snot!" he shouted. "I'll give you fifteen *and* the knife, how's that?"

"Twenty-eight and the knife," Eryyn countered, turning back with a grin on her face.

It was the beginning of a long and drawn out bargaining session, through which Sawyer, smart enough to let Eryyn do the haggling, and the other four children stood back to watch. The two dickered on and on, adding other items to their lists, dropping credits, then adding them back, hoping to bluff the other out with mock threats and gestures. Finally, after many minutes, when the two had run out of breath and ideas, Eryyn sold their plunder for twenty credits, the knife, and two new light-sticks.

Turning a grin to Sawyer, who rolled his green eyes in return, Eryyn pocketed the valuable knife, then watched closely as Master John ran the credit tab through his accounting machine, transferring the credits to the small computer chip inside the tab. A tiny screen beside the thumb pad flashed the number twenty and Eryyn glanced quickly at Sawyer, who nodded. Satisfied, she took the tab and pressed her thumb against the glowing pad. The color changed from green to red as the tab memorized her thumbprint, storing the image for security. Then the tab joined the knife in her pocket. She tipped her head to John, lied about how pleasant it had been doing business with him, then slipped out of the shop. Sawyer, his ears full of the broker's curses, followed right at her heels.

Outside, she pulled her knife from her pants and inspected it again, lovingly touching the slightly scratched surface of the casing and pulling out the longest of the blades to admire in the dying daylight.

"I hope you're satisfied with that," Sawyer groused as he followed her down the street. "That thing just cost us ten credits!"

"It's worth it!" Eryyn exclaimed, handing him the knife to look over. "It's a lot better than anything we can make sharpening pieces of metal against a brick."

Sawyer pulled out the file and ran his finger over its rough edge. He nodded after a moment and handed the knife back to the girl. It was useless to argue with Eryyn about something she wanted. Instead, he asked, "Can we get something to eat now? I'm really hungry, and it's getting late."

Eryyn, in a good mood because of her new knife, slung an arm over Sawyer's shoulders, pulling him close as she smiled. "Sure, and we'll camp out in Two tonight, it's the closest. So we'll get something we can actually cook, okay?" Without waiting for Sawyer to answer, she led the way down the street to a convenience market where food and other necessities could be purchased.

The clerk, a thin, scrawny man with just a little hair on his head and a short, bristly goatee on his chin, stood behind the dingy, yellowed counter and watched them closely as they wandered up and down the aisles. He cleared his throat loudly whenever they touched anything and his eyes narrowed as Sawyer longingly inspected the candy racks.

The boy, finally tiring of the gaze, turned and stuck his tongue out at the man. Even after years of living on the streets as a thief, Sawyer knew better than to steal from a store when they had money. Stealing was only for survival, and neither he nor Eryyn had any thoughts of taking something out of the store that wasn't bought and paid for. It bothered Sawyer that the clerk, who would eagerly take their money once they showed it, had to be so hostile and suspicious.

Joining Eryyn at the bread rack, he muttered to her in a low voice, cocking his head towards the pay counter. Eryyn turned to look at the man, who leaned on his elbows, glaring at them. She narrowed her eyes.

"Is something wrong?" she asked coldly, placing her hands on her hips.

The clerk pointed a long finger at her. "I'm watching you kids, so don't even *think* of taking anything. Unless you want to spend the night in an Enforcer station jail cell."

"I don't know, that might be a nice change," Sawyer quipped, tucking a loaf of bread under his arm. "At least the food there would be *fresh*, not something that came off the skimmer *six* weeks ago."

"That's fresh!" the clerk exclaimed, his sallow cheeks beginning to color as he caught the hint that his wares were old and stale.

Sawyer lifted his loaf of bread and looked at it skeptically, his brows raised. "Feels kinda hard to me," he mused.

"It was just shipped in this morning, and if it doesn't sell, I'd be throwing it out tomorrow. Nothing sold here is old."

Eryyn picked a can of soup off a shelf and blew a thick sheen of dust off the top. "Nothing?" she asked, grinning wickedly. Another breath set loose a cloud of gray that drifted slowly to the floor. Sawyer, standing too close, sneezed and started to laugh. He shook his arms and hands, brushing the dust away.

Bright spots of red now highlighted the clerk's cheeks and he hissed something rude under his breath. Eryyn, with a flip of her shoulder-length brown hair, turned away from the man and continued shopping.

When they finally brought their purchases up to the counter, after many minutes and much handling of other items, Eryyn whipped out the credit tab, with the flashing number twenty on the front, and held it out for the clerk to see. "And we *actually* have money…how about that, huh?" She smiled thinly as she leaned on the counter, waving the tab near the man's nose.

The clerk didn't reply and started adding up the items. When he was finished, Eryyn handed over the tab, which the man ran through his accounting machine. Eryyn then thumbed the small, electronic pad on the screen of the computer and eight of their credits were instantly deducted. Snatching back the tab, she accepted the crumpled bag the man pushed across the counter to her.

"It's been a real pleasure doing business with you, sir," she said, smiling brightly. "I do hope you have a good night."

Sawyer snorted back another laugh and held open the door for his friend. He, too, smiled sweetly at the clerk before stepping back out onto the street and, as a parting blow, pulled a candy bar out from his shirt pocket, held it up for the man to see, then tossed it on the floor.

"You should learn to watch better." He grinned and slipped out the door before the clerk could speak.

• • •

Of all the places they'd claimed for hideouts in the city, Nest Two was Sawyer's favorite. The closest of all their little nests to the central Mid-End marketplace, Two was situated on the top floor of a building doomed to be razed in the near future to make room for more Sky-End-like high-rises. Luckily for them, no one had yet seen fit to finish the job and the old apartment complex still stood, its windows and doors boarded up, the grass in the small front lawn overgrown and full of weeds. The only way into the place was through an upper window. The boards there had been torn away by a storm, revealing a space just large enough for the skinny bodies of street urchins to wiggle through. This window could be reached by climbing a diseased, old tree in the side yard, and crawling along one of the larger branches on the stomach until the window ledge could be grabbed. Then it was a simple matter of pulling oneself through the small space and dropping to the floor, taking care to avoid the littered shards of glass underneath.

Simple.

At least it was to Sawyer and Eryyn, who had been using the place as a nest for nearly a year. With practiced ease, they climbed the tree and shimmied out along the branch, sliding through the window one at a time.

The room they had claimed as their own was dry and stayed relatively warm for most of the day. They had stocked it with the best of their belongings: a few blankets folded into a sleeping pallet, a small paraffin stove rescued from a trash can and restored to working order, two dented pots and spoons, and a handful of light-sticks.

There were also three old books, the pages torn and dog-eared, the covers mostly missing, that belonged to Sawyer. These beloved prizes were kept tucked away safely under his side of the pallet.

When several of the light-sticks were operated, and the paraffin stove filled the room with warmth, the two children were quite cozy and comfortable. And, more importantly, they were safe, hidden from the dangers that lurked the streets outside at night. No one could climb into the room without their knowing, and, by the time the stranger made it, if they made it, the two would be long gone, hidden again in the lower levels of the house.

But it was not the safety of the house that made it Sawyer's favorite hiding spot, nor the little stove that kept them as warm as a heat-rod, or the collection of treasures they had stored there over the months. It wasn't the fact that while they were in the house, they were actually able to cook the canned soup and plain, starchy bread that had become the normal fare for the lesser folk since the decline of the original city and the old government. What drew him to the house, time and again, was the view.

One window in the room still had all its glass behind the wooden boards that covered it. One board had been pulled away long before, offering a grand view of the hill that was known as the Sky-End. This area, built after the Grand Election of Enforcer power, was filled with the houses of people who owned and operated the factories, or held a high government position, like Enforcer. It was splendid compared to the squalor that was the original city, now called the Dead-End. The houses were enormous skyscrapers, clean and bright and new against the smog-filled sky. There were no broken windows up there on the hill, no trash-littered alleys, or car-lined streets. The people of the Sky-End owned personal skimmers or flitters to take them back and forth to their businesses—from his spot at the window, Sawyer had often seen the flying vehicles winking in and out between the buildings. The Sky-End was rich and prosperous, thriving on the work done by the lower workers of the Mid and Dead-Ends.

And, up on the hill, the windows glowing with a warm, yellow light, was the house that constantly filled Sawyer's dreams. Even at a distance he could tell that it was one of the newer models, sided in pearly white metal, and rising more than thirty stories above the grass of the hill, but that was all he *really* knew of the place.

In his mind, he imagined a large lawn in front that was well manicured, lined with trees and flowers. Maybe a tire swing hung from one of the trees, just like in a picture of one of his books. The automated front door was made of frosted glass and never locked, and small pots with sweet-smelling flowers flanked the walkway. Up on the hill, the people had *real* houses, not the crumbling apartment complexes of the lower ends that were left over from more than a century ago. Up on the hill, children didn't have to worry about finding enough to eat or where to sleep, or whether they would grow up ignorant because they couldn't go to school. *They* didn't have to avoid gangs, who would just as soon kill them as allow them to join up. And *they* didn't have to hide from the En-forcers, who thought nothing of catching and selling homeless chil-dren to the factories for extra money and passing it off as keeping the streets clean of filth.

Life on the Sky-End hill seemed to be simple and happy and comfortable. It had to be—at night, the houses shone like the gems in the rings he stole, only much more beautifully. They stood high above the lesser ends, above the dirt and grime, the rats and dis-eased strays, above the gangs and the Master Johns, above the store clerks who charged too much for food no better than the rations the Enforcers doled out to all the legal citizens. The people of the Sky-End, with their gem-like houses, lived in paradise. At least as far as Sawyer was concerned.

And each time he and Eryyn bunked out in Nest Two, while the girl worked the stove and prepared the food that would keep them alive for yet another day, Sawyer would stand at the window, staring across the city to that distant hill.

Now, their day of theft and trading with Master John finally over, some of their overly expensive food simmering in one of the dented pots, Sawyer took up his usual position and gazed out at the growing night.

Eryyn was kneeling beside the stove, stirring a concoction of powdered soup and water while watching her young friend. She frowned darkly and bit her tongue, restraining the urge to scold the boy for his stupid fantasies. It went without saying that Sawyer was the imagination of their team—a dreamer, both sensitive and thoughtful, though sometimes overly so.

Eryyn was different. She was a planner, a worker, and she had long ago decided that fantasies and dreams were a weak substitute for *real* life. True, sometimes Sawyer's imagination had come up with a few good ideas to get them out of certain situations, but when it came to his constant daydreams, Eryyn had absolutely no patience. In her experience, if you couldn't use something to sur-vive the horrors and dangers of the city, it was useless.

Many times she'd told Sawyer this, hoping to break him of his fanciful beliefs before he got hurt, but he refused to believe her and always retorted that you *did* need dreams and that they were *every* bit as essential to survival as food and clothing.

Still, Eryyn was the unspoken leader of the pair, and her frown deepened when he showed no sign of leaving the window to help her. Finally, she lost her patience and snapped at the boy:

"Will you get *away* from there, Squirt! Do you *want* to be seen by the Enforcers?"

Sawyer jumped at her sudden, loud voice and he turned away from the window, looking slightly guilty. His cheeks flushed. "It's dark out, nobody can see us up here," he protested.

"Well, you could be doing something useful for once, like helping me here. Why should I do all the cooking?"

Sawyer's bright green eyes narrowed to slits and his frown easily matched Eryyn's. "If I remember right, *I* was the one who filched the watch from that guy on the street. *I* was the one who went into the house this afternoon and got the stuff. I don't remember *you* climbing through that window on Ninth Street. Actually, *you* just *pushed* me! I think I've done *plenty* of useful things today."

"Get away from that stupid window and fix the bed," Eryyn ordered, leaving no room for argument. Sawyer opened his mouth, then seemed to think better of it and stomped over to the pallet, where he began airing out their assortment of rags and blankets. Eryyn heard him mumbling under his breath and smiled thinly in satisfaction of being obeyed.

"I wonder if they have kids of their own," Sawyer spoke up suddenly, waving a blanket in the air to remove the creases and wrinkles. "Kids who have their own bedrooms and lots of toys. They might even have one of those little private flitters, you know, the ones that hold only two people?"

Eryyn held her tongue and he continued, taking a deep breath before saying, "But I'll bet they don't. I'll bet they're just a young couple up there, living together. I'll bet they want kids and they want to decorate rooms for them, with nice soft beds and lots of books and clean, fluffy blankets. And they gotta have lots of food there too—not rations, or convenience store stuff—but *real* food, bought from a *real* store. They cook every night and have meat and vegetables and fresh, *hot* bread. And they sit together and think about the kids they want to have."

"You're dreaming," Eryyn said shortly. "There's no young couple living up there. It's probably an old, fat Enforcer, and he goes home from work each day with extra money in his pocket because he grabbed a stupid kid like you off the street and sold him to a factory, one of the gang leaders, or a farm outta the city. And he lives there, with just his badge and his painstick and his energy binders. And he doesn't care about kids—*any* kids—because all he cares about is himself and his money and how he can make more of it by screwing all the lower folk, like us. There's your real dream family, Squirt, and I'll bet you anything that I'm closer to the truth than you are."

Eryyn paused in her stirring, suddenly aware that Sawyer had gone silent behind her and that the sound of his shaking of the blankets had stopped. Slowly, she turned her head and saw the boy kneeling on the floor, staring at her with wide, resentful eyes. She sighed, regretting her cruel words, while at the same time feeling satisfaction that Sawyer was *finally* hearing her.

"I'm sorry, Squirt," she said, hoping to soften his resentment and stop him from looking at her like that. "But you know it's true. The Sky-End is for the Enforcers and the factory owners and the crime leaders who run the gangs. There aren't any sweet, young couples up there hoping to adopt a little kid with green eyes and brown hair."

Sawyer stood up and walked away from the pallet, stopping at the farthest corner of the room, where he slid down to a crouch. Hugging his legs to his chest, he rested his chin on his knees and began chewing on his lower lip.

"It's okay to dream, Eryyn," he said after a long moment of staring at the dust motes on the floor. "Even a little. It sure beats the hell out of living." He fell silent again, staring at nothing but the cracks in the floor and the bits of dirt that made patterns in the glow of the light-sticks. It was a fight they had quite often, but normally they just traded angry words. This silence on Sawyer's part was something new. In the quiet room, Eryyn finished the soup, poured an equal portion into the second pot and carried it over to the corner. Sawyer glanced up when she approached, and shook his head at the offered food.

"You have it. It tastes like dirt anyway."

"Squirt, come on, I'm sorry." Eryyn tried to thrust the pot into his hands, but he stubbornly kept them tight around his knees. "Don't be mad at me. You were saying earlier that you were *starv-*

ing."

"I'm not hungry anymore. You can eat it," Sawyer muttered in a dull voice.

"Oh, why do you have to be such a stupid little bug!" Eryyn exclaimed. "I was only telling you the truth! But fine, if that's what you want, I *will* eat it. Just don't come complaining to me because you're hungry." Clutching the pot, she turned on her heel and stalked back to the pallet, flopping down to eat her dinner. "Sheesh, sometimes I wonder why I even bother keeping you around. If I wanted to, I could *easily* find another partner who knows how to keep his feet on the ground and his head out of the Sky-End."

"I'm sure you could," was the soft reply.

Eryyn ground her teeth together, gulped at the soup and winced. Sawyer was right—it did taste like dirt, and probably was just as healthy. Still, she swallowed it all, then tore a hunk off the bread, chewing it even though the effort made her jaw ache. Grumbling, she rolled up the package, leaving half of the loaf uneaten. She glanced back to the corner of the room, but Sawyer was still crouched in a ball, hugging his knees and staring at the floor. He didn't seem to notice her gaze and, not knowing why his silence made her so angry, Eryyn tossed the remainder of the bread at him, purposely aiming to hit his shoulder. Without waiting to see if he would look up or react, she curled up on her side, pulling one of the dirty blankets to her chin. Closing her eyes, she lay still, listening to the sounds of the city that continued throughout the night.

It was nearly two hours later when, having dosed off, Eryyn was roused from sleep by Sawyer climbing under the blanket on his side of the pallet.

She was instantly awake, but continued to feign slumber as Sawyer wrapped an arm around her, snuggling up close to her back.

"Sorry," he whispered, so softly she almost didn't hear him.

She pretended a sleepy moan and turned over slightly, accepting the hug. Sawyer cuddled against her side. Eryyn waited, still pretending, until the sound of her friend's breathing took on the deep rhythm of sleep. Only then did she carefully draw her arm out from under the blanket so she could drape it over the small boy.

Smiling wanly as Sawyer mumbled in his sleep, Eryyn held him close and stared across the dark room to the window that looked out to the Sky-End. The hole in the planking allowed a small bit of yellowish light to filter through onto the floor and she focused her attention on the spots of dust that drifted slowly through the shaft of light.

While her eyes watched the dancing of the tiny bits of debris that covered the floor of their nest, she thought over what she had said just a little while ago. She regretted her harsh words now, knowing them to be completely wrong. She would never leave Sawyer for another partner—she couldn't even imagine doing such a thing. Sawyer was her best friend, a part of her, just as she was a part of him and as they were a part of the city. They relied on one another to survive, and Sawyer was the only person in the world she actually loved. She would never tell him this, but she was sure he already knew, and she knew that he felt the same way about her. Sawyer was the only family she had and had ever known.

She hugged him tighter and continued staring at the dust until, finally, her eyelids started to grow heavy. Yawning widely, she dropped her head deeper into the bundle of rags that served as a pillow, then, running her fingers through the dark brown hair of Sawyer's ragged bangs, she whispered gently, "Goodnight, Squirt. Sweet dreams."

two

Looking down on the clouds

he lights of the city glittered in the night. From above, the lights resembled the people who used them each day, varied by order of the city district. North of the old city, the lamps and windows glowed radiantly with harsh, white brightness. The sky over this district was brightened by the glare and the tall, sky-scraping buildings stood out in stark, black silhouettes, like giant building blocks. Further to the south, toward the center of the city, the lights changed to pale yellow and were dimmer, warmer, as they shone through the windows of the stubby, square buildings that housed the market stores. Even further to the south, the lights became scarce and the streets were dim and gloomy. Aptly known as the Dead-End, the area looked empty and cold, dark and forbidding, when compared to the bright activity of the other sectors.

From the top floor of an immense building on the prominent Sky-End hill, in an immense room with glass walls, a man sat in a large chair, looking down at the night-darkened city. His black eyes scanned the different districts, keenly noting the variances in light, knowing when one end stopped and the next began, seeing the black fingers of the factory smokestacks to the west of the marketplace and the stumpy rectangles of the offices to the east.

The man did not need to look to his left or right to know the brightness of the lights that graced his own section of the city. The Sky-End was the wealthiest, most beautiful end. The buildings on the hill were enormous and new, bright and shining in the sunlight, and bright and shining at night.

The lights were still active to the east and west of the central Mid-End. The factories still spewed foul clouds of smoke into the sky and tiny silhouettes could be seen bustling behind the office windows.

Between the two "Business-Ends", the main Mid-End—the small houses and apartment complexes, and the giant market in the exact center—had darkened considerably from the bustle and flurry of activity that had filled it earlier in the day. The busiest of all the districts during the day, the central Mid-End was quiet at night, when most people returned to their homes.

Lifting his dark eyes slightly, the man scanned the city even more to the south and gazed upon the blackness of the Dead-End. This was the old city. The city built with bricks and wood, built before the Enforcers had come into power. The buildings were all near to crumbling and falling apart, their ancient designs unable to cope with the changes in the world. No lamps burned here—all the bulbs had long since broken or burned out. The only illumination came from the multiple trashcan fires that the homeless wretches of the Dead-End built for warmth.

There were some people in the city who wanted to do away with the Dead-End. Who wanted to tear all the old buildings to the ground and ship the inhabitants away to some other city, or, and this was always whispered, to simply exterminate them as one would exterminate any other pest, like a rat or a cockroach.

But the man felt differently about the Dead-End. He had no intention of letting that filthy, sordid section be destroyed until he was finished with it. The Dead-End belonged to him, just as the rest of the city did, though he was the only one truly aware of this. As he looked down from the window, he looked down upon his city.

A clock on the immaculate glass wall behind him began to chime a new hour and the man stepped away from the window, a scowl gracing his dark, angular features. Turning, he strode out of the room, following the hall down to an elevator, which took him to the street level. He had a meeting to attend at this hour and, as all his children knew, the Foreman never missed a meeting.

• • •

They were all assembled in the large room that served as the meeting place in their stronghold. Some had arranged themselves on the few chairs that had been stored in the room; others, less sure of themselves, slouched against the walls or curled up on the floor, taking care to keep near one another. Years of uncertainty, grief, and danger had a way of leaving its mark on a person, especially a child, causing a strange resemblance to peers who had suffered similarly. And the twenty-four children gathered in the room had certainly known uncertainty and fear in their young lives. The shifty, furtive look was matched in each set of eyes, whether brown or blue, gray or green. Ragged, unkempt hair of all shades and lengths hung over cheeks and brows, obscuring the faces beneath. Lips that should have been smiling and joyful with youth were pressed into thin, pale lines.

Clothing consisted of a motley assortment collected from old shops, stolen from houses, or supplied by the gang leader. Most of these garments were ripped, patched, and poorly fitted. Some of the children wore shoes, some did not. The only thing any of them wore in common with their fellows was a red and yellow, braided cloth band that was either tied into their hair or twisted around their upper arms. These bands were the symbol of their gang and its owner, and were worn at all times. No one wanted to face the consequences of being found without their band.

All eyes were now riveted on the doorway, where, with all the room and hall lights dimmed, the Foreman stood, obscured in deep shadows. The red and gold of the bands proclaimed this group to be his number three gang—his best, so he thought. But he paid no attention to the majority of the gathered thieves and focused his eyes on the boy he had personally appointed gang leader. This boy, a rough, tall youth of sixteen years, swallowed nervously, feeling the cold eyes on him. He shifted on his own seat, clearing his throat several times before finally saying in a strained voice, "Red and gold gang reporting, sir."

Two of the younger children were sitting on the floor near his feet and caught the frightened squeak that accompanied his words. One tittered slightly at his nervousness. To regain his composure, he lashed out with a foot, catching her in the side. The girl gasped in pain, then quickly fell silent, though large tears threatened to overflow onto her cheeks. Her partner looked up at the gang leader resentfully, but he, too, knew better than to say anything. He ducked his head in submission as the teenager looked down at him and quickly turned his attention back to the Foreman.

One chair in the dark room remained vacant. This chair, different from the folding metal ones used by the children, was large, soft, and covered in thick, red velvet. It stood in an alcove addition of the back of the room, where the weak light of the single bulb hanging from the ceiling could not illuminate the inky shadows. The Foreman, without a word of greeting or acknowledgement to his gang, crossed the room to this chair, keeping to a length of darkness along the wall, and sat down. Though his legs and waist could be seen, his face was completely hidden in the darkness of the alcove. When he was comfortable, he turned to the tall boy and said in a soft, raspy voice, "Were you successful in filling your quota?"

The boy stood from his chair and pulled a pair of boxes from behind him. Carrying them over to the alcove, he laid them at the man's feet, his eyes straining to see through the blackness to the secretive man's face beyond. Having no luck, he turned back to his seat and sat down again. All the children gathered in the room waited apprehensively as the Foreman sifted through the two boxes, inspecting the contents that their quick fingers had gathered. Pulling out a golden pocket-watch, he looked at it closely, then bit down on the chain. Satisfied with the quality, he opened it to inspect the inner workings. Then, he paused.

The tall boy sat up straighter, his face going pale as he realized that something was wrong. Quickly, he cast his eyes over the children in his gang, frantically trying to remember who had brought that watch in. His gray eyes finally came to rest on the girl he had kicked just a moment before—she was glancing up at him from under her black fringe of bangs, her blue eyes guilty and nervous. He scowled darkly at her and raised a hand curled up in a fist. If she had been the cause of the Foreman's anger, he would make sure she wouldn't do it again.

"Just how stupid can you be?"

The boy looked back to the alcove, startled by the angry voice.

"S-sir?" he stammered. "What's wrong?"

The watch was flung from the alcove, landing with a clatter at his feet. Trembling slightly, he leaned over and picked it up. The face was open and, as he inspected it, he immediately saw what had caught the Foreman's attention. The watch was engraved.

To my beloved Mitchell, for all the days, and all the dreams.

"How quickly do you think someone would recognize that?" the voice from the alcove spat coldly. "Even if the words were filed off there would still be a scar. It's worthless! Who was stupid enough to bring in something like that!"

Sensing a way to divert the Foreman's anger from him, the tall boy reached out and grabbed the girl by the back of her shirt. With a hard tug, he pulled her to her feet and shoved her towards the alcove. She stumbled to a stop a meter from the shadowed alcove and crouched down, her eyes full of terror.

"I- I st-stole the watch, sir," she said quickly, knowing that lying was useless and hoping that pleading would help her. "But I didn't realize it was marked. I wouldn't have taken it if I'd known! I'm s-sorry! I promise I'll be more careful from now on."

The man in the shadows was silent for a long, tense moment before rasping, "Name?"

The girl bit her lip and stared down at the concrete floor beneath her knees. She opened her mouth to speak, but fear turned her words into a weak gasp. Shaking her head dumbly, she glanced back at the other children, silently begging them for help.

"Otto, what is this useless brat's name?"

The tall boy, Otto, stood up and cleared his throat. He glared down at the frightened girl and clenched his fists to his sides while he answered, "Pammy, sir."

"Is she worth keeping in the gang?"

A quick gasp went up among the gathered children, and Pammy, still kneeling in front of the alcove, let out a small cry of despair.

Otto, his eyes flashing dangerously, stared at her, then looked around at the rest of his gang, as if challenging them to say something. The boy who had been sitting with Pammy at the start of the meeting had his eyes cast down. His face had gone pale and his cheeks were stained with tears. When Otto's gaze reached him, he glanced up and, chin trembling, whispered, "Otto, please?"

The anger in Otto's eyes flickered for an instant and he looked almost sympathetic. Then his gaze was drawn back to the dark outline of the man in the alcove and his lips tightened. Straightening his shoulders, he announced, "She has her uses, but she's no better than any of my other kleptos. In fact, she's a bit cheeky, doesn't really know her place. And she influences the other kids too. I...I think we can do better."

Pammy cried out in horror, a cry that was echoed by her young friend. The other children looked on, eyes wide, bodies tense. The life of one of their members was at stake here. The Foreman, sitting on his velvet chair, nodded thoughtfully.

"I see. That is a problem." He fell silent again for a time, then added, "I don't know how you little street brats manage to think you're so special." His voice, so soft at the beginning of the meeting, rose thunderously as he shouted at them. "You're nothing! Don't you realize that? Nothing! If it weren't for me, you'd have been sold to a factory long ago. And this is how you repay me? By bringing in useless junk that can't be sold, and risking my business! I think, perhaps, it is time I set another example for you useless pieces of trash."

Pammy bowed her head low and began to sob. She knew that she was to be the example. The Foreman, with a snort of distaste, waved a hand at Otto, who stepped forward to grab the girl. Just as he was about to grip her arm, she jumped up, slamming her heel onto his foot and driving a small fist under his chin. He choked, trying to catch his breath, and she bolted towards the door, running as fast as her thin legs and worn shoes could take her.

She would have made it if another girl, this one nearly fifteen, hadn't jumped up from her seat beside the wall and thrust out an arm, catching the younger and smaller klepto and pushing her roughly back into the center of the room. Wailing with fear, Pammy sprawled onto the floor near the livid Otto, who glared down at her, then dragged her to her feet. His fingers dug into her arm.

Sobbing, she twisted and struggled, turning to her fellow kleptos and reaching out with her other hand for help.

"Rane! Rane, please, don't let him do this! Dillan! Denny! Kit! Help me, please help! Please don't let him hurt me! *Please!*"

The other children were still—they dared not risk their own

lives now. Only the tearful boy by Otto's chair stirred, starting to reach a hand out to her, but his arm was grabbed by another child, who pulled him back before Otto could see the gesture. Stifling a sob, the boy turned away from his friend, not wanting to watch as Otto and Sasha dragged Pammy from the room. He knew that he would never see her again. He shuddered and bit down hard on his lip as Pammy's anguished, terrified cries echoed up the corridor. Then, abruptly, the screaming stopped and the stronghold was plummeted into silence.

The rest of the children sat silently in the dark, painfully aware that the Foreman, who still rested in his velvet chair, was watching over them, looking for any reaction to the loss of their fellow member. Despite the gloom, he did not fail to see that Pammy's friend was weeping softly, both hands clasped over his mouth to stifle to sound. The room was painfully quiet for several long minutes until Otto finally returned with Sasha.

Pammy was gone.

"I'm sorry, sir," Otto said, dropping into his chair. "It won't happen again."

"It shouldn't have happened this time," the Foreman said, in a tone harsh enough to make most of the children wince. "She should have known better! And now, because you failed to train a klepto correctly, your gang is short a member." A hand emerged from the shadows of the alcove, pointing to the boy at Otto's feet. "And *some-one* is without a partner and may become bitter."

The boy glanced up, startled, and quickly wiped at his damp eyes. Twisting around to look nervously at Otto, who was glaring again, he frantically shook his head.

"I don't think Rane will be any trouble," Otto said softly, reaching out to squeeze the boy's shoulder. "Not if he knows what's good for him. We'll start looking for a new kid tomorrow."

"Do that, and next time, bring me better stuff. I've seen more valuable things at street carts recently. Don't waste my time, Otto. It is more precious than your life."

Otto bobbed his head and jumped to his feet again as the Foreman stood. All the other children also rose, showing respect to their master as he left the room, his face still concealed in the shadows. Only when the door was closed behind him did they, with the exception of Otto, relax.

When the door closed, the tall boy immediately rounded on the smaller child standing nearby. He grabbed Rane by the shirt and snarled into his pale face, "And you better not be thinking of causing anymore trouble! If I so much as hear a *sniffle* out of you, so help me I'll..." He raised a fist in threat and was satisfied to see Rane flinch back. He chuckled dryly. "Do you have any objections with what happened here today, brat?"

Rane's brown eyes, swimming with tears, stared up into Otto's gray ones submissively and he shook his head. Pointedly, he raised a hand and wiped it across his eyes, drying them.

"N-no, no objections, Otto," he mumbled. "She-she got what she d-deserved."

Otto laughed bitterly and he released the boy with a shove that sent him stumbling. "Yeah, and don't you forget it." His gaze shifted to rake over the entire group. "Don't any of you forget it. If anyone else thinks they can make me look bad in front of the Foreman, I'll personally see that they have a lot more bruises by the end of the day. The Foreman won't even have to deal with you once *I'm* done. Now get out of here. Get to work if it's your shift, or go and get some sleep. Next time we're called to a meeting, I want to have some quality stuff to hand over." He paused thoughtfully, then added, "And forget about Pammy. It's over. I did it for the good of the gang. We'll be better off now."

With those words, he turned on his heel and stalked from the room. Sasha followed him closely. After them, the rest of the children drifted out of the dark room and started to head back to their places on the streets. In a few minutes, only three were left: Rane, another boy, and a small girl.

The boy, after a glance at the door, cocked his head at Rane and smiled sympathetically.

"Pammy wasn't that great a partner anyway," he said by way of soothing. "She was always getting into trouble with Otto. She never wanted to be a part of a gang. She didn't know how good she had it."

"How good *we* have it, Dillan," Rane said wearily, wiping at his eyes again. "How good *we* have it." Without another word, he started for the door. As he walked through the halls, his eyes grew dull and tired. By tomorrow, or the next day, he would be paired up with another partner and it would be his job to train the newcomer, just as Pammy had once trained him.

He sniffed softly, wiping his sleeve across his nose, but he didn't cry anymore. Pammy was gone, that was all there was to it, and it wouldn't help him to linger on her memory. Though only twelve-years-old, he had spent the majority of his life on the streets—three years in the Foreman's red/gold gang. Those years had trained him not to make a lasting relationship with anyone. It wasn't worth the pain.

Normally, it was his time to do a shift outdoors, collecting for the next payment. But without a partner, he was forbidden to leave the stronghold. Housebound, he made his slow way to the sleeping room instead. As he collapsed on his thin pallet, his preservation instincts had already started helping him forget what the girl had looked like. By the time Otto found him a new partner, he would hardly remember Pammy at all.

THREE

Five fingered discount

Sawyer and Eryyn wandered through the main market in the center of the Mid-End, walking slowly and looking at the shops. The glass windows of the stores were well scrubbed and displayed a vast array of items for sale. Expensive, imported clothing was arranged tastefully on old-fashioned, plastic dummies that had been rescued from ancient department stores. Skimmers and flitters were also displayed behind glass, their metal and chrome gleaming from daily polishing, the leather of the seats so realistic that some could be convinced that it had actually come from a real cow. Some shops dealt in special foods, others in jewelry, still more in shoes, bags, glassware, toys…

Enjoyable as it was to look through the stores at all the items up for sale, Sawyer and Eryyn never frequented the market to shop. They couldn't have afforded anything in the stores and, even if they could, their ragged, skinny appearances always put shopkeepers on instant alert. But the market was a great place to walk and work in relative safety. They rarely had to worry about being attacked by a gang, and, as long as they behaved well and acted like they were minding their own business, there was no reason for the Enforcers to bother them either. This assurance, as well as the fact that the streets here were usually packed full of people walking off their breaks, wasting time looking in the windows, or buying inexpensive items from the temporary pushcarts, made the market the perfect place for 'pocketing.

As always, none of the shoppers paid much notice to the pair of small children as they wound their way back and forth through the crowds. Sawyer and Eryyn had learned from experience how to be inconspicuous. They took their time in the market, walking around slowly. Usually, they separated, working the market in shifts from both ends. Walking towards the center, they gazed wistfully into the shops, stopped to listen to people chat, feigned interest in whatever stupid topic the adults had to talk about, then met again a few minutes later to examine what their ramblings had brought in. Quick, soft hands were never felt as the children passed by the middle class workers, and normally, when the rings or watches or wallets were discovered missing, the boy or girl would be long gone, vanished back into the press of people.

Now, after another walk along the length of the market, they stopped beneath an umbrella awning that sheltered the front of a jewelry store. Sawyer, pretending to look at a silver-plated bracelet displayed on a length of black velvet in the window, glanced up as Eryyn sidled closer to him.

"I got another watch," he said proudly, his voice pitched for her ears only. "This one's a beauty too. The guy looked like Sky-End material! He didn't even notice a thing. I could have pinched his wallet, or even his shoes!"

"Excellent." Eryyn took the watch he surreptitiously slipped into her hands and glanced it over. The face was large, dark blue, and appeared to be set with faceted stones. The band was tooled leather, probably real and therefore *very* expensive. Both of the hands were crafted in gold and silver. It really was a beauty of a watch and Eryyn guessed that the owner would not be pleased when he finally discovered it missing.

"I could kiss you, Squirt," she said, smiling and slipping the watch into her pocket. Sawyer, with a grin, took a step back, holding his hands up in mock disgust.

"So, do you think Master John will give us what it's worth?" he asked, glancing around to see if there were any eavesdroppers before speaking.

"Nah, MJ will cheat us, just like he always does. But *he'll* get a good price for it, that's for sure. And if *he* gets a good price, then he'll keep buying from *us* whenever we have loot."

Sawyer scowled. "I really hate that man."

"Me too, but don't worry, *I'll* make sure we get what's fair for this, and for what I found."

Her tone caught the boy's attention and his face brightened. "What did you get?" he asked eagerly.

Eryyn's lips turned up in a smile and she winked at her young friend. "I don't wanna show you here. See that woman over there? The one with the red hair and the yellow hat?"

Glancing in the direction Eryyn's chin pointed, Sawyer nodded, pulling a face at the horrible clash between the woman's hair and the bright canary yellow of her hat. She was standing in front of a large clothing shop, looking through the windows at a bright orange dress displayed prominently on a dummy.

"She needs some fashion advice," the boy noted. "I've seen kleptos dress better than that."

"Right, and we're two of them. But still, she had a few nice things on her that will bring in a few credits."

"Excellent! So, do we do another round, or try somewhere else?" Sawyer flexed his fingers and gave Eryyn a cocksure grin. She laughed and punched his arm lightly.

"One more round. You start here and I'll head up the other end. I'll meet you in front of the gem shop in…" She glanced up at the misty ball of light that was the sun hidden behind the smog that constantly hovered over the city. "…twenty minutes. Does that sound okay?"

Sawyer's grin turned to a look of uncertainty as he, too, squinted up at the sky. "Eryyn, you know I can't…"

"Ask someone, Squirt. It's not that hard. Just be your sweet, polite, little self." She patted his arm, giving him a small push in the process. "Honestly, how can a kid know how to read and write but still not know how to tell time?"

"Don't know," Sawyer retorted, sauntering off in the direction he'd been pushed. "Maybe the same way a girl can know how to tell the time from the sun, but can't read or write her own name." He heard Eryyn laugh at his remark and glanced back. But she had already moved away, disappearing into the crowd in the search for more loot. The grin returned to his face as he wound his way through a group of women clustered in front of yet another clothing shop. Purposely walking in front of their view and allowing himself to be shoved around and jostled, he made a point of bumping into each one, immediately excusing himself and moving away, his quick hands having already done their searching. When he was finally shoved out of the way by a heavyset, dark haired woman, his pockets were filled with odds and ends harvested from pockets, fingers, purses, and wrists. He was just walking away, heading towards a bottleneck of people trying to file through a set of street carts, when a piercing voice called out:

"Hey, you! You, street boy, stop right there!"

Sawyer paused, his heart taking a frantic leap in his chest, and slowly turned around. The chubby woman who'd pushed him out of the group had moved away from the others and was now standing just a few steps away. She had set her thick hands on her wide hips and her face was twisted into a rigid scowl. Struggling to keep a calm attitude, Sawyer offered her a bright smile.

"Me, ma'am?" he asked, pointing a thumb at his chest. He cocked his head to one side, and continued smiling sweetly to make himself look as innocent as possible. "Were you calling me?"

"I don't see any other filthy street trash walking around here," the woman retorted.

Sawyer frowned as several other people turned to look at him curiously—he hated being the center of attention. But the woman had started the fight, and, being a street kid, he couldn't resist answering in typical klepto fashion. Mockingly placing his own hands on his hips, he spat, "Maybe if you took a look in a mirror you wouldn't have that problem."

The gathering crowd laughed as the fat woman's face turned a deep scarlet. One hand fluttered to her chest as she hissed, "*You little beast!* How *dare* you speak to me like that!"

"You did it to me," Sawyer pointed out. He turned to leave, eager to disappear into the crowd, and the woman shrieked, "I didn't say you could go anywhere! I'm not finished here, you filthy little mongrel!"

Sawyer flinched, stung by the cruel words, but he did his best to ignore them. He kept walking, intent on getting out of sight and mind, but a bearded man, obviously enjoying the little show, stepped in front of him, blocking his way.

"I believe the lady was talking to you, boy," he said, chuckling.

"It's very rude to walk away when someone is talking to you."

Exasperated, Sawyer turned around until he was once again facing the fat woman. A careful look of confusion and hurt on his face, he asked, "What do you want? I'm not doing anything wrong."

"Look at what you did to my dress," the woman spat, holding up a handful of her long, blue skirt. Sawyer peered at it and noticed a small tear in the fabric. So did a lot of the people looking on. A murmur ran through the crowd and several people shot reproachful glares at the little boy, as if he had wronged them as well. Feeling surrounded and suddenly very nervous, Sawyer quickly decided that it would be safer if he held back anymore insults and maintained his look of innocence.

"I didn't do it," he said, clasping his hands behind him and cocking his head to one side.

The woman stepped closer and pointed a menacing finger at his face. "You went pushing past me and you caught my dress and ripped it! This is an expensive piece, you'll have to pay for it!"

"You can't prove that it was me! I didn't do anything!" Sawyer backed away from the pointing finger, his heart pounding, his cheeks flushed from the attention the woman had directed his way. He felt a flash of relief when no one else tried to stop him from moving away, but he hadn't counted on the chubby woman being as fast as she was. Snaking out a sharply-nailed hand, she grabbed the boy's thin arm in a tight grip and pulled him forward, nearly lifting him off his feet as she jerked upward on his elbow.

"I know all about kids like you!" she yelled, shaking him like a leaf. "You're nothing but a little street thief! I'll bet you were stealing from us! I'll bet your pockets are *full* of stolen things."

Swallowing hard, Sawyer tried to wrench his arm free of the woman's fist and twisted frantically to avoid her hand as it moved to search his pockets. Angry now, his captured arm throbbing with pain, Sawyer cried, "I'm *not* a thief! And even if I was, I wouldn't steal anything from you! Don't thieves have to take stuff with value?"

The woman's face colored again and her eyes narrowed, glittering dangerously. Shaking him mercilessly by the arm, she hissed, "I'm going to turn you over to the Enforcers right now, you smart-mouthed, little monster! *They'll* take you to a factory! Then you'll learn the value of a decent day's work."

Panic welled up in Sawyer as she began dragging him down the sidewalk. He struggled in her grasp, trying to pull free, and protested loudly to the people nearby, hoping *someone* would have a heart and step forward to help him.

"I didn't do *anything*!" he yelled, kicking uselessly at the woman's plump legs. "Let me go! I didn't do anything! *Stop*! Help! Someone help!"

"Hey, you there! Stop that this instant!"

The crowd that had gathered to watch the conflict between the fat woman and the small boy turned as a demanding voice cut through the noise and a tall, thin man strode into sight. An excited gasp and a flurry of whispers went up among the onlookers—this man wore the uniform and badge of office of a high-level Enforcer. His blue and gray pants and shirt were spotless and perfectly pressed. At his belt, he carried a painstick and a pair of energy binders. He was scowling as he pushed his way up to the angry woman and the struggling boy.

Sawyer's panic grew even greater as the Enforcer appeared. With a small sob of despair, he put all his strength into fighting the woman and looked desperately through the crowd for Eryyn or some other form of aid.

"What is the meaning of this?" the Enforcer asked, when the woman paused and turned to face him, a look of triumph in her glittering eyes. She held out her arm, dragging Sawyer closer to the man for inspection.

"Officer, this little rat is a thief! He rudely pushed his way past me and ruined my clothes, then had the audacity to insult me in front of hundreds of people. I want you to take him and lock him up to teach him a lesson."

Fighting back tears, Sawyer stared up at the Enforcer, mentally weighing his odds of escape as he studied the man thoroughly. The Enforcer was a young man for his high position, the name on his badge read *Level 3. Daved Connel* and he appeared to be only in his late twenties or early thirties. His hair was black and neatly combed and his eyes, which looked down at Sawyer curiously, were a bright, twinkling blue. He smiled briefly at the frightened boy, then looked back up at the enraged woman.

"And how would ruining your clothes and insulting you classify this child as a thief, ma'am?" he asked calmly, expertly narrowing directly to the woman's weak point. "Do you have any proof to back up these charges?"

"Why else would a ragged little urchin like this be hanging around the market?" The woman pulled up on Sawyer's arm again, yanking his wrist high above his head and momentarily lifting him off his feet. Sawyer yelped and frantically began struggling again, kicking and thrashing until the woman allowed his toes to reach the ground. White-hot agony lanced up his pinioned arm and the tears spilled over onto his cheeks. The fat woman, oblivious to the pain she was causing the boy, faced the Enforcer and stated, "It's obvious he came here to steal from good, honest working people. He should be locked up, or made to work in one of the factories, so the streets can be safe again. I was just going to bring him there now."

"I believe *I* am the authority here, ma'am," the Enforcer stated, as the woman made to walk off with the helpless child. "Now, release the child before you hurt him anymore and we'll get to the bottom of this." Reaching out a hand, he gently disengaged Sawyer's arm from the woman's grip, pulling him away and setting him back on his feet. "Are you alright, son?" he asked, kneeling on the street and placing his arm on Sawyer's shoulders.

With a small sniffle, Sawyer dashed at his tears and rubbed his sore arm. He glanced around furtively, wondering if he should attempt to run. He immediately decided against it. There were too many people around who'd simply grab him and drag him back, and to flee was to announce his guilt. Nervously, he forced himself to meet the Enforcer's blue eyes and bobbed his head in a small nod.

"Please, Officer, sir, I didn't do *anything*, honest! I was just walking around, and she started pushing me, then called me names and grabbed me! She hurt my arm but I didn't rip her dress, honestly I didn't!" Aware that he was babbling, Sawyer broke off miserably and wiped at his eyes again.

"Don't believe him, Officer! He's a liar! Look at this!" The woman held out her dress again, showing Connel the tiny hole. "Take the little thief away and make him work for once! One less *illegal* in the city is one less thing to worry about." Gasps immediately arose from the crowd and Connel looked up sharply. Beside him, Sawyer felt heat rush up to color his pale cheeks.

"I'm not an illegal!" he exclaimed, his nervousness at being so close to an Enforcer eclipsed by his anger at the crude insult.

Connel, keeping one arm around the boy's shaking shoulders, lifted Sawyer's right wrist with his other hand and pushed back his long sleeve. A silvery bracelet gleamed in the weak sunlight, and the small plaque on the top was engraved with a word and eleven numbers: *Sawyer 64021-503941.*

"Your name is Sawyer?" the Enforcer asked, purposely holding the boy's hand out so the crowd could see his identification.

Sawyer nodded stiffly, his eyes still locked on the angry woman.

"Then it's right here—this boy is as legal as you are, ma'am. He has an I.D. and a number and if I were to take him down to the station to test it, I'm sure it would prove to be valid. I believe you owe this young man an apology for such a grave insult. Illegality should not be taken lightly."

The fat woman looked taken aback and she scowled at the boy as Sawyer turned to look at the Enforcer in awe.

"I will not apologize to a dirty little street thief!" she said haughtily, tossing back her hair and straightening her shoulders.

Connel stood up, careful to keep one arm over Sawyer's shoulders, using the gesture to both calm the frightened boy and assure that he didn't try to run away. Raising his voice, he addressed the watching crowd, "Does anyone here have a complaint against this boy? Did anyone *else* see him steal from this woman? Did anyone see him *steal* anything at all?"

There were no answers from the crowd—no one had noticed anything until the woman had started to shout. Connel waited patiently for a moment, then returned his calm gaze to the accuser.

"It's your word against his, ma'am, and I cannot fairly search the boy because of one accusation from an obviously distraught person. It would be a violation of his *legal* rights. And if, by some accident, the lad did rip your dress..." The Enforcer's tone suggested that he thought this unlikely, "...I'm sure he is sorry for it." Connel glanced down at Sawyer and the boy nodded mutely.

"He should be made to pay for it," the woman pressed, feeling that she had somehow lost a battle she had thought already won. "It's completely ruined!"

"It's a small tear that a little needle and thread could easily fix. There is no need to pester this boy for something he may or may not have done. Still, I think you do owe him an apology. You accused him of grave offenses with no proof and you could have seriously hurt his arm."

The woman opened her mouth to speak, then closed it again with an audible snap. Turning on her heel, she stalked away without another word. Connel shook his head at her retreating back, then turned to the watching crowd.

"Alright, you people can disperse now. Go back to your shopping. And next time, don't be so quick to judge someone just because they're young. I'm ashamed that none of you thought to stand forward and aid this poor child."

The people began drifting away from the scene, mumbling amongst themselves. Sawyer watched them go, stunned by the strange turn of events. He could hardly believe that an *Enforcer*, a high-level Enforcer, had actually helped *him*, a street waif. Finding his voice, he murmured, "Thank you, sir."

Connel looked down at him and smiled. "Glad to be of service, son." His smile faded and was replaced by a look of concern as he watched Sawyer lift his shirtsleeve to inspect his aching upper arm. "I just wish I had gotten here sooner. Is your arm alright?"

Sawyer's left arm was still hurting badly from the woman's powerful grip. The area just below his shoulder was bright red, with a purplish band of bruising already beginning to show. He winced at the sight, knowing the bruises would be dark and incredibly tender by nightfall, but nodded at the young man.

"I'll be fine, it hardly hurts anymore," he lied. Then, deciding to keep the Enforcer on his good side, he added, "Thank you again, Officer Connel."

Connel stared at him curiously, his lips turning up into another grin. "How did you know my name, son?" he asked.

Sawyer frowned, confused. "It says it right on your badge, sir," he pointed out.

Connel laughed. "So it does. I'm sorry, I guess I just supposed that you couldn't read. These days, not many children your age can, especially children from..." he slowed, then stopped, not sure how to finish the sentence without causing further insult.

"Not kids from the low ends?" Sawyer asked, understanding. Connel nodded gravely. "Most don't consider it worth their time to learn. But if you did, I congratulate you." He patted Sawyer on the right arm. "I like seeing children trying to better themselves. Well, good luck, Sawyer, try to stay out of trouble now."

Nodding, Sawyer watched the man walk away, then let out his breath in a loud sigh of relief. Slowly, his knees stopped trembling and his heartbeat returned to a more normal pace. Considering himself extremely lucky, he turned and hurried down the street, eager to find Eryyn and get away from the marketplace.

• • •

"I still can't believe that an Enforcer helped you! Actually *stood up* for you against a grown-up!"

"Me neither, but it's true! He stopped the woman, then tried to make *her* apologize to *me*! It was so weird—you should have seen the faces of everyone watching. I think they expected him to drag me off to the nearest factory."

"You got lucky, Squirt! Real lucky!" Eryyn was shaking her head in disbelief. "I heard you yelling from across the market…but there was nothing I could do."

Sawyer nodded and fingered the bracelet on his wrist. "If I didn't have this…" he paused, swallowing at the thought, "…I'd be in a factory now, working for nothing but food, or I'd be in a gang." He shivered. "I can't think what would be worse."

Eryyn looked at the silver bracelet enviously, her dark eyes narrowed. She didn't have one on her wrist. If *she* had been accosted by the woman in the market, the Enforcer wouldn't have taken her side. No one ever took the side of an illegal.

Sawyer caught her looking at the bracelet and quickly hid it under his sleeve. It was a constant conflict between them—that Sawyer had come from a proper birth and had been recognized and certified as a citizen before becoming a street child. Eryyn was an urchin all the way, with hardly any memory of her parents and no bracelet to announce her legality in the city. If she were to be caught by an Enforcer, or even a common citizen, they would be completely within their rights to sell her to a factory.

Now, seeing Sawyer's look of shame as he pulled his sleeve down over his wrist, she sniffed and said bitterly, "You don't have to *hide* it, it won't change anything. Besides, you can't *help* being a legal."

"You say it like it's a bad thing," Sawyer complained, sitting back in his car seat and pulling his knees up tightly against his chest. The two, having caught up with each other outside of the market, had sought refuge in an old car parked in an abandoned lot, where they could sit and catch their breath while still being able to see anyone approach from all sides.

"And why shouldn't I? It *is* a bad thing."

"That I'm legal?" Sawyer looked up, his eyes wide with hurt.

Eryyn rolled her own eyes and slouched down further into her own seat. "Don't be an idiot, Squirt, not that. I'm talking about the stupid law! Think how much easier things would be if there were no legals or illegals."

"We can't change it, Eryyn," Sawyer whispered, still stung by her words.

"Yeah, well, we can change the subject. I don't want to talk about it anymore."

"You started it."

"Yeah, well, I wish I didn't," Eryyn retorted fiercely. "So drop, it, Squirt, alright? Just drop it!"

Sawyer nodded and fell silent. Wrapping his arms around his knees, he rested his head against the rotted back of the seat and looked out the grimy window. The lot was full of junked hulks: cars, buses, trucks, and other vehicles from before the Enforcers and the leap of technology. Most had been pillaged for any parts that might have still worked, but the hulks still remained. Other people were camped out in the rusted, broken machines—some actually lived in them on a daily basis. From his angle, Sawyer could see one such woman settling herself down in front of a trashcan fire near the bus she had claimed for herself. The woman, somehow sensing the boy's gaze, glanced up, her eyes wary, and huddled deeper into the blanket she was using as a shawl. Lifting a lip in a sneer, she showed off her broken, yellowed teeth, then raised a stick she used as a weapon, holding it up in threat.

Sawyer shuddered at the sight and sat up again.

"I have to get out of here," he said desperately. "I need to go for a walk. Can we go, Eryyn, please?"

Eryyn, caught in her own thoughts and staring dolefully at her naked wrist, was startled by the urgency in his voice and she looked up. The homeless woman was visible through the window beyond Sawyer's tensed shoulders and Eryyn, too, shuddered, getting a terrifying flash of her own possible future in the ragged, hopeless human. Immediately knowing what had caused her friend's upset, she shook her head and pushed open the door on her side, climbing out of the car. With a sigh of immense relief, Sawyer scurried after her.

"Never," Eryyn said, taking the boy's hand and leading him away from the lot and the eyes of the crazy beggar woman. "It'll never happen to us, Squirt. We'll figure something out, but *that* will never happen to *us*."

Sawyer, trotting along at her side, glanced back. Swallowing hard, he squeezed Eryyn's hand for comfort. "You promise?"

"Yeah, I promise. C'mon, let's go hit a house before it gets too late and everyone starts coming home. Then we'll go pay a visit to MJ."

Sawyer snorted bitterly. "Now *that's* something to really look forward to."

Eryyn grinned at the boy's dour look and pulled him along faster.

• • •

The place they chose was on Seventieth Street. An actual house, rather than an apartment complex, it held lots of promise and Eryyn had been planning to hit it for sometime. Three stories tall, with white paint that actually looked fresh and windows that were clean and sparkling, the house was the closest to the Sky-End they had ever risked.

"Feeling up to it?" Eryyn asked, watching Sawyer stare up at the house. He'd had no idea during the long walk through the Mid-End where she'd been leading him and now, hidden behind a doghouse in a neighboring yard, he swallowed and nodded. This would be exciting. From the appearance outside, the house was a possible treasure trove of little trinkets and knickknacks. With luck, they'd have plenty of stuff to sell to Master John and continue to stay in his good graces.

"There's no basement that I can see," Eryyn said, leaning out around the doghouse to peer at the house. "You'll have to go in through one of the ground level windows. That means there'll be a bigger chance of you being seen."

Sawyer's green eyes flicked around, surveying the house and all possible entrances. He could tell just at a glance that Eryyn was right—most of the lower windows were out in the open and would leave him exposed as he tried to climb in. Then he noticed something that could possibly be the answer.

"If I go through that one, near the tree, I'll be hidden by that ugly, old bush." Sawyer pointed to a low window on the far end of the house. "No one will see me then, and I can go in and out easily—the window isn't too high."

Eryyn surveyed the yard and thought over her friend's plan. "But to get there, you have to run across the yard. Someone may see you then."

"I'd have to run across the yard anyway, except at that one large window, and *that* one's in plain view of the building right behind us."

Eryyn nodded, feeling a flash of pride in the way Sawyer had thought things out. It had been *her* training that had turned him into such a careful planner when it came to a hit. She patted him on the head, earning herself one of his sweeter smiles, and whispered, "Okay, but try to sneak around the yard as far as possible before breaking for the window. It's still early and I don't think anyone's home around here, but this is closer to the Sky-End than we usually try. You never can know."

"Right." Sawyer stood up, brushing dead grass and dirt from his knees, and placed his hands on the roof of the doghouse, leaning over as he prepared to break cover. "Five minutes," he whispered to himself, taking a deep breath. "Three floors. I can do it. Five minutes."

Eryyn listened to his quiet mumbling and bit her lip. This house was big, bigger than most of the ones they robbed—it might take Sawyer longer to get through it and find anything worth taking. She sighed, hating to break her own rules, then tapped Sawyer on the arm, getting his attention. "Take ten," she said, "but no more, alright? I'll be right here, waiting. Whistle if you have trouble."

Looking shocked at the change in routine, Sawyer bobbed his head once. "Um… okay. Here I go." He slipped out of his hiding place and, keeping to the edges of the yard, where a line of scraggly, naked bushes grew, he began working his way toward the targeted window. At one point, just before a section where he would be visible from the street, he slipped on a patch of damp ground, nearly going to his knees before catching a handful of branches and steadying himself. Eryyn, watching from the doghouse, gasped and flinched sympathetically as Sawyer looked down at his hand, which now sported several long, bleeding scratches.

"Oh, sorry, Squirt," she murmured sympathetically. "But keep going, don't stop now."

As if he'd heard the whispered phrase, Sawyer glanced towards the doghouse, then up at the towering apartment building that was their greatest threat for being spotted. Wincing, he wiped his hand on his pant leg, then started moving again. An instant later, he reached the place where he would have to break cover and make a dash for the bush near the window.

At the doghouse, Eryyn held her breath, mentally counting the seconds it took the small boy to race from cover to cover. Instinctively, she glanced up at the building behind her, just as Sawyer had done after his near fall. When she looked back at the house, Sawyer was gone. For a second, she nearly panicked, then she saw a small hand, cocked in a thumbs-up, reach around the bush. Sawyer had made it and was now working on opening the window so he could slip into the empty house.

He had long ago perfected this part of the operation, using the old blade of a flat headed screwdriver he'd found in a Dumpster to pry up the outer window so he could slip his fingers under it and pull it all the way up. From there, he could easily pry open the inner window, if there even was one, and climb into the house. Now, wishing he was just a little bit taller, or that Eryyn was there to give him a boost, he gripped the sill, wincing again as his injured hand pressed against the hard plastic. With a quick, hard heave that sent his bruised arm into a loud protest of the sudden weight he was putting on it, he pulled himself up until he seesawed over the sill on his belly. Slowly, he wiggled in, holding his hands out until they came in contact with the floor. Crawling forward on his fingers, he managed to pull his legs through the open window and landed on all fours. For a long moment, he crouched where he had landed, ears straining for some sign of the owner of the house.

There was nothing. The house was silent. After another second to catch his breath and let the throbbing of his upper arm subside, he stood up and leaned back out the window, sending another thumbs-up signal to Eryyn. Then, he wandered off to explore the house.

• • •

Eryyn let her breath out in a loud whoosh as Sawyer's feet finally disappeared into the house. She knelt tensely in place, fingers crossed tightly, and felt a wave of relief when the little boy popped his head back through the window and waved to her. He was barely visible to her behind the bush, but she waved back anyway and watched him disappear again.

"Good luck, Squirt," she whispered softly, and sat back, glancing up at the sky to start her countdown of ten minutes.

• • •

Inside the house, Sawyer whistled softly under his breath, nodding his head appreciatively at the room that surrounded him. It appeared to be a sitting room. There was an oddly low couch, covered in thick, blue upholstery, and two black and silver lounging chairs arranged before an angular fireplace. A glass-topped table rested between the two chairs, its surface polished and gleaming in the pale light that washed through the windows and the door that led to the front hall. Black metal shelves were lined against two walls, filled with knickknacks and statues, odd looking objects that looked like large snail shells, candle holders, mirrors, and other fascinating bits of junk that instantly drew the boy's attention.

"Who needs all this stuff?" he murmured to himself as he ran his fingers delicately over a seashell. He'd never seen anything like it before and, having no idea what it was or if it would hold any value, he left it on the shelf and moved his gaze to a pair of matching stone statues. These, at least, could be sold to Master John for a fair price and he quickly pulled them down and stuffed them into the sack he had slung over his shoulder. A cursory glance at the rest of the shelf revealed nothing else truly worth taking and he moved away to another wall.

This one was empty except for a few paintings and a large potted plastic plant resting on the floor. The pictures were odd—bright colors were blended together and formed strange shapes and swirls that had no meaning Sawyer could think of. They looked almost as if a child had painted them, smearing the colors over the paper in a haphazard, messy way. Sawyer stared at them for a few seconds, his head tilted curiously to one side. Then his eyes started to hurt and he had to look away. The paintings were useless to him—ugly and too noticeable for sale in a pawnshop. The vase that contained the plant was pretty, painted with a design of interconnecting rainbow bands, but it was far too big for the small boy to lift and he passed it by with a wistful frown.

The hall beyond the room led to a large front door and was equipped with a glass-topped side table and a pair of ladder-back chairs, but nothing else of interest. Starting to feel disappointed, Sawyer hurried on. At the end of the hall, he found a set of stairs. Eryyn had always warned him to stay close to his original place of entrance, and to never get himself into an area that had no convenient escape route. But she had also given him ten minutes, and he knew that barely half of that had passed already, and it was still early in the day—the owners of the house would probably still be working. Plus, Eryyn would not be pleased if he went back with nothing worth selling, especially after his trouble in the marketplace.

With a small sigh and a backward glance at the front door, he rested his hand on the banister and started up to the second floor.

• • •

At first, Eryyn thought the noise was just a branch rustling in the wind. Then, as she heard the first strains of the whistled song, she realized with a start that there *wasn't* any wind. The day was calm and warm. The noise was not a branch in the wind. It was the sound of a branch breaking under a footstep!

She listened carefully, her body held rigid, her breath caught in her throat. Silently, she begged the unseen person to go away, to keep walking by. Sawyer had been in the house for only four minutes and the window, where he had climbed in, was still open!

Biting her lip with fear, she strained her ears and listened to the approaching person. He or she was whistling casually and ambling along the street nearby. Risking a peek, she stuck her head around the doghouse and surveyed the street. Her position in the yard next door to their target house had been well chosen. It gave her a view of both the front door of the house and the side window through which Sawyer had climbed. If she turned her head to the left, she could see a small section of the street and, eventually, the person who was walking down it. It was a man, dressed in a suit and carrying a briefcase. He passed by her hiding place, whistling jauntily.

Eryyn let out a sigh of relief, glad that he hadn't seen her crouched behind the tiny doghouse, but the sigh quickly turned into a gasp when the man continued walking, and turned off the street…straight up the walkway and towards the door of the house! Fumbling with a key on the stoop, he opened the front door and stepped inside, slamming the door behind him.

Eryyn gave a cry of dismay. Sawyer was still trapped inside the house!

• • •

The upper rooms of the house were showing far more promise than the first floor. After leaving the stairs, Sawyer found himself in a short hallway with four doors, two on each side. Choosing the first door on the left side, he pushed it open and entered a large bedroom.

The bed, an enormous waterbed with deep purple and red sheets, half a dozen pillows, and a down blanket, was amazing. Unable to resist, the little boy sank into the fluid confines of the mattress and blanket while surveying the room. The remaining furniture consisted of a large, gold lacquered dresser, a vanity table, a full-length mirror, a pair of plump, round, brightly colored chairs, and a card table. Very modern and up to date, there was also an expensive video screen on the dresser and a vid-phone on the card table.

On the vanity, Sawyer found a pleasing set of jewelry with necklaces, rings, bracelets, hair clips, as well a few nearly full bottles of perfume that Master John would almost certainly buy. Obviously the room belonged to the lady of the house…or one of them at least. A search through the drawers of the dresser only revealed an array of sweaters, skirts and blouses, but the video screen had a small section that detached and became portable. It fit easily in Sawyer's bag and went with him into the room across the hall.

In this one, he found an office of sorts, with computer equipment, another video screen, little bits of machinery that immediately joined the jewelry in the bag and, treasure above treasures, a wall completely lined with old soft-covered books!

The ten-year-old's eyes widened with delight at this amazing wall. He had never seen so many books in one place before—the three he owned had been stolen from three separate houses. Now, he was faced with *hundreds* of volumes! His mind reeled at the thought of being able to read so many books. The things he could learn from each one!

He scanned the shelves, his sharp eyes picking out the brightest covers and quickly reading the titles. Pulling four of the most interesting ones from their places, he looked them over carefully, then stuffed them down in the bag, which had, by now, become rather heavy on his shoulder. With a look of longing at the overflowing shelves, he selected one more book and turned to leave.

He had taken just two steps down the hall when he heard something that made his young heart skip a beat. Someone had just *opened* the front door and was now *walking* up the stairs! Hurriedly, not pausing to think or investigate, he ducked into the nearest room and shut the door as quietly as he could. Stepping away from the door, he felt his back come in contact with something cold and hard. Turning, he found himself backed against a porcelain sink. He was in a bathroom! Across from him was a toilet, and on his left was a deep, wide tub. The room was small compared to the others, and the only window was above the tub, and so tiny he doubted he could fit through it, even if he had been able to reach it.

He heard footsteps right outside the door and his breath caught in his chest. Fighting down panic, he stepped into the tub, pulled the curtain closed and crouched down just as the doorknob turned and the stranger stepped into the small room, shutting the door behind him.

Cursing himself for going upstairs, Sawyer squeezed his eyes shut and bit down on his lip. There was no way out of the tiny bathroom! The window was useless and, even if he could get it open, he would never get out without being noticed. Besides, he was *two stories above the ground!*

He could see the stranger's shadow through the curtain and wondered if he could be seen from the outside as well. The person was standing directly between the tub and the door back into the hall. There was nothing Sawyer could do now but stay low and quiet. He was trapped, and if he made so much as one peep, he would be caught! And, this time, there would be no fair-minded Enforcer around to help him.

• • •

Eryyn was in an agony of indecision. Sawyer was caught inside a house and the owner had returned early. If her friend was discovered, he would be sent to work in the factories, or worse!

She couldn't let that happen. She had been the one to select the house, and if she'd told Sawyer to stick to their original rule of five minutes, instead of ten, he would have been through and out by now. It was her fault that he was in trouble. She had to get him out somehow.

But how? That was the problem. She was too big to fit easily through the window, and what good would it do her friend if she got caught too? Things would probably be worse for her, because she wasn't legal. She certainly couldn't ask anyone for help. Briefly, she toyed with the idea of breaking a window on one of the lower levels. But that would only make the owner mad, and if he *still* found Sawyer...

Then she decided that there was only one safe thing she could do. With a glance around to see if anyone was watching, she left the cover of the doghouse, strode across the two yards and walked up the stone walkway to the porch. Taking a deep breath to calm her nerves, she mounted the steps until she stood before the door. Raising a trembling hand, she knocked loudly.

• • •

The person beyond the curtain turned on the water in the sink and was still unaware of the young boy crouched in the tub. Sawyer held his breath and squeezed his eyes closed, trying to stay as still as possible. It seemed to him that the person was taking an incredibly long time to wash his hands.

Beneath him, his legs began to get sore. He longed to move, to stretch them out a bit, but knew that any movement would reveal him. He tried to think of something else, to take his mind off the growing pain in his calves and knees. He pictured Eryyn, who was probably still hiding behind the doghouse, and wondered if she knew about his trouble. Then, suddenly, his leg cramped. He winced as a flash of pain raced through his muscles and instinctively stuck out his right leg, trying to relax the tension. His calf screamed in pain and he gasped, clapping a hand over his mouth a second too late.

"What the…?" he heard a confused voice say.

The running water on the other side of the curtain stopped abruptly and, as Sawyer looked up in horror, he saw the shadow coming closer to the tub. A hand reached out and grasped the curtain—he could see two large, gold rings on the thick fingers, and ducked down lower, biting his own finger in terror. The curtain started to open, he was about to come face to face with the owner of the house…but a loud banging suddenly sounded from downstairs.

"Damn!" The stranger pulled his hand back and hurried from the room to answer the door.

His heart pounding furiously, Sawyer sat up and took a deep, shuddering breath. He could hardly believe his luck. Reaching out, he pulled the curtain back a tiny bit and peeked into the now empty bathroom. The owner was gone…but for how long, he didn't know.

Standing up, every muscle in his legs protesting the movement, the boy climbed out of the tub, his sharp ears listening carefully for any sign that the man might be returning.

Fortunately, all was quiet and he stepped from the bathroom into the hall, peering down both directions before hurrying into the first room he'd pillaged. There was a window there, on the other side of the bed, and a rusty tangle of metal piping that could only be a fire escape. It was to this window that he ran, pulling it up and open. A quick test of the first rung told him that the fire ladder was still serviceable…if he was very careful. Dropping his sack out to land in the yard below, he swung his legs over the sill and stepped onto the fragile, rust-pitted contraption that was his only chance for escape.

• • •

Eryyn waited for a few breathless seconds after the pounding sound of her first knock faded from audibility, then knocked again, banging her fist against the door with enough force to make it shudder.

Please answer it, she thought desperately, *please answer it.*

She knocked again, so hard her hand grew sore against the un-yielding, smooth surface of the door. She wondered if this would do any good, if the man had already found Sawyer or not. She raised her hand again, then heard a loud voice call out, "Enough already, I'm coming. Don't break the damn door down."

Letting her breath out in a gasp of relief, Eryyn waited, hopping up and down on her toes, as the door was flung open and she was faced with the man of the house. He towered over her, more than six feet tall, his thick arms crossed over his broad chest. He frowned deeply as he looked down at her.

"What do you want?" he demanded.

Eryyn opened her mouth, but only a slight squeak emerged. The man looked seriously angry at having been interrupted. Had he discovered the little thief in his house? Was he impatient to get back to the boy who had been robbing him so he could turn him in to the Enforcers?

"Ex-excuse me, sir, I was just walking d-down the street and I found this in the r-road. I saw you come up here and I thought you might have dropped it." Eryyn held out the beautiful watch Sawyer had 'pocketed in the market place.

The man looked down at the offered watch and his frown deepened. As he contemplated it, Eryyn glanced past him into the house. *Which room are you in now, Squirt*, she thought, *Can you get out? Please be able to get out.*

"Yes, I believe that *is* mine. It must have fallen off—the clasp is always coming undone. I really have to get it fixed." The man reached out and took the watch from her, slipping it into his pocket. As he did so, Eryyn caught sight of his own watch plastered on his wrist.

"I-I'm just glad I could help," she muttered to the liar, wincing inwardly at the loss of the expensive watch. "It's such a beautiful thing, I didn't want you to lose it."

"You're lucky you didn't try to steal it, girl," the man growled. "From the looks of you, you don't belong around here. You'd get into a lot of trouble if you were caught with my watch in your pocket. Now get out of here, I was busy with something when you started banging on my door." He gave her a hard shove, throwing her off balance. With a cry, Eryyn tumbled down the stone steps, landing in a heap on the walkway. The man turned away and hurried back into the house, not even stopping to see if she had been hurt in the fall.

Picking herself up, Eryyn gritted her teeth against the pain that came from a scrape on her elbow.

"Jerk!" she yelled at the closed door. Turning, she limped away, her ankle sore from having twisted underneath her when she hit the ground. She went back to the doghouse and crouched down, twisting her arm up so she could see the scraped flesh and bits of dirt embedded under her skin. Flinching at the sting, she wiped her hand over the cut, then looked over at the house again.

"I tried, Squirt," she whispered. "I hope it helped."

• • •

Sawyer heard the footsteps coming back up the stairs just as he had eased his entire body out onto the fire escape. He was still clinging to the windowsill when the owner reached the top of the stairs and started back down the hall towards the bathroom where he had been trapped. Smiling thinly to himself, Sawyer let go of the window and started climbing down the side of the house, gripping the rusted bars carefully and testing each rung before putting his weight on it. He was still eight feet from the ground when the rung he'd been gripping with his hands came loose with a loud squeal. Losing his balance, he fell backwards, landing with a thump on the dry dirt of the yard.

The breath was knocked out of him on impact and, for a few seconds, there was nothing he could do but stay where he was, trying desperately to draw air back into his lungs.

"Squirt? Is that you?" Eryyn's worried voice reached his ears from across the yard. She was still behind the doghouse. "Hey! Are you alright?"

"Y-yeah," Sawyer managed to wheeze, turning over onto his stomach. He reached out a hand and grabbed at his bag, pulling it onto his shoulder before struggling to his feet. It was a short dash across the open yard to the doghouse, but he made it in a few seconds and dropped, gasping and trembling from the close escape, to the ground beside his friend.

"I thought you were going to get caught!" Eryyn said, nearly crying with relief. She threw her arms around him and hugged him tight, knocking the breath out of him again.

"I-I almost was," Sawyer stammered, quickly returning the hug and then pulling away from her so he could breathe. "I got stuck in a bathroom and the owner came home and...well, he came in while I was there. I hid inside the tub and..." Sawyer told her everything that had happened in the house during his close call. When he was finished, Eryyn squeezed her eyes shut and clenched her fists.

"It's all my fault," she spat. "I should have stuck to five minutes. Ten is just too long."

Sawyer nodded, agreeing with her now, and lowered his eyes. "I guess I shouldn't have gone upstairs either. So it was my fault too, not just yours. It's just that there was nothing good on the bottom floor. We were lucky."

"Luck had nothing to do with it," Eryyn said, pulling her hand away from her scratched elbow. Quickly, she told Sawyer what she had done to distract the man while he made his escape. "The jerk even *took* the watch and said it was his! He was *wearing* his watch, Squirt! Sheesh, and I used to think *we* were the robbers in this city! *He* took the watch and blamed *me* for stealing it, then pushed me down the stairs." She scowled deeply, crossing her arms over her chest. "I sure hope you got some good stuff from that house, I'd love to have cleaned him out."

"Not great," Sawyer murmured, pulling his bag closer. "But not really bad. Master John will like it enough. I got some video stuff—he always buys that."

"Well, let's get out of here so we can check it out. It ain't smart to stay so close. He's bound to notice that something's missing soon enough."

Sawyer helped her to her feet and allowed her to lean on his shoulder as they staggered away from the doghouse and down the street. Eryyn limped with every step, wincing, but she didn't complain. Still, it seemed an impossibly long time before they reached Nest Four and were able to stop and relax from their very close call.

ᛏᛜᚢᛉᚱ

There is no life without a gang

aster John's pawnshop was just opening up for urchin business when Eryyn and Sawyer made their slow way up to the door. The crowd around the back entrance was not as large as it had been the day before, but half a dozen other kids were clustered at the door, waiting for the greasy man to make his appearance so they could sell their stuff and go get something to eat. Among those waiting was a tall, auburn-haired girl both children recognized. Upon spotting them, she immediately hurried over. Sawyer groaned.

"Hey, Eryyn! I haven't seen you for a long time! You been hiding or something?"

Eryyn grinned, slapped Sawyer on the arm and moved over slightly to make room for the girl against the wall. "Hi, Aimee. Naw, we've just been working the higher ends, that's all. Mingling with the posh Sky-Enders. We've gotten some pretty good stuff."

Aimee nodded and her face broke into a sly smirk. "And a *lot* of trouble, so I've heard." She turned to face Sawyer, nudging the boy sharply with her elbow. "You had a run-in with an Enforcer today, didn't you, Squirt? What happened, did you try to grab something that was too heavy for you, or did you just give the old broad a friendly pinch on the…"

"Shut up!" Sawyer exclaimed, his face turning a deep red. "That's *not* what happened! She said I tore her dress when I passed her. And how the heck would you know about it anyway?" His arms crossed over his chest petulantly as he stared at the fourteen-year-old girl.

"Been chatting with Caulin lately?"

Aimee grinned at him and poked him on the tip of the nose with one finger. It was a gesture he absolutely hated and the reason he tried to avoid her as much as possible. "Yeah, but that doesn't matter, 'cuz everybody's heard about it, Squirt. And I mean *everybody!* You nearly got dragged away by some fat old lady in the marketplace and then you snatched an Enforcer's painstick and tried to stun her!" Aimee's brown eyes were glowing as she stared at the little boy with new respect. Sawyer's eyes were blazing with anger.

"I did not!" he nearly shouted, drawing the attention of the other waiting children. "Where did you possibly hear that? I never grabbed his painstick, for crying out loud! He stopped the fat cow from selling me to the factories. And if I hadn't had this…" Sawyer thrust out his arm to show the metal band around his wrist, "…even *he* would have sold me. He didn't take me 'cuz I'm legal. It had nothing to do with his stupid painstick."

Aimee looked far less impressed after this speech. Turning to Eryyn she muttered, "You poor thing, how can you stand it? He can't even take care of himself, can't even stay out of trouble. It's like having a helpless puppy tagging along with you everywhere."

Eryyn chuckled as Sawyer's face reddened even more and his teeth clicked together audibly as his jaw clenched. She patted her friend on the shoulder to calm him down, then said, "He does better than *you*, Aimee. What did you bring tonight? I'll bet the things Squirt swiped from the house we just hit are lots better than yours."

Her eyes widening, Aimee nodded her head. "I'll take that bet. How about…half of what Master John pays you?"

"It's a deal." Eryyn held out her hand and slid her palm across Aimee's, sealing the bet. Sawyer, standing nearby, hands on his hips, looked at her as if she'd gone crazy.

"You do realize that you are betting *my* money as well as yours," he said petulantly.

"What's the matter, Squirt, afraid to lose?" A hand came down on Sawyer's shoulder and he turned his head to look up at thirteen-year-old Caulin, a kid who had the reputation of being the city's best klepto gossip. Caulin grinned down at him, then looked to Eryyn. "Can I get in on the bet too? Squirt may be small and skinny, but that also means he can't carry as much. And I'm always willing to make more money."

"That's because you spend more time talking than stealing," Sawyer spat, shoving the hand off his shoulder. "Get lost, Caulin! No one was talking to you, and Eryyn is not betting anymore of our money." He turned to Eryyn, brows raised to turn the statement into a plea. Eryyn grinned wickedly.

"Who said I'm not? I'll take the bet, Caulin, but you're gonna lose, I should just warn you now."

"Oh, come on!" Sawyer yelled, outraged. "Eryyn! That's not fair!" Eryyn and the two others ignored him and, feeling overmatched by the older thieves, Sawyer turned away and leaned against the wall of Master John's shop. Crossing his arms across his chest, he frowned down at the dirty street and refused to talk to anyone else until Master John opened the door and called them in to sell their wares.

"Come on, Squirt," Eryyn said, pulling him up from his slouch and marching him forcefully through the back door of the squat building. "Have more faith in yourself. You could beat those losers any day. Don't worry, I know Aimee, and I know Caulin and we're gonna leave here today with more credits than we'll know what to do with."

"How can you be so sure? I've never seen you out with Aimee or Caulin. How would you know what they bring in each day? We could lose everything."

To his disgust, Eryyn simply laughed and draped an arm over his shoulder as they stepped into the gloom of Master John's dealing room. "But we won't, Squirt, 'cuz I have *you* working for me."

"That's still not fair, Eryyn," Sawyer said, a faint trace of a smile now beginning to show on his lips. "How can you possibly expect me to argue with that?"

"I don't. Now c'mon, let's go win some credits." She pushed him up to the counter and thrust their bag in front of the fat dealer. All the others, having witnessed the betting in the alley, stepped back to let Master John sort through the sack, eager to see who would win the wager.

As he pulled out the jewelry and pieces of electronic equipment, John managed to keep his fat, doughy face impassive, refusing to show the pleasure he felt at the haul. He would certainly be able to make a good profit hawking such things in his shop. He pawed deeper into the sack, already mentally calculating how much he could get for the items versus the price he would have to pay Eryyn. He risked a glance up at the girl and saw her watching him carefully, searching his face for any sign of interest. Sawyer stood beside her and slightly behind, but the look on the boy's face was apprehensive rather than shrewd. He looked like he simply wanted to get out of there, and, catching the dealer looking at him, he ducked further behind his friend.

"Well," John said, smirking at the nervous child and wishing it was Sawyer he was dealing with and not the self-assured Eryyn, "it's better than you usually bring in. And I guess you're gonna tell me that that one got it all, right?" He pointed a thick finger at Sawyer, who swallowed and tried to keep a brave face.

Eryyn nodded proudly. "Give me a *little* credit, MJ. Some of the stuff I 'pocketed, but all the electronics came from the same house and Squirt got them all." She ignored Sawyer's elbow jabbing into her side and said, "So, what's it all worth to you?"

John spent a long moment staring shrewdly at the two kids, his wet lips pursed and his dark eyebrows deeply furrowed. Finally, fingering the video screen thoughtfully, he nodded curtly, then quoted his price.

"You've got to be kidding!" Eryyn shot, raising her eyebrows angrily. "Come on, MJ, don't be such a drip. What do you really think its worth?"

"I told you what I would pay, and I'm not going to dicker either." John grinned. "That's all you're gonna get." He beckoned them closer, his grin widening as he whispered for only their ears, "I heard you bragging out in the alley, girl, so let me tell you this, anything I give to you, I'm gonna give Aimee more."

"You can't do that!" Sawyer exclaimed. "That's not fair! That's *cheating!*" He glanced reproachfully at Eryyn, who suddenly looked very angry, and *very* nervous. They both knew that John certainly could do it.

"Why?" Eryyn asked, her voice just as low as the broker's. "What's wrong with a little gamble. Street kids do it all the time. Why would you take Aimee's side?"

John's grin widened, "For fun. You kids have your fun, and I have mine, and you're getting a little too high headed for my liking, girl. I figured this would be a good way to bring you down a few notches."

Sawyer, his cheeks flushed, his hands trembling, whispered, "There are *tons* of other shops we can sell to. You aren't the *only* broker in the city, you know. You'll just lose all our stuff."

John spat on the floor and wiped his mouth with a dirty sleeve. "You think I don't got friends, Squirt? You try to sell your junk somewhere else, and I can guarantee that you'll get the same treatment."

"You're a liar!" Eryyn snorted. "Brokers aren't friends. You couldn't do *anything* to us."

"Willing to find out?" The broker scratched his nose with a fingernail, then tapped the nail on his counter. "Of course, I can be a nice guy instead. I could give you what this stuff is worth, and make sure you win your little bet, but I would want something in return. You see, a good friend of mine asked a favor of me this morning, a favor I think the two of you could help me with."

"And what would that be?" Eryyn said coldly. She was eyeing their items on the counter, already trying to decide which other pawnshop they could try that night if John kept up his stupid games.

"Well, when my friend sent his messenger here, I decided that you two would be perfect for him. I mean, you *are* some of my best kleptos. I figured my friend would be glad to have you. Of course, I'd hate to lose your skills and services." John linked his fingers in front of him, simultaneously cracking all the knuckles. His closely spaced eyes sparkled with greed. "But my friend promised me that my sacrifice would be worth my while."

Sawyer's eyes widened fearfully and he took a step back. "You're talking about a gang!" he exclaimed, his voice high and loud enough for everyone in the room to hear. "You made a deal to sell us to a gang!"

"Forget it, John! It isn't happening! We don't work for any cheating gang! You know that." Eryyn reached for the video screen, intent on shoving it back into her bag. She had just placed her hand on it when John grabbed her wrist, holding it so tightly she winced, unable to pull away.

"Hold on just one minute, girl. Don't you walk away just yet—

talk to the guy. You never know, you may learn to like it. At least you and Squirt wouldn't have to worry about being sold by an Enforcer." He looked meaningfully at Sawyer, who blushed deeply despite the fear that glowed in his eyes. He had instinctively stepped away from the counter, moving towards the safety of the door, but had stopped when John grabbed his partner's wrist. He wouldn't go any further as long as Eryyn was trapped.

Eryyn tugged at her wrist, trying to free it from the man's fat hand. "Let me go," she said evenly, hoping her own nervousness was not as apparent in her voice as Sawyer's was in his eyes.

"Not until you talk to the guy." John's voice had taken on a hard tone and his hand had tightened painfully. "Just a second, let's go see him." Dragging the girl down the counter to a small door, he gave a swift, cursory knock with his knuckle, then pushed it open and marched in, pulling Eryyn behind him. Sawyer, at a loss, followed along. At the door, he paused long enough to glance back at the other children, who were watching him curiously. Aimee and Caulin, standing together, raised their eyebrows at him in confusion.

"What's going on?" Aimee asked. "What was all that about gangs?"

Sawyer shook his head, stepped into the room and, on John's order, shut the door behind him.

A single light-stick lit the room and it took Sawyer's eyes a moment to adjust to the sudden dimness before he saw the other figure sitting comfortably in a large chair that obviously belonged to John. The stranger, a tall boy who looked older than Eryyn, had been leaning back casually, but he quickly sat up, a smile on his face, as they stepped into the small room. The slight movement revealed a gold and red band strapped around his upper arm.

Recognizing the gang symbol, Sawyer gasped and immediately stepped back, his hand straying for the doorknob. Eryyn, still held by John's fat hand, doubled her struggles and swore at the man.

"I should have known!" she shouted angrily. "You've been working for the Foreman all along! You filthy sleaze! Let me go! Let go! Squirt, get out! Run, hurry!"

As Sawyer started to turn the knob to open the door, the boy in the chair held out his hands pleadingly. "Stop, wait! You don't have to be worried. I'm only here to talk, that's all. Calm down, Eryyn, I'm not going to try kidnapping you or anything."

Eryyn ceased her struggling and gave the boy a scalding look. "But I thought that's what you did, Otto. Stole kids off the street and made them work for the Foreman. Turned them into little slaves and made them too scared to stand up for themselves. And if things don't work out with them…" she dragged her free hand across her throat. "Isn't that how the gangs work, Otto? Isn't that why you joined up with one?"

Otto laughed and Sawyer heard a definite ring of cruelty to the sound. "You're imagining things, Eryyn. The Foreman's gangs don't work that way." His tone of voice suggested that he was dealing with a much younger child than a thirteen-year-old street girl. "The kids are *cared* for, Eryyn. He protects us from the Enforcers and those jerks who run the factories and want to save a credit or two by getting themselves cheap labor. The Foreman's kids are paired up—kinda like how you and your little friend are paired up. It's so they have some protection when they're out on the streets. And they're given training. The Foreman makes sure they have someplace safe to sleep at night and food. He doesn't hurt his kids."

"Oh yeah?" Sawyer said, fixing the boy with a glare. "Then why are you out recruiting? What happened to make you short?" Like Eryyn, Sawyer's relationship with Otto was not a pleasant one. Previous meetings and several attempted captures had taught Sawyer not to trust the gang leader.

Otto's face darkened slightly and he returned the boy's glare. "We had a little trouble with one of our kleptos a few days ago. She wasn't happy with the arrangement, even though we did everything we could to make her happy, and she took off." He snapped his fingers. "Simple as that. We weren't going to keep her in the gang if she didn't want to stay." He shrugged, and tried to smile, but the look on Sawyer's face told him that the small boy wasn't falling for the story, and the smile quickly faded.

Eryyn, with a grunt, finally managed to jerk her arm free of Master John's grip, but she made no move to run from the room. Instead, she faced the gang leader, hands on her hips. "Don't be a moron, Otto. We may be street kids, but we aren't stupid. Your gang crashed our nest last week and tried to grab us, *both* of us. We had to split."

"So if your gang and your Foreman don't want to force kids to do anything, why would you put a raid on us?" Sawyer finished, stepping up beside Eryyn.

Otto rolled his eyes as if the two children before him were trying to be stupid just for spite. "That wasn't a raid, you two. I was only trying to get you to join the gang. If you hadn't run off so quickly, we would have had a chance to talk." He looked over at Eryyn, his eyes taking on a kinder look. "C'mon, Eryyn, we used to be such good friends. It bothers me that we aren't anymore. I just want it to be like old times. I want to make sure you're safe. And him too, since he's your friend now." He pointed to Sawyer, who was staring, stunned, at Eryyn, then cocked his head, smiling. "What do you say, Eryyn? John, here, says the two of you've become quite a team and that you bring in the best loot. The Foreman likes kids who know their stuff. He'd make sure you had no more problems in the market and were set up to hit houses in the Sky-End!"

Eryyn's eyes were cold as she said, "I'm *not* interested, Otto! I never was, and never will be. As for our friendship…well, that went down the gutter when you decided to chicken out and join up with a gang. Go find some other sap to fool, it isn't working with me."

Otto's smile instantly faded and a flash of anger sparked in his eyes. Quickly, he tried to hide it and turned to Sawyer. "Well, what about you, Squirt? I hear you have a lot of talent, thanks to what Eryyn taught you. You could go far in our gang. Wouldn't you like to wear one of these?" He tapped the band on his arm.

Sawyer gave Otto a look of annoyed disdain. "Oh, wow! A pretty armband, all for me?" he asked, his voice dripping with sarcasm. "Dream on. I may be littler than you are, but I'm not a dummy. I don't want anything to do with your gangs. Just leave us alone."

John, who'd been quiet during the discussion, tried to reach out and grab Eryyn again. "Now wait just a minute! The Foreman is a great guy—he gives me a pretty good cut for all the kids I send to him, and he assures me that they're well taken care of. You should consider it an honor that I decided to offer you two up. I think you would do well in his gangs."

"Who cares what you think?" Sawyer said.

"We're leaving," Eryyn spat as she nimbly evaded John's reaching hand. Whipping her pocketknife from her shirt, she brandished the weapon at the broker and gang leader while grabbing at Sawyer's arm. "Like I said, go find some other kid and leave us alone. And we'll find some other place to sell our stuff from now on." She hurried out of the room, dragging Sawyer with her, and paused at the counter just long enough for the boy to sweep most of their stuff back into their bag, which he slung over his shoulder. Behind them, Master John rushed out of the room, a deep scowl on his ugly face. Eryyn ignored him, walking across the floor to stand in front of Aimee, Caulin, and the other kleptos, all of whom looked genuinely apprehensive.

"Bet's off," she said to Aimee and Caulin. "Get out of here if you know what's good for you. Unless you wanna get sold off to one of the Foreman's gangs!"

"Eryyn! Wait a minute!" Otto's urgent voice rang through the back of the shop.

Shaking her head angrily, Eryyn took the bag from Sawyer, shifted it onto her shoulder, shrugged at Aimee's questioning look, then walked out of the shop, her very relieved young partner at her heels.

• • •

"All this time." Eryyn was fuming, pacing back and forth across the dusty floor, waving her arms dangerously. "All this time and that *fat* creep has been *working* for the *Foreman!*"

Sawyer sat passively on the pallet of blankets that graced the floor of Nest Two, watching Eryyn walk off her steam. Since they had sought refuge in the nest three hours ago, she had not been able to stop talking about their encounter with Otto, or Master John's treachery.

"Just last month, Fern and Peter disappeared. They *both* used to sell at Master John's and then, one day, they just stopped coming!" Eryyn rounded on Sawyer, her finger jabbing the air angrily. "I'll bet he *sold* them! I'll bet he made a deal with Otto and that *jerk* came and carted them off to the gang! I can't believe I was so stupid! I should have seen it! All that time we were selling there I was just setting us both up. Damn, I should have known!"

"I didn't guess either, Eryyn," Sawyer risked saying, his head starting to hurt from watching her frenzied pacing. "Neither did Aimee or Caulin or any of the other kids. 'cuz if they had known, they wouldn't have sold to the shop either. He kept the secret really good."

"Really good! Gosh, Squirt, do you know what would have happened if we hadn't gotten out of there when we did? Or what if Otto had brought the rest of his gang to make sure we went along with him? What if I hadn't bought that knife when I did? We could have been forced into a gang! All this time, we've been so careful and we've been able to keep away from them, and now, because of that fat, dirty, sleazy, no good *pig*…!" Eryyn grabbed a double fistful of her hair and tugged it angrily.

Sawyer continued to watch her, then softly said, "How do you know that being in a gang is so bad, Eryyn? Lots of kids are in gangs. If they hated them as much as you do, if the gangs were as bad as you say, then they'd just leave and become independents like us. Wouldn't they?"

Eryyn's pacing suddenly stopped and she flung herself onto the pallet to sit beside the small boy. Resting an arm on Sawyer's shoulders, she said, "Gangs *are* bad, Squirt. Don't even try to think different. It's not worth a little protection and food to lose all your freedom. It's just not. I know this, because *I* was in a gang once, and I *hated* it. I wanted to leave more than anything, but it's not as easy as it sounds. The grown-ups who run the gangs need the kids to steal for them. They don't wanna let the kids go. They trick them into staying, give them more food for awhile, or show them a body found in the street, so the kids think they're better off. They tried to trick me, but I saw through it. So, after that, they just threatened me, told me that if I tried to leave the gang, *I* would end up as a body in the street."

Sawyer turned wide eyes to his friend, his mouth hanging open in stunned disbelief. "You were in a gang? *You*? But…you never told me. You never told me you were part of a gang."

Eryyn snorted. "What did you expect? That I'd go running around bragging about it? Believe me, Squirt. I just wanted to forget."

"I-is that how you know him? O-Otto I mean?"

Eryyn nodded. "Yeah, we used to partner together, like you and I do. We worked as independents until Otto talked to this guy from one of the gangs. He fell right into the stories and begged me to join with him. Well, he was my best friend at the time, and he was older: I trusted him, so I went along with it. I was in the gang for nearly a year and it was only after a couple of months that I *knew* I had to get out. Otto loved it—he was big and strong and smart—they kept shifting him to higher levels and giving him more power. I went to him, asking if I could leave the gang and go back to being independent. I told him that I didn't like being bossed around and that I wanted to keep the stuff I stole." She looked away briefly and uttered a short, harsh laugh. "He told me to shut up and stop complaining. That's when I decided to run away."

"How?" Sawyer's large, green eyes were round and full of awe as he stared at his older friend. "How did you run away?"

Eryyn opened her mouth to reply, then closed it with an audible snap. Wrapping both arms around Sawyer in a tighter hug, she shook her head. "I don't really wanna talk about it. It wasn't anything special anyway—I just managed to sneak out after a time and a...a friend helped me hide until the gang lost interest." Eryyn shivered, sighed, then rested her chin on the top of Sawyer's head. "All I'll say, Squirt, is that gangs are no good; don't ever listen to liars like Otto when they try to tell you different. Got it?"

Sawyer nodded, speechless, having just learned more about his friend's history than he'd learned in all the years since they'd partnered up. He watched Eryyn, his mind reeling, as she stood up, wandered over to his favorite window and looked out at the Sky-End.

"You know, Squirt," she said after a long moment of silence, "there are a lot of people who don't even think the Foreman exists."

Sawyer blinked. "I...well...I always thought he was some kind of monster, something that hid in the alleys and went after kids so he could eat them," he said, blushing slightly at the nightmarish fantasy.

Eryyn laughed, but the sound was bitter. "Oh, he's real, Squirt, and he is a monster, but he's worse than anything you could read about in those books of yours."

"You've seen him?"

"No, no one *sees* him! No one! He keeps himself hidden all the time, even when he meets with his gangs. No one knows who he really is, or what he really looks like."

"Then how do you know he's real?" Sawyer asked, holding out his hands in question. "It's like ghosts. I've never seen a ghost, so how do I know they're real?"

"You've never seen a mountain, have you? Or a lake? Or a forest? But you know *they're* real. They're out there somewhere, past the city. Just because you haven't seen something doesn't make it fake or any less real. I know the Foreman is real because I've seen bodies lying in Dumpsters or behind crates in the alleys…"

Sawyer started, suddenly remembering something. "Alleys?" he whispered. "Like two months ago, when you went into that alley and wouldn't let me go in with you? You told me to stay out on the street. You saw something in there, didn't you?"

Eryyn looked at Sawyer grimly, also remembering that day, two months back, when she had slipped into an alley to scout out an entrance to one of the apartments they planned to hit. She had climbed onto an old trash bin, hoping to use its height to reach a window and had glanced down into its depths.

She shuddered at the memory of what she'd seen hidden partially beneath the bags of trash. The person had been young, not much older than she was.

Sawyer, seeing Eryyn shudder, took his answer from her reaction and looked away. He began toying with a corner of his blanket, tugging it and pulling worn threads free to set loose in the air. He watched them slowly drift down to join the dust on the floor. "You know," he said after a moment of silence, "you don't have to hide *everything* from me. How can you expect me to learn how to protect myself if you keep acting like I'm a baby?"

Eryyn shrugged and refused to reply. The room was quiet again for a long time until: "He's real, Squirt. Believe me. I hadn't been an independent again for even two months before Otto caught up with me on the streets. I was really surprised that he wasn't mad at me for leaving." She laughed. "He wasn't mad, no, he wanted me to come back with him. He'd joined a new gang, a bigger gang, and he wanted me to be a part of it. He told me that he'd just joined one of the Foreman's gangs, and that it was only gonna be a matter of time before he was made leader."

Sawyer looked up at her again, frowning. "How long ago was that?"

"I-I think I was just about your age…no, wait, I was younger than you then, about nine. I'd been Otto's partner since I was six and he joined up with that other gang when I was just past seven. At the time, I was like you—I thought the Foreman was only a story that kids told each other to scare competition away from prime hit spots. I thought he was just a monster that lurked in the alleys and tried to kill and eat kids. Then Otto told me he was every bit as real as the Enforcers who walk the streets, and every bit as powerful."

"And he made Otto leader of one of his gangs?" Sawyer shivered, even though the room was warm because of their little stove. "You think he'll try to force you into the gang again, don't you?"

"I don't know what Otto thinks anymore. I used to think that I knew him like I know you, but, well, he changed after joining the gang. Right now, I think it wouldn't do us any harm if we sold the stuff you got today at one of the other shops, maybe that one Fifty-eighth Street." She smiled as Sawyer wrinkled his nose at the mention of the Dead-End shop. "And then we should hide out for a few days, maybe head over to Nest Six. We'll stock up on some supplies and stay there for awhile."

Sawyer frowned. "But Six is the newest nest—we haven't even stayed there for a whole night yet. We don't really know if it's completely safe…" He paused, his eyes widening with understanding. "But…Otto wouldn't have had time to learn about it, would he? You think he knows about the rest of our nests? This one even?"

"Don't get all paranoid, Squirt," Eryyn said, as Sawyer glanced apprehensively towards their entrance window. "I just want to play it safe, that's all. But still, it wouldn't hurt to break up this nest and leave it behind. We've used it a lot and I wouldn't be surprised if someone had seen us come and go here."

Sawyer, all thoughts of Otto wiped instantly from his mind, turned to her, horror stricken. Pulling in a harsh breath, his eyes flicked towards the boarded window where he'd spent many hours simply gazing out at the city. Eryyn followed his gaze and her lips turned down.

"And another good thing may come of it too," she mused, resting her hands on her hips as Sawyer turned his bright eyes back to her.

"It's not fair!" he exclaimed, pulling his knees up to his chest and hugging them tightly. "This is the *best* nest we've ever found. Why should we have to leave it just because of your stupid old partner?"

"Because it'll keep us safe if we do. And it may help keep your head out of the clouds and on solid pavement where it belongs." Eryyn winced inwardly, immediately regretting her words as Sawyer's eyes darkened with anger. The last thing she needed now was a fight with her best friend.

"I don't see why this conversation had to turn into a lecture for me," Sawyer groused, pouting and refusing to meet Eryyn's eyes.

"It's just my way, my little dreamer," Eryyn murmured, hoping to dispel the sour mood she had caused in the boy. "I want you to end up street-smart, not street-fodder."

Sawyer blew out a heavy breath, then picked up one of the books he had stolen just that day and flipped it open to a random page, hoping the new story would calm him down.

Ignored now, Eryyn watched him, feeling a familiar jealousy rising up in her chest. "You nearly got caught today because you wasted time picking out those stupid books," she pointed out, her tone causing Sawyer to look up. "Really, Squirt, what good is it to drag those things around with us from place to place? They're just heavy and they have no sale value."

"They have value to me," Sawyer protested, holding the book against him protectively. "I-I have to read, Eryyn, or I'll forget how."

"And why would that be so terrible?"

Sawyer ducked his head as he answered, "I just like knowing how to read. It's something special *I* can do and it makes me feel like I have a chance to do something else, to *be* something else." The minute the words were out of his mouth, he wished he could take them back. Clapping a hand over his lips, he looked up to see Eryyn glaring down at him, her eyes narrowed dangerously. "Sorry, I didn't mean it like that," he said miserably.

"Yes, you did," Eryyn hissed accusingly, all thoughts of keeping peace vanished under a wave of hot temper. "You think because I can't read and don't want to learn that I'll never be anything but a thief! Well, let me tell you something, Squirt, I'm a *lot* smarter than you are. You wouldn't even *be* here right now if it weren't for *me*. You would *never* have survived out there if I hadn't come along! You'd have been caught and sold off to a factory or a gang!"

Sawyer knew Eryyn's temper all too well from previous experiences, and now, his cheeks paling in the face of her anger, he swallowed hard and hugged his drawn-up knees tighter. "That was harsh, Eryyn," he whispered softly. "Really harsh. I didn't mean it, *honest*. I *know* you're smart—you're the smartest person I've ever met, even if you *can't* read. I just…" Sawyer sniffed, trying to hold back impending tears, and bit down hard on his lip before continuing, "I just don't wanna live like this for the rest of my life. I don't *like* stealing from people, Eryyn—it's not right! And I-I don't like being afraid of the Enforcers or the gangs. I wanna have a family again, a real family, in a real home. But everyday I see kids like Aimee, or Caulin, and I keep wondering if anyone would actually *want* them. But, if…if I don't let myself become like them…if I don't think of the streets as my whole life…well, then maybe…"

"You'd have a chance to be picked up by some Sky-End couple who live in a beautiful house and want a little son of their own to love and spoil? *Wake up, Sawyer!* Are you really still thinking about that?"

Sawyer glanced up, startled by her use of his real name. Unable to cope with her angry eyes and flushed face, he looked down again and two tears slid down his cheeks.

"It's not going to happen!" Eryyn raged on, caught up fully by her temper and not caring anymore if she hurt his feelings. "No one is going to come along, adopt you, and take you into their home. If anyone takes you off the streets, they'll be marching you right into a factory! That's a fact of life, Squirt, and you just have to *live* with it, just like you have to live with being *poor* and being a *thief*. None of that's going to change just because you know how to read and dream your little fantasies. *Just get it out of your head already!*"

These last words, shouted so loudly that a bit of the dry, crumbling plaster sprinkled to the floor, made Sawyer wince and cry even harder. Hiding his face in his hands, he began to sob.

His reaction startled Eryyn, whose anger immediately cooled in the face of her young partner's grief. Despite all his difficult years of living on the streets, facing daily dangers from the Enforcers and gangs, Sawyer rarely cried. But Eryyn's harsh words, coming so soon after the close call in the house and the scare at Master John's shop, had opened a hidden reservoir deep inside him. Overwhelmed by his tears, he didn't even notice that Eryyn had wrapped her arms around him until she spoke in his ear.

"I'm sorry, Squirt! I didn't mean it. Please don't cry, I didn't mean it! I was just upset, that's all. We just had such a hard time today—you almost getting caught twice, and then Otto showing up at Master John's. Well, I just wasn't in the mood to hear your stories. They make me feel funny, and I just couldn't handle that, not now, not today. Please don't be so upset, it's not that bad."

"But it is!" Sawyer cried, his words muffled by his hands. "It is that bad, Eryyn." He finally looked up, sniffling, and Eryyn winced at the expression in his reddened, tear-puffy eyes. "I miss having a real house to live in, and toys, and good food, and a real bed. I miss my family!"

His words hit Eryyn like a blow and she bit her lip as her own eyes grew misty. Sawyer, seeing this, had to stifle more tears just so he could continue.

"I hate this!" he cried, slamming his fists into the rags of the pallet. "You're all I've got now, Eryyn, and I hate making you mad at me. I didn't mean to make you feel bad." Another wave of sobs rose in his throat and he covered his eyes again helplessly.

Eryyn sat frozen, one arm wrapped around his shoulders, her eyes filled with tears that she refused to release. She knew that she could truthfully echo Sawyer's words; the fight was *her* fault, not Sawyer's, and she should apologize, but her throat had seized up and she couldn't bring herself to speak. Beside her, Sawyer finally managed to control his tears and, when Eryyn didn't reply to his outburst, he became morosely silent, staring at the floor.

"We'll leave now," Eryyn said finally, wiping quickly at her eyes when Sawyer lifted his head to look at her. "We'll pack up all the stuff here and we'll go to Six. We won't use this nest anymore. It's caused us nothing but trouble anyway. Alright?" She tightened her arm around him briefly and cocked her head, waiting for his answer.

Sawyer's green eyes narrowed into slits as he stared at her. He opened his mouth to speak, then seemed to think better of it. With a deep sigh, he looked away and nodded.

Eryyn, sensing that the fight wasn't really over, just put on pause for the time being, gave her small friend a tighter squeeze, then stood up to begin the packing of their meager belongings. She was just stuffing their stove into one of their sacks when Sawyer spoke, his voice pitched low so she had to pause in her work to hear it.

"I don't care what you say, I'm not gonna stop believing that there's something better than all this. But if it makes you happy, I promise I won't talk about it anymore. And I won't argue about leaving the best nest we've ever had, just 'cuz you don't like the view." He stood up and grabbed the other bag, stuffing his books deep inside it before rolling up their blankets. Eryyn stared at him, but he refused to meet her eyes until they were completely packed up and the room was empty except for the dust.

As she headed for the exit window, Eryyn suddenly realized that Sawyer wasn't following. Turning back, a scowl already forming on her face, she saw the boy standing by his window, staring out at the Sky-End view that had been the cause of many of their disagreements. Sensing her gaze on him, Sawyer finally turned to look at her and shrugged.

"I won't forget, Eryyn, and I won't give up, no matter what you say. I'm not like Caulin or Aimee…or even you for that matter. This isn't it and *I* know it." Sneaking one last, longing look at the house on the hill, Sawyer hefted his bag over his shoulder and joined Eryyn to leave.

• • •

Night had fallen in the city, and the street lamps that still functioned were turned on to illuminate the streets and alleys to the people returning to their homes. Yet, even with all the lamps turned to their highest, there wasn't enough light to dispel the darkness that lay over the city like a blanket. If anything, the lights made the surrounding shadows seem even darker.

Or, at least that's how it felt to Aimee as she made her way down the street, searching out the tiny doorway that led to one of her own hiding nests. The night air was chill and the skin on her arms broke out into goosebumps that sent a shiver through her. But, even as it happened, she wondered if it was really the cold that caused them, or the amazing things that had happened in Master John's shop just a few hours ago.

She'd been shocked when Sawyer and Eryyn had started yelling about the Foreman and his gangs, and even more shocked when the two burst out of the small back room, angry and pale. Eryyn's words had been puzzling and, seeing the look on Master John's face, Aimee had decided to pawn her goods at one of the other shops for that night. Tomorrow, she'd find Eryyn and ask her what had happened and if her suspicions were true; and if Master John was working for the Foreman and selling kids off to the gangs, well, she'd just have find herself a new regular shop.

But now, she was simply too tired to worry about it any more. It had been a long day for her—she made most of her loot by 'pocketing and had walked from the Dead-End straight through the Mid-End in search of likely targets. Her feet hurt, she was hungry, and she hadn't found a shop worth selling to, so she would continue to be hungry until the next morning.

Silently cursing Eryyn and Sawyer for ruining her plans for the day, she picked her way down the street, taking care to stay in the milky light of the lamps as much as possible. There were dangers far worse than Enforcers and gangs lurking in the shadows, especially at night.

Aimee paused and looked back over her shoulder apprehensively. Not seeing anything, she cocked her head to one side. She could have sworn she'd just heard footsteps behind her. Frowning, she shrugged it off, hugged herself for warmth, then started walking again.

She had barely taken five steps when she stopped again, sure this time that she had heard someone following her—someone who stopped every time she did.

"Caulin! Is that you?" she called, thinking it was her friend trying to play a trick on her. Caulin knew that she didn't like the dark and used every opportunity he could find to scare her. "Come out, you dummy! I'm not in the mood to fool around!"

"Alright. I'm coming."

Aimee drew her breath in sharply—that voice was not Caulin's!

She began walking backwards, edging away from the source of the voice.

"Who are you? What do you want?" The voice was familiar to her, she had heard it just recently, but she couldn't place it with a face.

"My name's Otto." A shadow appeared in the darkness before her, slowly growing more distinct until a tall, handsome boy stepped into sight. He smiled warmly at Aimee and held his hands out to show her he meant no harm. "I'm a friend of Eryyn's. I just wanted to talk to you, that's all."

Aimee was instantly wary. The boy's name was familiar to her, but not in a good way. "Er…Eryyn? How do you know her?"

"The same way you do. We're all thieves—Eryyn and I used to work together. We were very good friends."

"Were?" Aimee had not missed the use of the word and raised her eyebrows at the boy.

Otto shrugged. "We had a few small disagreements and decided to part ways. Anyway, I was talking to her earlier, but it seems that she doesn't have a lot of fond memories of me. She left in a bit of a hurry. Very rude." He started shaking his head sadly.

"Talking to her?" Signals started going off in Aimee's mind and she took another step back. "She was shouting something about gangs; so was Squirt. You're from the Foreman's gang, aren't you?"

Otto smiled and crossed his arms over his chest. "Wow, that's very good! Yeah, I was smart enough to join a gang. Best decision of my life, if you ask me."

"What do you want?" Aimee demanded, taking another step back. She didn't need to listen to his answer. She already knew what he wanted. All *she* wanted was to get away.

Otto laughed scornfully to see her backing away. "You've already got it figured out, you flake. I'm out hunting, you might say. Looking for smart, talented thieves. You wouldn't happen to know any, would you?"

Aimee continued to retreat until she bumped into something hard and unyielding. Hands grabbed at her arms, holding them tightly as she started to struggle.

"*Let me go!*" she screamed. "I don't wanna be a part of your *stupid* gang! Leave me alone! *Help*, someone help me!"

Otto sighed and cocked his head towards a nearby alley. Aimee's struggles were useless as she was dragged off in that direction, away from the main street, away from the protecting lights. A hand clamped over her mouth, cutting off her screams, and she was pulled down the alley, where several other shadows waited.

At the mouth of the little passageway, Otto paused and glanced back, looking up and down the street, and up at the windows in the buildings all around. No one else was in sight. No one had witnessed the abduction. With a grin, he picked up a stone and threw it at the nearest street lamp, breaking the glass of the globe and shattering the bulb within. The area beneath the lamp, and the mouth of the alley, was plunged into darkness as the boy slipped after his friends to see to their new member.

• • •

"I was in the market today, and you'll never believe what I saw. It was absolutely horrible!"

Gregory Paulson looked up at his wife while she placed a dish of potatoes on the scarred top of their small table. Tucking a napkin into the collar of his shirt he said, "Do I really want to know about it, or is it just going to make me even more depressed after a bad day at work?"

His wife glared at him and set a pitcher down with more force than was necessary, splashing water over the table. "No matter how bad your day was today, it couldn't be nearly as bad as that of this little boy I saw."

Gregory groaned loudly and started dishing himself some of the potatoes. "Not another of your charity cases, Liz?" He scanned the table, looking for something more substantial than the mashed potatoes and settled on a piece of the fatty meat that was all he could afford.

"And just what do you mean by that? Greg, if you had seen this boy you wouldn't be so quick to shrug him off. He was just minding his own business, walking around the market, and then this woman goes completely crazy, grabs his arm, and calls him a thief. She was *hurting* him, Greg, and she would have dragged him off to the factories if an Enforcer hadn't been nearby to stop her! I was right there, watching, and no one, I repeat, *no one* stepped forward to help this child. They all just gathered around like it was a show, like this little boy's fear and pain were entertainment. I kept trying to get closer and put a stop to it, but everyone just pushed me back! But I could *see* him, Greg! I saw his face, and how terrified he was." Liz ground her teeth together and clenched her hand into a tight fist. "And I would bet *everything* that the woman had no intention of taking him to the Enforcer station for a fair hearing. I'll bet she would have taken him right to the factories so she could sell him, and the boy was *legal*—he had a *bracelet* and a *number* and everything!"

"Having a legal I.D. doesn't mean he isn't a thief, Liz. Why do you think he was walking around the market? He was probably picking pockets." Greg bit into a piece of meat, swearing under his breath at the lousy quality and how he wished he could have a *real* steak for once. He was just about to take another bite when he felt angry eyes upon him and looked up at his wife. He groaned again and dropped his fork onto his plate with a loud clatter. "Oh, c'mon, Liz. Don't look at me like that. You know I'm telling the truth. It's a sad fact that most of the kids out on the streets are thieves. And if they're not doing that, then they're doing *something* that's even *worse*."

"And you don't feel sorry for them? Those kids have no chance. Nobody takes care of them. Of *course* they have to steal, if they want to survive…" Liz shuddered, remembering with painful clarity the pleading look that had been sent her way by the frightened boy in the market. She had seen everything: from the boy being accused and insulted, to the woman grabbing his arm and trying to drag him out of the market, to his near interrogation, and it hurt that she hadn't been able to do anything to help.

"The Enforcers do what they can to round them up and take them someplace where they'll be given good work to sustain them." Even as he said the words, Gregory knew what Liz's response would be. He sighed and steeled himself for her tirade.

"Good work? Sustain them? Most of the Enforcers line their pockets with the profits made from selling illegal street kids to the factories. They don't take *care* of them! They don't train them for the future. They make them slaves is more like it! Force them to work in the factories for no pay and no hope of a real *life*, of an *education*. Will you listen to yourself, Greg? It's your job to oversee those factories everyday. You get paid to see to the workers and make sure everything is done fairly and correctly. And everyday you come home complaining about the conditions in those places— and that's just the conditions for those who get paid and can quit if they choose to. What about the children you see working there? The ones who were sold there by people like the woman in the market? The ones whose only alternative is stealing on the streets, or *something worse*? What conditions do they live under? What fears do they have that keep them there, even though they're underfed and overworked?"

Greg pushed his plate away—the image his wife had conjured had just lost him his appetite. And it was because he knew the words were true that made the images so terrible. Everyday he saw the children who were forced to work in the factories to avoid being deported. Small, skinny, unhealthy waifs who staggered back and forth at the odd jobs they could find the strength to do. Most of them bore the bruises and cuts of the older workers who had no tolerance for slow, clumsy efforts. Most of them were sick from lack of food. Most didn't live past their fourteenth birthday.

Again, he felt Liz's eyes upon him and, again, he looked up into her deep blue gaze. "Alright, alright, I agree, it's a *horrible* life for them. But is it anymore horrible than leaving them on the streets where they're beaten and *killed* by older kids, or forced to scrounge through the trash for food? I know you want to help them all, Liz, and I want to help them too, but what can we do? We barely have enough money to feed ourselves, and heaven knows the Enforcers don't help with their cheap rations. And the law forbids more than two children in the household under the age of sixteen, so adoption wouldn't help more than a couple of them."

"But I've been talking with Carmen and Olivia and they feel the same way about the kids. They think that helping the street kids would do a big part in helping to make our city safer. If there was only a place where these kids could go and get food and an education, a place where they could live and be safe and…possibly adopted."

Greg rested his chin on one hand and raised an eyebrow at his wife. "Sounds like a dream come true. And who would pay for this?"

"We would! Well, I mean, we would collect funds and donations to run it."

"No one would donate anything. People don't want to waste their money on someone else's thieving illegal."

"But we can try at least!" Liz exclaimed, giving her husband an impatient, exasperated glare. "Even if it doesn't work, we would have still tried!"

"And where would you put this special charity house?" Greg leaned on the table and looked at his wife, a grin playing on the corners of his mouth. "Right here in this apartment? Or, no, maybe in Carmen's place—that one room flat. Or maybe in a factory break room, yeah, I could see that happening."

For a moment, Liz looked like she was about to argue, but she managed to hold her tongue and turned away to take her own plate from the counter. "I know we haven't planned out everything yet," she murmured, staring through the window over the sink. "But we will eventually, and then we'll help straighten this filthy city out."

"And what about the Enforcers?" Greg persisted. "What's to stop them from shutting this place down, rounding up those poor kids, and deporting them or carting them off to the factories? Most street kids spend their lives avoiding notice for that very reason."

Liz sighed. "I *know*. I know there are a *lot* of details left to work out. But, Greg, I...I just feel like I have to try *something*. For that little boy's sake...for the sake of all of them."

Gregory stood up from his seat and wrapped his arms around Liz before she could take her place at the table. Squeezing her tightly, he pressed a kiss to her neck then whispered, "I know you'll figure it out. You'll come up with something, and when you do, I'll be right there beside you, ready to help in any way that I can. But...until then, please don't make me want to starve myself."

Liz snuggled into her husband's arms and nodded. "Alright, I won't mention it again until we're able to do anything about it." Then, turning around, she poked a finger into his belly. "But when that happens, I'll *expect* you right there beside me."

"You have my promise," Greg gasped, bent over slightly from the jab.

Liz sat down to her dinner, a smile forming on her full lips. She would be certain to keep Gregory to that promise, and hoped she could call upon it very soon.

• • •

It was dark and cold. Aimee didn't know where she was, or how long she'd been there, or when she would be let go, but she *did* know that it was dark and cold.

Her wrists hurt because she'd pulled too hard against the bindings that held her arms to the chair and had chafed her skin. Also, her head was swimming with imagined lights in the darkness and her ears pounded with the sound of blood rushing from her frantically beating heart.

"Is somebody out there!" she screamed. "You can't *do* this to me! Let me *go*, please! *Please*, whoever you are, let me go!"

"But I don't want to let you go. If I let you go now, you'll only try to run away."

Aimee gasped and whipped her head around. She'd been locked up in the small room for a long time, she was sure of that. But during that time, she had never seen, or heard, a door open to admit another person. Yet the voice that had just spoken was directly behind her. Had the person been with her in the room for the entire time, just standing there silently, watching her struggle and cry with frustration? The very thought made her shudder and more tears popped into her eyes.

The speaker went on, "And right now, I don't want you to run away. I just want to have a nice talk with you and tell you what is going to happen. But for me to do that, I need your cooperation, Aimee. Will you give it to me?"

Fighting back her fears, Aimee managed to stammer, "H-how do you know m-my name?"

The faceless voice chuckled nearby. "I know more than anyone in my city. I know *everything*. I know *who* you are, how *old* you are, that you are an *illegal*, with no true name or identity of your own. I know where you nested, and where you preferred to work 'pocketing…shall I go on?"

"What do you want? Who are you?" Aimee's voice was anguished as she shouted out into the dark. Once again, she began struggling against the ropes that held her to the chair and kicked out her feet, hoping to strike the unknown and unseen speaker.

"I guess you're not the smartest child on the streets, or else you would have guessed who I am already. As to what I want…that, too, is easy to answer if you just think about it. My head gang is short a klepto. One of my children is unable to work because he has no partner. You, girl, are going to rectify that situation."

Despite her terror, Aimee did her best to sound tough and sure of herself. She failed miserably. "You *can't* make me! I don't care if Master John sold me out or not. He doesn't own me. I don't work for *gangs*!"

A dry chuckle filled the air around her. "Definitely not the smartest child on the streets. You work for a gang *now*, girl. You work for one and from now on you will work harder than you ever have before or…well, I'll just allow your fellow kleptos to tell you about the consequences. Especially the boy who will soon be your partner. You should ask him what happened to his *former* friend. I can assure you, you wouldn't want the same fate."

Aimee felt her breath tighten in her chest and she looked wildly into the dark, desperately trying to catch a glimpse of her captor.

"And what makes you think I'll stay in your stupid gang? Once I get out of this chair and back on the streets, you can bet that I'll…"

"Run away? Hah, they all try to run away. Most don't make it and the few that do…well, they're found again…maybe a week later, maybe a month…in a box tucked into an alley, or maybe hidden under trash in a Dumpster. It's an obvious truth—there is no life without a gang. You'd do better to learn this very quickly."

Aimee let out a small sob and threw herself against her bonds with a new strength.

"It won't work. No one can get out of that chair. You'll just sit there for awhile until you've had a chance to calm down. Then you can meet your new friend. I'm sure he will be happy to meet you as well. Around here you don't get fed unless you work, and he hasn't been able to work for several days now."

The voice suddenly grew faint, and Aimee realized the man was leaving. Leaving her alone, tied to the chair, in the dark room.

"*No!*" she screamed. "Let me go! I don't wanna be here! I don't wanna be in a gang! *Let me go, please!*"

"Sleep well. Hopefully a few days in the dark will mellow you out some."

"I know who you are!" Aimee cried. "I'm not stupid and I know who you are!"

"Of course you know who I am. Once they meet me, everyone knows. There's only one Foreman, girl. Be proud that you have been given the honor of working for him."

Sunshine in a rainstorm

After the fight in Nest Two, Eryyn and Sawyer hardly spoke a word to each other that wasn't related to work or theft. Both hurt by the other's words, both feeling they deserved an apology, they withdrew into their own thoughts and the days and nights became painfully quiet and strained.

On Eryyn's order, they had moved into Nest Six, a desolately small nest compared to the one they'd just been forced to abandon. Situated in a broken-down car, they had removed the backseat to make a small cave of sorts that they could sit, crouch, or sleep in. It was cramped and smelled of the nearby sewer. The only saving grace was that after they had covered all the holes and windows with rags, pieces of old fiberglass, and wood, their tiny stove managed to fill the entire place with satisfying warmth.

After a long day of 'pocketing in the market, Eryyn sat awake, even though the hour was late and the streets were black as pitch from lack of useful and working lamps. Beside her, wrapped in a motley of spare clothes and pilfered blankets, Sawyer was sound asleep, his eyes closed, a hand tightly gripping one of his treasured books. One finger was still marking the last page he'd been reading when he'd given in to slumber.

Eryyn watched him closely, wondering how he always managed to sleep so deeply. Life on the streets had taught her to be constantly alert, even while resting. She napped at best, waking up instantly if a sound or smell caught her attention. In a way, she had become like the wary animals that still lurked in the shadowy parts of the city—the cats, rats, and stray dogs that were always prepared for some danger. Sawyer, on the other hand, seemed to trust that if *he* was asleep, then so were the dangers.

Eryyn shook her head as she looked at him. Briefly, she toyed with the idea of shaking him awake, just to tell him off for not being alert and more careful. There had been times when she'd done that, to Sawyer's great annoyance. Now though, with the way they had been acting towards each other, she had the suspicion that Sawyer would not laugh it off after a few minutes and go back to sleep. He'd be angry. And he'd continue to be angry throughout the entire day, ruining their chances of making a good profit by working together.

Sighing deeply, Eryyn wrapped one of their blankets around her shoulders and nestled down, trying to get comfortable in the tight quarters. Accidentally, one of her feet, looking for some spare bit of space, scraped against Sawyer's cheek. The boy was awake in an instant—apparently, he didn't sleep as deeply as Eryyn thought— and clasping a hand to his sore cheek. His wide eyes glared at her.

"Why'd you do that?" he accused, sitting up and blinking back tears. A red mark was already beginning to form beside his nose. "Just because you can't sleep doesn't mean you can…"

Eryyn held out her hands helplessly. "Squirt, I didn't mean it, honestly. I was just trying to get comfortable. There's not a lot of room in here."

"And you just noticed this?" Sawyer asked sarcastically. "We had *plenty* of room in Two."

Eryyn groaned. "Don't start that again—it was an accident, alright! If I'd wanted to hurt you, I would have done a lot worse."

"Oh, that's a nice way to put it!" Sawyer rubbed at his cheek. "And the least you could have done is say sorry!"

"It was just a little scrape! Sheesh, you don't have to make such a big deal over it!"

"If I had kicked you outta sleep, you'd be climbing the walls, and you don't want *me* to make a big deal of it?"

"Oh, just shut up and go back to sleep."

"So you can kick me again? Forget it, I'm up now, and I'm hungry."

"Well, that's tough because we have nothing to eat. That junk we sold yesterday didn't bring in enough to get dinner *and* breakfast. Besides, the stupid dealer cheated us more than MJ ever did."

"That's not *my* fault. *You* picked him." Sawyer pulled himself to his knees and made for the hole that had once contained the car's driver side door. Pulling aside the slab of fiberglass they had found to cover up the hole, he climbed out onto the street.

"Where are you going?" Eryyn asked, shifting slightly so she could see him out the door. "It's still dark."

"As if I couldn't figure that out for myself," Sawyer muttered, stretching after the cramped quarters. "But then again, you *are* a lot smarter than me, aren't you?"

Eryyn winced to have her words thrown back at her. "You know it's not safe to wander around at night. Get back in here and stop being an idiot."

"I'm not an idiot," Sawyer replied heatedly. "I'm hungry, and I'm gonna go find something worth pawning so I can have something to eat."

Eryyn stared at her friend, wondering how he could have become so angry that he was willing to risk walking around at night, alone. Their last fight hadn't really been resolved, and he had taken the loss of Nest Two badly, but to actually risk walking around at night, just to get away from her for a few hours…? He really couldn't be holding *that* much of a grudge?

"Squirt! Get back here, are you crazy! C'mon, it's not worth it, just because you're a little mad."

"A little mad!" she heard Sawyer mutter. He had started heading down the street—she had to lean out the door to see him. Sawyer ignored her and kept moving. Afraid of losing sight of her friend, Eryyn scrambled out of the car and ran after him. Catching up, she reached out and spun him around to face her, causing him to flinch as her fingers dug into his tender, still bruised arm. Loosening her grip only slightly, she spoke in a rush, "Okay, Squirt, I'm sorry! I'm *really* sorry! Just don't go out now, it's too dark. Please, come back!"

Sawyer scowled briefly, then let out a long sigh and nodded. Not letting go of his arm, Eryyn turned, greatly relieved, and led him back to the car.

"I hate this thing," he muttered, climbing into the small space.

Without another word, he crawled back to his little bed and flopped down, curling up into a small ball. He pulled his blanket over his head.

"Well, at least you came back," Eryyn sniffed, climbing in after him and moving the slab of wood back over the exit hole. She leaned against it, determined to block any more attempts to take a late night walk.

"I told you that I'm not stupid. I just thought I deserved an apology," Sawyer's muffled voice said from under his blanket. Eryyn turned and stared at his huddled shape, her eyes wide with shock.

"You mean… you set that whole thing up! You wouldn't have walked off? You were just looking to get me to say sorry?"

Sawyer's tousled head appeared again and he flashed Eryyn a smug grin. "I *told* you I'm not stupid! You should have apologized days ago. *I* did. Please don't kick me anymore. I'm going to sleep."

Eryyn's mouth dropped open, but she was speechless. Sawyer's grin widened and he dropped his head down on his arm, closing his eyes. Eryyn stared at him silently for another minute before she finally found her voice again.

"Oh, Squirt, one day I'm gonna…"

"Treat me like I have a brain of my own?" Sawyer quipped, without opening his eyes. "I sure hope so. Goodnight, Eryyn."

With a cry of annoyance, Eryyn threw a handful of rags at the boy, covering his head with tattered cloth. Sawyer began to giggle and tossed his head to dislodge the rags, which he rearranged over the blankets he was already using.

"Thanks, I was a bit chilly. Though I thought you would have wanted these for yourself." Turning again on his side, Sawyer snuggled down beneath the blankets as, behind him, Eryyn realized her mistake and was left to curl up in the few tatters she had not thrown. Grumbling to herself about being outsmarted by a ten-year-old, Eryyn wrapped the largest of her rags around her shoulders and slumped down against the wall of the car, trying to get comfortable while keeping her feet well away from the soundly sleeping boy.

• • •

"It's not that bad, Aimee, once you get used to it. You just have to remember that whatever Otto says is what's right. If you follow his orders, and don't try to upset the Foreman, you'll get along fine."

"Yeah, just like your last partner got along fine?"

Rane flinched at the stinging words and took a step back from the angry girl he had been trying to comfort. "That's not really fair," he said softly.

"No, what's not fair is that they can grab me off the streets and force me to work for them. It's not going to happen, so just *get lost*, alright! I'm not your partner, I'm not a gang member, and I'm going to get out of here the *first* chance I get."

Rane shook his head wearily. Ever since Aimee had been released from the darkroom, two days ago, he had been locked up with her with the orders from Otto to convince her to accept her new position within the gang. So far, she hadn't shown any sign of caring about what he said and Rane was beginning to get desperate. He didn't want to call Otto's wrath down on himself again—the gang leader had only *just* forgiven him for Pammy's disobedience.

Also, he was very hungry, and it was a rule in the gang that new members were not fed until they were "tame", as Otto put it. Unfortunately, this meant that the partner locked up in the room with them was also forced to go without food. This was a cruel blow to the boy, since Otto had seen fit to punish him for Pammy's mistake, and that punishment had included the withholding of his already meager rations. He was on the verge of getting on his knees and begging the stubborn girl to listen to him, if it would just get him something to eat.

"Please, Aimee, just think about it. What choice do you have?"

"Shut up and leave me alone!" Aimee raised a fist and threatened to hit the boy if he came any closer.

Again Rane flinched, and he took another step back, giving up on what seemed an impossible task. When *he'd* first been added to the gang it had been Pammy's job to talk to him and convince him not to give them any trouble. He'd made it easy for her. He'd only been nine and had just lost an older friend, who'd taken him in and protected him, to illness. Being in a gang had sounded much easier than making his own way on the streets, and, after two days of being tied to the chair in the darkroom, he'd been more than willing to listen to what Pammy had had to say. Unfortunately, Aimee was not a shy, timid, little nine-year-old who was afraid of the streets and the dangers they posed. She was tough, fourteen, and had been making her own living as a thief for more than six years. She had proven to herself that gangs were not needed and best avoided.

But that didn't mean she had to be so difficult and risk them both getting into trouble with Otto. Sighing deeply, Rane turned his back on her and walked over to the far wall, where he leaned his head against the flat, rough surface, completely out of ideas. His stomach rumbled and the last of his patience dissolved.

"Fine!" he shot back over his shoulder, barely keeping his voice from breaking with his emotions. "Be like that! I really couldn't care. But when that jerk Otto comes in, I hope you tell him that I did *all* I could, and that you were just too *pig-headed* to listen. Not that he'll care—I'll get a thrashing for it anyway." His voice faded off into angry, depressed mumbles and he closed his eyes tightly, unaware that Aimee was staring at him from across the room.

For some reason, the boy's impatient voice had broken through her anger and she had suddenly realized that none of this was *his* fault. *He* hadn't been one of the kids who'd kidnapped her. He didn't want to be here any more than she did, and if he was trying to convince her to accept the gang as her new life, it was only because he feared the boy called Otto.

And she really couldn't blame him for that. In the first hours of their imprisonment together, he had told her about his life in the gang, including that his last partner, the girl who had taught him everything he knew about gang life, had angered the Foreman by bringing in an engraved piece of jewelry. Otto had been admonished by the Foreman for not noticing the item sooner, and he, in turn, had punished Rane for something he hadn't even done, just because Pammy had been his partner.

Looking at the boy, Aimee shook her head sadly. He was only twelve, and already he'd seen eight kids come and go in the gang. Just where they went, he didn't say, but Aimee was wise enough to figure it out for herself. They were the kids who ended up hidden in the trash or the river. All because they had done something to anger the gang leader, or worse, the Foreman himself. Kids who had made stupid little mistakes, like bringing in engraved items. Or kids who had been too stubborn to take orders. Just as stubborn as *she* was being now.

"Wh-what'll happen if I don't listen to that Otto guy? If I don't just settle in and start working for the Foreman?" she asked when Rane showed no sign of moving.

"Take a guess," was Rane's curt reply. "Which means that I'll be without a partner again, which means that I can't work, which means that I won't get any food and will probably be punished again." He turned around, leaning against the wall, his arms crossed over his chest, and fixed his dark brown eyes on her face. For the first time since they had been paired together Aimee studied him closely. Seen like this, with the light of the tiny, barred window shining on him, she noticed that his clothing, faded and patched, was too large for his small frame. He was very thin and not unattractive, but with the furtive, wary look of one who has learned the hard way that there are few who can be trusted. At twelve, he looked as though his life, only two years shorter than her own, had been filled with more hardships than she wanted to imagine, and considering that he had spent three of those twelve years under the Foreman's command, she didn't doubt that. But now, on top of all his wariness and fear, he looked angry. And that anger was directed at her.

"But it wouldn't matter to *you* if I got punished by Otto," he continued, his eyes narrowed to slits. "You wouldn't care if he locked me up in a closet for *three* days after slapping me around like a punching bag. You wouldn't care if he gave me *another* black eye, or maybe broke my arm so I couldn't work. You wouldn't care if he refused to let anyone give me food and just left me locked up to starve. And do you wanna know *why* you wouldn't care, Aimee? Do you want me to *spell* it out for you? It's actually rather simple. You'd...be...dead! Just like Pammy! Just like Carlos and Vicky, or Quint and Judey! And you wouldn't have to worry about Otto or the Foreman ever again. But I'll just tell you this, Aimee, *that's* the only way you're ever gonna get out of here, 'cuz they'll *never* let you go, and *no one* escapes from the Foreman."

He broke off, out of breath, and the room was plummeted into silence. Aimee sat on the floor beneath the window, her eyes wide and stunned as she stared at the boy. Everything she'd ever heard in rumors about the Foreman's gangs had just been repeated to her by a long time member, someone who knew firsthand that they were *not* rumors—that everything was, in fact, true. Dropping her face into her hands, she began to cry.

Almost immediately there were hands on her shoulders, tapping her frantically and awkwardly.

"Don't cry, Aimee. I'm sorry if I sounded mean. But you wouldn't listen to me and I had to get you to understand." Rane's voice was rough with tears of his own and he knelt beside her, unsure of how to stop her from crying and attracting Otto or his lackeys. "I just didn't want you to get in trouble with Otto. I-it's really not so b-bad, once you get used to it."

"You're a *liar!* And you're not a good one," Aimee said, her voice muffled by her hands. "You *hate* it here, just as much as I do. If you had the chance, you'd run." She suddenly looked up at his startled face, catching his wide brown eyes with her own. "Wouldn't you?"

Rane's eyes flicked nervously towards the door and he licked his lips before answering, "You shouldn't talk like that. It'll get you in trouble. No one *talks* about escaping."

Aimee stared at him curiously for a moment, trying to ponder out his meaning. She, too, glanced towards the closed and locked door, and suddenly realized what Rane had meant. No one actually *talked* about trying to escape from the gang. It was too easy for the wrong people to overhear. No, you didn't *talk* about escaping, you just *did*. That is, if you were smart enough to find a way.

Looking back at Rane, Aimee smiled wanly. This boy was slightly taller, and his eyes were brown, not green, but for some reason he reminded her of Eryyn's little shadow, Sawyer.

Well, maybe it was time for her to have her *own* little shadow.

Lifting one arm and draping it over Rane's thin shoulders, she allowed her grin to grow a little wider.

"Alright, kid. I get your point. It's useless to fight back, so I'd better just get used to it, right?"

Rane, shocked speechless by the sudden change in the girl, nodded mutely and did a weak job of returning her grin. Something told her he didn't get many chances to smile—it looked forced.

Shrugging, she said, "Okay, I understand and I'll be good from now on. You can go tell them that and get us out of here, alright?" She gave Rane a slight push to his feet and, still stunned, he obediently wandered over to the door to call out for Otto. With his back to her, Aimee's grin disappeared, to be replaced with a thoughtful frown. Sure, she would be good and she would get along in the gang. She'd even be a model member: sweet and polite and hard working—she'd eventually get Otto and his thugs to let their guard down. And the minute they did she would be *gone*, running as fast as her feet could carry her. And she would take Rane with her when she went.

• • •

"Yuck, I hate the rain! Why does it always have to rain when we really need to go 'pocketing?" Sawyer pulled his head back into the car, his hair wet and dripping from the downpour that had started sometime near dawn. Scowling, he shook his head vigorously, spraying the inside of their nest with water before he grabbed a torn blanket to dry his hair and face.

The rain was so heavy Eryyn couldn't see the other side of the street through the windows of the car. The water was coming down in sheets, nearly flooding the roads with channels draining quickly into the overflowing sewers. The noise of the droplets hitting the metal roof of their hiding place was deafening and Eryyn could hardly hear herself think, let alone listen to Sawyer gripe about going 'pocketing in the mess. She shook her head at him, holding her hands over her ears. He nodded, sighed, and leaned against her side, preparing to get comfortable as they waited out the storm.

• • •

"Gosh, would you look at it out there? It's like the sky is trying to wash the entire city clean!"

Gregory looked up from the coffee cup he'd just drained and smiled at his wife. "It would take more than rain to get this slum clean. It would take a damn miracle." He dragged himself out of his chair and looked out the window, scowling at the amazingly wet weather that had blown in during the night.

"Damn, I don't want to go out in that. I'll drown!"

"Same here," Liz said, peering through the shimmering runnels of water that tracked over the glass of the windows. "But at least *you* don't have to walk." Gregory sighed heavily and kissed Liz on the top of her head before walking to the door and grabbing his coat from where it hung on a loose hook.

"Well, I'd better get going. You too, but be careful. I don't want you to be washed away just because you have to take notes for some brainless Enforcer. The only reason you should risk getting washed away is while trying to get home in time to make my dinner."

Liz laughed and threw one of her slippers at his head as he ducked out the door. Chuckling faintly to herself, she stared back out the window for a few minutes more as she drained her own cup of coffee. Only when the hot liquid was gone, and she had found all the hidden pictures and shapes in the patterns made by the running water, did she head for the door to gather her own coat. Slipping a hat over her hair, she, too, sighed and slipped out the door into the torrent.

Fortunately for him, Gregory was able to catch a public skimmer to his factory, sparing himself the worst of the rain and cold. Liz did not have that convenience. Nor were she and Greg well off enough to afford a private flitter. She had to walk to her job, and the Enforcer station where she worked was more than fifteen blocks away. She had a long walk ahead of her, and a lot of rain to do it through.

Swearing under her breath, she stepped out onto the sidewalk and was immediately drenched. By the time she reached the station, she was wishing she'd thought to bring a change of clothes with her. She gathered smiles from the other secretaries as she made her way to her desk, leaving a river of cold water on the floor behind her with every step.

"I hate this city," she complained, shaking out her wet hair and hanging her coat over a heater. She took her seat, feeling horribly wet and uncomfortable, and started working on the forms that covered her desk from the night before.

She was halfway through a 493, a necessary force form, when the door opened again and one of the Enforcers walked in. Glancing up absently, Liz noted that it was Captain Connel. She smiled in greeting, then remembered that the captain was the very Enforcer she'd seen help the boy in the market the other day. Her smile broadened and she stood up quickly as the captain started past her desk.

"Captain Connel?"

The captain stopped and turned around, a small smile breaking the stern mask of his face when he saw who had spoken.

"Morning, Liz. I'm in a bit of a hurry."

"I know, sir, sorry to stop you, but I just wanted to say thank you."

Daved Connel's smile disappeared under a confused frown. "For what?"

"For being a kind, decent person. I was on my lunch break in the marketplace the other day."

Daved's frown deepened for a moment and then he smiled again. "Oh yes, the little boy. Sawyer, I think his name was. Cute little kid, for a Dead-Ender."

Liz nodded. "You probably saved his life. I thought that was very kind of you. Most people would have just stood by and allowed him to be dragged off to the factories."

"He was a legal citizen. It would have been a crime to forcefully employ him. Besides, and this is between you and me, I just wanted to pop that old bat's bubble. I hate it when civilians think they can take the law into their own hands. They don't have any idea of what they're doing. If they were meant to make decisions concerning the city, they would have been picked to be Enforcers. Now, if you'll excuse me, I have some work I have to do. Good day, Liz." Connel nodded his head briefly, then turned and walked into the offices beyond the secretary alcove.

Liz sat back at her desk, happy to know that at least one Enforcer working for the city had a civil bone in his body. She felt eyes looking at her just as she started in on the forms again and glanced up. The two other women in the room were staring at her, stunned and awed that she would have the audacity to talk to an Enforcer as though they were close friends. She smiled at one.

"You should have seen it, Carmen. That little boy was going to be dragged off and no one was doing anything to help him. Then Captain Connel showed up and he stopped everything. He actually *listened* to the boy's side of the story, and checked the child's wrist, proving that he was a legal civilian, even if he *was* a Dead-Ender.

And then he told the *woman* who'd started the whole thing to *apologize* to the *boy*! It was amazing!"

Carmen grinned widely and dropped her pen, neglecting her forms in order to listen to Liz's story, which the young woman was perfectly eager to tell from start to finish.

"It's seems too good to be true," she said wistfully when Liz finally ran out of breath. "Who knows, we may actually have a high-level ally." Carmen glanced at the door through which Connel had disappeared, her eyes narrowed slyly.

A scornful laugh drew their attention to the third woman in the room, who was watching them with her painted lips drawn up in a skeptical sneer. "Oh, *right*. You two are going to ask an Enforcer, no wait, an Enforcer *captain* to help you with your little mercy mission. What is it again? The Beggar Thieves Liberation Association?"

"Becka, if I wanted your opinion, I would have asked for it," Liz said coldly. "And it is the Street Child Protection Agency. And it *will* work, once we get it in motion. Just you wait and see."

Becka laughed again and pointed her pen at Liz. "Sure. Once you actually *find* a building to set up shop you're going to spend all your hard earned money to take in a bunch of *illegal* street brats, who would just as soon *steal* you blind as look at you, and teach them to read and write. What makes you think those kids even want your help? They'll probably be afraid of your little charity group. How will they know that you won't just sell them off once they step through the doors?"

"Don't be so stupid, Becka. If just *one* child is saved by that place, then it will have been a success, and if *one* child is saved, then *others* will want to be saved. News travels fast among the lower classes," Carmen stated. "Once they hear from their own peers that we want only to help them, then they'll be streaming through our doors."

Becka shook her head. "Whatever helps you sleep at night. Myself? I prefer to just turn the other way. There's nothing you can do for the kids who live on the street. There's just too many of them. You'd do better to save your money for your own kids and stay away from the kleptos."

"We'll do what we want, Becka," Liz announced, lowering her eyes to the form on her desk again. "And just you wait, our Agency will be a success and it will be a big step to making this city safe for everyone." She picked up her own pen and started writing on the sheet, signaling to the other women that the conversation, as far as she was concerned, was over. Yet, even as she filled in the appropriate columns and signed the certification numbers, she could feel Becka's incredulous and pitying eyes on her. Shrugging it off, she bent herself to her work, filling in forms and applications while the clock on her desk ticked its slow way towards lunchtime.

• • •

"I'm really surprised, Aimee, and really happy. You're good. I never would have guessed that you were so good. From what Master John said, you only brought in cheap, simple stuff. You certainly weren't *my* first choice for a new klepto."

Aimee, sitting beside Rane on the lumpy, broken-legged couch that resided against one wall in Otto's room, scowled at the left-handed compliment. Then, as Otto's grin threatened to turn into a frown, she quickly wiped the anger off her face and pretended a weak, humble smile. She had only been on one job since agreeing to become a willing member of the gang—she and Rane had been assigned a house in the Mid-End and had managed to bring back several nice items, mainly jewelry. Otto had been very pleased and Rane had been very grateful.

"Can we go out again soon? You guys were right, working for a gang *is* better. It's useful having a partner." She draped an arm over Rane's shoulders and the boy, puzzled, glanced at her. As far as he'd been able to tell, Aimee *hated* having a partner, even though they got along together well enough. When it came to hitting the house she had thrown away all the gang's rules concerning partnership and had actually become annoyed when he had tried to help. Wondering what she was up to, he turned to Otto, but the tall boy had only noticed the smile on Aimee's face and the pile of goods that she had dumped on the table for his inspection. Leaning over the loot, he surveyed it yet again, then looked up at Aimee, one eyebrow raised.

"I thought Rane told you that new members don't work as often as seasoned ones. It takes time for the partner bond to form so that you two know how to signal each other during a job." He fixed his gaze on the boy and Rane immediately nodded, sensing that if this went the wrong way he would get into trouble.

"Of course I told her," he insisted. "Several times."

"But I'm already a seasoned klepto," Aimee protested, sitting up straighter and shoving Rane away from her. "I know *how* to steal, *wha*t to steal, *when* to steal, and what *dangers* to look out for. I'm not some little *baby* fresh to the job, Otto. I know what I'm doing. And you're just wasting my time keeping me locked up. I'm sure the Foreman wants people with talent out on the streets bringing him stuff."

Rane's dark eyes widened at the girl's spunk and he briefly wondered if Otto would somehow try to blame it on him. Warily, he watched Otto's face for any sign of annoyance, readying himself to give Aimee a hard pinch if she got too cocky.

But, to his surprise, Otto gave the girl a quick searching look, smiled, and nodded. "You know, you're right. If you've got the skills, you should use them. The more stuff brought in by payment day, the happier the Foreman'll be. What do you have in mind next? Another house? I have one in mind that may be just up..."

"I want to do some 'pocketing," Aimee interrupted hurriedly. "The park, or the marketplace. I used to bring in good stuff from those places, and I'm actually better at 'pocketing than I am at housing. What do you say, Otto? Rane told me that he doesn't care much for 'pocketing, so I could give *him* a few lessons for once."

Rane's mouth dropped open as Otto's searing gaze swept over him once again. "Is that so? And why didn't you ever tell me this, Rane?"

"'Cuz it's not true!" Rane exclaimed. "She's lying!"

"I am not," Aimee protested, placing a hand on Rane's chest and giving him another shove so he fell back against the couch cushions. "He was just afraid to tell you, that's all. He told me *all* about it when we were in that room together. That other girl, Pammy, or whatever her name was, never gave him a lot of training in 'pocketing."

Otto's eyes swept from one to the other, finally coming to rest on Rane's pale face.

"She's lying," Rane said again, though the look in Otto's eyes told him that he wasn't being believed. Rane really *wasn't* very good at 'pocketing—his hands always started to tremble just as he was about to lift something free—but he'd *never* told Aimee about that. She was making everything up, *trying*, for some crazy reason, to get him into trouble.

Otto grunted loudly, leaning back in his chair, and Rane took the opportunity to flash Aimee a wounded look, asking her, with one glance, why she would do that to him. She shrugged and immediately focused her attention forward again as Otto cleared his throat to speak. After a quick glance of annoyance in Rane's direction, he smiled again and nodded at Aimee. "Alright, it's breaking rules, but like you said, you know what you're doing. And you can teach him…" he pointed at Rane, who slumped down sullenly in his seat, "…a thing or two about 'pocketing. I'll give you four hours in the park. And if you're not back on time…well, Rane can explain all that to you, can't you, Rane?"

Rane nodded miserably and looked down at the hands he was ringing together in his lap.

"Right. Four hours, starting now. Have fun, and make sure you bring back something useful, got it?"

"Got it," Aimee said, flashing a bright smile and standing up. She pulled a scowling Rane to his feet and half dragged, half led him out of the room and down the hall to the street. Once they had slipped out of the building and were on their way to the park, Rane spoke, his voice full of hurt and anger.

"You're a real *jerk*, you know that?"

"Am I?" Aimee turned to him absently as they walked together. "And why is that?"

Rane gaped at her. "Oh, yeah, that's good. Go ahead and play innocent. You know what I'm talking about! Why would you say that to him? You've never been out 'pocketing with me, you don't know if I'm good or not! You lied to him, and you nearly got me in trouble!"

"Oh, don't be such a dummy, Rane. You're not in trouble. And I only said that stuff so he would let us go out 'pocketing."

Too hurt and upset to catch the meaning of her words, Rane murmured, "Well, why did you have to lie about *me*? What did I ever do to you?"

"Nothing. You were there, it seemed like a good plan at the time, and it worked! We're out 'pocketing, just like I wanted."

Now Rane was completely confused. "Why would you want to go 'pocketing? It's more work to get the same amount of stuff you could probably get in one hit."

Aimee rolled her eyes and drove her knuckles into the top of Rane's head, making him yelp. "Wake up in there!" she said witheringly. "Sheesh, haven't you figured it out yet, Rane? We're not going 'pocketing. That was just an excuse to get that idiot Otto to let me out of the stronghold. Now that we're outside, we're gonna find my friends, Eryyn or Caulin, so I can have a chat with them."

"C-chat with them?" Rane swallowed hard, finally beginning to understand. "You mean talk them into helping you…"

"Escape? Good boy, you've finally caught up! Of *course* that's what I wanted. But we only have four hours to find them. That's not much time, so just help me out a bit and go along with me on this, okay, Raney?"

Rane stopped in his tracks and turned to face her, his eyes wide with indignation. "What did you just call me?"

Aimee grinned and poked him on the nose. "You heard me. Now hurry up, we've wasted enough time already." She grabbed his hand and pulled him along down the street before he could protest. They ran off in the direction of the market, unaware of the fourteen-year-old girl walking just a dozen steps behind them, who had been sent out of the stronghold with the strict orders to follow them both *very* closely.

• • •

"We haven't been to the park in ages! Why would you want to go now, especially after a heavy rain?"

"Because people are going to wanna come out and walk around, especially after all that rain. It's a freedom thing."

Sawyer stared dolefully at the dripping trees and sodden grass that made up the park, and grumbled, "It's a *stupidity* thing, if you ask me. It's not even sunny out. It's still cloudy and it looks like it's going to rain again. Nobody would be dumb enough to go walking around on a day like this. The grass is wet and slippery and the trees just drip on you. It's no fun."

"Stop complaining so much, Squirt. Don't worry, there will be people walking around, I'm sure of it. The park is a place to escape for them. They come here because they don't wanna stay where they work." Eryyn glanced up, marking the cloudy sky and the pale spot of light that managed to filter through the haze. "It's still early. Lunchtime isn't for another thirty minutes or so. We just have to wait and then the people will start coming out."

"You'd better be right. I'm freezing, and I think if we stay out here too long, we'll get nothing more than a cold. Can you afford to get sick?"

"No, but we also can't afford to waste another day cooped up in the nests. Aren't you hungry? I know I am, and the only way we're gonna get food is if we get credits to buy it with, and there are only two ways for kids like us to get credits in this city. We either steal the tabs for hacking, or we steal stuff for exchange."

Sawyer rolled his eyes and rubbed his cold arms. "You ought to write a book, Eryyn, *How to be a Dead-End Thief.*"

Eryyn gave him a push that sent him stumbling onto a wet patch of grass. Slipping on the slick stalks, he fell, landing on his rear with a cry.

"Jerk!" he muttered, pulling himself back up and wiping off the mud and broken grass that had stuck to his shirt. Scowling, he took a step towards Eryyn, ready to give her a shove in return. Eryyn giggled and retreated from her friend, holding up her hands in defense. Sawyer had just backed her up before a good-sized mud puddle and was just about to push her when a frantic voice called out, yelling their names, and footsteps splashed through a puddle very close by.

"That's Caulin!" Sawyer said, giving up his attempt to make Eryyn very dirty while he looked around the dreary park for the other young klepto. He pointed in the direction of an old playground, where Caulin was just ducking under a broken and extremely dangerous looking slide. The boy raced towards them, his shoes splashing in the mud and puddles and sliding on the grass. Finally, he skidded to a halt in front of Eryyn, nearly falling as his feet slipped and sent him crashing into Sawyer.

"*Whoa!* Sorry, Squirt, thanks for the cushioning." He pushed himself upright, knocking Sawyer back into the mud in the process. "Eryyn, I've got news, and you are *not* gonna be happy with it!"

"What news?" Eryyn asked, reaching down to help a grumbling and incredibly muddy Sawyer to his feet. The smaller boy tried vainly to wipe the mud off his clothes, then scowled at Caulin. There was a streak of dirt across the bridge of his nose.

"It better be good," he spat. "Or you have to buy me some new clothes."

"Aw, just steal them somewhere like you always do," Caulin said absently, giving Sawyer another shove that threatened to send him back into the mud. Only by pinwheeling his arms frantically was the boy able to stay on his feet. "And don't worry, this is *really* good! Have you seen Aimee lately, Eryyn?"

"It would have to depend on what you mean by 'lately'," Eryyn replied, sticking her cold hands into her pockets. "The last time I saw her was that night in MJ's shop, when Otto showed up. But that was awhile ago. I haven't seen her since then. But then, Squirt and I have been holed up for the past few days—it's not much fun working in the rain."

"Ditto there," Caulin said, grimacing at the thought. "And actually, that was the last time *I* saw her too. She went off on her own after you left the shop, looking for another broker. Pretty much *everyone's* been looking for a new broker since you two ratted out MJ as gang-paid scum. Nobody will trust him now."

"Is that your *news?*" Sawyer asked. His dirty nose had started to itch and he rubbed his fist across it.

"What? Oh, not even! I was just getting to it."

"And sure taking enough time doing it."

"Shut up, Squirt, and listen. Like I said, I haven't seen Aimee since that night, but I just saw her this morning! She was in the marketplace and she had this other kid with her. Some scrawny twelve-year-old named Rane. Weird name, if you ask me, but anyway, *he's* her new *partner*. And that's not even the *whole* of it. The only reason those two are partners is because Aimee is now a member of the Foreman's red and gold gang!"

"What!" Eryyn and Sawyer shouted in unison. Stunned, they glanced at one another, then turned back to Caulin, who was clearly enjoying the attention.

"It's *true*! She told me with her own mouth, and then she asked me to find you. I think she wanted to find you herself, but the other kid, Rane, was looking really nervous 'cuz they were supposed to be working—'pocketing, not talking. So Aimee told me to tell you that she'll be looking for you, and that she's gonna need our help. She wants out."

"'Course she does!" Eryyn exclaimed, bunching her hands into fists. "How could she possibly be *dumb* enough to get herself stuck in a gang!"

"But, Eryyn, you were…" Sawyer's words were cut off as Eryyn pushed him, sending him, howling in protest, toppling into the mud again. Slowly, he dragged himself back to his feet, then stood, silent and scowling, as Eryyn coerced as much information from Caulin as he was able to tell her.

When the boy finally started to repeat himself, Eryyn held up a hand. "I already heard that. I'm gonna head over to the place you said you saw her. Maybe she's still there. You coming?"

Caulin shook his head. "I'm gonna find Trent and Gabbe; they'll scream when they hear this!" He took off, running through the mud and puddles, splashing as he went. Sawyer watched him go and shook his head.

"Caulin's a real flake, isn't he?" he asked. He wiped his hands over his shirt, trying to remove mud, and only succeeded in making himself dirtier.

"You're only just figuring that out now? I'm surprised that *he* hasn't ended up in a gang yet."

"None probably want him. He never shuts up."

"He just likes to gossip. C'mon, I wanna find Aimee. I can't believe she got herself taken by a gang."

Sawyer made a face. The last thing he wanted to do on a wet, cold, cloudy day was go looking for a girl who enjoyed making him feel like he was two inches tall. "I thought we had to do some work!" he protested. "I'm still hungry, you know. And the only way kids like us can get credits is to…"

"Shut up, Squirt and get moving!" Eryyn gave the boy a hard push that sent him staggering, then passed him at a run. Grumbling loudly, Sawyer quickly gained his balance, tried one last time to wipe some of the mud from his clothes, then hurried after his friend.

• • •

"I knew it! It was too easy! She was *way* too peaceful—after all that fighting, she was just way too peaceful." Otto sat on the couch in his room and stroked his chin thoughtfully.

"She's a sneaky little rat. And I'll bet she's got Rane in on her plan too. Everybody knows how much that kid hates the gang…and you."

Otto sneered. "Rane is not the problem, Sasha. He's perfectly gang-tamed, you know that. *Aimee* is the problem. I *knew* she was going to be trouble."

Sasha frowned. "The Foreman will be coming to collect soon. If Aimee isn't allowed out to work, then neither is Rane, and that means everyone else has to work harder to make up for what *they* should have brought in. And if the quota isn't made, the Foreman is gonna be upset. And after last time, with all that trouble Pammy caused…"

"I'm aware of that!" Otto snapped, clenching both hands into angry fists. "In case you've forgotten, *I'm* the gang-leader, not you. I know the Foreman will be pissed, but don't worry, it won't come to that. Aimee was a mistake. She's not going to get along here, and we'll only waste time trying to wear her down. But there are plenty of other kleptos out there who'll be easier to tame. We can start again, before the Foreman realizes that anything went wrong. But first we should get Rane and Aimee in here for another little…pep talk." He slammed one fist into his palm with a loud slap and Sasha grinned.

"Dillan and Kit are off duty," she said, glad to be in on Otto's planning. "I'll have them keep a watch and send Rane and Aimee here when they come in."

"Good idea. And, Sasha, nice work *persuading* info out of that kid Aimee talked to."

Sasha's grin widened. "All in a day's work, chief! I just find it hilarious that that little idiot actually thought she would get away with it." She laughed loudly, then left the room, closing the door behind her.

Once he was alone, Otto opened his clenched fist and stared at the half-moon impressions made in his skin by his fingernails. He grimaced. Aimee should have realized that her sweet-faced insistence that she was *happy* to be a member of the gang and that she truly *wanted* to do her best for the Foreman hadn't fooled anyone. He had known all along that she was planning something and Sasha had proven it when she had seen Aimee talking to one of the boys who'd been at Master John's on the night he'd talked to Eryyn. According to his second-in-command, the boy had run off like a rat with a cat on its tail, probably to pass on the news.

Well, Aimee didn't know who she was dealing with. Otto hadn't been made a gang leader because he was stupid. If Aimee thought she'd given herself a chance to escape by being agreeable, then she was wrong! And now she was going to get herself a little surprise when she and Rane returned to the stronghold.

• • •

Sawyer was not enjoying the morning in the slightest. The rain, though it had finally stopped, had left the park a labyrinth of deep puddles, dangerously slick grass, and heavy, dark mud that clung to shoes and pant legs. He was filthy from falling in the mud earlier, thanks to that idiot Caulin; the mud was uncomfortably itchy and he was gathering looks from the few people who had actually proven Eryyn's theory by coming to the park. He wanted to go back to the nest, warm up, dry off, and get into some clothes that didn't have enough dirt on them to plant a garden. But Eryyn wouldn't listen to his pleas and just kept walking through the park, her eyes forward, mumbling under her breath about gangs and Aimee.

Sawyer scowled darkly as he trotted behind the girl, wondering why Eryyn should care so much about Aimee being taken into a gang. Sure, gangs were something to be avoided, but why should *Aimee's* troubles be any of *their* business? Eryyn *should* have been pleased—it just meant one less free-lance klepto to compete with.

Lifting his gaze from the mud, he started to ask Eryyn this question, but the words were quickly strangled in his throat as he stared past his friend.

The lady was perched on a bench, a paper bag held on her lap. She was dressed plainly, practically, but the clothing all matched and looked elegant on her slender frame. Her hair, neatly brushed and styled, was a fluff of blonde curls that surrounded her beautiful, oval face. Sawyer stopped following Eryyn and openly gaped at her, stunned that such a beautiful woman would be in the park on such a dismal day. She seemed out of place, like a delicate flower growing in a junkyard, or a bright ray of sunshine in a rainstorm.

Slowly, he began shifting through the mud, moving in a circle around the lady's bench, looking at her from every angle.

It's amazing, he thought, cocking his head to one side, unaware that Eryyn had continued on without him. *She looks just like the lady in my dreams! The lady who would live in the house on the hill!*

He continued walking around the bench, careful to keep at a safe distance, while he looked at her wistfully. Seeing her on the bench, his dreams immediately came back to him—dreams of being adopted into a happy family, with a beautiful woman who wanted to be his new mother, and a nice man for a father. People who would take care of him, feed him, and give him clean, brand new clothes. People who would take him to live in their enormous house, where he would have a bedroom all for his own, with clean sheets and blankets on the soft bed. And if these people were kind enough to take him in as their son, they would think nothing of taking Eryyn, an illegal, and adopting her as their daughter, making her an officially legal citizen and giving her an I.D. bracelet of her own. Then they'd *all* be happy.

Caught up in his dream, Sawyer didn't realize that he had sunk down into the mud with a sigh. He sat with his legs drawn up to his chest, his hands clasped around his shins and his chin resting on his knees, watching the woman as she ate her lunch. He wondered what her name was, and if she liked children. Especially little boys with green eyes.

• • •

Liz ate her lunch slowly and deliberately, hoping the little street child would come closer. She had been aware of his presence ever since he had stopped following the girl and had started circling around her bench, staring at her.

She smiled to herself, watching the child through the corner of her eye. From what she could see, the little boy was filthy, covered in mud nearly from head to foot, like he had fallen or had decided to play in a puddle. His clothes, hair, hands, even his face, were streaked with mud and dirt. It was hard to see what he really looked like beneath all the filth, but she *could* judge that he was young—by his size, he was probably not older than nine or ten.

At first, she had wondered if the child meant to rob her. It wouldn't have been surprising. Most children who grew up on the streets resorted to theft in order to survive. But, after a few minutes, it became apparent that the boy did not have theft on his mind when he lowered himself into the mud, curled into a ball, and sat, staring at her as if he were seeing a ghost.

He must be homeless, she thought to herself. *His clothes alone can attest to that—they're filthy—and even if they* were *clean, none of them match, or fit him. He must live on the streets, maybe with that girl he was walking with. I wonder if he would let me talk to him, I could tell him a bit about the Agency.*

She stood slowly and turned towards the child, raising one hand to beckon him closer. "Hi there! Come here, little boy, I want to talk to you for a moment." She took a step closer to the sitting child, holding her hands out to show him she meant no harm. Unfortunately, the boy didn't read her intentions in that way. He jumped to his feet, his eyes wide and scared. He was gone in the next instant, running away through the mud, slipping on the grass. When he had put twenty yards between them, he stopped and turned around, giving her one last, lingering gaze, before taking to his feet again and disappearing from view.

SIX

Sibling Rivalry

Eryyn had traveled more than half the length of the park before she realized that Sawyer was no longer following her. Stopping in her tracks, she turned in a circle, scanning the muddy terrain in search of the small boy. Not seeing him, she swore under her breath, stamping a foot in frustration and splashing a wave of muddy water on a man seated nearby on a drying bench. With a roar of indignation, the man surged to his feet, exclaiming about dirty, foul-mouthed street brats who had no respect for anyone. Cursing loudly, he took a step towards Eryyn, who quickly kicked another glob of mud onto his suit, then took off as fast as her feet could carry her.

"Squirt, when I get my hands on you..." She was panting hard by the time she stopped. A glance over her shoulder showed her that the man had not pursued, but she still didn't see her friend anywhere. Swearing again and adding a more colorful assortment of words just to spite the man she would probably never see again, she turned and started again in the direction Caulin had told her to go. She didn't like being out of sight from Sawyer, but if he couldn't keep up with her when she was in a hurry, then that was his fault. He knew enough to go back to the last nest they had used if they became separated. She'd simply meet him at Nest Six after she'd found out more about Aimee.

Still, she grumbled to herself and kept glancing back over her shoulder every few steps, hoping that the boy would show up. Ten minutes later, she had reached the end of the park and stood on the sidewalk separating the grass from the street. Sawyer had not appeared yet. She was beginning to get really worried and would have started retracing her steps if a voice had not called out her name. She spun around quickly, facing up the street, and saw a girl of about twelve running in her direction.

"Eryyn?" the girl asked, coming to a halt just a step away. Eryyn nodded and the girl smiled, relieved. "I'm Meghyn; a girl named Aimee asked me to find you. She was waiting for you, up there." Meghyn turned and pointed in the direction of the market. "She wanted to talk to you. She said you were supposed to meet her, that she'd asked someone else to find you, but you never came."

Eryyn swore loudly, attracting disapproving glances from people passing by. "Damn! Caulin, that *idiot!* He was supposed to bring me to her, not go running off to tell everyone about what happened! Ooh, when I get my hands on him…"

Meghyn cocked her head and gave Eryyn a rueful grin. "Caulin? Hah! You should have *known* better! Anyway, this Aimee girl, she said she would have looked for you herself, but she had this other kid with her and she didn't want to run too much of a risk, or something like that. She waited for you as long as she could, but she couldn't stay out too long, she said she'd get into trouble and she couldn't risk *that* either." Meghyn was speaking with her eyes closed, as if trying to remember everything Aimee had said word for word. "So, she asked me to find you—told me what you looked like and all—said that she was going to need your help, and to meet her by the big horse statue in the Yellow plaza at noon tomorrow…yeah, that was it, tomorrow at noon."

Eryyn nodded, letting the information sink in. "Alright, I'll do that, though between now and then I'm going to try my hardest to find and strangle Caulin. Thanks a lot, Meghyn. I've gotta go now." She patted the girl on the shoulder, then turned to run back through the park, eager to find Sawyer and tell him their new plans for the next day.

"Hey! Wait a minute!"

Eryyn stopped before she had even gotten started and turned back to face Meghyn, who was standing with her hands on her hips, her mouth open in indignation. "Aimee didn't have anything to pay me, and neither did the boy she was with. She said that in return for the message, *you* would give me something."

Eryyn's mouth dropped open and she tapped her empty pockets. "Oh, of all the mean, dirty, rotten...*Aimee, you brat*! I haven't got anything. I didn't do any work today, so far."

"Eryyn! Eryyn!" Suddenly, Sawyer was at her side, still covered with mud and smiling radiantly. He tapped her arm, trying to get her attention. "Eryyn, you'll never guess what happened! Who I just saw...! It was *amazing!*"

"Where have you been?" Eryyn asked crossly. Sawyer blinked in surprise and opened his mouth to answer, but Eryyn waved a hand, silencing him. "Oh, *never* mind right now. Have you got anything good on you? I know you always keep something around. Empty out your pockets."

Stunned by her harsh order, Sawyer stuck his hands in his pockets without question and pulled out whatever hodgepodge of junk he had collected since the last time he had changed his clothes. He held his full hands out to the girl, who sifted through them carefully. Among the string, pebbles, feathers, and stray pieces of paper, Eryyn found an old coin that was tiny, thin, and silvery in color, with the profile of a man on the front. Nodding with satisfaction, she handed it to Meghyn and said, "You might be able to get something for that in a shop. It's really old, from before the Enforcers came, I think. Old fashioned credits. Some people collect them."

Meghyn looked at the little coin with a frown, finding it hard to believe that the tiny circle of metal she held could be worth anything. Then she glanced at the items still held in Sawyer's hands and figured that she had gotten the best of what was up for offer. With a shrug and a smile, she turned and left.

Sawyer looked after her, pouting slightly. "I liked that," he muttered. "It's the only one I've ever found and you had to go and give it away?"

"Shut up, Squirt," Eryyn said, and Sawyer, hurt by her tone, fell silent. "Where have you been all this time?" Eryyn asked, her arms flung out in frustration. "I didn't even realize you had stopped, and I have better things to do than go looking for you. Now where have you been?"

Sawyer stared at her and crossed his arms over his chest. His face took on the stubborn look Eryyn felt she was seeing entirely too often lately. He shrugged, but didn't speak.

Her fragile patience stretched close to the breaking point, Eryyn leaned down and grabbed Sawyer's shoulders, resisting the urge to shake him as she said, "Come on, Squirt, don't start this now. What happened to you?"

"You just told me to shut up," Sawyer replied glibly. "How can I answer you if I'm supposed to shut up?"

Eryyn stared at him, then buried her face in her hands, groaning. "I can't believe you. Aimee gets caught by Otto, she needs our help, and all you can do is get yourself lost and make stupid jokes."

"It wasn't a joke," Sawyer said defensively. "I was just doing what you told me to do. And besides, I *didn't* get myself lost, Eryyn. I can find my way around the stupid park without getting lost. I stopped because I had to look at something, or actually, some*one*. I was trying to tell you earlier, but you told me to shut up, and then you gave away my dime."

Eryyn cocked her head. "What *are* you talking about, Squirt?"

"We were in the park, walking, and I stopped because I saw this lady."

"Lady?"

"Yeah, she was so beautiful, Eryyn! She was sitting on a bench and she had this golden hair and it was in curls, and she looked just like the lady who would live in the..." Sawyer drifted to a pause and swallowed hard. Eryyn was looking at him, her eyes narrowed dangerously. He had forgotten, in his excitement at seeing the woman, that Eryyn had no patience for his dreams and fantasies. "Never mind," he concluded miserably. "It wasn't anything special." Then added under his breath, "Not to *you* anyway."

Eryyn stared at him, piecing together what he had been about to say. Her lips pursed angrily. *Like an adult*, Sawyer thought grimly. She shook her head.

"It's just *not* worth saying it over and over," she finally spat. "Now come on, we have to get to work or we'll go hungry tonight. And I always think best when I'm working. Tomorrow, we have to meet Aimee."

"Meet her? Tomorrow?" Eryyn had started walking away from the park and Sawyer, relieved to have escaped a lecture, hurried to follow, looking up at her curiously. "What do you mean, meet her?

I thought she was in the Foreman's gang, how can we meet her?"

"In the Yellow plaza. By the big horse statue. She'll be waiting there for us tomorrow at noon."

"And then we'll help her...how?" Sawyer's voice showed the skepticism he was feeling. "That old friend of yours, Otto, he's a lot bigger than you, and a *hell* of a lot bigger than me! Plus, he has his whole gang on his side! Who will we have...Caulin? I'd feel safer taking my chances alone."

Eryyn's frown turned into a wry grin. "So would I. But Aimee wants us, or me actually, to meet her, so she must have some sort of plan. All she has to do is get away from Otto and the rest of his thugs and then hide out for a few weeks, until they lose interest in her and find someone else to bother. Still, it's easier said than done. She'll need our help getting away, and then hiding. At least that's what I think she has in mind. Also, she's paired up with a partner in the gang, some boy, and I don't know if he'll be any help or not. He may decide to cause us trouble, or Aimee may want us to help *him* too."

Sawyer clutched at his head and rolled his eyes. "How simple," he said sarcastically. "And I don't even *like* Aimee—she's always teasing me."

"We have to get her out of there, Squirt, believe me, we have to get her out of there." Eryyn went down on her knees and, taking Sawyer by the shoulders again, looked into the boy's eyes. Her own eyes were pleading and damp with tears. Sawyer gaped at her, stunned to see her so upset. Kids they knew got taken everyday, either by gangs or, more often, by the Enforcers for factory work. Eryyn had never gotten overly emotional about it, and now she was crying!

"Why, Eryyn?" Sawyer asked, confusion and nervousness lowering his voice to a whisper. He glanced around at the people walking down the sidewalk and streets; a few had stopped to look at the two children, one covered in mud, the other in tears. Uncomfortable with the scrutiny, afraid that someone would eventually notice the absence of a bracelet on Eryyn's wrist, Sawyer grabbed his friend's arm and pulled her to her feet. "Come on, let's go back to the nest," he murmured, tugging on her arm and moving her forward a few steps.

"No, I'll be okay, Squirt. I-I'm just scared, that's all."

"Over Aimee?" Sawyer was thoroughly perplexed now.

"Yes, over Aimee." Eryyn said, putting more energy into walking so Sawyer didn't have to drag her. "I can't leave her with those jerks, Squirt, I just can't. I've never told you this... I've never told *anyone* this, but Aimee is really special to me and I can't stand to see her hurt.

"Why?" Sawyer asked, looking over his shoulder so he could see her face.

Eryyn, worried and pale, was silent for a moment, then muttered, "Um, well, you see, Squirt... Aimee's my big sister."

• • •

Newly cleaned and changed into a set of spare clothes, Sawyer sat quietly in the rusted car, leaning against the back of the passenger seat, his head cradled against a rolled up blanket. His feet were tucked up beneath him and he had wrapped another blanket around his shoulders. Surprisingly, he was pretty warm and cozy, a nice feeling after the chill damp of the park. Unfortunately, his thoughts were nowhere near as comfortable. He was listening to Eryyn tell the story of how she, and her older sister, Aimee, had come to live on the streets.

"You see, Squirt," Eryyn murmured, picking at a hole in the knee of her jeans, "my mother and father, um, I guess they were part of one of the rebel groups that started up when the Enforcers invented the "Two Child" law. When people were told that only two of their kids would be allowed to have legal status, a lot of people got angry. Some decided that it wasn't any business of the Enforcers to tell them how many kids they could have. In a way, that's why there are so many kids like us on the streets, 'cuz these *illegal* born kids have no where else to go. People who break the law and have more than two kids are cut off from rations and sometimes thrown out of their jobs. I think that's what would have happened to *my* parents, if they hadn't decided to wimp out and get rid of the *extra* kids. That meant Aimee...and me.

"I was the fourth kid my parents had. Or, well, I *think* I was the fourth. All I remember is a crowded room where four people had bracelets and two didn't. Me and Aimee. And then we were on the streets—just like that, no goodbye, no warning. Nothing. One minute I'm inside with a family, the next, I'm a street kid.

"Aimee and me, we stuck together for a little while, but we never really got along very well and always fought a lot. So, we decided to split up, and I met Otto and started hanging with him. But Aimee and I always kept in touch, even after I was in the gang. *She* was the one who helped me escape when I needed to. *She* was the one who hid me from the rest of the gang members. I would have stayed with her after that, but you know what she's like. She's a pain! *You* can't stand to be around her for long—think about how it is for me, being her sister. So I struck out on my own after awhile, and one day I ended up at the dump and went looking for someplace to hide out for the night, and I found you in that car... and you know the rest from there."

Sawyer hugged his knees to his chest and stared blankly at the ripped and stained upholstery on the floor of the car. "Do I?" he murmured. "I used to think so, but right now, I'm not so sure."

Eryyn frowned. "What do you mean?"

"I've always told you everything, Eryyn. *Everything.* I've never kept secrets back from you; I always thought we were too close for that. But, from all the stuff you've been telling me these last few days, I guess you didn't feel the same way. All the time we've worked together and been friends, you didn't trust me enough to tell me that you had been in a gang, were friends with a gang leader, *and* had a sister among the kids we used to see every night at Master John's." Sawyer finally looked up at his friend and his eyes were sad. "I've *always* trusted you, Eryyn, and it really hurts to know that you didn't trust me."

Eryyn sighed and reached out a hand to touch Sawyer's arm. He flinched away. "Squirt, you don't understand..."

"No. No, I guess I don't." His eyes narrowed and his voice took on a sarcastic tone. "Maybe I'm too little and not smart enough to understand."

Eryyn paused, fully realizing how much her words from the other night had hurt Sawyer's feelings. Looking down at her hands, unable to meet his narrowed eyes, she swallowed hard, then murmured, "It's not that. I didn't think like that. I-I just didn't want to talk about it, that's all."

Sawyer looked at her witheringly. "Great save, Eryyn, that makes me feel a *whole* lot better."

"I'm sorry." Eryyn shrugged. "The time I spent in the gang is something I just want to forget, along with my old partnership with Otto. And when it comes to Aimee, well, after the Otto thing, she thought it would be safer if no one knew that we were related. She didn't want anyone going after *her* because of *me*."

Sawyer laughed. "That was real nice of her."

"I thought so too," Eryyn said with a snort. "But, you know, there *are* things you haven't told me, Squirt. You said you tell me *everything*, but that's not true. You've never told me why *you*, a legal citizen of the city, have to live on the streets."

"That's not the same thing!" Sawyer exclaimed. "I never told you about my family because you make me feel like having a citizenship and a bracelet makes me a criminal." He pulled his sleeve up to expose the silvery piece of jewelry on his wrist and scowled darkly at it. "Every time we start talking about my bracelet you go and get all huffy. You did it just the other day, when that Enforcer let me go because I'm legal. I've never told you about my family because I didn't think you'd want to hear about them. I thought you'd just get mad at me!"

Eryyn hesitated, thinking, then shook her head. "You could tell me now. I promise not to get mad at you, and we won't have anymore secrets."

"It's not a secret," Sawyer grumbled. "And it's really not much of a story. I had a family, just like the one I like to picture in my mind. I had a mom and a dad, and an older sister. I was happy. But one day the Enforcers came to our house and knocked down the front door. Smashed it right out of the wall, Eryyn! They arrested my dad, and my mom when she tried to stop them. Then they went after me and my sister. We hadn't done anything wrong, but my dad must have, I guess, and 'cuz he was under arrest, there wouldn't be anyone to take care of us. The Enforcers must have decided to save themselves some time, and they were probably gonna ship us both off to a factory or something. I think my sister figured on that and she grabbed my arm and pulled me away from the table and into one of the bedrooms. Then she opened a window and made me climb out onto the fire escape and yelled at me to hurry down to the street and to run as soon as I reached the ground.

"I climbed down, but I didn't run, not right away. Instead, I turned and called back up for her to hurry and come with me. I didn't wanna go without her, I was too scared. I could see her head sticking outta the window and I know she started to climb out, but then this arm, all covered in a blue and gray sleeve, reached out and grabbed her by the hair." Sawyer's eyes were bleak as he swallowed hard past a lump that had climbed into his throat. "She *screamed*, Eryyn, when they dragged her back into the house, and then there was someone else looking out the window, staring down at me, and the arm pointed and I heard the man yell for someone to go after me, to catch me before I got away. *That's* when I started running. I know I was crying, and that I was scared, but I don't know how long I ran, or where I actually ran from. I don't even remember where our house was. But I ended up on the streets, alone, without my family. I didn't know how to steal, and begging just gets you in trouble, and I was really scared of the Enforcers. I kind of thought they were all the same man—they all dress alike—and I thought that if any of them saw me, they would recognize me and I'd get caught and dragged to a factory.

"After all that, I don't really remember a lot, except for this one time, when I was *really* hungry and it was raining and wet. I thought that if I just let the Enforcers catch me, I'd at least be warm and have something to eat, and maybe I'd find my sister again. But then I remembered what my sister had told me about the factories, how they work people so hard and how big and loud and smelly they are, and how people are always getting hurt or sick or killed and no one even cares! I wanted to find my sister again, but I didn't want to risk a factory to do it. I wanted to stay free. So I hid, everywhere I went, I hid from people, and I slept in alleys and ate out of the trash," Sawyer's nose wrinkled and he wiped tears from his eyes, "and then I found the dump, and it seemed like a pretty safe place to be. I was little, and if anyone tried to grab me I could just hide in a lot of places where they couldn't fit. So I stayed in the dump, sleeping in that old car, scrounging for food, until that day when you came along, and decided to use my car as a hiding place."

Eryyn's lips turned slightly up, but it was a poor excuse for a smile. "And you said it wasn't much of a story? Sheesh, Squirt, you had it worse than I did."

Sawyer shrugged. "I don't know."

Eryyn's smile quickly turned to a frown and she turned to look out the window. Staring at the rain-soaked city, she took a deep breath and stated, "If you think about it, none of this, *any* of this, would have happened if it weren't for those stupid Enforcers. They ruin everything. Because of their laws, Aimee and me are illegals and forced to live on the streets, and because they didn't like something your father did, *you*, a legal citizen, are forced to do the same. They say *they're* trying to keep the city safe and clean, and they're the ones who are making it the way it is!"

Wiping his eyes on his sleeve, Sawyer shrugged again. "They're Enforcers. People have to do what they say. It's the law." He hiccuped and took a deep breath. "And just because *we* don't like 'em doesn't mean everyone else feels the same way. How could they stay in charge if everyone hated them? Wouldn't everyone just stop listening to them, or fight back or something?"

Eryyn shook her head. "Not if they're scared. *We're* scared of being sent to a factory or deported, and *we're* street kids, we don't really have anything to lose. What would it be like to have a family and a home and a job and suddenly the Enforcers come and take it all away from you, just because you did something they didn't like? Everyone is afraid that it will happen to them, so no one thinks of fighting back, right? They're just too scared."

"I can't imagine grown-ups being scared. I think they're happy with the Enforcers and they like things the way they are. They don't care about us, so they don't care if the Enforcers take us to factories, and if someone like my dad gets in trouble, it's because he must have done something wrong and he deserved what he got." Sawyer looked depressed and very pale. "That's what *I* thought. That my dad did something wrong and the Enforcers punished him for it. I just don't know *what* he did that was so bad. And I don't know if *I'm* in trouble with the Enforcers because of it."

Eryyn was silent for a long time after listening to Sawyer's story, leaning back against her seat, staring at the bent and warped wheel that had once been used to steer the car. As she gazed at the rusted circle of metal, she found herself wondering if the one time owner of their hiding place had used the car to drive to work everyday and had parked the car in a driveway at a house when he came home at night. Or maybe a woman had owned it, driving it around after work, visiting friends. Maybe a family had taken the car on trips out of the city—had visited a lake, or a forest, or had driven through the mountains. It was possible that the car had gone all the way to the ocean. The family might *have* gone to the beach, to see all that water stretching on for miles and miles and miles; the sun had shone down on them and they'd watched it set, all the colors blending, red and orange and yellow and gold, turning the water into a rainbow. Sawyer had a picture in one of his books of the ocean, with the sun setting over it. Eryyn had looked over his shoulder once while he was reading that page. He'd told her about the picture, since she couldn't read it for herself, and now she wondered if the one time family that may have owned their hiding place had sat on that distant beach, staring out at the water, smiling at one another and being happy...

Realizing what she was doing, Eryyn snorted and shook her head at the steering wheel. Angrily, she slapped out at the metal and hurt her hand. Squeezing her lips together, she shook her wrist in a vain attempt to stop the pain, then, suddenly, she started to laugh.

"Doing a Sawyer," she muttered through giggles. "How bad is that?"

"What?" Next to her, Sawyer sat up, his brows raised in confusion.

Eryyn glanced at him. "Huh?"

"You...what did you just say...something about me?" Sawyer frowned, and Eryyn, realizing she'd spoken out loud, laughed again and punched the boy on the arm.

"It's nothing, I was just talking to myself."

Sawyer leaned back again, rubbing his arm, and looked at her curiously. "You're batty," he said. "Did you knock something loose?" He twirled his finger over his ear, indicating a loss of wits. "Or did too much water get inside your head during the rain?"

"Funny," Eryyn said, chuckling in spite of herself. She stared at Sawyer, thinking back at her temporary lapse into dreams, and how pleasant it had been, how different and calming. She smiled. "Are you still mad at me, Squirt?"

"Huh? You have gone batty!"

Eryyn shrugged. "Maybe. But I was just thinking that we shouldn't fight anymore, Squirt. It doesn't do us any good and you and me need to stick together if we're gonna keep living out here with all those Enforcers around. Do you get me?"

"I think so…" Sawyer cocked his head to one side, still looking thoroughly confused.

"Well, you know I have to do something to help Aimee, right, because she's my sister? Even if we don't always get along and she didn't want anyone to know, she's still my sister: we have the same blood. We have to stick up for each other and help each other."

"What *are* you talking about, Eryyn?"

"Us, you and me. We fight, but we still get along with each other really well, and if *anything* happened to you I'd do whatever I could to help you, just like I would Aimee."

"Me too," Sawyer said with a frown. "But…"

Eryyn waved away his interruption. "We're friends, Squirt, but we aren't brother and sister—we aren't related."

"That's obvious," Sawyer said, getting slightly impatient.

"So, I'm gonna do something about it."

Before Sawyer could puzzle out her words, Eryyn pulled her penknife from her pocket, flipped open one of the blades and reached over to grab Sawyer's left hand. Then, to his astonishment, she slashed the knife across his the ball of his thumb, slicing open the skin. Blood immediately began to well up and flow into his palm and he stared, shocked and silent, at the wound as Eryyn opened a similar cut on her own right palm.

"The way I see it, Squirt," Eryyn muttered, closing the penknife with her teeth and thrusting it back into her pocket, "you might as well be my little brother. I feel like you are. If it came to choosing between you and Aimee, you'd always be my pick. So…" Eryyn reached out and clasped Sawyer's bleeding hand with her own, pressing their palms together.

The boy's green eyes widened in distaste as the blood in their hands mixed and several drops dripped down onto the brake lever between them. He opened his mouth to speak, but was too stunned by the sight of his own blood and Eryyn's staining the floor of the car.

"W-why…?" he finally managed to stammer, wincing as the

cut began to sting.

"We share blood now. You're my blood brother, and that means we can't fight *anymore*, that we have to take care of each other from now on." Eryyn's warm brown eyes held Sawyer's startled green ones for a moment before she pulled him forward and crushed him against her in a tight hug. His breath knocked out of him by her tight embrace, Sawyer held still, dumbstruck by Eryyn's odd behavior. Then, as the meaning of her words and actions finally became clear, he smiled and returned the hug.

"No more fighting?" he asked, dropping his head onto Eryyn's shoulder.

"No more fighting." Eryyn gave her friend one last, hard squeeze, then pulled away, quickly wiping tears from her eyes before Sawyer could see them. "Now, let's get going and visit some pockets before it gets too late. I'm starving."

• • •

"And what makes you think Otto is gonna let us go out again tomorrow? I *told* you the rules of the gang—we cycle and pairs are only allowed to work on *certain* days and then they switch and rest while someone else takes their place. Otto thinks it's safer that way—we aren't so noticeable. I doubt he'll let us out again, 'specially since we didn't bring back anything good." Rane looked glumly into his hand, staring at the single bracelet and pair of silver rings he had managed to 'pocket. He shook his head at the meager amount of loot, knowing that Otto would not be pleased and wishing that Aimee had kept her mouth shut about going 'pocketing.

Walking beside him, Aimee glanced around and, seeing the dour look on her younger partner's face, playfully swatted him on the arm hard enough to make him yelp and drop the trinkets. Swooping down, she scooped the jewelry up and stuffed it in her pocket while Rane glared angrily at her, rubbing his sore arm.

"We'll be fine. I think Otto will let us go out again, if you can keep your mouth shut about me wanting to meet up with Eryyn."

Rane opened his mouth to speak, but Aimee clamped her hand over it and shook her head. "Shut up, I mean it. You can't tell Otto *anything*, or we'll both be in big trouble. Got it?"

Rane frowned, his brown eyes narrowed, but he nodded and Aimee pulled her hand away.

"Good, at least you have some brains. And don't worry about not going back with anything good. Once Otto sees *this*, he won't care about the other stuff we got." Aimee held out her hand under Rane's nose, brandishing a long brown object fitted with metal clasps: a wallet, made from real leather.

"Where'd you get that!" Rane exclaimed, his eyes darting around quickly to see if anyone was watching them as they walked down the sidewalk of a Mid-End market street. "Put it away before any-one spots it!"

Aimee laughed and tucked the wallet back into her pocket. "I told Otto I was good at 'pocketing. It's got *four* credit tabs in it. And just you wait until you see the numbers on them!"

Rane ducked his head nervously and pressed his finger against his lips. "Could you have possibly said that any louder?" He pointed across the street. "I don't think the people over there heard you. How long ago did you get it? Why didn't you show me earlier?"

"I thought it would be better to keep it as a surprise. So, do you think Otto will be happy with it?"

Rane started to nod, then stopped and bit down on his lower lip. "Credit tabs can be traced though. Otto's mentioned it a few times—it can be dangerous hacking into someone else's credits."

"Otto's an idiot!" Aimee sang happily. "I've done this lots of times and I've never been caught. Tabs can be traced, yeah, but all you have to do is fiddle around with a few circuits and you can change the thumbprint."

Rane didn't look convinced. "I don't know. Otto doesn't like it…and neither does the Foreman. That's, umm…that's how Pammy got into trouble, remember? And why Otto is still kinda mad at me. Pammy brought in that watch but she didn't check to see if it had writing on it, you know, how some people put a message on some-thing? It had a guy's name on it and the Foreman got really mad. He said that it could be traced if he tried to sell it, and then he could get in trouble. He got mad at Otto for not noticing and Otto got mad at Pammy and…" Rane licked his lips nervously and ran a hand through his hair. "I just don't think we should risk working with someone else's personal credits. I don't want to get into trouble, not again…not so soon." Suddenly, he reached out a hand and grabbed Aimee's arm, pulling her to a halt. "Aimee, please forget about going to the statue tomorrow! Forget about meeting that Eryyn. It'll only get us *both* in trouble! Can't you just get along in the gang? Give it a little time to see if you could get to like it?"

"Like *you* like it?" Aimee's voice was cold as she pulled her arm away from Rane's grip. "Like *you* get along, cowering for Otto and following his orders so he won't beat you up? Get real! I *have* to get out, and I'm going to."

"But if you just waited a little longer…"

"No! I'm not gonna be owned by a gang. Just forget about it!"

Faced with Aimee's amazing stubbornness, Rane's temper flared again and he crossed his arms over his chest. "Then why don't you just go now, huh? We're here, outside. Otto's not around! Why don't you just run away and get it over with!"

Several people looked around at Rane's raised voice and Aimee snarled at them before grabbing the boy's arms and pulling him off the street into a doorway. "Because I know how things *work* in gangs, you little *idiot!*" she hissed. "I know from experience how hard it is to get away from a gang once they decide to come after you. And I *know* Otto will come after me and now he knows all my hiding places and where I worked the crowds. I'd have *no* place safe to hide from him. I'd have to start new and then I'm vulnerable!"

"So why bother?" Rane asked sullenly, not even bothering to break free of her grip. "You know you can't get away, and you'll only get yourself *and* me into trouble. Why?"

"Because Eryyn will help me, I know she will, and then I'll have a bit of a chance." She looked at him shrewdly for a moment, then released his arms with a contemptuous little push. "Unless you're too much of a *coward* to keep your mouth shut."

Rane looked stung and bit his lip, torn between the prospect of freedom and feeding Otto's wrath. Turning, he stepped back onto the sidewalk and started walking again, quickly blending into the crowd as he wound his way back to Otto's chosen stronghold. After a moment, he felt a hand on his shoulder as Aimee caught up and fell into step beside him. He sighed deeply, thrust his hands deep into his pockets, and whispered, "Would you take me with you?"

"Yeah," Aimee said, her voice carrying no surprise at the question, telling the boy that she had planned to all along. Rane looked up at her, his brown eyes softened by this knowledge.

"And this Eryyn, your friend, she could help us both?"

"I think so."

"I hate Otto," Rane confided in a whisper, as though this had been a great secret. "I *hate* him more than *anything*. For what he did to Pammy, and how he hit me. But he scares me too. I want to get away from him *so* much."

Aimee's hand tightened on the boy's shoulder. "We can. It's possible, believe me. We can get away."

Rane glanced at the crowd around them, then turned back to Aimee and, again, he sighed. "I think you're crazy, and something tells me I'm making a big mistake, but don't worry, I won't say anything."

Aimee replied with a smile and followed Rane back along the streets to the meeting place of Otto's gang.

• • •

The stronghold was quiet by the time Rane and Aimee slipped into the sleeping room. The pilfered and salvaged couches and pallets that lined the room were all empty.

"Everyone who was supposed to be working today is still out, and I think Otto sent most of the first shifters out again too. He needs more stuff to give the Foreman on payment day."

Aimee looked around the empty room. "What about Otto? Where's *he* right now?"

Rane shrugged; he didn't know what the gang-leader did with his time. Didn't care usually, as long as it didn't concern him. "He's probably in his room, sleeping on his couch," he muttered.

"So what do we do now?" Aimee asked as she dropped down onto one of the empty sofas. The springs squealed angrily under her weight and she sank deeply into the moth-eaten cushion.

"Wait," Rane said with another shrug. "We can't eat anything until Otto looks over our stuff and decides that we've earned it, and we aren't supposed to go back out again, the four hours are up, so I guess we can just sit and…"

"Umm, no, you have to come with me, Rane." A tall, red-haired boy stepped into the room and faced the pair. His blue eyes were troubled. "Otto's been wanting to have a talk with you both."

Aimee glanced quickly at Rane, who had paled. "W-why, Dillan?" he asked, reaching a hand into his shirt to grasp at the meager items he had managed to 'pocket.

Dillan shrugged. "How should I know? Do you think anyone tells *me* anything around here? Sasha just came up to me a few hours ago and told me to keep an eye out for you and to bring you in to Otto when you came back." His freckled face broke into a frown as he added, "She didn't look too happy, I'll tell you that. You getting into more trouble already?"

"*No!* At least, I *hope* not." Rane glanced at Aimee again, his lip quivering nervously. "I don't think so," he finished doubtfully.

Dillan cocked his head, puzzled, then sighed deeply in sympathy. Waving an arm at the pair, he muttered, "Let's go," and stepped out of the room.

Rane followed obediently, an instinctive response to three years of taking orders from those older than him. Aimee looked back towards the door, but nodded and hurried to follow when Dillan called out, "You too, Aimee! Are you coming?"

A slight tap on Otto's door yielded a cheerful order to enter and Dillan opened the door and gestured the two inside.

"Good luck, kiddo," he muttered when Rane stepped past him timidly. "From the look on Sasha's face earlier, you two are gonna need it." He smiled pityingly at Rane's look of dismay, tapped a finger to his temple in a gesture that many of the younger gang kids used to wish each other luck, then stepped back into the hall, closing the door behind him. Seeing his last hope of escape disappear behind the wooden barrier, Rane turned around to face the gang leader, a hard knot of worry choking his throat.

"So, how was the 'pocketing job? Get anything good?" Otto's smile was wide as he leaned forward in his chair. His eyes locked first on Aimee, then on Rane, staring piercingly at the boy until he began to squirm and hurriedly reached into his pocket to pull out the bracelet and rings that he had 'pocketed earlier. Stepping forward, he handed them to Otto, who looked them over critically.

"This is it?" he said skeptically, holding up the bracelet and playing with the links of the chain. "I gave you four hours to work and this is all you come back with?"

Rane blushed, actually ashamed by the words. Looking down at the floor, he muttered, "It's only just stopped raining. People weren't really out because of the wet and cold and those who were walked around really fast, hurrying. It was harder to 'pocket."

"And you think *that* excuse is going to work for the Foreman? You think he'll be sympathetic if you stand in front of him and tell him that the reason you brought in crap is because it's been raining and people don't like walking in the rain?"

Rane's blush deepened, even as he felt a strange sense of relief. In the agony of watching Aimee talk to the two kids on the street, planning her escape, he had forgotten what she had told Otto that morning. Otto was just checking up on them.

"It wasn't his fault," Aimee said suddenly, reaching into her own pocket to pull out the wallet. "I was working with him, on 'pocketing, like I said I would. I just wanted to make sure he had it down before I let him try for anything. It took up a lot of time, that's all." She glanced at Rane and scowled. "He's a slow learner."

Otto chuckled and accepted the wallet she held out to him. As Rane scowled back at Aimee, he thumbed through the compartments, pulling out the credit tabs and looking carefully at their number screens.

"These are personalized, Aimee," he said, holding up a credit tab. "They're traceable."

"I can hack them," Aimee said proudly. "I learned a couple of years ago. It's a lotta work to change the print-pad, and it will only last for an hour or so before the memory erases completely, but I can do it."

Otto stared at Aimee, toying absently with the credit tab between his fingers. His forehead was furrowed thoughtfully, his lips pressed into a thin frown. To Rane, it looked as though he were trying to decide something and having a difficult time doing it.

Feeling nervous in the silence, Rane slid his hand into Aimee's and squeezed her fingers, then took a furtive step back when Otto's eyes caught his. The gang leader stared at him for a long, tense moment, then sighed and shook his head. Rane took another instinctive step back, his heart pounding. Otto had just made his decision and something told Rane that it wasn't a good one.

"I thought you had learned a lesson the last time about proper gang behavior, Rane," Otto said finally, dropping the credit tabs onto the table as he stared at the pair. "So I'm going to give you a chance to come clean." The gang leader tented his fingers on his table and smiled at the boy. Rane thought his teeth looked like fangs. "Why don't you tell me the *real* reason Aimee wanted to go 'pocketing."

"I-I don't know w-what you're talking about," Rane faltered. "Honest, Otto."

"You're lying, Rane," Otto sneered. "I can tell just by looking at you. It's not good to lie to your gang leader," his gaze suddenly shifted to Aimee, "or to make plans behind my back."

At Rane's side, Aimee shuddered, not liking the look in Otto's eyes.

"What are you talking about?" she asked, tightening her grip on Rane's hand until he flinched. "We haven't been making any plans."

Otto shook his head. "That's not what my source found out," he replied.

At his words, the door behind Rane and Aimee opened to admit Sasha, who stalked up to the children, smiling slyly. She held out a hand to Aimee, who, trembling slightly, reached out and took the item she offered. Holding it up, she saw it was a battered and stained cap…a very familiar cap…the cap Caulin always wore on his head and had been wearing that morning when she had asked him to find Eryyn.

"Your dumb friend was really helpful," Sasha said with a cruel chuckle. "He sure does talk a lot."

Rane clapped a hand over his mouth to stifle the cry that had risen in his throat. Desperately, he looked from Sasha to Otto, whose eyes had taken on a hard edge. His chest felt tight and heavy as he realized that he was now in much more trouble than he had *ever* been in when Pammy was his partner. Otto *knew;* he knew *everything!*

"Oh no! No… Aimee!" he moaned, dropping Aimee's hand and stepping back in terror. "They followed us. They followed us!"

• • •

Sawyer blinked in the early light drifting through the window that had been his pillow. His neck was sore and stiff from the odd position and he made up his mind, as he sat up, to tell Eryyn that they would have to look for a more suitable, comfortable place to hide.

Still, for the first time in several days, he had food in his stomach, the rewards of a few hours good 'pocketing, so he couldn't bring himself to feel very sour about the morning. Granted, the shop where they had sold their stuff hadn't been nearly as good as Master John's and, in Sawyer's mind, that was saying quite a lot. A cheap shop meant they didn't make many credits for the pile they placed on the counter. This, in turn, meant cheap food, bad quality, not very tasty, bought in the seedy, dirty stores that catered to the low class peoples. Still, the feeling of a full belly more than made up for the lack.

Sawyer gazed out the window for a few moments, thinking about the dream he'd been having when the sun had hurt his eyes, causing him to wake up. The lady in the park had been in his dream, and she had been his friend, talking with him, laughing, joking, inviting him to her house, where she cooked fabulous meals for him to eat.

Beside him, Eryyn snored loudly, breaking through his thoughts and bringing them back to the reality of the streets. Again he was in the car, nestled against the broken seat back, an old, tattered blanket wrapped around his shoulders for warmth. He sighed heavily and rested his chin on his up-turned palm. It had been such a nice dream.

Eryyn snored again and Sawyer winced at the noise. She always snored when she had been cold during the night. He couldn't explain why, but it meant that Eryyn snored almost every night, and when she snored, she snored *loud*.

Shaking his head and pressing his fingers to his ears to blot out the noise, he kicked open the door and crawled out of the car, looking around quickly to see if anyone who might pose a potential danger was within sight. Things looked safe for now, and, since it was early morning, with few people out on the streets to notice a small boy, Sawyer decided to take a walk and work some of the aches out of his muscles.

Whispering his intent back to a sleeping Eryyn, who mumbled an incoherent reply, he started down the street, heading, without really thinking about his destination, towards the park.

• • •

Liz didn't know exactly why she went back to the park. It was so early in the morning, normally she would still be at the house, fixing breakfast for herself and Gregory, and the recent bad weather didn't make the dirt paths of the park very pleasurable for a walk. Still, she had told Greg that she needed some air and had gone out, her coat wrapped over her arm, her work case in her hand, and had headed straight for the bench where she had been sitting the day before, when she had spotted the boy watching her.

This is silly, she thought to herself as she sat down on the damp metal and tried to make herself comfortable. *It's so early. He probably won't even be awake yet, and don't street kids migrate around the city to avoid being caught? He probably won't even come to the park today. I'm just wasting my...*

A rustling in some bushes across the path stopped her thoughts and her breath caught in her throat as she caught sight of a small figure crouching behind the branches and leaves.

• • •

Sawyer was stunned. He couldn't explain why he had bothered taking this early morning walk, or why he had chosen the park for it; so early in the morning, the park was usually devoid of people, so it wasn't even a place to practice 'pocketing. He certainly hadn't expected to find himself at the same bench he'd been circling the day before, with the same beautiful woman sitting on it!

Ducking into a bush near the bench, he blinked rapidly and rubbed at his eyes, wondering if they were playing tricks on him. No, everything was real. She was really there, sitting on the bench, holding a coat and what looked like a shoulder bag. She was looking around, seeming to search for something... and then she looked right at him!

Sawyer froze, his heart pounding. Could she see him in the

bushes? Did she know that he was watching her? He glanced to his right, spotting a pigeon walking along the grass, searching for dropped crumbs. Maybe she was just watching the bird.

"Hello in there. You can come on out. I don't bite."

No luck. Sawyer turned back to the woman and bit down on his lip. Should he dare? Was she really speaking to him? He knew from Eryyn's warnings and from experience that he should just melt back through the bushes and run away, that he shouldn't even get close to the woman. But, looking through the leaves at her pretty face and at the hand she held out to him…he swallowed hard and crawled out onto the path.

• • •

Liz watched the boy as he stood up before her, taking note that he was keeping a safe distance from the bench, his muscles tensed to flee if anything frightened him.

Like a cat, Liz thought to herself. *An alley cat who's afraid someone will throw something at him.*

She shook her head, looking at the child's comely, but wary, face. For some reason, she felt that there was something definitely familiar about him—the thin face, the brown, wavy hair, the look of fear in his bright eyes. She could have sworn she had seen them somewhere before…she gasped suddenly, lifting both hands up to her mouth. "Sawyer?" she breathed.

The boy's eyes widened and he took a hurried step back, stumbling over the stone border of the path. Pin-wheeling his arms to keep his balance, he turned, about to run, and Liz, half rising from the bench, held out a hand. "Wait! Please, Sawyer, I won't hurt you, don't worry! Please, don't go yet!"

The boy turned back to her, stared at her, then whispered, "How do you…?"

"Liz! Well, what a surprise to see *you* here this early in the morning! This is *wonderful*. I have some great news that I'm *dying* to tell you!"

Liz turned quickly, startled by the loud, braying voice that belonged to her co-worker, Carmen. She spotted the woman hurrying towards her, waving her arms over her head, a wide smile on her face, then whirled back to the boy who'd been just about to speak to her.

He was gone, fled at the first cry from Carmen. Liz scanned the bushes again, and the paths leading away from the bench, but he was nowhere in sight. And if anyone would know how to disappear in the city, it would be a child of the streets. She sighed deeply, hating the loss of the chance to talk, then favored Carmen with a weak smile as the woman plopped down onto the bench beside her.

"Were you just talking to someone?" Carmen asked, her eyes following Liz's to the bushes.

"Well, sort of, but not exactly."

Carmen looked at her curiously, then waved it off with a bright, toothy smile. "I don't have time to try and figure you out right now, hon. I have to tell you, Liz, we got it! We've got a place for the Agency! We can finally get started organizing it, because we have a place!"

Liz stared at Carmen uncomprehendingly. "What?"

Carmen's fingers were drumming excitedly on her knee as she explained, "After you left work yesterday, I got up some courage and asked to talk to that Enforcer, Connel. I got permission and went to his office…he was just leaving for the night, but I asked him to wait for a minute and told him about our idea for the Agency. He listened, and said that he thought it wasn't a bad idea. In his mind, the streets would become a lot safer and easier to control if something were done about the homeless and illegal kids, but he doesn't agree with shipping them off to factories as slave work. He thinks there should be something better, and that our Agency may just be it. He called in a few favors, used some of that famous En-forcer authority and now an old building in the Mid-End is ours. It used to be a gymnasium, so he said, and needs a lot of cleaning up. But once it's finished, it'll have *plenty* of room for what we need— offices, main room, dorms, that sort of thing. And he even prom-ised to try and raise some of the money we'll need to get it fixed up!"

Liz was dumbstruck. She opened her mouth, but no sound came out other than a small squeak. All she could do was reach out and take Carmen's hand in hers, squeezing it tightly.

Carmen laughed and gave her a hug. "Isn't it great, Liz? We're finally getting somewhere. And, since you're out early, we can take a walk over and check it out!"

"I'd love to," Liz finally managed to say. "Let's go, right now!" She jumped up from the bench, quickly smoothing down her skirt, and grabbed Carmen's hand, pulling the older woman up and hurrying her along. As they left the area of the bench, she glanced back once, towards the bushes where the boy had been hiding just moments before. She smiled. Now she had a way to help the children of the city, and she knew the name of the first child she wanted to help.

• • •

Sawyer was kneeling behind a bent and rusted trash can, frowning slightly as he listened in on the conversation at the bench. The beautiful woman he'd been watching had a name now. Liz. At least that was what the other woman had called her. And the two of them were trying to organize some type of agency, one that had to do with the street kids…kids like him.

He swallowed hard, remembering that the woman, Liz, knew his name. How had she known it? She'd never seen him before; at least, he didn't *think* she'd ever seen him before.

He jumped, startled, as the two women left the bench and started walking away. Scrambling to his feet, he followed them, careful to stay out of sight. If they had something in mind for the street kids and the kleptos, it would benefit him and Eryyn to know about it.

They left the park behind, taking to the streets of the Mid-End, where more people suddenly appeared, heading to their jobs for the day. Sawyer suddenly had trouble keeping the women in his sight while he dodged around hurrying adults, most of whom thought nothing of shoving past a small boy in their way. One man, large and muscled from factory work, even stooped so far as to give Sawyer a push that sent him sprawling into a trash can. It hurt, and Sawyer yelped in surprise as he, and the trashcan, tumbled off the sidewalk and into the street, directly into the path of an approaching skimmer. Luckily, the driver of the vehicle spotted the boy and, swearing loudly and blasting the warning siren, he cranked up the hover mode, swerving the skimmer up and over Sawyer, barely missing him.

Laughter bubbled up from the people who had paused in their walking to watch as Sawyer, pale and breathing hard from the near accident, painfully rolled onto his knees and stood up, his clothes now covered with bits of garbage.

"Yahoo! How about that! Just the way to start the day off right," the man bellowed. "Slam a stinking little thief before he has the chance to lighten your wallet. What do you think, boy? Wanna take another bath in the trash?" The man held up his hands as if readying himself to push the boy again.

Scowling, Sawyer wiped off his hands, leaving two lines of filth on the front of his shirt. Sore from the fall and afraid that he had lost sight of the two women, he muttered something to the man that made the bystanders gasp. The factory worker's beefy face turned an astonishing shade of red and he took a step forward, rolling back one sleeve as he prepared to punch the much smaller child. Having learned a valuable lesson from the woman in the market, Sawyer danced out of his range and flashed his I.D. bracelet.

"You better not touch me!" he shouted. "I'm legal, you fat pig, and I can call an Enforcer over here and have you arrested for assault! You can't prove that I was doing anything wrong. *You* were the one who attacked *me!*"

The man paused, uncertain now that he saw the boy's bracelet. When looked at from Sawyer's point of view, it *did* look like assault and could probably cause him plenty of trouble if any Enforcers were called in to investigate. There were plenty of witnesses, and the kid, though dirty and ragged, was legal...

"Get lost, brat!" he snarled, waving his hand as if Sawyer were a fly pestering him.

"What, no apology?" Sawyer, still a safe distance from the man, stuck out his tongue at the man, then hurried off, weaving his way through people who quickly stepped aside to avoid his dirty clothes. Unfortunately, Liz and her friend had continued walking while he had been stopped. He couldn't see them anywhere and didn't know whether they had stayed on the same route or had turned off on one of the many side streets that branched from the main avenue. He'd never find them now, and he didn't have much time left. It was still early, but Eryyn would almost certainly be up by now, and she would be worried, and angry, because he had left without telling her where he was going. His best bet, now that he had lost track of Liz, was to return to the nest for the day and try again tomorrow.

Swearing under his breath over the lost opportunity, he spun around and started running back the way he had come, passing the factory worker, who shied away from him with a loud oath. Sawyer twisted around just long enough to flash the enraged man a bright smile, then sped up, reaching the park and running through it, finally coming to the street where their most recent nest was located. He wound through the much smaller crowd that traversed the narrow road and was just within sight of the old car when a hand suddenly shot out of an alley, grabbed the front of his shirt, and dragged him into the gloom.

Sawyer yelped with fright and started to scream, but was stopped by a hand clamping tightly over his mouth, muffling any sound he could have made. Strong arms spun him around, striking his back against the wall, driving the breath from his lungs.

Desperate and terrified, Sawyer bit down hard on the hand covering his mouth, drawing a scream from the stranger, and struck out blindly, catching his assailant in the stomach and forcing the person back a few steps.

"*Ow!* What the hell was that for?" Eryyn's enraged voice asked.

Sawyer's eyes widened and he gulped down a hard breath. "Eryyn?" he asked, pushing away from the wall. He winced sympathetically as he watched his friend, bent over from his blow to her belly, clutch at her wounded hand.

"Yeah, who'd you think it was, you little idiot?" Eryyn snarled.

"Me?" Sawyer pointed to his chest incredulously. "How about you? Sheesh, Eryyn, don't *ever* grab me like that! I thought you were Otto, or some jerk working for the factories! *You scared the living daylights out of me!*"

"I scared the daylights out of you? How do you think I felt when I woke up and you were nowhere in sight? You didn't even tell me you were going anywhere. I thought…" she paused and straightened up, fixing the boy with a stern glare. "You know we shouldn't walk around alone! Where did you go!"

Sawyer blushed as he realized why Eryyn was so mad. "Sorry, you were asleep, and I didn't think I should wake you. I just went for a walk, that's all. The park, where we were yesterday. I-I was looking…oh, never mind. I'm sorry, I should have told you, I know. It was stupid."

"You're damn right it was. What if I *had* been Otto, or some creep out to make a few quick credits? What would you have done then?"

Sawyer shrugged. "Don't know, which is why you shouldn't scare me like you did."

Eryyn stared at her friend, then shook her head slowly. "I'm never going to understand you, and I keep telling myself that I shouldn't even try—all I get from it is a headache."

Sawyer grinned.

"But," Eryyn continued. "I still want to know where the hell you went to!"

"The park," the boy answered. "I told you."

"Why?"

"Don't know, just felt like it. And don't try to understand, you're not much fun when you have a headache."

Eryyn stamped her foot petulantly, then burst out laughing. "Not much fun, am I?" She darted at the boy, caught his head under her arm, and dug her knuckles into his scalp while he squirmed, yipped in pain, and tried to bite her hands. Finally, she released him, jumping back as he rubbed his sore head and pouted. "And let that be a lesson not to wander off without telling me."

"I did tell you!" Sawyer retorted, though he was laughing. "You were just sleeping at the time, and *snoring* like a factory whistle."

"Oh, you little…I do not snore!"

Sawyer snorted and raised his eyebrows at her, his hands on his hips. Eryyn frowned. "Well, I don't snore *that* loud."

"I'm hungry," Sawyer said, abruptly changing the subject so he wouldn't be forced to agree. "And we don't have any credits, do we?"

Eryyn shook her head, allowing the subject to drop since she had had the last word. "None, spent them all. We need to do some work before we go meet Aimee."

"Houses, or 'pocketing?"

"Umm, let's hit a house, it's quicker and we can get more stuff. But first," She eyed his filthy clothes, her nose wrinkling as the smell of garbage reached her, "you should change. We can't go walking around with you dressed like that. What did you do, go Dumpster diving?"

"You could say that," Sawyer replied, glancing down at his grime-streaked shirt and pants. "But the rest of my stuff is still covered in mud."

"It'll be dried by now. Better to be dusty than smelly." Eryyn followed Sawyer as he headed towards their recent nest, then waited on the curb as he rummaged around in the old car for the set of clothes he had disdained after the day in the mud. The boy pulled the shirt and pants out and held them up, frowning as chunks of dirt and clouds of dust dropped down to form a small drift around his ankles. Sighing and mentally cursing the man who had pushed him into the garbage can, Sawyer shook the worst of the dirt out of the clothes, then slipped back into the car to change.

"I think we should search out a house with kids," he murmured, climbing back out onto the street. "We need to get some new clothes."

Eryyn cocked a grin at her dusty little friend. "Yeah, but on the way to this specific house, would you mind walking a few yards behind me?"

Sawyer scowled, confused.

"Why?"

"I don't want anyone thinking that I'm associated with such a little ball of dirt."

"Ha ha."

• • •

Sawyer felt his feet sinking into the plush carpet that lined the floors outside of the room he was scowling into. This house was definitely the most luxurious he'd ever encountered in the Mid-End, and, looking into what could only be the children's room, he felt an odd flash of insane jealousy. Life just wasn't fair!

The room was almost as large as the parlor he had recently plundered and was completely *covered* in toys. Dolls and tiny clothes were draped over the miniature table and chairs. Collectable, shiny metal skimmers and flitters of all brands and colors lay across the floor—one was so large that Sawyer could have sat in it. Fluffy animals were arranged in piles in the corners along with papers and puzzles and games. The list went on and on, the room was packed!

But one thing was missing. Sawyer stood in the doorway, heedless of wasting his five minutes, and tried to puzzle it out. Finally, he came to a conclusion: the room had no beds. All it had were the toys, which meant… He walked a few feet down the hall and pushed open another door, finding his suspicions confirmed. Two beds, one covered in blue blankets, the other in pink and yellow, were arranged against the walls, each laden with even more toys. A pair of plastic dressers stood at the foot of each bed, the drawers hanging partly open. Colorful clothing had been jammed in haphazardly, overloading the drawers and spilling out over the toy littered floor.

Two rooms to hold all the toys! Sawyer let out a whistle through his teeth. Whoever lived in this house sure had it going well for them. He even spotted a pocket- sized viewer on the blue bed. Stepping into the room, he snatched up the expensive piece of machinery, stuffed it into his sack, then turned his attention to the overfilled dressers. Surely they wouldn't miss a few shirts and pants…

He had just finished his selection, relieving the dressers of six shirts, four pairs of pants and two sweaters that looked so warm and soft he couldn't resist, when he happened to glance up at a shelf hanging over the pink bed. There he spotted a picture of the family he was currently robbing. A balding, middle-aged man; a round, pallid, awkward boy with a frown on his face; a chubby girl who appeared to be scratching her rear, and…Sawyer did a double take, his mouth falling open as he stared at the woman beside the girl.

"That witch!" he exclaimed, nearly dropping his bag in shock. "No wonder…!"

He wheeled back, running out of the room and down the hall, pushing open doors at random until he found another bedroom. This was obviously the master room, with an enormous four poster bed, spread with a white lacy canopy and elegant yellow and cream sheets and blankets. Another picture, identical to the one in the children's room, only much larger, hung over a very rare wooden dresser. The details in this picture were much better and now there was no doubt in Sawyer's mind. The woman in the photo was the very woman who had accosted him on the street at the market. The fat woman who had claimed he'd ripped her dress and who had been so eager to drag him off to justice. Now he understood just *why* she had been so eager. How else would she be able to afford all the luxuries of her house if she didn't round off her income with a little illegal money made from selling kids to the factories?

Sawyer felt sick, realizing just how close he had come to adding even *more* toys to the collection in the neighboring rooms. Angrily, he grabbed an ugly glass figurine of a girl in a wide skirt from the top of a nearby table and flung it at the picture, shattering the glass. A few more statues—birds, cats, more people—followed the first, breaking windows and a large mirror that occupied a place of honor above the headboard. When every statue had been thrown and all the available glass had been broken, all that remained on the table was a wooden jewel box, which he swept into his sack.

By now, his five minutes were definitely up, and Eryyn would be starting to get worried. Throwing one last contemptuous look at the smiling family in the photo, he turned and hurried back down the stairs, found the window he had used as an entrance, and threw his bag out to the waiting arms of his friend. Scrambling over the sill, he dropped down into a yard that was just as littered with toys as the rooms had been. Still angry, he kicked at a child's toy flitter, one that was powered by pedals rather than fuel, and managed to break off one of the fiberglass air-wings.

"What took you so long?" Eryyn was asking, clutching the bag to her chest. "I told you to take only five…" She paused, watching her partner kick at the flitter, and frowned. "Squirt?"

"Let's go," Sawyer said shortly. "I wanna get out of here. Now! I hope I took them for enough; if I'd had a few more minutes I would have…" He shook a fist at the house, then spun around and ran through the bushes that separated the house from the small side street they had used to find the place. Confused, Eryyn followed, keeping silent until they were several blocks away and safely hidden behind a metal column in a parking garage. There, she sat on the ground and dumped out the contents of the sack, whistling appreciatively at the myriad of junk Sawyer had managed to collect during his short time in the house.

Sawyer watched her impassively, leaning against one of the nearby walls. His cheeks were damp with recently wiped tears, but he was slowly calming down. After a few more minutes, he dropped beside

Eryyn, rested his head on her arm, and pointed out the jewel box, which had yet to be opened.

Eryyn glanced at the boy, then dumped out the box onto one of the sweaters. It contained a collection of valuable rings, pins, bracelets, earrings, and one long necklace with a very tacky red stone pendant.

"Nice job, Squirt," Eryyn said, nodding appreciatively. "Though I wonder if it was worth it." She gave Sawyer a meaningful look and he nodded slightly.

"You'll never guess who owned the house, Eryyn," he murmured.

"Probably not, but whoever it was sure didn't make you happy, that's my guess."

"It was that creepy fat woman from the market."

Eryyn's eyes widened in remembrance. "The one who…"

"Tried to blame me for ripping her dress and then tried to drag me off, yeah. You should have seen the inside of that place, Eryyn. It was amazing! The kids must have every type of toy ever made! Half the furniture is *wood* and they have a *huge* collection of music equipment. Must have cost a *fortune*."

Eryyn was quick to catch on. "Not a problem if you have plenty of money coming in from selling helpless little street kids."

Sawyer nodded grimly, too upset to protest being called helpless. "I could have been another toy for her kids. Or another of those ugly rings." He pointed to the jumble of jewelry. "She wouldn't have taken me to an Enforcer station, she would have *sold* me!"

Shaking her head sadly, Eryyn gathered up the stuff and shoved it back in the bag. "But she didn't get the chance, and you'll never see her again, probably."

"Still, she *sells kids*, Eryyn! Someone should stop her. Maybe if we tipped off an…"

"Enforcer? No way! We're not going to do anything. It's not our problem anymore. If she gets a few kids it just means less competition at the shops."

Sawyer's eyes widened at the callous words. "You can't mean that? What if she *had* gotten me? Or what about Aimee? We're gonna try and help Aimee. Wouldn't you try and help…?"

"Not a stranger. Not if it puts *me* at risk. What's the use, Squirt? Even if we did tip off the Enforcers…well, there are probably a thousand more like her in the city who'll still keep working. It's useless. I hate saying it—I'd love to see some Enforcers march into her house and drag her away in binders—but what can we do? We're just kids…and only one of us is legal."

Sawyer sighed deeply, clenching his hands into fists. "And what can kids do?" he muttered. "No one'll listen to us."

"Nope. So it's best to just stay nice and quiet and not do anything to attract attention." She smiled faintly and patted the boy on the shoulder, sending up a waft of dust from his dirty clothes. "But, if it had been *me* in the house, I would have done something to get back at the old witch."

Sawyer brightened instantly. "What makes you think I didn't?" he said through a smile. "She's gonna have a lot of glass to clean up when she gets home." He tilted his head to one side, his expression hopeful. "Maybe she'll cut herself."

"I've really rubbed off on you." Eryyn nodded with satisfaction. "There's hope for you yet, Squirt."

"Why, thank you." Sawyer dipped a little bow. Eryyn, laughing, gave him a small shove, making him wobble precariously before regaining his balance.

"C'mon, Squirt," she said. "Let's go find a broker and dump this stuff, then go meet Aimee."

• • •

Moving hurt. *A lot!* It was safer to sit quietly, hugging his knees to his chest, avoiding any sudden movements that might make his bruises scream out. Besides, it was too dark to see anything, and the closet, for that's where Otto had thrown him, was too small to allow much movement anyway.

So he sat, leaning against the wall, feeling cold, hurt, betrayed, and very scared. He didn't know how long he'd been locked in the tiny storage room; it seemed like hours, days, but darkness and depression had a way of distorting things. Still, he believed that *some* time must have passed because his stomach hurt, like he was hungry. Although *that* could also be attributed to fear and sadness.

There was only one thing he did know for sure—Aimee was gone. That fact could not be changed by the dark, or the cold, or the punch he had taken to the side of his head that had made stars flash before his watering eyes. He knew what they had done to her: just before Otto had dragged him back into the closet, he had seen the triumphant look on Sasha's ugly face.

He clenched his fists, digging his fingernails deep into his palms, not caring about the pain. What was a little more after what he'd just gone through? At that moment, he hated Sasha even more than Otto, hated her for what she had done, and because she was proud of it. Hated her for ratting them out, causing trouble.

But actually, it had been *Aimee* who'd caused all the trouble. If *she* hadn't insisted on trying to escape, and had just *accepted* life within the gang, wouldn't Otto have left them alone? Wasn't it her pig-headedness that had led to…?

He shook his head, wincing, and pressed both hands to his temples. He didn't want to remember what had happened after Sasha had come into the room, carrying Caulin's cap. He didn't want to think about it…but thinking drove away some of the pain, and right now, in the dark and the cold, there was nothing else.

There hadn't been any chance for them at all after Sasha had come in with the cap. Otto had grabbed him, while Sasha had gone for Aimee. Aimee, of course, had fought, giving Sasha a few good punches before her arms were twisted behind her back and she was pushed to the floor. *He* hadn't fought at all, which was just as well, for Otto was twice his size—he didn't stand a chance against the gang leader. Still, he thought it was to his credit that he hadn't started crying. Considering what they faced, that had been an accomplishment.

But he'd probably just been too stunned, and too frightened. After the initial attack, Otto had started talking calmly, telling him how it had been obvious all along that Aimee had been planning something and that he, Rane, had been in on it.

"Did you really think I'd be stupid enough not to notice?" Otto had said, shaking him so hard that his neck had hurt. "You're lucky you're small enough to get into houses with no problem. I've decided to keep you around for a little longer. Aimee, though…" Otto had broken off and looked at Aimee shrewdly, "…she's expendable, I guess."

Aimee had screamed and panicked, fighting against Sasha's grip on her arms.

"Get her out of here!" Otto spat. "You know what to do, go do it!"

"What about you?" Sasha had asked, twisting Aimee's arms up to her shoulder blades.

"Do it without me. I'm going to be busy for awhile. Rane and I have some…talking to do."

With those words, the punishment had begun. Aimee, cursing and fighting, was dragged away by Sasha. That was the last he had seen of her. Her eyes, desperate and terrified, had looked back at him, and he was sure he had seen regret in them. Two of Otto's other thugs had been waiting in the hall; he'd seen them through the opened door for a second, and he knew perfectly well what they had been waiting for.

That had left him alone with Otto, a terrifying concept even when not in trouble. As Otto had twisted him around, towering over him with a dangerous glare on his face, Rane had fleetingly wondered if Aimee was, in fact, the lucky one. For her, the trouble would soon be over; for him, it could only get worse.

The beating had been typical of the gang leader, interspersed with loud curses and oaths. When, after many excruciatingly slow minutes, it was finally over, Otto had pulled him off the floor by his hair, forcing him to look at the door.

"You got off *easy* this time!" he snarled. "Remember that. And if you ever get it into your head to try something stupid again…"

Otto had pointed to the door where Sasha had just appeared. The girl was carrying the red and gold band that had previously adorned Aimee's arm. Grinning wickedly, she had thrust it into his trembling hands. His second partner had stood no more chance of surviving than the first one had.

After that, he had been locked away in the closet while Otto had probably gone out to supervise the disposal of Aimee. Now, he had nothing to do but sit. Sit and wait and think about what had happened. It had all been over so quickly, and, thinking back, he decided that it was *his* fault too. If he'd just had the guts to go to Otto. If he'd just told the gang leader about Aimee's plans, none of this would have happened. Aimee would have been punished, that was inevitable, but at least she would still be alive. It was his fault.

In the dark closet, his small body reduced to a mass of pain and his head throbbing with dreadful memories and fear, Rane dropped his face into his hands, and started to cry.

• • •

"One…two…three…four…" Sawyer counted the cracks in the sidewalk, hopping on them playfully as he kept pace with Eryyn. The older girl laughed at the simple game he had invented, which consisted of jumping from crack to crack, over the solid portions of concrete. Since the sections of whole sidewalk were uneven in length, Sawyer's hops varied from short steps to long jumps that threatened to land him on his backside.

"Five…six…oops, seven…" Sawyer nearly tripped on a small stone, then had to leap to the next crack because the sidewalk here was incredibly well kept, "…*eight!*" he said, landing hard and nearly falling again. "Nine… ten!" He paused, out of breath, and Eryyn stepped up beside him, grabbing his arm to keep him on his feet.

"The statue is just ahead," she said, becoming more sober. "I can see it from here, but I don't see Aimee anywhere. Do you?"

Sawyer peered ahead and saw the statue in question. It was a large, rusty monument of a man, holding a sword aloft and riding a magnificent stallion into the face of the enemy troops, ready to fight for his freedom and happiness. Or, at least that's what the plaque on the stand said. Sawyer had read it several times while passing through the small plaza that had been built about the statue. He'd spent long minutes staring up at the ancient sculpture, trying to imagine what life must have been like back when people had fought with swords, on horses, and had tried to win freedom and happiness for themselves and their families. It was difficult, even with his great imagination, to picture such a man existing in the flesh, but that was probably because the statue had stood in the plaza for so long. Over the years, the face had been weathered smooth and the large sword and magnificent steed had become a favorite roost and bathroom for pigeons. Not much glamour in that!

"She's probably late. Aimee's never cared before if she's left people waiting for her," he quipped, cocking his head and continuing to stare at the statue.

"She's never been in this much trouble before," Eryyn retorted. "I find it hard to believe that she would be late showing up when she needs our *help*."

"But that's Aimee," Sawyer pressed.

Eryyn shook her head. "No, she wouldn't. She'll be here real soon. C'mon, let's sit and wait for her." She grabbed Sawyer by the arm and dragged him over to the statue. She would have pushed him down onto the immense metal stand if he had not yelped in protest, tearing his arm out of her grasp. "I am *not* sitting there!" he exclaimed. "It's covered in bird stuff! And these are new clothes!" He held out his arms, displaying the stolen clothing, which, while clean and comfortable, did not fit his skinny frame, hanging off him like a scarecrow's shirt. The boy in the house had been considerably plumper— twice Sawyer's small size.

Shaking his head in disgust, Sawyer turned around and marched to a nearby bench, where he sat down, pulling his legs up to tuck beneath him. Eryyn glanced at the bird droppings covering the statue, shrugged, and joined her friend on the bench. She sat quietly, staring at the small, ornamental trees that still attempted to survive in the small plaza. After a moment, she noticed that Sawyer was being unusually quiet. She glanced at the boy and saw that he was staring at the ground, his lower lip caught between his teeth, his hands clenched into loose fists.

"You okay?" she asked, placing an arm over his shoulders. Sawyer jumped as though he'd been burned.

"Wha-what? Huh?" He turned, his green eyes wide and nervous before they cleared and focused on her. "Oh, yeah, I'm fine...I guess."

"You guess?"

"Well, I just realized...what if this is all a trap? I mean, if Aimee *was* caught by Otto's gang, wouldn't he...well, wouldn't sending her out to ask you for help be a perfect way to nab you...and me, and force *us* into the gang? What if Otto set the whole thing up, and Aimee is just the bait?"

Eryyn stared at him intensely; she had not considered this. Then her attention was distracted by two men walking nearby, both talking loudly. In fact, the whole plaza was quite loud. People seemed to use it for a place to hold their breaks and lunches, just like the park, or the market. There were quite a few factory workers wandering around, even though the nearby buildings were all worn down and dilapidated, the stores long since closed or turned into sleazy bars or pleasure clubs.

"Otto doesn't know about me and Aimee. He probably thinks we're just friends. And look around, Squirt," she said, grinning slightly. "This place is trashy, but it's busy too. Otto would have to be a complete idiot to try and grab us in broad daylight with people walking around. That's probably the main reason Aimee chose it."

Sawyer chewed on his lip for another moment, then shrugged and nodded. "Alright, but let's hope Otto *isn't* just such an idiot."

• • •

They waited, and Aimee never showed. For five hours they sat on the bench in the Yellow plaza, watching the crowds of people diminish as work started again after lunch, until they, and a few adult low-lifes, were the only ones remaining. The air had become chill and breezy, and, since they were in the shade of a tree, a damp smell rose from the fallen leaves, which had been left to wilt and rot on the ground. It was not a very pleasant afternoon.

Finally, towards the end of the fifth hour, Eryyn groaned and stood up, stretching out the kinks that had accumulated in her legs during the long wait. She was hungry and tired, and cold...and worried. *Why didn't she show?* she wondered silently.

On the bench, Sawyer started and looked up, blinking rapidly. He had fallen asleep against her shoulder sometime during the third hour. By standing up, she had left him nothing to lean on. He had tipped over, banging his forehead against the bench. Rubbing at the sore spot, he glanced at Eryyn, then looked up at the sky.

"What time is it?" he asked, his voice slow and confused. Even *he* could tell by looking at the hazy ball of the sun that a lot of time had passed. "Did she come? Why didn't you wake me?"

"You're too cute when you sleep. And a lot quieter," Eryyn said absently. Sawyer scowled, then stood up, groaning as he straightened his legs. Pins and needles raced up his limbs. "But no, she never showed," Eryyn continued. "Not even a message sent by Caulin."

Sawyer limped up beside her, wincing. He had fallen asleep with his legs tucked under him and they had similarly dozed off, but were taking a lot more time to wake up again. "So what's that mean?" he asked. "That she didn't show?"

Eryyn shrugged. "Don't know. Could mean that she didn't find a chance to get away. Otto may be watching her or something. Or she might have forgotten where we were supposed to meet…"

"I doubt that," Sawyer interrupted. "She's a jerk, but she's not stupid. Not *that* stupid, anyway."

"…or it could mean trouble. In fact, it *probably* means trouble."

"Trouble?" Sawyer bit down on his lip uncertainly. "So what do *we* do?"

Another shrug. "I don't know, Squirt. Aimee would have known, if things were like they were last time, but *I'm* just not good at this kind of thing."

Sawyer wrapped his arm around his friend's waist, offering a scant bit of comfort.

Eryyn looked down at him, her brown eyes troubled. "I think the only thing we can do right now is just wait, Squirt. I hate it, but I can't think of anything else."

Sawyer nodded. "I-I guess we'll hear something from her eventually, right?"

"We'll hear *something* eventually, but if there was trouble, it may not be from her. C'mon, I don't like this place after dark—it's not very safe." But she made no move to leave the plaza. Sawyer watched as she wrapped her arms around her chest, hugging herself, protecting herself, but not from the cold.

"Eryyn?" Sawyer ducked a little, even to himself, his voice sounded small. He touched her arm, causing her to jump. "It'll be dark soon. Let's go and get something to eat, okay? Please?"

"Umm, yeah…yeah, okay." Eryyn shook her head dazedly and allowed herself to be led from the plaza. Several people watched them, but these weren't the people they dealt with in the busy markets—the people who ignored them if they didn't try to cause any trouble. The people who occupied the plaza at this hour looked at them with dangerous interest and Sawyer put speed to his steps, knowing that he and Eryyn each had a credit tab in their pockets from the morning's hit. Such people would think nothing of robbing a couple of children. As quickly as he could without actually running, he led Eryyn out of the plaza and through the city to their hideout. After the greedy hunger in the eyes of the people in the plaza even the ugly, uncomfortable car looked inviting.

"You're really worried about her, aren't you?" Sawyer announced from his passenger side seat. Eryyn had been eerily silent on the trip back to the nest. Now, hearing the concern in his voice, she made an effort to control her nervousness.

"Yeah, Squirt, yeah, I am worried about her. I don't trust Otto anymore, and I would *never* trust the Foreman. Aimee should have showed up, and since she didn't, it just proves that there is trouble. Yes, I'm worried about her."

"What are you gonna do?"

Eryyn shrugged. "What *can* I do? Storm Otto's stronghold and demand he give my sister back? I don't think that would work. Can you imagine what kind of power Otto would have if he knew Aimee and I were related?"

"So we wait?"

Eryyn nodded. "We'll find out something eventually, but until then, it won't do her any good to get ourselves in trouble. I think the best thing we can do is act like nothing's wrong, keep working and hawking and such. And I think we should get ourselves a new nest, just to be safe."

"No complaints from me there." Sawyer tried to stretch in his seat and only succeeded in bumping his head against the window.

Eryyn sighed and nodded her head as she watched him rub the bruise. "But we'll keep our eyes open, alright? We'll listen around. Someone's got to know something, and then we'll find out what went wrong."

• • •

They found out two weeks later, from Caulin. The older boy caught up with Sawyer on First Street, falling into step beside him as he walked about, surreptitiously 'pocketing.

"Aimee's dead," Caulin said solemnly, his eyes on the sidewalk. He ran a hand through his black hair and Sawyer frowned for a moment, taking note that his cap was gone. Then the message reached his brain, and he gasped.

"Dead?" he repeated dumbly. "She's dead? H-how d-do you know?"

"I saw her," Caulin murmured quietly, glancing around to make sure no one was listening in. "Blake saw a crowd of Enforcers hanging around a big, old packing crate in the east Dead—they were pulling a body from it. It was a kid. Blake called me over, I was across the street 'cuz we were 'pocketing together, and I got a good look. She was pretty beat up, not very pretty, but it was Aimee, no doubt. Someone killed her."

Sawyer felt sick. Catching Caulin by the arm, he dragged the older, larger boy down the street to where he knew Eryyn was working. The girl was just reaching for a woman's wristwatch, but the sudden appearance of the two street boys startled the woman. She turned, and Eryyn had to pull her hand back quickly. Angry for the missed opportunity, she cast a glare at her partner.

Sawyer ignored the look, then pushed Caulin forward. "Tell her," he said. "Tell her what you told me."

Caulin looked bleak and stared down at the sidewalk. "Can't you?" he muttered. "That's why I told *you* first."

"*Tell her!*" Sawyer kicked Caulin in the shin, but the boy only flinched and ducked his head lower.

"Tell me what?" Eryyn placed her hands on her hips and looked at the two boys suspiciously.

"They...found Aimee, Eryyn," Sawyer said, giving Caulin a scathing, disgusted look. "The Enforcers found her...umm, found her..." Sawyer sent another look to Caulin, hating to be the one to give Eryyn the bad tidings. Caulin continued to avoid his eyes and, knowing that he'd said too much to back out, he blurted it all in a rush, "She's gone, Eryyn. She...Caulin saw her and..."

"She's dead," Eryyn finished for him, her voice dull. "Otto killed her."

It wasn't a question, but Sawyer nodded.

"Where is she? How long ago did they find her? Take me there." Eryyn rounded on Caulin and the boy didn't hesitate this time. Eryyn's face warned him that it wouldn't be a bright idea. He turned and led her along the roads until they reached the place where he had seen Aimee's body pulled from the crate. The area was not cordoned off, nor were there any Enforcers around to keep curious onlookers back. The body had already been taken away for disposal, and, since it was nothing more than an illegal street kid, no investigation would be made into the death.

Eryyn stepped up to the crate and peered inside. It was full of old trash, but one item caught her attention and she reached in to pull out a thin scrap of green fabric. It was filthy and speckled with a few dark stains, but Sawyer recognized the color immediately.

"Aimee was wearing a shirt that color the last time we saw her, remember? That night at Master John's, when Otto was there."

Eryyn winced and clenched the fabric into a fist. "The night Otto nabbed her," she said. "He actually killed her!" She shook her head, as if disbelieving the obvious. "That *creep* killed my sister! When I get my hands on him…"

"*Sister?*" Caulin, who was standing at the mouth of the alley, spoke up, surprised. "Aimee…?"

"Shut up," Sawyer warned, elbowing Caulin in the chest when Eryyn glanced in boy's direction. Sawyer stepped forward and gently took the scrap of cloth from Eryyn's hand. "Otto killed her, Eryyn, but she was in the gang because of the Foreman."

Eryyn stared at him, stunned. "You're right! The Foreman…*he's* behind it, behind the gangs, and the killings. If he hadn't…she would…Aimee'd never have…"

Sawyer stepped back to a careful distance, sensibly keeping his thoughts to himself. Eryyn was mad now, madder than he'd *ever* seen her, even when they were fighting about his little wish/dreams or about what made a legal or illegal. He glanced back to Caulin, who shrugged his shoulders and cocked his head to the street, asking silently if he could leave. Sawyer shook his head.

"It's wrong!" Eryyn finally exclaimed. "And you want to know why?" Sawyer stared at her, realizing that she was talking to him. He bobbed his head, knowing she would tell him why, even if he had answered no.

"Because no one fights back!" she said in a low voice. "It's always been everyone for themselves, one against one, and that's why the gangs have gotten so strong. Because no one ever *fights* back. Well, guess what, Squirt…I think it's time someone did. I think it's time someone gave the Foreman a run for his fortune."

Sawyer felt a shiver pass through his body, even though the day had actually been pleasantly warm for the late season. "We're someone, aren't we?" he said miserably.

Eryyn nodded, and smiled, her eyes glowing. "You're damn right. You're here to witness, Caulin. I officially declare a street war against the Foreman!"

Swallowing hard, Sawyer turned to Caulin, who was white-faced by the oath Eryyn had just sworn. No one had ever considered calling a street war against the Foreman. Another shiver swept over the small boy and he looked down at the scrap of green cloth he still held in his hand. "I think this is just the start of a *lot* of trouble," he murmured.

Eryyn smiled grimly and clapped him on the back.

SEVEN

Owning it all

A tour through his factories always brought a glimmer of a smile to his face. It was wonderful to walk through the enormous, hideously ugly buildings, a kerchief held to his nose to keep out the smell, and oversee the workers who, each day, added more and more credits to his accounts.

Granted, the inside of the factories were so filthy and run down he would have to throw away whatever suit he had been wearing. But the *thrill* of walking through the halls, watching the scores upon scores of wretched people go about the dreary, mind-numbing routine of piece work, and knowing, *knowing*, that they survived because of him, made it worth the waste. Their miserable little lives, and those of their families as well, would probably cease to continue if he said the word and had them thrown out. *That* was power.

That was even better than watching the credits pile up. Just that little bit of knowledge itself was mind-numbing, and incredibly satisfying. After even the greatest disappointment, such as the necessary loss of a useful gang kid, he could always lighten his spirits with a trip to a factory.

The one he was visiting today made skimmer and flitter parts, both metal and plastic. These parts, once molded and refined, would be shipped to one of his other factories, to be made into the hovering vehicles that were so prized by the wealthy, and brought so much profit. But the entire process started here, with the Dead-End workers who labored over the melting vats and ovens and polishers. Here, where the fumes from solvents and molten metal and plastic were so strong his eyes watered and his nose stung, even behind the protective layer of cloth. It was worse for the people working the vats and ovens, people who remained in the fumes for hours on end, vainly trying to protect themselves with pieces of rag tied around their heads. He had to replace dozens of workers from this particular factory every year just because of the fumes and the bloody coughs they caused.

But there was still always a profit, no matter how many workers had to be called to fill in, so there was no harm done. To him anyway.

He walked by a vat where plastics were being stirred and melted until ready to pour into the molds used for engine parts. A girl, perhaps fourteen, was standing on a small, rickety platform that hung over the vat, stirring the gray, molten concoction with a long handled paddle. She was barefoot, badly dressed in rags that hardly covered her skinny form, and hunched over. Her blonde hair hung in clumps and tangles down her back.

Sensing his gaze, she lifted her head, locking her eyes with his. She frowned, her lips trembling, then put more effort into her work.

The man raised a hand and snapped his fingers loudly. An overseer who'd been following along at a short distance hurried forward.

"Yes, sir, is there anything I can do for you?" he asked, bobbing his head like a pigeon. He even looked like a pigeon, fat and squat with a short neck and dark, beady eyes.

The man nodded and pointed to the child on the platform. "What is this child doing?"

The pigeon-like overseer glanced at the girl. "She's blending the plastics for carriage parts. She stirs the stuff, keeping it from clumping until it's ready to be molded." He paused, trying to evaluate the man's frown. "I guess it *is* a difficult job for one her age. I can put her somewhere else and get someone bigger and stronger to take her place."

"Don't be a fool! She's fine where she is. The platform would collapse if someone heavier were put on it. She stays there. But get rid of that hair—it's too long, could get in her eyes, cause her to trip, and then a whole vat would go to waste."

"Oh, right, sir, I should have thought of that." The overseer frantically signaled another worker over and ordered the man to find a pair of shears and to clip the girl's hair close to her skull for safety. "And do the same with the rest of the stirrers and those who work the vats!" he called as the worker hurried to comply. The girl on the platform scowled deeply but didn't dare complain. She continued her frenzied stirring as the man and his flunky wandered on.

In another aisle, they came across two smaller children—a boy and a girl—struggling to push a small wagon loaded with a large basket full of finished metal gears and fittings. The boy rested his shoulder against the edge of the wagon and pushed, leaning against the basket and shoving hard with his feet. The wagon rolled forward a few steps, then ground to a halt. Gasping with exhaustion, the boy collapsed beside it and lifted a small hand to wipe away the sweat from his grimy face. The girl, who had stood by watching her partner work, sat down beside him.

Glowering, the man stalked over and gestured for the two to stand. Glancing quickly at one another, they obeyed and stood before their boss, trembling.

"I see no bracelets," the man said after he had instructed them to hold out their wrists. "Illegals. It's a favor that I let you work here, where you have food and a roof over your heads at night, safe from those idiot Enforcers. All I ask in return for this favor is good, honest work. I would say that's a fair trade, wouldn't you?"

The girl nodded rapidly, "We know, sir, but it's so heavy! We're trying, honest we are!"

The overseer sliced his hand through the air, cutting off the child's excuses. The girl fell silent and turned her eyes to the floor, where her bare feet scuffed at the concrete miserably.

"I will return in a month or so," the man stated to the overseer. "I expect to see things handled differently in the future."

"Yes sir, certainly." The overseer followed the man, bobbing his head submissively. They continued their walk, but had only gone a few paces when a low voice caught the man's sensitive ears.

"Hah, honest work…that guy wouldn't know *anything* about honest."

The man turned and smiled at the boy who had spoken.

"Since you are so unhappy here, perhaps you'd prefer to be working in one of the fire pits, boy? Those bellows have to be kept running at all times, don't they?" The child pulled in a harsh breath at the threat and his eyes immediately flooded with tears. He would never survive long in the fire pits. If an accident with the flames or the highly dangerous fuels and bellows didn't kill him, then the deadly fumes and heat eventually would.

As the girl touched her friend's arm in sympathy the man turned to the overseer. "Have that boy moved this afternoon. Let's see if a month in the fire pits can burn away that cheeky attitude." The overseer bobbed his head again, casting a glance at the frightened boy, and the man moved on once again, pleased with his work so far. One could not tolerate shoddy work, or shoddy workers. The latter had to be taught to obey and respect orders, or cleared away cleanly and efficiently. The boy, if he survived his month in the fire pits, which was unlikely, would have learned a valuable lesson about talking back to a superior. Either way, the problem would be solved.

He made a quick inspection of the assembly rooms, where adults and children alike, legal and illegal, sat for hours on plastic benches before long tables covered with screws, switches, spark plugs, transistors, wires, and tiny gears. Each person was given the simple, mind-numbing duty of fitting a single type of wire or gear or toggle to the switch plates and memory boards that would eventually grace the cockpits of wonderfully expensive skimmers and flitters. Tiny welders and drills whirred constantly under the flickering lights as the workers bent painfully over the tables, hour after hour, day after day, squinting at the pieces of their monotonous job.

After the assembly room, he moved on to inspect the time watchers, who stood before the exits throughout the entire day, checking the bracelets of the legal workers against the times on their schedules to make sure the shift changes were accurate and that none of the illegal workers could escape.

Satisfied that all was in order and heartened by his short visit, the man left, boarded his private skimmer and headed back to the glittering lights and buildings of the Sky-End. After a day of inspecting his property, he found he was in great need of a good meal and a long bath.

• • •

The piece of property acquired for the Agency was more than Liz could ever have hoped for. Once an old recreational building, it was simply *enormous* when compared to the other houses in the area. A perfect place for homeless children to make a home.

It *did* need a lot of work, however, since disuse over the years had left it in bad shape. Walking through the main room on the first floor, Liz mentally listed the various jobs that would still need to be finished before they could even think of bringing children here. The stairs to the second floor were rotted in many places, a hazard to anyone, big or small. The ceiling over the main upstairs room was leaking. The kitchens and bathrooms were in need of new plumbing. The wiring throughout the entire building needed to be replaced. Several windows were broken. All the walls needed to be painted…the list went on and on. Not to mention the necessary furniture—chairs, tables, kitchen equipment, desks for the school, beds. Also blankets and sheets for the beds, new clothes for the kids, books for the school, paper, pencils, and most importantly, good food and toys.

It was a large load, but not impossible. Already, because of the money they had received from donations, coupled with a small sum from the Enforcers, the stairs and ceiling were beginning to receive their repairs. Liz and Carmen had debated over certain fundraisers to bring in more money and each had added most of their savings to the pot. Even Greg, who was still grumbling over the idea of wasting money on someone else's kids, had pitched in what little he had.

All in all, the Agency was beginning to look more like a definite possibility instead of the far-fetched dream of two secretaries. Just a few more months and they would probably be ready to take on their first client. Liz wanted it to be the little boy, Sawyer, whom she'd met in the park. If ever there was a child in need of a good home and the assurance of a caring adult, it was that boy. She still thought about him, remembering the look of shock and awe that had come over his face when she had said his name. She hadn't seen him since that day, though she spent an hour each morning waiting at the bench in the park, hoping he would return.

"Sheesh, are you still here? It's past seven o'clock, Liz! That husband of yours is going to pitch a regular fit."

Liz smiled at Carmen, who was walking across the room, swinging the hammer and wrench she had been using to play with the plumbing. *Play* was the only word Liz could think of for what Carmen did when she was under the sinks, because the woman certainly wasn't doing a very good job of fixing anything. In the two days since she'd started on the plumbing, Carmen had managed to break three pipes and two fingers. However, she hadn't let the injuries dampen her spirit and continued to go about the renovations with a will.

"You're still here," Liz pointed out. "And Greg will be fine; he has something to reheat for dinner. He understands." She pulled a wry face. "Although, I had to agree to not nag him about his gaming nights to make him understand. I have a feeling he got the best of the deal."

"Aww, just take half his winnings. You're entitled."

"Ha! That's if he ever *has* any winnings!" Liz laughed. "Greg likes to gamble, but he's no good at it. Still, I can't complain, he's definitely been doing his share helping us."

Carmen nodded and looked around the room. "It won't be long, especially if we can get more volunteers. This place is gonna shape up just fine."

"It sure is." Liz grabbed her purse from the corner where she had stowed it upon entering the room and slung it over her shoulder. "But, you're right, there's not much I can do here by myself, I might as well go home and get some rest. I'll see you tomorrow."

"Sounds good, I'll hang around a little longer, see if I can actually get some water running to the upstairs. Have a good night."

"You too," Liz called, already halfway out the door. She took her time walking home, cutting around to the park and taking a short breather by the bench. The boy didn't show, but she refused to lose hope. She went home for the evening, knowing that she would be up, bright and early, to again head down to the park, to sit and wait.

• • •

The man jokingly considered the room as his "Vault". It was where a great quantity of his credits were stored, along with deeds of property for his houses and factories. It was also where he stored his secret information—his records of the gangs, and how well they fared each month when he went for collections.

He kept the records meticulously. Each disc contained all the information on each gang, and there were four discs, each displaying the gang colors, in a protective case on his desk; four discs, four gangs, all situated throughout the city, gleaning a little each day from the three districts. He flipped through them, reaching the disc emblazoned in gold and red—the colors of Otto's gang. He pulled it out of its plastic jacket and inserted it into the drive of his comp station. Instantly, columns of words appeared on the previously gray screen—the previous month's inventory of collections. Otto's gang, a high Mid-End group, was his best, there was no mistaking that. Each month they brought in more loot for payment than any of the others, and also got into less trouble.

Until recently.

Recently, it seemed that Otto was having trouble controlling the brats in his gang. There was that girl, the one who had been stupid enough to bring in the marked watch. Stupidity made a kid expendable. She'd been taken care of. But then her partner had had to be paired up again. That brought in another girl, the red-head. The man scrolled down the screen until he reached the personal profiles that he kept of each kid in his gangs. The girl had been named Aimee, fourteen-years-old. A call from Otto, coming in on his private line, had informed him that Aimee was gone, eliminated. Otto had claimed that he'd caught her stealing loot from the collection boxes. He'd taken care of her, and had punished her partner for not noticing and reporting the theft.

It had been the right move; Otto knew enough to make such decisions and to not bother the Foreman with the details until afterward. Aimee had been trouble from the start; it had been apparent to him from the amount of time she'd taken to submit in the dark room. She'd been expendable too.

But he hated losing kids, especially new ones. Each kid "released" from the gang was a potential threat. If the body was found too soon, or if someone spotted the kids sent out to hide the body, or, the man shuddered to think this, if something went really wrong, and a kid managed to survive and was able to give information to the Enforcers... It was too simple for things to screw up. Better to nab the brats and keep them in the gang, keep them working.

And now, because of Aimee, he had a gang member without a partner: a young boy who was unable to do his share of the work. He'd seen this boy during his visits—he was timid, obedient, had been successfully broken into gang life. And the boy, Rane, was a good worker—intelligent, and skilled in burglarizing houses.

Two weeks had passed since Aimee had been disposed of. The boy would probably be suitably recovered from his punishment, ready to work again.

The man reached out a hand, found, and picked up a link receiver. He dialed the code of Otto's personal link, all his gang leaders carried communicator links so he could reach them when needed, and spoke a few curt words to the boy who answered.

That finished, he closed out the red/gold file, switched off the comp unit, turned off the single light in the small, closet-like room, and left, taking special care to close and triple lock the door behind him.

• • •

Otto replaced the tiny communication receiver on his belt and rested his chin in his hand. He sat quietly, forgetting the conversation he'd been having with Sasha and ignoring the girl who still sat on the sofa across from his small desk.

"What did the Foreman want?" Sasha asked, miffed at being forgotten.

Otto glanced up at her, then shook his head absently. "Go and get Rane for me. Bring him here," he ordered.

"Rane?" Sasha frowned. "What do you want with that little rat?"

"I didn't ask you for your opinion. *Now get off your fat butt and go get him!*"

Sasha's frown deepened, but she didn't dare say anything else to enrage Otto more. She stood up, taking what little revenge she could in moving slowly, dusting off her clothes, and sauntered towards the door. A few minutes later she returned, shoving a nervous-looking Rane before her. She pushed the boy to stand in front of Otto's desk, then returned to her seat on the sofa, smiling smugly.

Otto ignored her and looked at Rane. The twelve-year-old had been released from the closet ten days ago and had been grounded to the stronghold ever since. Unable to go out for lack of a partner, and as added punishment, he had spent his time cleaning the numerous rooms of the old building and doing any tiny, insignificant chore that the other kids were able to imagine. His bruises from Otto's beating were fading, but still visible, and, since his rations had been cut, he'd lost weight. Completely miserable from his mistreatment and very frightened by this sudden, unannounced meeting, he wisely kept his eyes lowered while Otto contemplated him.

The scrutiny lasted for a painfully long moment before Otto finally smiled and said, "So, Rane, long time, no see. How ya been, buddy? Having fun around the stronghold? I have a feeling the others have kept you busy, huh? I think they like not having to do their chores."

The boy nodded briefly and swallowed.

"Think you've learned your lesson?"

Rane finally looked up, his brown eyes showing his confusion and pain. "I really didn't do anything wrong," he said softly. "None of it was my idea."

"You knew about a possible mutiny and escape and didn't inform a superior. That's wrong. That calls for suitable punishment. Do you think yours was suitable?" Otto asked with a grin.

"More than," Rane mumbled in reply.

Otto laughed. "Feeling wronged, Rane? *Pity.* But I have some news that might cheer you up. How would you like me to release you from grounding? Wouldn't that be nice…you could go back outside and do real work, and the others wouldn't be allowed to boss you around anymore. Wouldn't you like that?"

On the sofa, Sasha's smirk was replaced with a look of puzzlement that nearly matched the one on Rane. In *her* knowledge, Rane was supposed to be grounded to the stronghold for at least another month. The other kids enjoyed having someone do their boring work for them and, though Rane was unhappy—not that *that* mattered he was *supposed* to be unhappy—the spirits of the other kids were buoyed by having someone to step upon. Even Rane knew this, for his look was not just one of confusion, but of wary fear. Otto was talking about an early reprieve from punishment—that just *didn't* happen; surely the gang leader had some other trick in mind to torture him, something that would take him from bad to worse.

"What's this all about?" he asked tentatively, not willing to commit himself yet with a straight answer. "You never let anyone off punishment early."

"*I* never do, that's right, but I have orders from a superior," Otto said, tenting his fingers before him on the desk. He watched, grinning with satisfaction, as Rane and Sasha figured out his words. Rane's eyes grew wide and he glanced around the room, as if expecting to see a sinister shadow in the corners. Otto held out a hand, indicated the sofa. "Take a seat, Rane, and I'll explain."

Looking like a mouse that was cornered by a cat, Rane sidled over to the sofa and perched on its edge. Sasha glanced at him, then slid over a few inches, separating herself from the "traitor". Rane, his attention riveted on Otto, ignored her.

"It would seem," Otto started, "that you have caught the Foreman's eye, Rane. I don't know how a timid little traitor like you could be anything but an embarrassment to the boss, but hey, I don't tell him how to think. He called me just a few minutes ago and told me to stop wasting workers and to put you back to work. Not only that, he told me to put you to work with either me or Sasha."

"What!" Sasha jumped up from her seat. "Why should I take the little snot with me?"

"Foreman's orders. Rane's small and has skill with houses, so he shouldn't waste his time hanging around the stronghold. And since there are no other kids free to be his partner, well..." Otto let the sentence hang and grinned at Sasha, daring her to defy him.

The girl's face, never pretty to begin with, turned ugly with rage. She turned a glare on Rane, as if the Foreman's decision had been his fault, then sank back into her seat. His face pale, Rane edged a little further from her.

Seeing the movement, Otto turned his grin on the smaller boy. Rane went still and looked at his leader. The grin was not a friendly one, not a happy one. It was a dangerous one, one that meant Otto was steadily reaching the point where he was perfectly capable of doing *anything* if he were pushed just a little too far. But this time the Foreman was doing the pushing, and the Foreman would not bear the brunt of Otto's anger. Rane would. He knew it.

"So, Raney, how about if we go and hit ourselves a house? Hmmm? Doesn't that sound like fun? I'll be your watcher, outside, and you can go in and get us some quality stuff."

Rane, not failing to catch Otto's use of the nickname Aimee had given him, allowed himself a tiny nod. Otto's grin widened, showing off his teeth. No, that wasn't a friendly grin—it was the grin of a sick dog that wanted to bite!

"And I do mean quality stuff, Raney boy, because if you waste my time by getting nothing but useless junk that no broker would take…hah, well, those bruises you've got now will seem like a *tickle* compared to what I'll do. And this time, I'll tell all the others that the Foreman is mad at the gang and it's your fault, and then I'll let *them* have a go! Sound like a deal?"

Rane felt tears stinging his eyes and struggled not to wipe at them. Sasha was watching him, her face caught in an ugly smirk of triumph, just waiting for a chance to insult him. Slowly, he nodded. "All quality stuff," he whispered.

"That's right. So, let's go have ourselves some fun." Otto pushed back his chair and stood up. He jerked his head once at Sasha, then headed for the door. Still smirking wickedly, Sasha grabbed Rane in a vise-grip, digging her fingernails painfully into his arm, and dragged him across the room.

"Cheer up, Raney boy," she whispered in his ear. "This is going to be *loads* of fun!"

• • •

He'd been right. Otto *had* taken him from bad to worse. As he walked silently through the house, Rane puzzled over the turn of recent events. What had made the Foreman go and do a thing like that? Sure, he understood why the man would want him back working. He *was* a good worker, despite what Otto and Aimee had said, especially when it came to hitting houses. And the Foreman would never want to risk losing any credits because a kid didn't work. But why pair him up with Otto and Sasha? What was the reason for that? More punishment? That seemed likely, but not just for him.

For Otto too, because he'd failed to find a good enough replacement for Pammy. So now, as punishment, Otto, the leader, the gang boss, had to go out and work the streets like any common klepto. Yeah, that was the most probable answer. But it still didn't make him feel any better, or make Otto any less dangerous.

Absently, he picked up a portable communicator link and stuffed it into the bag Otto had handed him outside the house. He already had a good motley assortment of items at the bottom of the bag— bracelets, necklaces, earrings, small pieces of machinery from a room that had had a comp unit in it, a handful of silver from a drawer in the kitchen, a disc player. And he still had about a minute left to get out. At least Otto had given him a chance and chosen a good house. He wouldn't have put it past the jerk to pick a Dead-End place, just to get an excuse to beat him up.

Not, Rane thought bitterly, *that he ever really needs an excuse to do that.* His head had only just stopped ringing from the punch he had taken there, and the area around his right eye was still tender to the touch. He shuddered to think about another, worse, beating so soon after the last one. He probably wouldn't even survive, just end up like Aimee, hidden in an alley somewhere.

He snatched at a watch left carelessly on a small table in the hall, added it to his loot, and turned around, starting back down the stairs to the first floor. The door he had used to enter the house was in the cellar, and he headed down there, treading carefully on the worn steps while looking around at the myriad of boxes piled against the walls. There was probably some nice stuff hidden away in those boxes, maybe antiques, the brokers really went for antiques, but he didn't have enough time to check through them. Otto was waiting, and Otto was just looking for the slightest excuse…but Rane was determined not to give him one.

"*Get back!*"

Rane stumbled away from the storm door at Otto's hissing voice and instinctively raced across the room. He flung his bag into a crevice made by the boxes against the wall and slid in after it. Trembling in his hiding place, he listened nervously as footsteps traced a path outside and the hinges of the storm door suddenly squealed in protest as the door was slammed shut. The basement was flooded in darkness.

Perfect! Rane thought miserably. *What else can possibly go wrong?*

The darkness seemed to grow thicker with each passing minute and the silence echoed thunderously in Rane's ears. He wondered if the owners of the house, who were suddenly making a lot of noise upstairs, could hear his heart pounding or the whistling of his breath through the floor.

Minutes passed, though to Rane they felt like hours, days, *centuries!* He started to fear that Otto and Sasha had run, leaving him to get caught and bear the consequences. Maybe *this* was all just another part of Otto's sick method of punishment…maybe Otto and Sasha were just trying to get rid of him…maybe they *wanted* him to get caught and dragged off to the Enforcers…maybe…

The storm door opened abruptly, spilling light across the cellar floor.

"Rane? *Rane, get out here!*"

Rane didn't know whether to breathe a sigh of relief or burst into tears. Deciding against both, he crawled around the box, dragging the bag of loot after him, and stood up on trembling legs.

"*Now!*"

Rane cast a quick, tense glance at the stairs leading to the first floor, then hurried across the basement to the storm door. A hand reached through the flat, ground level door and helped him out. He had hardly stepped onto the grass of the yard when Sasha tore the bag from his arm and began pawing through it eagerly. After a moment, she glanced up, her face stretched in a smile.

"He didn't do none too bad, Otto. I guess you were right, the little shrimp *can* be useful."

I'd rather be a shrimp than a stupid, fat cow, Rane thought bitterly. *You'd probably get stuck in a window if you tried to do a hit.*

He was jolted from his thoughts by a hand, Otto's, that slapped him sharply on the shoulder.

"Good work. Looks like you spared yourself for a little while anyway. Now let's get out of here before that happy couple realizes anything is gone." Otto gripped the boy's upper arm and sneaked out of the yard. Sasha, the bag of loot hanging from her shoulder now, matched him step for step.

As if their first step onto the sidewalk were a cue, somebody in the house behind them gave vent to a loud yell of anger. Otto glanced back, grinning, and hurried them along.

"You must've gotten some *really* good stuff. Lucky you, I might even give you back your rations."

"Hooray," Rane muttered sourly. He had fallen into place beside the two as they walked down the sidewalk, but that was only because Otto was gripping his arm so tightly he feared there would be more bruises there by evening.

"What's the matter, Raney boy, not enjoying yourself?" Sasha poked him hard on the back of the neck. "Don't you like ripping off the lousy Mid-Enders?"

"Not with you," was the truthful reply, as Rane used his free hand to rub at his neck; that was all he needed right now, more soreness and bruises. And leave it to Sasha to find what was pretty much the only place on his body that had been spared the beating.

Otto laughed and gave Rane's arm a little tug. "Better get used to it, brat. I haven't done a hit on a house since I made gang leader. I've missed this! We could probably hit five more houses before the work whistles go off."

"And let me guess, *I'm* the one who goes in on each job?" Rane raised his eyebrows at the older boy.

"You got it! See, I knew there were some brains in that little head of yours. Being small ain't all bad, now is it?"

Rane scowled, causing Otto to laugh all the harder.

"I've never tried to hit more than two houses in a day," he murmured.

"Well, you never had a good partner before, did you?" Sasha grinned to see the small boy wince at her cruel words. "Only deadbeats who didn't know how to work. Didn't know much of *anything* if you ask me."

"No," Rane whispered.

"But now, if a day goes by when you don't hit at *least* two houses…" Otto held up a fist in front of the boy's nose. Rane leaned back slightly, looked at the tightly clenched fist, and his eyes filled with tears.

"Why are you doing this?" he asked. "Didn't you already punish me enough?"

"Oh, this isn't punishment, Raney boy, this is *incentive.* To make you work harder. To make our quota on payment day bigger. To make the Foreman happier. 'Cuz when the Foreman's not happy, then I'm not happy. And when *I'm* not happy…"

"Then I'm in pain."

Otto's grip on his arm loosened slightly. "You *do* catch on quick when you have to, don't you?"

Rane said nothing as Sasha giggled.

Otto looked around to make sure there were no eavesdroppers nearby, then stopped suddenly and his grip became tight again as he turned Rane to look at him. "You just have to remember, Raney boy," he said, his voice low and serious, "*I* may own *you*, but the Foreman owns us *all!* Better get that branded into your brain, because *whatever* the Foreman wants, he gets. So it's best to stay on his good side. You'll live a lot longer and a lot better if you do. You got me?" He punctuated each of the last three words with a hard shake of Rane's shoulders.

Two tears escaped from Rane's eyes while Otto was shaking him and ran down the sides of his nose. Feeling hopelessly trapped by the truth in the gang leader's words, the small boy nodded. "I got you."

Otto grinned. "Alright," he clapped his hands and rubbed the palms together eagerly, "Then let's go hit ourselves some houses!"

EIGHT

Rob from the rich and make allies of the poor

Sawyer wasn't sure when he and Eryyn had discovered the tiny restaurant that was situated between the Mid-End and Dead-End. All he knew was that it was one of their better finds, and that was because the owners of the restaurant didn't seem to care who they served, as long as the patrons had money to spend. Therefore, two street kids who'd just cashed in their loot to a broker were able to sit quietly at one of the outside tables, have something to eat, and talk in relative peace and safety. Not much could be said for the food, but that was to be expected from a lower end place. It was still better than most of the meals they bought from the stores with the suspicious clerks.

As he thought about this, Sawyer poked disdainfully at a wilted piece of lettuce that had been a garnish for the snack he and Eryyn had purchased to gain the right to sit in the restaurant. On either side of him, Eryyn and Caulin talked in low tones, discussing Eryyn's plan. Sawyer listened with half an ear. He'd heard it all already. Caulin was really having a difficult time imagining a group of street kids getting revenge on the Foreman.

"But he's the *Foreman!*" Caulin was saying for what must have been the twentieth time.

"I know that, Caulin," Eryyn snapped. "You keep saying that! Can't your puny little head hold more than one idea at a time?"

"Not when there's food around," Sawyer piped. He and Eryyn had had enough credits to buy themselves something to eat, but

Caulin was currently broke. And, since he was not a partner, they hadn't shared. In the minds of the street kids, Eryyn and Sawyer had earned the money for the food, so the food was theirs and only theirs. Caulin knew this unspoken rule as well as the other two. He hadn't asked to share any of their meal, but his stomach had started rumbling loudly at the smell and had not stopped for half an hour. Teasingly, Sawyer held up the remainder of a piece of bread. "Maybe this would help you concentrate better."

Caulin snatched at the bread contemptuously. "This isn't worth feeding to a pigeon," he muttered.

"Well, you're a bird-brain, not much difference."

Caulin scowled, but bit into the bread quickly before Eryyn saw fit to take it away.

"Okay, so now that your head isn't being run by your stomach, can we get back to business?" the girl asked impatiently.

"What business?" Caulin asked around a dry mouthful. "All the stuff you've been telling me is a joke. Do you really think that a bunch of street kids could *possibly* do anything to the Foreman? Nobody even knows *who* the man is, not to mention *where* he is. And he has a bunch of gangs of his own. We wouldn't stand a chance."

"We would if we were organized," Sawyer said, finally adding to the conversation. He'd been thinking hard the night before and had come up with a small idea that might give them a little chance, but hadn't yet told Eryyn about it. Now was his chance. "The kids in the gangs only stay with them because they're scared, right?"

Eryyn and Caulin both nodded. "Yeah," said Eryyn. "They're either scared of the gang leaders, or they're scared of what will happen to them on the streets if they don't have the…I guess you could say, *protection* of the gang."

"Uh huh, so that's why they stay *in* the gangs. But what about the kids like us, the partnerships, like me and Eryyn, or the independents, like you, Caulin, or like Aimee. What keeps kids like us *out* of the gangs?"

"Out?" Eryyn's brows furrowed. "Well, that's easy. There's no freedom in a gang. Only the leaders get to make decisions, and if the kids don't follow orders…" she punched her left fist into her right palm. Caulin winced, but nodded and added, "And nobody ever gets to *keep* what they get in a gang. All stolen stuff either goes to the gang leader, who decides what to do with it, or in the case of Otto's gang, to the Foreman."

Sawyer smiled brightly. "And who ever said you were a bird-brain, Caulin? Sounds like you know what you're talking about."

Caulin punched him playfully on the arm. "You've got to remember, Squirt, I've been around longer than you. I've talked to people. I know kids who have been in gangs."

"So do I," Sawyer replied with a sideways glance at Eryyn. "But that's it—kids like us don't wanna be in a gang 'cuz we can't do what we want, and have to give up whatever we make. Not much fun in that. But what if..." He paused for a moment, staring at the table, then continued in a rush, "...what if there was a gang where the kids got to keep all the stuff they stole, or at least some of it? What if there was a gang of kids that stole, but took the loot and used it, not to make the leader rich, but to keep all the kids alive and happy? You know, kinda made sure everyone was taken care of?"

"Doesn't sound like any gang I've ever heard of," Caulin said, leaning back in his chair and raising his eyebrows skeptically at Sawyer.

"What are you getting at, Squirt?" Eryyn asked. "What kind of gang would do that? A gang leader is always the biggest or strongest kid in a group. What kind of gang leader wouldn't take a huge cut and make himself rich?"

"You," Sawyer answered quickly. "'Cuz you want something else." He leaned down and dragged his bag onto the table. Rummaging through it, he pulled out a soft-covered book, old and tattered, the pages ripped or dog-eared at the corners; the foil on the cover was worn off, leaving the name barely visible. He held it up for them to see.

Eryyn stared at the cover. She could see that it was one of Sawyer's older books, she recognized the faded colors—green and brown and gold—and knew that he had read it often. But he had never told her what it was about, and she had never asked. Now she glanced at him, brows raised like Caulin.

"What is it?" Caulin asked. Like Eryyn, he couldn't read and didn't like knowing that Sawyer could do something he couldn't. "It's too worn out to see the name."

Sawyer chuckled. "You wouldn't know the name even if the cover was brand new, Caulin. Don't think you're fooling me."

"Well…?"

"This is a book called *Robin Hood*. It's really good. I've read it lots of times. But this is the first time I ever thought it would be any *use* to me."

"How?" Eryyn plucked the book from her friend's fingers and looked it over curiously. She flipped it open at random and peered at the pages. All the words and lines looked hopeless to understand. She handed it back. "How can a *book* help us beat the Foreman?"

Sawyer smiled and, for the next hour, told them the entire story of Robin Hood and his men of the forest, who lived happy, carefree lives and stole from the rich to feed the lesser people of the world. And how Robin and his men were loved and praised by the poor people, how they gained their honor and respect just by showing them a little kindness.

"See?" he said, finally finishing the tale. "He got himself a gang by being nice to them. He treated them like friends, not slaves. And because he gave away all that he stole, he had more and more and more people who wanted to be around him."

"And join him," Eryyn whispered, in awe. "All the poor were willing to help and protect him, because they thought he was…"

"Their friend," Caulin finished for her, his eyes wide and wistful.

Sawyer's lips were turned up in a small smile. "Sound good?" he asked, flicking a crumb off the empty plate and onto the ground, where a fat gray and white pigeon quickly pecked it up. He watched the bird, then nudged it with his foot until it moved away from the table.

"I think it sounds great, Squirt," Eryyn replied, patting his hand happily. "I just don't know how to start it. I mean, that guy, Robin whatever, how did he start? Who did he give to first? How did everyone find out about him?"

Sawyer looked pointedly at Caulin, one of the klepto grapevines. "People talked, I guess. They told their friends, who told their friends, who told *their* friends, who…"

Eryyn clapped a hand over his mouth to silence him. "Okay, I get the point. So, if I got this right, we start taking what we get from hits and 'pocketing and give it away to other kids, right? And then we let blabbermouth here tell everyone about it, and hope that everyone comes running to us for handouts."

"Hey!" Caulin protested. Eryyn ignored him.

"But *instead* of more handouts, we offer them the chance to join a gang, *my* gang, where everyone will get a piece of the loot, and nobody has to worry about getting hurt."

"I'm *not* a blabbermouth. And when did I ever say that I was going to be a part of this stupid plan?" Caulin asked sullenly.

Sawyer and Eryyn fixed him with angry eyes.

"You have no choice," Eryyn said, pointing a finger at his nose. "If you don't help us, I'll personally tell *everyone* that it was your fault that Aimee died. I mean, you *did* tip off Otto's gang about her escape plan, and that was probably what got her in trouble." She rested her elbows on the table, and perched her chin on her hands. "So, Caulin, would you rather I tell everyone that you're a bawling little coward who spilled his guts at the first question, or do you want me to say that you've been a member of Otto's gang all this time, and you're nothing but a spy?"

"That's not true, Eryyn, and you know it!" Caulin exclaimed, half rising from his chair. Several people at other tables looked around and the restaurant owner glared in their direction. He'd been glaring, actually, for the past hour, since they were taking up a table even after having finished their food. Sawyer, spotting the dangerous glint in the man's eyes, nodded briefly and jerked his head towards the street, signaling that they would leave in a moment. The man nodded back and returned to cleaning his counter.

"Are you trying to tell me that you *didn't* tell that girl about Aimee, and how she wanted us to meet? Funny, that was the story not too long ago. But now you have a different explanation for losing your hat?" Eryyn reached out and ran her hand through Caulin's messy, exposed hair. The boy blushed deeply.

"I didn't mean to tell, Eryyn, honest. I didn't know it would get her hurt, or killed. I just didn't want any trouble for myself."

"It was *Otto's gang!*" Eryyn raged. "How could you possibly think Aimee wouldn't get into trouble? Just how dense are you, Caulin?"

Caulin looked down at his hands, ashamed and regretting that he had mentioned his forced conversation with Sasha.

"Umm…" Sawyer tapped Eryyn's arm and tilted his head in the

direction of the restaurant owner. The man had taken to watching them again, and the boy feared that they would soon lose their right to use the restaurant if they didn't leave quickly.

Grumbling, Eryyn stood up and stalked out of the fenced-in eating area, stepping immediately onto the main street of the Dead-End. She glanced across the street to the avenue that would lead to the Mid-End, then looked up the road both ways. It was better to play it safe—you never knew when a skimmer would show up and plow you down in the middle of the street.

A touch on her arm alerted her of Sawyer's presence at her side. Caulin, looking very subdued, stood on the other side of the small boy.

"Do you think it will work?" Sawyer asked softly. "I mean, I was only fooling around with ideas in my head and this was one of them, but do you think it could *actually* work?"

"I'll tell you the truth, Squirt. It's not the *best* idea in the world, but it's still a *really* good one, and it's better than anything I've come up with yet."

"And if Otto catches on that *you've* started your *own* gang?"

"Let him try to figure me out. We'll fix that problem when it comes up. Our *first* problem is getting enough loot to start giving away. Feeling up to hitting a few houses today?"

Sawyer flexed his fingers. "Possibly," he answered with a lop-sided grin.

"Then let's get busy. We go Mid-End, and work straight until work whistles go off. Hit as many houses as we can. Then we stash the stuff at..." she paused, glancing at the second boy. "Get lost, Caulin," she said after a second. "Go put that big mouth of yours to good use and start spreading it around that Eryyn and Squirt are gonna be giving stuff away. Tell everyone you can find that if they're interested in making a few quick credits, then they can come find us."

Caulin didn't say anything, just nodded and walked off. Eryyn watched him until she was sure he was out of earshot, then continued, "...we'll stash the stuff at Nest Seven. It's the biggest yet, and I think the best hidden. Of course, that means we'll have to move again..."

Sawyer rolled his eyes, but smiled as Eryyn pushed him off the curb and into the street. Careful to watch for oncoming skimmers, they made their way quickly to one of the residential areas of the Mid-End, where the houses were just perfect for supplying them with the bribes they would need.

• • •

Eryyn slept deeply that night, and didn't wake up when the first light hit the city streets and started pushing back the pale yellow glow of the street lamps. Curled on her side against the crumbling wall of the abandoned store they had adopted as Nest Eight, she snored loudly and mumbled in her sleep.

Sawyer, awake and alert despite his fatigue, sat watching the light creep along the street as the sun rose. He knew he should still be sleeping—his whole body *screamed* for sleep, he was so tired from the previous day's hits. But his mind was too full to rest, at least now that the sun was up.

He stood up and stretched, then padded quietly over to the window they had used as an entrance. It opened into an alley, where a series of trashcans made an effective staircase and screen. Turning around, he scooted out on his belly until his feet touched the cans. He let go of the sill only when he was sure of his balance, then scrambled the rest of the way down to the ground. Once there, he wiped his hands free of the mildew they'd acquired from the moldy sill, and dusted off his clothes.

It was pretty useless, being out on the streets so early in the morning, and without Eryyn. It was too early for most people to be up, or if they were, the work whistles wouldn't go off for a few hours yet, so they'd be in their homes. And, not only was it not profitable to be walking around so early, it was dangerous. Out here, when it was still dim and quiet, he was vulnerable to the lowlifes who scoured the city in the night. Those people who didn't have jobs in the offices and factories and made their living in much the same way as the street kids: by stealing. However, those people, grown-ups usually, drunks and druggies, didn't bother to go for the houses. They waited for stupid people to walk by and simply threatened them until they got what they wanted. Sawyer knew this from experience—he'd been held up several times and had had to relinquish all his credits or whatever loot he'd 'pocketed to keep the creeps from hurting him.

So, why am I out here now? he wondered to himself as these thoughts raced through his mind. *If it's so early and dangerous, why don't I just go back in and get some sleep? It's not like I don't need it with the way Eryyn had me hitting the houses yesterday.*

He glanced back up at the window, contemplating climbing back through it into the grungy room.

But the lady at the park, Liz, she came out this early and sat by the bench, he answered himself. *I might be able to see her again if I go to the park for an hour.*

Sawyer knew the idea was dangerous—the park was an ideal place for the nocturnal predators to lurk for potential prey. But the thought of seeing Liz again, seeing her pretty face and her kind smile, and maybe finding out how she knew his name, convinced him. He turned away from the window and skirted along the alley until he reached the street. Then he ran as fast as his legs would take him towards the park. He reached the bench just as the light became strong enough for the street lamps to become useless and for their automatic sensors to shut them off. Without them, the park was still slightly gloomy and unwelcoming, but Sawyer shook off any trepidation and made himself as comfortable as possible on the dew-laden bench.

He didn't know if Liz would come to the park that morning. *He* hadn't been there since the last time, when she had beckoned him out of the bushes and had called him by his name, but he was hoping. And he hoped she would come soon, if she were going to come at all. He didn't relish the idea of Eryyn waking up back at the nest and finding him missing…again. She never took too kindly to that.

He pulled his legs up onto the bench and hugged them tightly to his chest, resting his chin on his knees. Mornings and nights were chilly now; summer was over and, though they still had another month or so of mild afternoon weather, winter was not long in coming. That was an idea he relished even less than Eryyn waking up and discovering him gone. Winter was never kind to street kids. Each year, many of them died from cold or lack of food. People were harder to 'pocket in the winter, because they tended to walk faster in the cold, not hang around in one spot so long, and gather their clothing close to keep them warm. Most kleptos had to resort to house hitting during the winter months, and some kids just weren't suited for it. Each year the competition would falter a little during the cold, only to rise again when spring and summer came and new kids showed up, seemingly from nowhere.

But that wasn't true, so Eryyn had said, they *had* to come from somewhere. Probably from other cities, hoping to find better pickings, or possibly kicked out of their homes, like he and Eryyn had been. Or maybe they had been employed in factories and had managed to run away, though that possibility seemed the least likely of them all.

He heard a noise—footsteps!—and sucked in his breath with a hiss. Sitting small and quiet on the bench, he glanced around furtively, trying to spot the newcomer. If it *was* some creep out for quick money from a kid, he would do better to spot the mugger first, so he could try and run away before *he*, in turn, was spotted.

A shadow was heading his way from up the path, dim in the weak morning light. Sawyer slipped his legs down to the ground and tensed his muscles, ready to jump and run if he needed too. Then the shadow morphed into an old woman, wrapped in a ragged shawl, pushing a shopping cart before her as she walked up the path with shuffling steps. She was muttering absently to herself, and paid him no attention. After a moment, she was gone, slipped back into the shadows.

Sawyer let out his breath slowly, relieved that it had only been a bag lady. No *real* danger there, unless she happened to look at you and her crazy mind took you for a demon, or something else that might harm her. Then it was safer to keep a distance and stay to a crowd. Even complete strangers would usually protect a kid, even a street kid, from a sick old loony with a shopping cart.

"You came back."

Sawyer, who'd been looking after the retreating bag lady, twisted his head around so rapidly his neck creaked. He instinctively leapt from the bench and ran a few steps before realizing that the voice was somewhat familiar. Slowing, he risked a glance behind his shoulder and saw that Liz was standing behind the very seat he had just vacated. The woman was watching him, her eyes wide and happy, her lips lifted in a smile. Sawyer pulled to a stop and turned completely around.

Seeing that he wasn't going to run away from her, Liz stepped around the bench and held out her hand.

"I was hoping you'd come back," she said softly, sitting down. "I really wanted to talk to you, but you ran away last time before we had a chance. I've been coming here every day, hoping you'd come back."

Every day? Sawyer gaped at her.

Liz must have seen his shock because she smiled and patted the bench beside her. Sawyer took a small step forward, closing some of the distance between them, then stopped and shook his head. He wasn't stupid. He wanted to talk, but would be ready to run if she decided to turn mean.

Liz nodded, understanding. "That was my friend Carmen who interrupted us last time. She's rather loud, but she would never hurt anyone, especially not a child. If she had known, she wouldn't have shouted like she did."

"You knew my name," Sawyer said quietly, changing the subject. He didn't care about the woman who had yelled and startled him the last time. All he cared about was that Liz was here, in front of him, and she had been looking for him *every day* since their last meeting. That had been at least two weeks ago, before they'd found out about Aimee, and she'd been coming back to the park since then, looking for him, hoping *he* would return. "How did you know my name?"

"Sawyer? It is Sawyer, right?"

He nodded.

"I was in the market awhile ago, and I saw a woman attack you, claiming that you ruined her dress. I saw the Enforcer stop her and help you. He read your bracelet," she pointed to his wrist, where the silver bracelet gleamed slightly, "and then asked you your name. He said Sawyer, and you nodded. Then he let you go."

"Officer Connel," Sawyer murmured, nodding his head.

Liz's eyes widened. "You remember?"

"Yeah, 'cuz he helped me. I doubt he remembers *me* though."

"Oh, he does!" Liz said quickly. She immediately regretted her words when Sawyer's face lit up with alarm and he stepped back. "No, no, don't go! He doesn't want to hurt you, or anything," she amended quickly. "I work for Officer Connel, and I mentioned what I saw to him, and he remembered your name. He said he thought you were a pretty cute kid." She cocked her head at the boy, her eyes merry. Sawyer blushed, but smiled in spite of himself. He took another step towards the bench.

"Why did you come back?" he asked curiously. "You said 'every day'. Why?"

"I wanted to talk to you again. Every time I see you, I want to talk to you, but you end up running away. I kept hoping that you would come back, and we would get a chance to talk, but you've never come back until now."

"We don't hang around the park that much," Sawyer muttered with a shrug. "What do you mean, 'every time'?" He moved a small step closer.

"Well, there was last time, when Carmen interrupted us, and then there was that time after the rain. At least, I *think* that was you. I might be mistaken—the boy I saw was absolutely covered in mud. But I…"

"It was me," Sawyer whispered, ducking his head in embarrassment. "I tripped in a puddle. I was surprised when you noticed and tried to talk to me. Most people don't really notice when street kids are around."

Liz smiled warmly at the wary child. "How could I not notice a little boy who stops, sits in the mud, and stares at me like I'm a painting on the wall?"

Sawyer's blush deepened. "You were just so…so *beautiful*," he blurted. "Everything was so gross and messy after the rain and the mud, and you were there, all clean, and… and, you were just so pretty that I…" He broke off miserably, shaking his head. "Oh, it just all sounds so *stupid!*" He started to back away, intent on running before he made a bigger fool of himself.

Afraid of losing him again, Liz acted without thinking and moved quickly. She jumped off the bench and rushed over to the boy, catching his wrist before he could flee. Sawyer's eyes widened in apprehension for a moment, but she smiled and whispered, "That's probably the sweetest thing *anyone* has ever said to me. Please don't say it was stupid. And please don't run. Not again, not when we're finally getting to talk."

"I...I have to..." Sawyer glanced over his shoulder, back in the direction of the latest nest, and Eryyn. "I can't stay long. I'll get in trouble."

"Trouble?" Liz looked at him worriedly, and he quickly stammered, "N-not *real* trouble, but Eryyn'll get real mad if she wakes up and I'm gone and..."

"Eryyn? Who's Eryyn?"

Sawyer clamped his mouth shut, wondering if it was dangerous to tell this woman too much. Eryyn wouldn't like it. Liz was a grown-up, not to be trusted, someone who could betray them to the Enforcers. And Eryyn wouldn't care if Sawyer didn't think so, because *she* had never seen Liz, and *she* wouldn't trust her, and that was all that mattered to her.

Feeling miserable again, he shook his head. "Nobody." He tried to tug his wrist from Liz's grip, but she held on tenaciously.

"Is Eryyn your friend? Is she a street kid, like you? Is that why you said 'we' earlier?"

Sawyer winced and looked away, refusing to speak. Liz sighed.

"Alright, I'm not going to force you. I wouldn't do that. If you want to tell me, you will, eventually."

Sawyer looked back at her, his green eyes large and round. "Eventually?"

"Well, after we've gotten to know each other, I mean."

"Gotten to know each other?" Silently, he scolded himself for repeating everything she said—it sounded so dumb—but Liz only smiled.

"I don't know if you'll believe me yet, Sawyer. In fact, you probably won't...but I want to help you. My friend Carmen and I want to help you, and all the kids like you. Kids without homes or families. We've come up with an idea, but we still have a long way to go before we can use it. But I *know* it'll work, if we can just get the kids to trust us. To believe that we're friends. I would like to keep seeing you, so we can become friends. Would you mind that? Can you believe that I wouldn't do anything to hurt you?"

Sawyer bit down hard on his lip. This was a little more than he could understand at the moment. But he nodded. Yes, he *wanted* to believe that Liz would be his friend.

"Can you keep coming here, to the park? To this bench? I will if you will. We can meet, and talk, and get to know each other. I'd like to know more about the little boy who thinks that I'm beautiful." She earned a shy smile for that. "And I can tell you all about our plan. Does that sound good to you?"

"When?"

"This time is good. Before I have to go to work."

"It's…" Sawyer glanced back towards the nest, fearing that, with every minute that passed, Eryyn would wake up to find him missing. He had to get back soon.

He turned back to Liz. "It's kinda hard to get here so early," he muttered. "It's a long walk and there's not a lot of light, and…" *And Eryyn will scream my ear off about being stupid if she finds out,* he added to himself. He stared up into Liz's face, seeing her disappointment, and realized that any other time would be hard for her. Despite the danger of invoking Eryyn's anger, he nodded quickly, desperate to keep Liz happy. "But I'll come anyway. I want to come."

Her smile returned and Liz released his wrist. "Okay, each morning, same time, same bench. I'll bring us both something to eat. Alright?"

Another nod. Sawyer began backing away. When he was out of reach, so she couldn't grab him again, he turned and started jogging down the path.

"Wait!" Liz called out behind him. He stopped and turned around, looking back curiously. "I want to tell you my name."

Sawyer smiled. "It's Liz!" he shouted back, and had the pleasure of seeing the shock on her face. "I followed you and your friend and listened to you talking. She called you Liz."

Liz waved to him. "That's right. I'll see you tomorrow, Sawyer."

Sawyer lifted his own hand, then turned and ran away.

• • •

He headed straight back to the nest, not thinking about the possibility of being followed. The conversation with Liz had left him shaken. *She* had actually wanted to talk to him. *She* had returned to the park everyday, hoping he would show up. *She* wanted to be his friend. That right there was the most important thing. She wanted to be his friend, and she wanted to help him. And he believed her; even though it went against *everything* he'd learned about survival on the streets, he believed her.

But that was also the reason he couldn't tell Eryyn. At least not yet. Because Eryyn *wouldn't* believe Liz. Eryyn hadn't seen the look on the woman's face, hadn't been able to see the joy in her eyes as she talked about helping the street kids and being their friend. Eryyn would call Liz a liar, and would tell him to stay away from her. And, though he knew it was wrong, he would probably listen to her, because Eryyn had been his friend first, and had never intentionally tried to hurt him.

He glanced at his hand, where the scar of Eryyn's sibling ceremony streaked a white line across his skin. Eryyn was his *sister* now, and she had sworn to take care of him, even if it went against what he wanted. So, if Eryyn knew about Liz, she would find a way to stop him from seeing her. He had to keep it secret. At least until he understood more of Liz's plan.

"Hey! You! Hold up for a second!"

Sawyer turned around to see a girl running towards him, waving her hands. For a second, he thought the girl planned to beat him up, or rob him, or both. He tensed, preparing to run, and the girl shouted, "Wait! Are you Squirt, Eryyn's friend?"

"Y-yeah," he said, finally stopping to let the girl catch up. She did, panting, and was silent for a moment, trying to catch her breath. Then she looked at him shrewdly. "I've been looking for you all over the city."

"Why?" Sawyer couldn't recognize the girl, who was short, raven-haired, and husky, with sharp gray eyes, a missing front tooth, and a scar across her eye, probably gotten from a previous fight. He didn't understand why she would be searching *him* out, and that made him cautious. He instantly measured the distance between them, keeping just out of arms reach.

"'Cuz I want some stuff. And Caulin said you were giving loot away for free. I had to see if it was true."

Sawyer let out his breath in a relieved whistle. So *that* was what the girl was after. His conversation with Liz had made him completely forget their plan to start a gang of their own with the independent kleptos. He offered the girl a weak smile. "Yeah, it's true. But we're not giving it away *completely* for free. Eryyn is asking something for payment. It's your choice to decide if you want to pay or not."

"What payment?" the girl demanded. "Caulin didn't say anything about payment. He said it was free!"

"It is!" Sawyer said quickly. "Kind of. Maybe you should talk to Eryyn. She's the leader."

"Leader?" The girl looked confused, but was intrigued enough to let Sawyer lead her back to the nest where Eryyn, awake and very angry, greeted them with a scowl and a hard pinch to Sawyer's arm.

"I thought I told you not to wander off so early," she groused. "Where have you been this time?"

"Nowhere," Sawyer answered sourly, rubbing at his arm and scowling darkly at his friend. He indicated the girl. "This is…" he glanced at her, his brows raised.

"I'm Cinder," the girl answered shortly, as if insulted that Sawyer hadn't already known that. Sawyer nodded and said to Eryyn, "Caulin told her about our plan. But he didn't tell her that…"

"What's all this about a payment now?" Cinder interrupted, stepping forward and shoving Sawyer to one side. "I thought you were giving out stuff for free. But now this little rat says that you're actually charging." She sneered at Sawyer, who, taken by surprise, had tumbled to the ground after her shove.

"You won't get *anything*, payment or not, if you ever push him or call him a rat again," Eryyn warned, reaching down a hand to help the boy to his feet. Sawyer glared at Cinder, but didn't say anything. He had already decided that he didn't like Cinder one bit, but she was tough, and she seemed strong. At least, the push she had given him had had enough power behind it to knock him down. That would make her useful to Eryyn, and their plan. But being useful didn't mean Sawyer had to like her. He kept silent while Eryyn explained their ideas to the black-haired girl.

"I'm trying to start a gang," Eryyn stated. "Not a normal gang, but one where all the kids, no matter how small, or clumsy, or stupid, or whatever, get a share of loot. I want as many kids as possible to join up, no matter who they are, and I'm willing to pay them for it. Squirt and I have collected a lot of stuff, and we'll get even more today, that we plan to give away to anyone who wants to join up with us. The catch is, you don't get the free stuff until you've been in

the gang for a month. After that, you can pick your payment, whatever you want, and you can leave. But during those four weeks,
we're hoping that you'll learn to like our gang and will want to stay
in it."

Cinder scoffed. "What makes you think I'd want to stay, after
I'd collected?"

"Our gang is not going to be like the others," Eryyn said. "I'll
be the leader, but I won't take all the collected loot for myself or my
friends. Instead, I'll take it to get pawned and use half of the credits
to feed the gang and to keep them in clothes and everything else
they'll need."

"What about the other half?"

"Squirt and I divide it up and give it out to the kids. Everyone
will get a fair share, depending on how much work they put in to
helping the gang survive."

Cinder looked thoughtful. It seemed like a great deal. But often
times what seemed perfect eventually turned out to be dangerous.
What could the two possibly gain from plying their own thieving
talents just to give the stuff away? Curious, she asked them.

"I have my reasons," Eryyn said cryptically. "Squirt's are the
same. But mostly, we want protection. The kind of protection you
can only get within a gang. 'Cuz the more people gathering for the
gang, the more loot at the end of the day, so gang members protect
each other, right?"

Cinder nodded. "And if, after the four weeks, or maybe after a
little longer, I wanted to leave the gang?" she asked.

Eryyn shrugged. "Your choice. *I* won't stop you. Squirt won't
stop you. We'll make sure none of the other kids try to stop you. We
only want members who *want* to be part of the gang. We're not
going to force anyone, or nab lone kids off the street, or beat up
kids who want to leave."

Sawyer chuckled and Cinder glanced at him. Then she giggled
too. It was funny to imagine small, skinny Sawyer beating up another kid to convince them to stay in the gang. This realization put
Cinder more at ease.

"It sounds too good to be true," she said, placing her hands on
her hips.

"But it is true," Sawyer replied. "Honest. The other gangs are getting too tough now. And the Foreman's gangs are the worst. Nabbing kids and forcing them into the gangs doesn't bother them. And if the kids don't want to be in a gang…well, they either learn to live with it, get beat up and learn to live with it, or…" Sawyer pulled his finger across his throat.

Eryyn winced, but Cinder didn't notice. She was too busy calculating the gains of this venture.

"So," she said after a few minutes of silent thought, "I join your gang, hang around for four weeks, and I get free loot? No other deals attached; if I want to go, I can go?"

"Yep. But for the four weeks, you can't just *hang* around. The gang won't survive if kids think they can be lazy. You wanna collect a share of loot at the end of the day, then you gotta put in the work. You need to be a klepto, and a good one. You need to bring in stuff every night. You may feel like you're losing out at first, but the way I have it planned, you'll soon learn that it's worth it."

"So you hope."

Eryyn grinned and nodded. "Yeah, so I hope."

"You in?" Sawyer asked, getting impatient with Cinder's delay. It wasn't *that* hard to decide on joining or not, and he was getting hungry standing out in the alley near their nest.

Cinder bit on her lower lip, tilted her head thoughtfully and, finally, nodded. "Yeah, I'm in. Sounds too good to be true, but too good to pass up. So, what do I do?"

Eryyn held out her hand and Cinder accepted it. Sawyer's friend stared at the girl with serious, brown eyes. "Say that you'll do anything to protect and aid your gang."

"I'll do anything to protect and aid my gang."

Eryyn grinned and her eyes sparkled. "Welcome to the gang, Cinder. You're my first new member. And I hope you're not my last!"

• • •

Eryyn and Sawyer showed Cinder their most recent nest, which would serve as a stronghold for the gang. It was a perfect hiding place for a group of children—for comfort, they simply had to cover the broken windows with pieces of fiberglass, glass, or dark cloths to shut out the cold and hold in any light. The floor, once padded with as many blankets and rags as they could find, would be fine for sleeping on.

The little paraffin stove, carried along since the departure of Nest Two, was given a place of honor in the middle of the main room, where it could warm the area reserved for sleeping and general meeting. The tiny second room, reached through a small door in the left wall, was also carefully boarded up and it was decided that the collected loot would be stored there until Eryyn pawned it.

Cinder liked the idea of the kids all sleeping in the same room. It meant protection from any possible attacks, and it also meant more warmth. She mentioned that she had a few things at her own nest that would be useful, and ran off to find them, leaving Eryyn and Sawyer alone again.

Eryyn slapped Sawyer on the back. "One, Squirt! We've got one! And where there's one, there has to be another, and another, and another. For once, Caulin's big mouth was actually useful for something."

Sawyer gave his friend a weak smile. "I hope we collected enough stuff."

"If not, we'll just have to collect more, today, after we eat. C'mon, let's go get some breakfast." Eryyn clapped her hands and bounced several times on her toes before heading for the window. The smile on her face was enormous. "Excitement makes me hungry."

Sawyer followed Eryyn out of the stronghold and out onto the street, where they headed towards a nearby store that provided daily rations to legal citizens, as well as extras that had to be purchased. Eryyn waited outside while Sawyer ducked into the store, showed his bracelet, and was given a packet containing an allotment of dried goods that made up his day's rations. A few extra credits went to buy some bread and an apple to fill out the meager portion that they would share, and to add some flavor to the otherwise bland and tasteless meal.

They took the food to a corner and settled down on the sidewalk, out of the way of foot traffic. Sawyer had only just torn open the paper of the ration package when they were hailed by another kid, a boy, who hurried down the street to stand in front of them. He had just talked to Cinder and was now curious about Eryyn's gang. He told them that Cinder had said the gang was a sure thing, a perfect chance, and he wanted to know how to join.

"You're in," Eryyn said, causing the boy to raise his eyebrows in surprise. "As long as you can live with my rules." She went on to explain the laws of the gang, and the conditions the kids were expected to keep.

"That's it?" he asked, incredulous. "We get a cut of half the credits brought in, and the other half is used to feed us? So we don't even have to use our cut for that? And if we don't like the gang, we can just leave, and *still* get something for free?"

"Not a bad deal, eh?" Sawyer said, leaning back against the brick wall behind him and biting into the apple with a loud crunch.

"Not a bad deal at all!" The boy, who called himself Lex, didn't hesitate to take Eryyn's oath and join up. Once he was in, Eryyn told him to make some rounds about the city, talking to his friends or any other kids he saw who weren't already in a gang. Lex got the idea immediately, and ran off, eager to do his new job as recruiter.

"You're pretty good at this, Eryyn," Sawyer complimented as he watched Lex run down the street. "Who knew that kids would be willing to take orders from a skinny, rude, shifty-eyed, beak-nosed girl?"

Eryyn chuckled and gave him a shove. "I've had lots of practice. With *you*. Now hand over that apple!"

Sawyer obediently surrendered the half-eaten fruit to her and she took a large bite, letting the juice run down her chin as she chewed thoughtfully. "And I'm *not* shifty-eyed," she stated after a moment.

Sawyer cocked his head and pretended to scrutinize her. He grinned brightly. "Maybe not. But all the rest is sure true." He jumped to his feet then and ran off, laughing as he listened to the pounding of Eryyn's feet on the pavement as she chased him.

• • •

Amazingly, when they returned to the nest that night after dropping off a supply of recently stolen goods to their storage nest across the end, they found Cinder and Lex waiting for them with four more kids, all of whom were eager to join the gang.

"Caulin stopped me at the Green plaza," one girl said, following Eryyn up to the nest. "He said that a new gang was being formed, one to beat all the other gangs out of the city. I didn't care at first, but then he said that *you* were going to be the leader. I remembered you and Squirt from Master John's, and how much you always brought in, and how much you were able to get Master John to pay, and…well…" She broke off, and another boy finished for her, "If what Caulin says is true, then we got nothing to lose. If you're lying…" He crossed his arms over his chest, and Eryyn nodded—he was pretty big for a street kid. He stood nearly a head taller than her, and simply *towered* over Sawyer. If he ever chose to leave the gang, she wouldn't be able to stop him, even if she wanted to.

"We're *not* lying," Eryyn stated, holding up her hands to make sure all attention was on her and her words. "Everything is true. I'm not starting this gang to get power over other kids, or to get rich. I'm starting this gang so kids like you and me won't be afraid of who will attack us every time we go around a corner. If we have the protection of a gang behind us, a gang that's fair to *everyone* in it, then we won't have to fear the other gangs, will we? How can the kleptos who work for the Foreman try to beat a kid up for money if that kid has four or five friends nearby who're willing to help him out?"

The tall boy nodded slowly at this. "Makes sense. But why would you care about what happens to us?" He jabbed one thumb at his chest and the other at the three kids who were hovering beside him. "Why would you want to protect other kids? Each klepto taken out by the Foreman and his gangs is one less for us all to compete with."

There were a few murmurs of agreement among the other new arrivals and they all looked at Eryyn questioningly. The girl opened her mouth to answer, but Sawyer beat her to it. Mimicking the tall boy by crossing his arms over his chest, he stepped forward.

"What's your name?" he asked.

The other boy made a show of looking down at him, craning his neck and squinting his eyes as though he were trying to look at an ant on the pavement. Some of the kids thought this was funny. Sawyer didn't. He frowned.

"What's it to you?" the boy asked, smiling at Sawyer's sour response.

Shrugging, Sawyer answered, "I guess nothing. I was just curious. But could you answer one simple, little question for me? How much loot do you usually bring in at the end of the day?"

The tall boy paused, frowning. He hadn't expected a question like that. "Why?" he demanded.

"I was just thinking. You're really big, so hitting houses can't be very easy for you. What do you do, 'pocket all day? Rob other kids? *Mug* people heading home after evening work whistle?"

The newcomer looked indignant at this suggestion. "I've never mugged anyone, shortie. I 'pocket." He blushed a little. "'Cuz you're right. I can't hit houses, so I 'pocket what I need."

Sawyer grinned. "So *how* much loot does 'pocketing get you?"

"Enough," the tall kid hedged.

"Not much at all, eh?"

"Shut up, or so help me I'm gonna…!"

Sawyer quickly held up his hands in defense and stepped back, closer to Eryyn. "I'm just trying to make you see that if you were in our gang you'd have a cut of *everything*. Even stuff brought in from hits by the smaller kids," he stopped for a second, his brows knitted thoughtfully, then grudgingly added, "like me."

The boy nodded, and laughed loudly. "Yeah, I'll bet *you* have *no* trouble getting into houses!"

Sawyer wrinkled his nose. "You don't have to rub it in! How do you think we got the stuff that we plan to give out? I'm little, but I'm not useless, right, Eryyn?" He turned to his friend, who smiled broadly, nodded, and put a hand on his shoulder.

"Squirt's the best partner I could hope for. We almost never have trouble getting stuff to sell. Now imagine a group with ten or fifteen kids Squirt's size, who can get into the houses easily and bring out the good stuff, while we older, bigger kids work the crowds in the market. At the end of the day…"

"The collection would be huge," one of the others, a boy Sawyer's age and size, piped up from beside the tall youth. "I think it sounds great! I'm in!" He held out his hand for Eryyn's, and she accepted, then had him repeat her improvised oath.

"Name?" Eryyn asked.

"Jay." He was smiling brightly as he stepped up beside Sawyer.

"I'm Krista," said the girl who had spoken first. She disengaged herself from the other two new arrivals and stuck out her hand. "I want in too."

"Yeah, I could learn to live with this," the tall boy said, nodding. "If anything, I could be a bodyguard for the…" he glanced, grinning, at Sawyer and Jay, who smiled right back, "…little kids." He joined Krista in the promise, stepping across the small alley to stand on Eryyn's side, now a part of her group. A moment later, the remaining kid, a slender, dark-skinned girl named Foxy, increased their membership by yet another.

Six in one day. Eryyn turned to show the new members the nest, then shot a glance and smile back at Sawyer. Her eyes were glowing.

· · ·

Six was the number for the first day. They were approached by other kids, but most didn't like the idea of being in a gang, *any* gang, while others, though the description of Eryyn's plan appealed to them, shook their heads and said they'd have to think it over.

Still, Sawyer thought that six was a good number; he honestly hadn't expected to get even one new member on the first day. Caulin's power of gossip through the city was better than he thought.

Sitting against the far wall of the newly filled nest, he watched Eryyn, who was busy talking with Foxy, Cinder, and Rick, the tall, tough guy. She wanted them to continue the recruiting job the next morning, talking to as many kids as they met while they were out. Cinder and Foxy were nodding vigorously, while Rick, who already seemed to have established himself as Eryyn's second-in-command, started asking questions. Seeing that Eryyn had everything under control, Sawyer blanked them out and leaned his head back, closing his eyes. He was still tired from yesterday's frantic collecting spree; and his early morning meeting with Liz, along with the work they had done today, had worn him to near exhaustion. He didn't care right now what Eryyn did with her new gang as long as it didn't involve him moving from his spot for at least an hour.

Someone plopped down beside him, rustling loudly on the pile of blankets he had arranged into a bed. Feeling a gaze on him, Sawyer opened one eye to see Jay looking at him expectantly. He sat up.

"Aren't you going to help Eryyn plan what to do tomorrow?" Jay asked, pointing to the center of the room and the four kids sitting closely around to the small stove.

Sawyer looked at his partner, caught her eye when she happened to glance up, and smiled quickly at her. She smiled back and he shrugged at the new boy. "Eryyn has thought out everything she wants to do. If she needs me, she'll call me. Until then, I ain't moving."

Jay grinned. "Aw, all worn out?" he asked, giving Sawyer a friendly poke on the arm.

"Uh huh. Collecting stuff to pay *your* fee if you decide to leave." Sawyer smiled as he shoved Jay back, nearly tipping him over. "Be grateful."

"Sure. I just hope you got me something good."

"Always the best." Sawyer cocked his head at the boy and squinted. "But if things go well you won't have to collect, will you? You'll stay in the gang, and Eryyn will just sell that stuff and you'll still get a cut."

"Yeah. I guess you're right. It *does* seem like this is actually a gang that you'd want to stick with. But let me ask you, Sawyer…and I want the truth…"

"I only lie when I get caught with a hand in a pocket."

"Why *is* Eryyn doing this? What use is it to her to make a gang of all the independents? I mean, she's planning on taking in *anybody* who wants to join, even the real little kids, or the ones who are so dumb and clumsy they couldn't pick the pockets of a dead guy. How can *they* help the gang?"

Sawyer was silent as he thought about the question for a minute, pondering the best way to answer it and convince Jay of Eryyn's good intentions. "Well, I'm little…and I'm good at doing hits on houses. I can fit through the windows better than Eryyn can, and if someone comes home, I can hide better. So the little kids *are* useful, as long as someone tells them what to do. As for the dumb and clumsy ones…Eryyn wants them anyway."

"Why?"

"She wants the gang to be big."

Jay let out his breath in a loud sigh and scowled. "That's not much of an answer, you know?"

"It's the answer you'd get from Eryyn." Sawyer looked pointedly at the girl and Jay, following his gaze, nodded.

"But if she wants us to trust her…?"

"Eryyn's not gonna be like the other gang leaders. You've heard of Otto, right?"

Jay bobbed his blond head emphatically. "He terrifies me! I heard that the girl they pulled out of the alley recently was a part of his gang and that she pissed him off, trying to escape, and he had his gang kill her."

"Where'd you hear that?"

Jay shrugged his shoulders. "Can't remember. *Someone* told me. But they didn't say where they had heard it."

Sawyer frowned. So, Caulin the blabbermouth had struck again. Not that it really mattered. He continued his explanation.

"Otto came after me and Eryyn one night. We got away, but Eryyn was mad 'cuz it was a close scrape and we had to run from one of our nests and leave some good stuff behind. She hates it that Otto can just take whatever he wants," he paused, chewing on a fingernail, "or *whoever* he wants. I mean, kids like us have enough trouble having to deal with the Enforcers or the jerks that try to nab us and sell us to the factories. It makes things a lot harder when we also have to worry about being grabbed or robbed by a gang."

Quiet now, Jay turned to look at the far wall, staring blankly at it for a long moment before finally saying, "I know what you mean."

In answer to the curious look on his face, Jay told Sawyer about the time some gang kids had singled him out and beat him up in an alley just so they could get a ring he'd 'pocketed.

"I couldn't move," he explained, his voice rising slightly. "When they finally left me alone, *I couldn't move!* I hurt *that* much. I had to stay there, in that alley, all night, until I could finally get up and find someplace to hide." There was another long pause while Jay stared down at his hands, his blue eyes bright with bad memories. Sawyer instinctively kept silent, looking at the boy, waiting for him to continue. Finally, he did:

"I've never told anyone about that. It took me a long time before I could work again. I had to hide out until the bruises went away and I almost starved in the meantime. When I finally came out, I grabbed the first kid I saw who was littler than me and I robbed *her*. I took a bracelet she'd just 'pocketed, then pushed her down and ran off."

Sawyer held his breath, then let it out slowly. "And I thought *I'd* had some hard times. At least I've never been beat up. I've been *robbed* a couple of times, but that was by grown-ups."

Jay laughed, but there was no amusement in the sound. "Yeah, you never have a chance against a grown-up, unless maybe if they're really drunk. And it's worse if you're alone. You got no one to help you if you get hurt. That's why I wanted to join up. It sounded like a dream come true, you know? I'd never have to worry about getting beat up again if I had a gang to back me up." He kept his eyes lowered and squeezed his hands together. "And I'd never have to stoop to being a bully just to get something to eat."

There was more silence. Sawyer didn't know what to say. His idea of forming the gang had been to help Eryyn get her revenge against the Foreman for Aimee's death. When he'd thought of the plan, reading his book on Robin Hood, he'd never realized what such a gang would mean to the kids who joined it. He'd never thought that some would join up just to get the assurance of protection, and friendship, without even having to be bribed. He'd been Eryyn's shadow for so long, counting on her for help and companionship, that he'd forgotten how difficult and scary it was to be alone. He didn't know if he could have survived on the streets without Eryyn at his side. He'd been lucky.

He said this to Jay, who nodded grimly. "You're damn right there. I never had nobody."

"So you'll stick around then, huh?"

Jay looked surprised for a moment, then bobbed his head again. "Yeah. Unless your friend turns out to be a real jerk, I'm here to stay."

"Eryyn can be a jerk," Sawyer said truthfully, "but she's not Otto. She'll never be like Otto: she knows better." He stopped for a moment, then puffed out his chest proudly. "Besides, *I* won't let her. This gang was my idea first, and I don't want to play Foreman."

The sadness left Jay's eyes at Sawyer's pompous attitude and he smiled, shaking his head. "You're not scary enough."

"Thanks."

Jay shifted himself a little closer to his new friend, leaning over as he asked in a conspiratorial voice, "So, what's Eryyn really like?"

Sawyer glanced towards the center of the room and noticed that Eryyn was looking right at him. It slowly dawned on him that she'd been listening to every word he'd said; in fact, the whole room was silent now, waiting for his answer. He grinned brightly and winked at his partner. "She's great, but she snores louder than a trash grinder."

• • •

"Collection day is tomorrow, and look at this! This is the junk you bring in? This is the stuff you expect me to hand over to the Foreman? Do you really think he's going to accept this crap, say thank you, and leave with a smile on his face?"

"How would we know if he were smiling or not? It's not like any of us have ever seen him."

There was a ripple of laughter through the meeting room that was quickly silenced as Otto glared at the boy who had spoken.

"That's not funny, Dillan. Would you be brave enough to say that to the Foreman when he comes here tomorrow to see the crap you expect him to take? What do you think, Raney boy? Would the Foreman find Dillan funny?" Otto glanced at the boy who sat by his left elbow. Rane shook his head mutely.

"You'd end up just like Aimee," Sasha added, hoping that, by threatening Dillan, Otto wouldn't notice that she'd laughed at the boy's joke. Otto and Rane were the only two in the room who hadn't thought the joke funny. She had the immediate satisfaction of see- ing Dillan blanch. He'd been one of the kids chosen to hide Aimee after they'd finished with her. He'd *seen* what had been done, and it made the bruises Otto gave to Rane look like a scrape on the knee.

"Sorry," he muttered, lowering his eyes.

Otto gave him a curt nod, forgiving the matter. He went back to questioning the group about the quality of the loot they had brought in.

"The only good stuff I see in this pile are the things Rane nipped, and *I* was with him when he got them. Does that mean that Rane and I are the only kleptos in this room who have any sense of qual- ity? Is my entire gang made up of lazy idiots who just grab the first thing they see and make a run for it before the big, bad grown-ups come home?" He leaned back in his seat and glared at the gathered children. "Maybe I should just talk to the Foreman and see about getting myself some new kids. I don't want to be known for leading a group of worthless failures."

The room was silent as the kids glanced at each other or at their hands. The threat was too obvious, and too soon after Aimee, not to be effective.

"Go get me a pen and some paper," Otto demanded with a small wave of his left hand. Without a word, Rane immediately got up and left the room. While he was obeying the order, Otto continued to berate his followers and, by the time Rane returned with the paper and a stubby pencil, several of the children where close to tears.

Otto took the paper and pencil and set it on the desk while Rane returned to his seat.

"I'm making a list," Otto said ominously. "All your names will be on it. Tomorrow, when you bring in your loot, I'm going to check it over and write down what you got beside your name. And if the Foreman isn't satisfied with the haul, then the kids who brought in the least will be the first ones I replace." He began writing quickly on the page, glancing up every now and then, looking from one kid to the next. "And I'm going to put a mark beside some of the names, because those were the kids who brought in the least today. If you're smart, you'll do better tomorrow, because I'll be checking your stuff closely. And, just so you know who you are..." he began reading down the list of selected children, "Dillan, Kit, Neomi, Luke, Jerri, and Karl."

Rane's eyes flicked around the room, locating each of the targets easily. The children looked stunned, terrified, as they caught his eyes—a few seemed to be silently pleading for help. But Rane, though nervous and somewhat sorry for them, wasn't about to show any sympathy. None of gang kids had been very kind to him while he'd been under punishment. He didn't see any reason to be different. He stared longest at Neomi. Of all the kids, she had been particularly mean to him during his grounding. She met his eyes with a glare, but quickly looked away, chewing her lip worriedly.

"You all better start shaping up," Otto said, looking pointedly at the five targets. "I'm sick of you *children* wasting my time." He folded the list, jammed it into his shirt pocket, then stood up. "Let's go," he ordered. Rane and Sasha both jumped up and followed him out of the room. Just as he stepped past the door, he called over his shoulder, "You're dismissed! Get out and go to work."

Stunned, the gathered children sat where they were for a few minutes, recovering from the threats and insults. Then, in ones and twos, they slipped out of the room, until only the six who had been checked on the list were left. One of the girls, Kit, was crying.

"He's going to kill me!" she sobbed. "I couldn't help it, and now he's going to kill me!"

Dillan, looking like he wanted to be sick, sat beside her on the floor and put an arm around her shoulders. "No, he's not," he said, trying to calm her. "He's just mad, that's all."

"He's been mad before, but he's never been like that," Luke complained while biting on a ragged fingernail. "He's never put anyone's name on a list. Never threatened more than one or two at a time."

Karl agreed. "He's such a jerk. For the longest time he just sat around, playing leader and handing the stuff over to the Foreman like he had collected it himself. Now, just because he's started to go out and actually do some work of his own, he sounds like he wants to replace the whole gang."

"Not all the gang," Neomi said with contempt. "He wouldn't get rid of his little friends, Sasha and Rane. Then who would he have to kiss up to him?"

"Who said I was his friend?"

The six in the room turned to see Rane silhouetted in the doorway. Slowly, quietly, he stepped forward, eyes dark and angry, hands held to his sides in fists. Looking at him, Dillan felt Kit start to tremble in his arms, and wondered just how much Rane had heard...and if he would tell Otto. Apprehensive, he made an effort to smile at the other boy.

"Hey, Rane. We were just..."

"Talking about Otto." Rane's brown eyes locked onto Dillan's and he raised his shoulders in a small shrug. "Yeah, I know, I heard everything. Otto was watching everyone leave from down the hall and he sent me back to ask why you six haven't followed his orders yet. The way he figures it, since you guys are the ones in the most trouble, you should have been the first ones out of the room."

"We're going now," Neomi spat, rising to her feet. "You don't have to go report to your new buddy that we don't follow orders." She marched across the room, pushed roughly past the boy, and headed out into the hall. Luke, Karl, and Jerri followed her, though they skirted around Rane as if touching him would hurt. Rane clenched his teeth and watched them go, then looked back at Dillan, who was leading Kit across the floor. He stepped aside to let them pass, then grabbed Dillan's arm before he could leave.

"I'm *not* his friend, Dillan," he whispered brokenly. "You *have* to realize that."

Dillan wanted to just walk out, wanted to ignore Rane, but the desperation in the whispered voice stopped him. He glanced at the boy who'd always been his friend and was stunned to see tears in his eyes. Rane looked genuinely unhappy.

"I hate him," he continued to whisper. "I hate him just as much as you do, more even, but I don't have a choice, Dillan. He'd *kill* me if I didn't do what he says. I know he would. Do you think I like being his little sidekick? Do you think I *like* following him around like a puppy, jumping every time he gives me an order? I want to live, Dillan, but that doesn't make me his friend."

Dillan thought for a moment, wondering if he should say something to comfort Rane…but then he remembered Otto's danger list. He sighed heavily. "You may not be his friend, *Raney boy*, but like you said, you're still his little sidekick. And that's just as bad. You're *not* a regular klepto anymore and that means no one can trust you. So just go back to waiting on Otto hand and foot and leave us alone."

Rane flinched back, stung by the cruel tone, and Dillan took the chance to shrug the hand off his arm. He pushed Kit through the door, leaving Rane alone in the room. As he walked down the hall towards the exit, he heard a loud thump from behind as Rane kicked the wall. Kit flinched, but Dillan kept her walking. They didn't look back.

• • •

Eryyn couldn't believe her luck. Only a day had passed since

Sawyer had first brought the story of *Robin Hood* to her attention and already her gang had six new members. It was an impressive and encouraging start.

Night had fallen over the city and her new gang had settled down for some much needed rest. Yet, even though it was late, and she was exhausted, Eryyn found it impossible to sleep. Instead, she was leaning against a wall, a blanket wrapped around her shoulders. Sawyer's book was in her hands and she stared at the cover, wishing she could read it. Maybe she should ask Sawyer to teach her. He'd offered enough, but she had always refused, thinking it a waste of time. But if there were stories and ideas like *Robin Hood* to be gotten from reading, then it couldn't be *all* bad, could it?

Chewing thoughtfully on her finger, she stood up and wandered over to the closest window. All the windows in the nest were filthy, covered with street grime and black dust from the nearby factories. Opening the glass, Eryyn gazed out at the dark street, so lost in thought that she didn't hear the rustling behind her as Sawyer woke up, missing the warmth she had provided. An instant later there was a hand on her arm and a second set of eyes staring out into the dark.

"Can't sleep?" Sawyer asked quietly.

Eryyn shook her head and rested an arm around the boy's shoulders. "No. But you were, why'd you wake up?"

"You moved. I got cold."

Eryyn chuckled.

"Think anymore kids'll join up tomorrow?"

"I'm hoping. Six was a good start, but it's not enough. We need to make sure every kid in the city has at least heard of the gang and for that we need more members who'll go out to the different ends, spreading news. Caulin's good, but he can't talk to *everyone*."

"He'd try if you told him to. I think he's feeling guilty about Aimee and wants to make up for it."

Eryyn snorted. "Cinder, Lex, and Foxy can help. I talked to them earlier, and they're gonna do 'pocket work tomorrow, so they'll be drifting enough to see a lot of other kids. And all three used to sell to different pawnshops, so they all have different friends that they'll talk to."

Sawyer was impressed. "You've got it all planned out."

"What can I say, I'm brilliant."

"Don't kid yourself."

"Go back to sleep!" Eryyn pressed her knuckles onto the top of his head. Sawyer yipped and frantically ducked down, giggling. "Gladly. You coming?"

"In a bit. I'm still thinking."

"About what?"

"Just stuff, Squirt. What to do tomorrow. I have a gang to feed now."

"You've got your work cut out for you: Rick could eat more in one dinner than I could eat in a week."

"Yeah, but it's good to have a big kid in the group. We won't be bullied as much by the smaller gangs that have been around longer. Rick'll make sure none of our members get hurt while they work."

Sawyer nodded and rested his head against her arm, closing his eyes. He yawned widely. Eryyn hugged him close for a moment, glad for the companionship, then, when he yawned again, gave him a slight push back to the wall. "Go back to sleep, Squirt. You need it. Here," she pulled the blanket off her shoulders and handed it to him, "use this if you're cold."

Taking the blanket, Sawyer headed back to the spot he had left at the wall. He tiptoed around Rick and Lex, who were sprawled out on the floor, then paused and turned around. "Are we gonna have a name?" he asked, his voice a loud whisper.

Eryyn looked away from the window and fixed him with curious eyes. "A name?"

"Well, something. A lot of the gangs have names, and something the kids wear to show that they belong. Otto's kids have that yellow and red band. They tie it in their hair, or around their arms."

"The Foreman's gang, you mean."

Sawyer shrugged. "It works though. Everyone knows that a kid with a yellow and red band belongs to that gang. I think we should do the same thing, once we get enough members, and we should have a name."

"A name? Hmm…" Eryyn grinned. "Like Eryyn's Crushers, or the Mid-End Killers?"

The boy across from her turned solemn. "No. Not like that. Can I get you to promise me something, Eryyn?"

"Depends on the promise."

"I want you to promise that, no matter how big or powerful your gang gets, you will never, *ever* kill another kid. Even if you're fighting with another gang. We started this gang to be different from Otto, but if you get Rick, or Lex, or Cinder, or any of the others to kill a kid to make a point, then you'll be just like Otto and the Foreman. So please promise me you'll never hurt anyone? It's not right!"

Eryyn stared at Sawyer, stunned by the thought. But she nodded. "Okay, Squirt. I promise. I feel the same way."

Looking extremely relieved, Sawyer continued back to his little bed.

"Squirt?"

He stopped, and turned around again. "Yeah?"

"How about the Sherwood gang?"

Sawyer raised his eyebrows, confused for a second, then caught on and smiled. "Yeah. Yeah, I like that," he murmured, peering around the dim room at the six kids who slept on the floor or against the walls. "The Sherwood gang. Nice."

"See? Brilliant!"

Laughing, Sawyer flopped down on his pile of rags and pulled the blanket closer around him. In just a few moments, he had gone back to sleep, and Eryyn had turned to the window again, staring out at the dark.

• • •

Liz had kept her word, and Sawyer had been on the bench for only a few minutes before he spotted her walking up the path towards him.

"Good morning," Liz called, waving and hurrying to reach him. She smiled brightly and pointed to the seat beside him. "May I sit?"

Sawyer hesitated briefly, then nodded. What did it matter? He'd already agreed to meet her each day, why shouldn't he trust her enough to sit with her?

Liz's smile widened as she sat down, and she risked a pat on his hand. Sawyer tensed, but didn't jump or try to pull away. Instead, he lifted his face up to look at her and grinned shyly.

"It's gonna rain later," he said, pointing to the dark clouds that kept the park dim, even after the sun had started to rise. "How can you call it a good morning?"

"I think every morning is a good morning," she answered.

Sawyer frowned. "Not me. If it's gonna rain, then it's a bad morning. If it's gonna be sunny and dry, *then* it's a good morning. It's no fun walking around in wet and muddy clothes."

"I think I can understand that," Liz murmured. She reached into her coat pocket and pulled out a paper bag. "Are you hungry? I promised to bring breakfast."

Sawyer's eyes widened and he nodded, mutely accepting the bag. Inside was a warm pastry stuffed with eggs and cheese—it was a better meal than anything Sawyer had eaten since he'd come to live on the streets. He couldn't even remember the last time he'd eaten an egg. He bit into the flaky crust, his mouth watering.

"Good. You like it," Liz said with relief as she watched him eat. "I was wondering what to bring you. I don't know what kinds of foods you like to eat."

"As long as it's not too rotten, I'll eat it," Sawyer mumbled around a huge mouthful. "I'm not picky when I'm hungry."

"Rotten?" Liz looked green.

"Not *too* rotten," Sawyer repeated. "I won't eat it if it'll make me sick. What's the use of that? Besides, I haven't dived a trash bin since I was little. I can usually buy food, and I always have this…" he held out the arm that bore his bracelet. "So if I'm *really* hungry, I can get rations."

"Why wouldn't you just eat the rations, so you wouldn't have to eat…rotten stuff?"

"Have you ever tasted the rations?" Sawyer wrinkled his nose. "I'd rather eat from the trash—it tastes better. I think the shopkeepers can tell when someone's from the Dead-End and they have a special ration packet that they give 'em—old ones, or cheaper ones, or something. And I try to get by without having to get rations. I don't *need* the Enforcers to take care of me!" He spat the sentence out like it tasted bad, took another large bite of the pastry and chewed silently.

"Do all the kids like…" Liz paused, wondering how to phrase her next question correctly. Sawyer, still chewing, looked up at her, his green eyes expectant and understanding of her dilemma. Finally, deciding not to spare the words, she said, "Well, do all the homeless children eat rotten stuff, Sawyer? Do they all eat out of the trash?"

Sawyer swallowed and, not looking offended, said, "No. Not if they have the credits to buy food. Like I said, I haven't eaten out of the trash for a long time. It's nasty. The shopkeepers don't like kids in their stores, 'specially kids like me and my friends, but they'll take our credits and sell us the leftovers that no one else wants. It's not much, but it *is* better than the trash."

Liz realized that she was staring at him with her mouth hanging open. She closed it with an audible click, drawing a small smile from the boy, and blushed. They sat quietly for a few minutes, Sawyer working his way through the pastry while Liz watched him and pondered her next question. As he was swallowing the last bite, she cleared her throat and tapped his hand to get his attention.

"If you don't mind me asking, how do you get the credits to buy food?"

Sawyer stared at her for a moment, then shifted his gaze to a tree across the path and mumbled, "It depends on the kid."

"What do you mean?"

"Some kids bully other kids. Little kids. They beat them up to get food or money, or whatever else they want. Other big kids like to gang up on grown-ups and steal from them. Some kids are really wimpy and only beg, and others pick through the junk on the streets, looking for lost stuff they can sell…and then there're the ones who 'pocket or do hits."

"Hits?" Liz had an idea of what he meant, but was stunned to think that the cute little boy beside her could be a thief. Hoping to disprove the notion, she asked, "What are hits?"

The boy began to look uncomfortable. He fidgeted on the bench, squirming and drumming his fingers against the metal as he avoided meeting her eyes. "Do we have to talk about it?"

"It's just a question, Sawyer. Nothing to be upset about."

"I don't wanna talk about it. May-maybe some other time. You said you were gonna tell me about your plan. That you wanna help some of the street kids." He finally looked her in the face, his eyes wide and pleading. "Can we talk about that?"

Liz cursed silently, but nodded. She couldn't force the boy to talk to her. He was here only because he wanted to be and if she pressured him too much, he would just stop coming. She didn't want that. She wanted him to trust her. Once he trusted her he would open up and start to tell her more. She just had to be patient.

"Okay, we can talk about that. What do you want to know?"

Sawyer brightened and his fidgeting immediately stopped. Grinning sweetly, he said, "Everything!"

• • •

His belly was pleasantly full as he made his way back to the nest, but Sawyer's mind was troubled. He liked Liz's idea of a home for the street kids, a place where they could stay safe and have food and clothes and learn to read. It sounded perfect to him.

But that was the problem—it *sounded* perfect, and when something *sounded* perfect Sawyer was every bit as much like the children who had come up to Eryyn the day before, asking her about the new gang. Suspicion flowed like blood through a street kid and anything perfect and easy *always* caused suspicion. Just like the idea of the gang, so nice, so *ideal,* had made the kids somewhat suspicious of Eryyn, so Liz's plan of starting a children's home aroused suspicion in Sawyer. He *knew* what Eryyn had to gain from starting a gang, but Liz's reasons, other than that she wanted to, were a mystery. And the kids who had joined their gang would be fine, even if Eryyn *had* planned on being a jerk of a leader—there were six against her, including Rick, who almost counted as seven. The odds would not be the same against grown-ups.

So, as he walked back to the nest, bracing himself for the anger he *might* get from Eryyn, and the orders he *would* get from her, Sawyer decided that he would keep his secret about Liz a little longer. There was no need to stir up possible trouble, not when Eryyn had her hands full leading the gang. He would just continue meeting with Liz alone, and keep hoping that she was a grown-up that he could, in fact, trust.

• • •

Eryyn split the gang into groups and sent them out into the city immediately after breakfast. Cinder and Foxy went to visit their latest haunts, where they would do 'pocket work while talking to kids they knew. Jay and Krista took off towards the boundary between the Mid and Sky-Ends, where the streets were lined with small trees and the single family houses all had a tiny yard. Being the two smallest kids in the gang, next to Sawyer, they were most useful sneaking into houses, and that was the job Eryyn had assigned them. Rick and Lex were given the Dead-End neighborhoods. Eryyn knew that the houses and people found in that district weren't worth robbing, but lots of kids set up their nests there, in the crumbling, run-down buildings of the old city. She was a little unsure about sending the two boys into the dangerous neighborhoods, but Rick and Lex were willing, eager to recruit some of the kids who were tough enough to survive in the worst of the ends.

"Think any of them will come back with new kids?" Sawyer asked, when he and Eryyn were the only two in the nest.

"I'm keeping my fingers crossed," Eryyn answered. "And my toes."

"That's gotta hurt."

"It's worth it." Suddenly, she turned and pressed Sawyer up against the wall with one hand. "Okay, now that everyone's gone, why don't you tell me where you went this morning. Don't make me have to wrestle it out of you."

Amazed at Eryyn's ability to sense when he was gone, Sawyer ducked under her hand and headed for the window. "For a walk," he said as he climbed over the sill to drop into the alley. He landed lightly and jumped a few paces away. A second later, Eryyn dropped into the space he'd just vacated.

"A walk?" she asked witheringly as she straightened up from her leap. "You've been going for a lot of walks lately. You never used to go for walks."

"Why is that a problem?"

"I didn't say it was, I just wanna know where you go on these little walks of yours."

"The park. I just go to the park." He and Eryyn started walking down the street. They'd decided earlier to head to the neighborhoods just below the ones where Jay and Krista had gone. "It's nice and quiet there in the morning. I like it."

Eryyn looked at him out of the corner of her eye. "You need quiet?"

"It was just a little walk, Eryyn. I don't need to tell you everything."

"I'm your gang leader. If it concerns the gang, yes, you do."

Sawyer stopped in his tracks and gaped at her. "Gang leader? You're not *my* gang leader, Eryyn. It's your gang, but I'm *not* one of your kleptos. I'm your partner, and your friend."

"Then you can tell your friend why you had to take a walk by yourself this morning."

Now Sawyer was beginning to get annoyed. He loved Eryyn with all his heart, but that didn't mean she could interrogate him about everything he did. "Sheesh, Eryyn! What are you getting so freaked about? It's not like I'm a spy from a rival gang! I wasn't reporting to my leader about what goes on in the nest! I was just taking a damn walk! What more do you want?"

"Alright, alright! Don't get all upset!" Eryyn dropped her arm over his shoulder in an attempt to make things peaceful again. "I was just curious, that's all."

"Nosy is more like it," Sawyer muttered.

"That too. Forget about it, okay? I'm sorry."

"Sure, whatever." Sawyer suddenly stopped and looked around at the street and the apartment buildings lining the sidewalk. "You have any houses in mind?"

Eryyn followed his gaze and did a quick survey of the multi-leveled homes. "Don't know. We haven't spent much time in this particular neighborhood. I want to scout around, see what we find. We'll do a hit if we see something worth it. Sound okay?"

Sawyer didn't answer. They were currently walking past the far west point of the park and he had turned his head, staring through the bushes and trees. Eryyn nudged him. "Squirt?"

Sawyer jumped, blinking. "What?"

"Does that sound good to you?"

"Does what sound...? Oh, yeah. That. Sure, that's fine, whatever you want." He turned back to watching the park, ignoring Eryyn as they made their slow, leisurely way through the Mid-End, carefully studying all that they passed.

Not finding a house they wanted to risk hitting that morning, they decided on a rotation of the marketplace. It was busy when they arrived and they were instantly able to melt into the crowds.

"Jewelry," Eryyn said, pulling Sawyer off to one side. "Try to get good jewelry, stuff that would really bring a good price at a shop. Don't be wimpy, but don't be too risky either. And stay away from fat women in ugly dresses."

Sawyer scowled at the joke and moved away. He trotted down the sidewalk, glancing disinterestedly at the shops, humming under his breath, all the while keeping a sharp lookout for a possible mark. He spotted a potential target standing by a trashcan. The man was looking around as if he were lost, tapping his foot impatiently and checking the watch on his wrist. Sawyer guessed that he was waiting for someone who was late. Good, if the man was distracted, he would be less likely to take notice of the theft.

Sawyer sidled up behind him, moving slowly, careful not to look too eager or intent on his mark. One woman standing nearby caught his eye and he paused, flashed her a shy smile, and lifted his right hand to pretend scratching his nose. The sight of his bracelet put the woman at ease. She grinned back and looked away, and Sawyer moved forward again, until he was standing directly behind the man. Another furtive glance around and he stepped smartly off the curb, passing the man and bumping into him slightly.

"Watch it," the man growled as he lost his footing and was forced to step off the sidewalk into the street. "Keep your damn eyes on where you're going, you little idiot."

"Sorry, sir. Excuse me," Sawyer mumbled, glancing back timidly. He offered another smile, but the man was not impressed. He glanced at his watch again and swore under his breath as he stepped back onto the curb. Sawyer did his best to look wounded, then moved away again, carefully concealing his smile as he fingered the money clip he had lifted from the man's pants pocket. Unfortunately, there were no credit tabs in the clip, but Sawyer reasoned that that was just as well. Eryyn claimed that while credit tabs could be hacked, even when personalized, it was a difficult process that most brokers didn't think worth the effort. Master John had never accepted thumbed tabs, and had usually insulted the kids who'd brought them in to his shop. Sawyer was sure that there were some brokers in the city who specialized in stolen tabs, but it probably wasn't worth the effort to find them, or the danger of possibly being caught with tabs that were personalized to someone else.

His theft completed and unnoticed, Sawyer blended back into the crowd. He knew that, once he realized he'd been robbed, the man would remember the little boy who had bumped into him, but what good would it do him then? Sawyer grinned to himself as he searched out his next target.

He and Eryyn spent three hours walking up and down the market streets. Several times they caught sight of each other and would wink or smile to signal that they were doing well. By the time the crowds started to dissipate as the midday breaks ended, and he and Eryyn met at their assigned place in front of a clothing store, Sawyer's pockets were heavy with stolen goods.

"Have fun?" Eryyn asked, turning away from the window where she had been examining a skirt and blouse set. Sawyer jangled his pockets meaningfully and Eryyn grinned, her eyes bright. "Wanna go visit a broker?"

"Not really. But I'd do anything for you," Sawyer replied in a sweet, innocent voice. He cocked his head at her and smiled charmingly. Eryyn laughed and flung her arm over his shoulders, nearly causing his legs to buckle. The success of the day had put them both in good spirits.

"A quick stop, a fast couple of trades, and we'll head back to the nest with enough credits to buy everyone dinner. Sound good?"

"Brilliant."

Eryyn rubbed her knuckles into his head at the joke, then struck a path for their most recent pawnshop. The owner was a man named Rogers who worked the shop with his wife, Delle. Rogers was far from a very pleasant person, but he didn't terrify Sawyer like Master John always had. Sawyer found that he could talk to the man and had even helped Eryyn with some of the bargaining.

Delle, however, was another case. She hated kids and never had a kind word to say when Rogers called them in. She'd sworn at them many times, called them names, threatened them if they happened to wander too close to a display, and had even thrown a plated belt buckle at Eryyn. Fortunately, the girl had ducked just in time, and, when she stated that they'd take their business elsewhere, Delle had been banished from the back room.

Unfortunately, she was in the front of the shop when they stepped through the door, and she glared deeply, brandishing a broom as she snarled, "Don't even think of taking anything that ain't yours."

"We already did that," Sawyer retorted, slamming the door behind him. "But we took stuff with *value*."

"Always glad to hear that," Rogers said, hurrying out of the small back room where he stored the stolen items for a few days before attempting to sell them. He sent a fierce look towards his wife, but this time Delle did not leave. She planted her feet to the floor and glared back.

"We don't have a lot of time," Eryyn said, taking a few things out of her pockets and placing them on the counter. "We'll go somewhere else if there's going to be a problem." She glanced pointedly at Delle, whose glare had centered on Sawyer.

"Stop it," Rogers growled at his wife. Delle's glare deepened for a moment, then she turned on her heel and returned to her sweeping. She circled the room slowly, keeping her eyes locked on the two young thieves while making a point to stay near the displays to protect the wares. Her husband scowled briefly, then stepped behind the counter and began inspecting what Eryyn had laid on offer with a critical eye. He nodded slightly, glanced at Eryyn, then looked back to the watch he was holding. Another long minute of staring and he put it down. "Is this all?" he asked with a contemptuous sneer.

"Squirt?" Eryyn held out her hand to her friend, who was standing just inside the door.

Sawyer, eyeing Delle and her broom warily, stepped up to the counter and emptied his pockets of the ten items he'd managed to collect. These were added to Eryyn's pile and looked over carefully. Rogers was somewhat more critical than Master John—he only bought from a few select kleptos and would only take the best of what was offered.

"Not half bad, girl," Rogers said, nodding his thin head. "Not half bad. What do you want for it?"

"Sixty," was Eryyn's prompt answer.

"Not a chance! I'll give you twenty."

"That's stealing!" Sawyer cried, outraged.

Rogers fixed him with a withering stare. "And what do you think you did to get this stuff, boy? *That's* stealing. I'm just trying to out-weigh the risks I take for you kids with profit."

"Don't do us any favors," Eryyn said acidly. "We want fair pay. That pile is worth fifty at least. And I know you'll turn around and sell it for much more. You'll probably get fifty just for that watch you were holding."

"Twenty-two."

"Forty-eight."

"Twenty-five."

They finally settled on thirty-six and Rogers swept the items into a box for later sorting. Eryyn handed over their latest credit tab, which still contained a few credits from their last sale, and watched carefully as Rogers added in thirty-six with his credit register. When he was finished, and the digital screen read twenty-four, Eryyn snatched the tab back and shoved it deep into her pocket.

"You're a wonderful guy to do business with. You should get together with Master John. You two cheapskates would be great friends."

"Your business here is done," Delle snapped, raising her broom threateningly. "Get out."

"And we've been having so much fun, too," Sawyer replied sarcastically. He followed Eryyn out of the shop, then stopped and handed her the few items—a watch, a bracelet, and the money clip—that he had held back from the sale.

"Excellent," Eryyn said with a smile. She took the loot, stuffed it into her pocket with the tab, then sauntered off down the street, Sawyer at her side. "We'll stash these things with the rest of the payment stuff at the old nest, then go buy something to eat. Any choices?"

Sawyer made a face. "Not dried soup."

"Aww, but it tastes so *good!*" Eryyn laughed. "We have forty-four credits, that'll get us something good from one of the stores, if we pick the right store. I'll bet we can get bread and cheese and make sandwiches."

Sawyer raised his eyebrows appreciatively. "That should keep the others happy."

"My whole point."

The others *were* happy—all eight of them. The new arrivals, Nissa and Ivy, were nervous and skeptical at first, but quickly warmed to the idea of being in a gang, especially when Eryyn gave them their sandwiches first.

The gang equaled ten now, a safe number, and there was a pile of loot in the middle of the floor that Eryyn picked through expertly while she ate. She nodded with satisfaction, claiming that she would personally pawn the items in the morning, and thanked the kids for contributing. Rick, who had been the one to convince Ivy, a Dead-Ender, to join up, swelled with pride at Eryyn's praise.

"I think we'll be okay, Squirt," Eryyn murmured a few hours later, when she crawled under the blanket that she was sharing with her partner. "We have more kids, which means we have to keep buying more food, but they brought in enough stuff today to take care of that. The deal pretty much takes care of itself, doncha think?"

Sawyer nestled down, hiding his nose under the rough cotton; it was going to be a chilly night and he was cold already. "Mm hmm," he murmured, shivering slightly and wriggling closer to Eryyn. "And if we have any trouble, I can still get rations. We can stretch a packet pretty far when we need too."

"Yep." Eryyn had already thought of that. Sawyer was the only kid in her gang who was legal and had a bracelet. She had always scorned the important piece of jewelry, claiming that Sawyer, as a street kid, didn't need it to survive and was only trying to cling to his pampered past by keeping it. Now, however, she could see the benefits in the free food that it provided. Granted, it only brought one packet of rations a day, which equaled three small meals intended for a single person, but it was still better than nothing. Normally, she and Sawyer disdained using the bracelet, choosing to work for their own food, but now she wondered if she should have him collect everyday. It would be one less bit of food that she would have to provide, and the kids would have the assurance that there was always a source, even if it was meager.

Eryyn snuggled under the blanket and cuddled up beside Sawyer, using him for warmth, just as he was using her. All around on the floor, she could hear the sounds of her gang as they settled in for the night. Some tossed, turned, and shifted on their thin pallets of rags, others snored, one talked in her sleep. But they all seemed content as they sprawled around the room, comforted by the gentle heat shed by the stove, and the knowledge that they weren't alone. Soon, Sawyer added the gentle rhythm of his breathing to the sounds, as he fell asleep beside her. Eryyn rested her head on a fold in the blankets, flung an arm over her sleeping friend, and closed her eyes, sighing contentedly. After a few minutes, she, too, was asleep, and that night she slept deeply enough to dream.

小本小丘

You shouldn't have made him angry

he bunkbeds were delivered in the middle of the week and set up around the walls of the second floor main dorm room. None were in very good condition—they'd been discovered by a construction crew assigned by the Enforcers to clear out an abandoned building down in the Dead-End for destruction—but Liz was glad to have all of them. The two story beds would help the dormitory house twice as many children in the same amount of space.

They needed a lot of cleaning though and she spent a full morning on her hands and knees, wielding steel sponges, trying to remove the worst of the rust and tarnish from the metal frames. It was hard, tiring work, and when Greg walked in to tell her to take a break, she did so gladly, throwing the sponge to the floor and standing up for a much needed stretch.

"You're doing good in here," Greg said, looking around at the bunks she had already finished. "Now you just need the Enforcers to find a building full of mattresses so they can donate those too."

"We already have that covered. Olivia cashed in the credits she'd been saving. The mattresses are being delivered tomorrow."

"Cashed in the credits?" Greg shook his head, hardly daring to believe how far his wife and her friends were willing to carry the project. "How much did that cost her?"

"Enough." Liz raised her arms over her head, working out the soreness in her shoulders. "And it's a big help."

Greg gazed around the room, admiring the work they had done. The house was almost finished. The plumbing and foundation had been fixed. The window glass had been replaced. The cracks in the walls and ceiling covered up. The smell of mildew and rot scrubbed away. Fresh paint had been coated over every surface and Carmen had managed to construct some curtains out of cloth scraps for the windows. The stairs had been repaired—there was no longer a danger of falling through to the first floor if one of the boards gave out—and the kitchen had been supplied with pots, pans, and other equipment for cooking and keeping the kids fed. They had even convinced, with a few well-placed hints from Enforcer Connel, some of the local Mid-End schools to donate old desks, books, and supplies for the schoolroom, all of which would be delivered within the next week. The Agency was close to being livable.

"You've done a great job here," he said. "At first, I thought this Agency idea would just blow over. I really didn't think anyone would go for it. But I was wrong—it's amazing how many people are willing to pitch in a few credits."

"They just want the kids off the streets," Liz said with a grin. "Though I really wish they'd pitch in a few working hours with those credits. Let's go downstairs, I really want a drink."

The stairs let out by the front room, the room they intended to use as a main activity place. The front entrance was on the north side of the room and, as Greg stepped off the last stair, he happened to glance in that direction and noticed a small shape moving in the shadows by the partially closed door. He paused to allow Liz to catch up with him.

"What's the matter?" she asked, unable to go any further with her husband blocking the stairs.

"I think we have a visitor," Greg replied, pointing towards the door. "A rather small visitor."

"Visitor? But who…?" Liz peered into the shadows where Greg pointed and she gave a small gasp. "Could it be?" she murmured to herself. "But he doesn't…Sawyer? Is that you, honey?"

The shape by the door moved slightly, becoming smaller as it hunched down. Liz pushed past Greg and hurried over. "Sawyer? It's okay, come here. What are you doing here?"

Greg watched his wife kneel down beside the door and heard

her whispering softly. After a moment, she stood up and came back towards him, leading the shadow by one hand. When they stepped into the light, he saw that the "visitor" was a small boy.

"Greg, this is my good friend, Sawyer," Liz stated as she led the child further from the door. Sawyer, his hand caught in Liz's gentle grasp, stared up at Greg with wide, green eyes. He looked nervous, chewing on his lower lip. "And this, Sawyer, is my husband, Greg."

Casting a confused look at Liz, Greg held out his hand to the little boy. "Nice to meet you, Sawyer."

Sawyer looked at him apprehensively, then reached out with his free hand to accept the shake. "Um, yeah," he murmured. "Same here."

"Sawyer's one of the children who could benefit from the Agency," Liz supplied. "I met him a couple of weeks ago when I was taking a walk."

Stunned by this surprise, Greg didn't answer right away and stood, studying the boy, for a long moment. It was easy to see that Sawyer was a street child. He was small and underfed, dressed in a motley of ill-fitting and unmatched clothes. He wasn't filthy, like some of the kids Greg had seen, but he didn't have a freshly bathed look either. Most of all he had the wary, nervous eyes of someone who doesn't know many people he can trust.

"Is he going to be our first candidate?" Greg asked, taking care to smile at the child to put him more at ease.

"I was hoping." Liz released the boy's hand and wrapped an arm around his shoulders. "But I never told you where we were, Sawyer. How did you find out?"

Sawyer blushed. "I f-followed you. When I left the bench this morning, I only went around the corner, then turned back and watched you leave. Then I followed you. The door was closed when I got here, but a woman just left and she didn't lock up, so I came in. I didn't know there'd be anyone else here." He continued to stare nervously at Greg. "I just wanted to see..."

"That was Olivia," Greg told Liz. "She went out to get some lunch."

"So you've been waiting outside since this morning?" Liz was surprised. She hadn't gone in to work that morning, choosing to take the time to finish the bunks instead. If Sawyer had followed her from their meeting in the park, then he'd been sitting outside for at least five hours.

But Sawyer shook his head. "No. I followed you, found out where you were, then went to see my friends. I only came back a little bit ago and hid in the bushes out front until I could get in." He looked down the hall towards the main room. "But I wasn't sure if this was where you worked, or if this was…"

"The Agency?"

He nodded.

"This is the Agency, Sawyer. I work further north, in an Enforcer station. I took the day off to come and do some work here."

Sawyer perked up a tiny bit. "So I got lucky. Following you today."

Greg laughed and Liz smiled warmly. "Yeah, I guess you could say that. Well, now that you're here, would you like a tour?"

The boy looked back towards the door, the only means of escape. He hesitated, then gave a small nod.

"Great! I've been dying to know how a child would take to everything. They see things differently than grown-ups."

Sawyer's slight grin returned at that and his nod was stronger. He followed Liz away from the front hall and into the main living room, where she showed him everything from the sofas and tables, to the toys and games she and the others had collected at local shops, to the shelves that she planned to line with books. She noticed how Sawyer's eyes shone at the mention of books and shot a small grin at Greg, who was tagging along.

They moved on to the kitchen and the office, both of which were on the first floor, then back to the front hall, where they took the stairs up to the second floor, and the dormitory and classroom. Sawyer looked curiously around the classroom, carefully examining the desks, but there were no books on any of the shelves yet, so he soon lost interest. The dormitory was better. He stepped to the middle of the long room, turning in a circle as he tried to see it from all angles, then sat on one of the lower bunks.

"Real beds?" he asked, tilting his head back to peer at the bunk above him. His eyes were very wide, as if the idea of real beds was unbelievable.

"Of course," Greg said from the doorway. "What did you think, that we would have the kids sleeping on the floor?"

Sawyer looked down at his feet, which were dangling off the side of the bunk. "You get used to it," he mumbled, shrugging.

Greg was stunned to silence and Liz had to think quickly to clear up the sudden awkwardness.

"Um, Sawyer? By now you've probably worked off breakfast, haven't you? Are you hungry? Thirsty? We have some drinks downstairs in the kitchen, in the cooler. Would you like one?"

The little boy shook his head, then glanced up, saw her face, and changed his mind. "Sure," he said, not sounding very enthusiastic.

"Why don't you head on down and pick anything you want. Greg and I will be just a minute, I have to show him something I was working on up here." Liz winced inwardly at the lame excuse. In the weeks since they had started meeting in the park, she had come to realize that Sawyer was far from stupid. He wasn't falling for her story, this she could tell from the way he narrowed his eyes. He was smart enough to know that she wanted to talk about him, but he stood up anyway and slipped past them to go downstairs. As he did, Greg stuck out a hand to ruffle his hair. Sawyer flinched a bit, then turned and favored the man with a weak grin before disappearing out the door.

"He's cute, isn't he?" Liz asked, once she was sure Sawyer was out of earshot.

Greg stared at the door for a second, then turned to his wife, his face confused. "How do you know him? You said a couple of weeks...when did you meet?"

Liz hurriedly told him the story, from sitting on the bench after the rain and realizing that someone was watching her, to figuring out that Sawyer was the little boy she'd seen accosted in the marketplace, to her daily morning visits with him in the park.

"It's taken awhile—he's really slow to trust—but he's talking to me about more things now. He told me about his best friend, a girl named Eryyn, and how they've been living together on the streets for years, moving around to different hideouts while they work to get food."

"Well, here's what I'm confused about. You just said work, but that boy can't be any older than nine or ten. What work does he do?

It can't be factory work, because then he wouldn't be free to wander around the streets."

Liz sighed, remembering the exact day when Sawyer had finally confided in her what he had meant by 'pocketing and hits. "It's the one thing about Sawyer that I don't like, that I really hope to change if he moves in here. He and his friend, Eryyn, the two of them work as…"

"Thieves." Greg nodded with certainty. "I had a feeling."

Liz looked bleak. "They call themselves kleptos and make their credits by pick-pocketing, or breaking into houses and taking little things. He doesn't like it. He knows it's wrong. But he would never have survived if he hadn't learned how."

"Has he ever stolen from you?"

"Wha…?" Liz was taken aback by the question. It had never crossed her mind to think that Sawyer would try robbing her. "I…well, I don't know. I've never found anything missing after our talks. I honestly don't believe he would do that."

"Why?"

"I'm his friend."

"And you think that would stop him from picking your pockets if he saw the chance?"

"Please, Greg. I *know* Sawyer. You don't. Not yet. He's really a sweet boy: he just got dealt a bad hand, that's all. He steals because it keeps him alive. Keeps him and his friends alive. He wouldn't do it if he didn't have to. If he had a nice place to live with plenty of food and warm beds, then he would act just like any normal little boy. We can't judge him just because he wants to survive—we would do the same thing in his place."

"Why doesn't he go to the Enforcers for help? He's legal, he has a bracelet. They'll place him somewhere until he's old enough to make a life for himself."

"I think he's afraid of the Enforcers," Liz said with a little shrug. "It has something to do with how he ended up on the streets, but he won't tell me, no matter how much I ask. And I have a strong feeling that his friend, Eryyn, is an illegal, and he won't leave her. So he can't go to the Enforcers."

Greg shook his head. "I wish I had known about this. Why didn't you ever tell me? When *were* you going to tell me?"

"I'm not sure. I probably would have brought him here once the house was finished. He can be really useful, Greg—once we're ready to open the Agency to the kids, he can help us find and talk to them. They'll be more apt to trust a child, and Sawyer really knows his way around the city, he knows where all the kids meet and live. Which is one of the reasons why I'd like to keep him as a friend, keep him trusting me. Understand?"

"I suppose. But just watch out, okay? Check your pockets after you talk to him. He may be a sweet, intelligent child, but he's still a thief."

Liz had just nodded when a small voice spoke up from the stairwell.

"Liz? I have to go now."

Liz and Greg froze. It sounded like Sawyer was much closer than the front hall. Had he heard them talking about him? Liz rushed to the door and hurried down the steps, encountering the boy sitting halfway up the stairs, a can of soda in one hand. He grinned at her and stood up.

"I've been gone for awhile and Eryyn's gonna be worried, so I should go."

"Oh. Oh, well, alright, Sawyer. Let me walk you down." Liz fell into step beside him, putting one hand on his shoulder as he made his way down to the front hall. "Did you like the house? Does it seem like a place where kids would want to stay?"

Sawyer bobbed his head and smiled. "It's wonderful."

"Do you have any ideas for things we should change?"

"I don't really know. Anything would be better than what we have now. I mean...you have *beds*. We don't have those, and there's gonna be food, and it's clean and warm. I don't really know anybody who wouldn't want that." They had reached the door by then and Sawyer stepped out on the porch. He turned around, blinking up at Liz in the sudden, hazy light. Clasping his hands behind his back, he grinned slyly. "All you need is someone who knows where those kids meet and live, right? Someone who can talk them into coming here and giving it a try."

So he *had* heard. She should have known he'd try to listen in, given the way he'd looked at her when she'd sent him from the room. Liz hid her eyes behind her hand. "I'm sorry, Sawyer. I didn't mean it to sound like I only wanted to use you." She glanced up. "I really am your friend."

Sawyer's eyes twinkled mischievously. "I know. I listened in on everything, and you said that that was only *one* of the reasons. And I want to help you."

Liz knelt down and hugged the boy, running one hand through his hair. "And I want to help *you*. That's why we're working on this. I'll see you tomorrow?"

Sawyer nodded against her shoulder. Liz let him go.

"Okay. Be careful." She kissed her fingertips and brushed them against his cheek. He smiled and jumped down the stairs, walking off in the direction of the market. When he had gone a dozen steps, he turned and waved to her, then broke into a run.

Liz watched him until he vanished around a corner, then went back inside to finish scraping the bunks.

• • •

In the weeks since Eryyn had begun collecting kids, the gang had grown to a number of sixteen, not including herself, as leader, and Sawyer, who had adamantly insisted that he was her partner and not just a member of the gang. Eighteen of them bunked out in the nest at night, after handing over the loot collected during the day and eating whatever meal Eryyn managed to buy with the half profits she saved. Eighteen kids scoured the streets each day, working together to bring in loot, protecting one another from possible trouble, and always keeping an eye out for new recruits.

They were beginning to be known around the neighborhoods and were easily recognized by their dark green armbands, which Sawyer had made by tearing up a blanket he'd stolen from a house. There had been at least two fights with rivals, both of which had been won with the help of Rick, and four of their newer members had escaped from gangs just so they join up with Eryyn.

It truly seemed like Sawyer's Robin Hood idea would work. The street kids were eager for protection, friendship, and a leader who would treat them fairly, like equals. Rick was the largest of the kleptos, a girl called PJ was the smallest, but both were entitled to the same quality food and a fair cut of the loot, as long as they did their share of the work. Eryyn played no favorites.

So their gang was strong, and happy, and worked well together. Sawyer had managed to get into several houses with Rick's help, standing on the boy's shoulders to boost him up to a window that he couldn't have reached otherwise, and Jay had once saved Eryyn and Foxy from being caught while 'pocketing by catching sight of an Enforcer and whistling a warning to the girls. It was a good system and it worked so well that they were soon among the higher ranking gangs in the Mid-End.

On the day Sawyer took the tour around Liz's Agency house, Eryyn was out with Foxy and Cinder, working a small shopping plaza on the border of the Mid and Sky-Ends. After a few days of experimenting, Eryyn had come to the conclusion that Foxy, Cinder, Rick, Jay, and Melody were some of her best 'pockets. She assigned them to the plazas and marketplace often while the others worked houses. Now, she was wandering about with Foxy and Cinder on one end of the plaza while Jay and Melody worked the other end. They had plans to meet in the middle.

"Good pickings today," Cinder stated as she slipped her hand out of a woman's purse, holding a small portable link receiver. The woman moved on, stepping off the curb, none the wiser of her lightened purse and Cinder handed the receiver to Eryyn, who slipped it into her shirt with a smile.

"That's dinner tonight," Foxy said happily. "Receivers like that are worth a fortune."

"Yeah, too bad we won't get a fortune for it," Eryyn griped. "But you're right, we'll get dinner." Despite her bitter words, she was quite satisfied. Already she and her two friends had gathered enough stuff to pay for food for at least two days, and she didn't know how the others were faring. The cuts for everyone, after pawning, would be great. In fact, they would probably be able to afford a day or two of rest after such success.

"Ooh, this is nice!" Foxy held up a ring she'd just pilfered. A small blue stone glimmered in the gold setting. "I'd love to keep this! It's not fair. How come these drips have pretty stuff like this and we don't?"

"'Cuz these drips are Sky-End and we're not. They probably notice us as much as they notice the pigeons." As she spoke, Cinder kicked at such a bird, sending it flying off in a flurry of feathers and angry coos.

"But the pigeons don't grab stuff like this right off their fingers," Foxy said, slipping the ring onto her finger and holding up her hand to admire the sparkling blue stone. She yipped, startled, when a loud, piercing whistle shot through the air, and hurriedly slipped her hand into her pocket, hiding the ring as they all turned to see Jay pelting down the street towards them. He was smiling broadly and waving his arms, trying to catch their attention.

"Eryyn! Eryyn! Come on, I've got a *huge* surprise!" Jay grabbed her hand and spun around, running back in the direction he had come. For a scrawny eleven-year-old, Jay could be pretty strong when he was excited. Eryyn was nearly jerked off her feet as she struggled to keep up. She managed a quick, confused glance back to Foxy and Cinder, who, looking just as perplexed, broke into a run to follow.

Jay dragged her through the plaza, heedless of the people who muttered angry exclamations as he shoved past, and ran straight to the mouth of an alley, where Eryyn could see Melody waiting. Seeing them coming, Melody waved, and turned to say something to someone behind her.

"You're never gonna believe this!" Melody exclaimed when Jay finally slowed to a stop. "Eryyn, you're gonna love it!"

"Wh-wh-what is it?" Eryyn gasped, doubled over at the waist to catch her breath. Jay, hardly even winded, pointed to the alley. "New recruits," he announced, looking elated.

Eryyn immediately perked up. "Where are they? Get them out here." she demanded as Cinder and Foxy caught up and ground to a halt behind her. Jay shook his head.

"No?" Eryyn was perplexed. "Why not?"

"They're scared. They don't want anyone to see them. Not yet," Melody answered.

"Scared? What are you talking about? Are they in there?" She pointed to the alley; Jay and Melody nodded in unison. Eryyn swallowed and stepped past them, into the gloom of the alley, where she could just barely see two dim figures huddling against a wall. Behind her, Cinder and Foxy started forward, ready and tense, just in case Jay had been deceived and this was an attempt of a rival gang to hurt their leader.

But there was no problem. The kids waiting in the alley did not want to hurt Eryyn—they were just terrified of being seen talking to her. The gold and red bands around their arms made them too conspicuous.

"You're from one of the Foreman's gangs! Otto's!" Eryyn exclaimed when she could see them clearly. The boy dipped his head in a nod. He appeared to be about twelve or thirteen, tall and lanky, and was standing beside a girl of possibly nine. He had one arm draped over her shoulders protectively.

"Not by choice," he murmured. "We heard about you. You started a gang that kids like. You let the kids take some of the profits."

"And you take in kids from other gangs," the girl piped up, "and hide them if someone comes after them."

"Yeah," Eryyn said. "That's right."

"We want to join…if you'll let us."

Eryyn eyed them carefully, keeping a cool front while just barely containing her excitement. Kids from Otto's gang! She was almost afraid to believe it.

"Would you be willing to take orders from me and work for your cut of the profits?" she asked, unsure of what to expect from kids trained by Otto.

They both nodded.

"Once you feel safe, will you be willing to help protect the rest of your gang, and any other kids who join?"

More nods.

"Do you promise to help recruit as many kids as you can convince? Even kids from other gangs? Like the Foreman's?"

"Yes," the girl said, while the boy continued to nod.

Eryyn stuck out her hand. "What's your name?" she asked the boy.

He shook hands with her and said, "I'm Dillan. This is Kit, my partner." Kit grinned shyly.

"Welcome to the gang."

"Really?" Kit's eyes widened. "You'll take us? That easy?"

"I'll take anyone who's serious about helping and working. You're serious, right?"

"Yeah."

"You're in." Eryyn turned back to Jay and Melody. "How'd you two do?"

"Loot wise?" Melody smiled, and patted at her pockets. "Not bad, Eryyn. We got some stuff."

"We did pretty good too. Okay, we can head back to the nest and get Dillan and Kit settled in." She held out her hand to the little girl and Kit timidly stepped away from the wall. Dillan followed closely, but hesitated at the mouth of the alley, looking around warily.

"Take off your bands," Cinder said. Dillan looked at her, nervous and uncomprehending. Jay, however, caught on and touched the boy's arm, where his braided band was visible over his shirtsleeve.

"You aren't the Foreman's anymore. Take off the band and no one will pay you any attention. It's the band that tells everyone you're part of Otto's gang. Get rid of it."

Dillan's freckled face brightened with a grin of understanding. "You're right!" He touched the band that he'd worn everyday for nearly two years, then wrapped the cloth in his fist and tore at it, pulling the knot loose. He held the strip out before him for a second, staring at it with intense hatred, then he dropped it. Kit, watching him with wide eyes, was quick to copy.

"All gone!" Foxy sang, as Dillan stepped on the braid. "You'll get a new one soon. A *better* one."

Dillan eyed the band around Foxy's arm. "I always did like green more than red."

Eryyn laughed. "Dillan, I think you're gonna fit right in. Come on. Let's go back to the nest so you can meet the rest of the gang."

• • •

Sawyer heard the voices in the nest before he'd even pulled himself over the sill of the entrance window. As he dropped down to the floor, Eryyn called out, "Hey, Squirt, come meet our new members—former kids of Otto's gang."

Struck dumb, Sawyer climbed to his feet and padded across the room to where Dillan and Kit lounged against a wall. The two kids were already wearing their new armbands and beaming from ear to ear.

"This is Dillan, and this is Kit," Eryyn said, pointing to each in turn, "and this is Squirt, my partner and my blood brother."

The look on Dillan's face showed the surprise he felt that Eryyn would choose such a little kid as her partner. From his experience in gangs, only the biggest and the strongest held positions of power. With Rick and Lex having recently returned from the Dead-End, it was obvious that Sawyer was *not* among the biggest or strongest. The exact opposite in fact—he looked as young as Kit, and she was only *nine!*

Sawyer understood the look, having seen it before on some of the other new kids; he shrugged. "We run things differently in this gang. Eryyn's leader, I'm her partner, but I'm not really her second-in-command."

"You'll get used to it," said Ivan, one of the other kids who had escaped an abusive gang. "There really isn't a second-in-command—*everyone* gets a say around here."

"I don't care!" Kit claimed loudly. "I'm out of Otto's gang, and he can't hurt me or threaten me anymore. That's the only thing that matters. Now he can't say he'll do to me what he did to Pammy, or Aimee…" Dillan elbowed her in the ribs and she immediately quieted down, looking chagrined. Then they both seemed to realize that Eryyn wouldn't punish them for talking and they sighed, relaxing visibly.

"What did he do to Pammy and Aimee?" PJ asked, sitting on the floor by Sawyer's feet. Only seven, she hadn't been on the streets long and still didn't understand many of the dangers. It had been an act of mercy on Lex's part when he had brought her in.

"He killed them," Dillan replied fiercely, his blue eyes flashing with sudden anger. "'Cuz they weren't good enough. Pammy brought in stuff that the Foreman didn't want, and the Foreman ordered her out of the gang, so Otto killed her and dumped her body out by the factories. Then, just awhile ago, Aimee…" The boy stopped, his voice choked off by the memory of hiding Aimee's body. Kit, giving her partner a look of sympathy and a pat on the arm, continued for him, "Aimee tried to escape with her partner, Rane, but Otto caught on and he punished them both. Rane got beat up really bad and was locked in a closet for a week, but Aimee was killed. Otto even made Dillan help hide her body."

"Shh!" Dillan hissed, looking fearfully at the gang. He didn't know how they would react to the part he'd been forced to play in Aimee's death. Luckily, most of the kids were sympathetic and staring at their shoes or at the walls, painfully aware of the awkward topic. But Eryyn was staring at him, her eyes cold and angry, and Sawyer was staring at *her*, looking worried. The small boy glanced at Dillan, biting on his lower lip, then touched Eryyn's arm and whispered under his breath. Dillan couldn't hear what he said, but it had an effect on Eryyn. She looked away, turning towards the wall, and quickly wiped a hand across her eyes.

"It's okay, Dillan," she said after a short, tense silence. "No one here will blame you for anything Otto made you do. Right?" She turned her head to look at each of the kids. All of them mumbled something in agreement. Dillan relaxed a little more.

"Thanks," he muttered. Kit leaned over and hugged him, smiling.

Eryyn clapped her hands. "Now we have twenty. And we're reaching some of the biggest, most important gangs. If we keep this up, we could put all the others out of business."

Rick, Lex, Cinder, Foxy, Melody, Jay, and Ivan all cheered at the thought. The kids of the Foreman's gangs had heard about them and were willing to run now, knowing that they would have protection if they did. Each new kid added more strength to the gang; Eryyn was right, soon they would be the best group on the street and everyone would know the green armbands. At that moment, the thought of leaving the gang and collecting the payment seemed amazingly stupid. They were Eryyn's gang now, and they all planned to stay that way.

• • •

Otto's fist slammed hard into his desk, knocking a pad of paper and a glass to the floor. The glass shattered, sending razor sharp shards throughout the room.

Sitting on the sofa, Rane swiftly lifted his feet, avoiding the glass that flew near him. He peeked briefly at Sasha, who, for once, seemed to share his trepidation. The girl sat beside him, clasping her hands in her lap tensely.

"It's not that bad, Otto," she risked saying.

"Not that bad!" Otto roared. "Are you stupid! Of course it's bad! Do you have any idea what the Foreman is going to think!"

"We haven't lost that many. We may be able to cover it, like we did yesterday."

Otto raised his brows and gave her a scorching look. "We aren't the only ones who have lost members, idiot. Jason has lost five of his kids in the last weeks, and most of the others have lost at least one or two. We lost Dillan and Kit last week and now Deb and Shawn have vanished. Of *course* the Foreman is going to notice!"

Sasha flinched and Rane struggled to hide his smile. This was one problem that Otto couldn't blame on him.

"Who's running this new gang?" he ventured to ask. "All I know is that they all wear green armbands." Rane had seen some of the kids on the street when he went out with Otto. None of the green bands were ever alone, which made it harder to question or intimidate them. Rane knew that none of Otto's spies had been able to get much information, so he already had the answer to his question. Still, he managed to get a small bit of satisfaction in seeing Otto flustered.

"I don't know," the gang leader replied shortly. "They never talk about their leader. They must be trying to keep him hidden."

"Or her," Rane pointed out.

Otto stared at him, eyes narrowed. Then he nodded. "Could be. That's what I'm determined to find out."

"Before the Foreman does?"

"Shut up." Otto stared at the blank top of his desk for a moment, clenching and unclenching his fists rhythmically. He pushed his chair back and stood up. "Sasha, go and watch the other kids, see what they're up to. Rane, you come with me."

Rane and Sasha glanced at each other, then jumped off the couch to obey. Sasha disappeared down the hall to the room where the kids slept, while Rane joined Otto at the front door.

"What are we doing?" Rane asked.

"We're gonna do a little 'pocketing, Raney boy."

But what you really mean is a little spying, Rane thought. He didn't say anything out loud, however. He knew better than to goad Otto too much. Instead he followed the older boy out of the stronghold and into the streets.

. . .

Sasha had been listening at the door of the sleeping room for less than five minutes and she knew that they were in trouble. All the kids in the gang had heard of the green bands and *most* were intrigued with the idea of cutting out on Otto and seeking safety. It was a bad situation. Otto hadn't been able to track down Dillan and Kit when they had run off the week before, and now he couldn't find Shawn or Deb. It was obvious that they had joined up with the green bands, and it was even more obvious that the new gang was protecting them, hiding them, so they couldn't be caught and brought back. Otto's gang knew this as much as she did and now they were all tempted to run.

And if they ran, then the payment day collection would dwindle, and if it dwindled, then the Foreman would be mad. And he would figure it out; he'd realize that Otto wasn't able to control his kids, and Otto would be in trouble. And if *Otto* was in trouble, then she, as his second, would be in trouble as well.

The thought did not appeal to Sasha. She rested her head against the door for a moment, thinking quickly, trying to decide what she would say when she went into the room.

A hand dropped on her shoulder and she jumped, a small scream erupting from her throat.

"Shut up!" a voice growled in her ear. "Where's Otto?"

The Foreman! Sasha's heart skipped a beat.

"I asked you a question. Where's Otto?"

"H-he to-took R-Rane and went out 'p-pocketing," she managed to stammer. The man's hand had moved up to her throat.

"He didn't tell me about this new gang," the Foreman muttered, close to her ear. "He didn't tell me that my kids have been deserting to join to up with this new gang. I don't like having secrets kept from me."

His hand tightened a bit on Sasha's throat and she gasped. She was still facing the door, the man was behind her—she couldn't see his face. How had he found out?

"I-I'm sorry, s-sir. Otto d-didn't w-want to b-bother you."

"Shut up," he warned again. Sasha fell silent, trembling.

"Now, here's what you're going to do. You're going to go out for a walk and find Otto. Tell him to come back here, that I'm waiting for him. Understand?"

Sasha nodded, tears stinging her eyes.

"Good. I'll give you one hour. I'll just make myself comfortable here until you get back. Get going!" He released Sasha's neck and, not risking a glance back to see the man, the girl took off down the hall, running as if a pack of dogs were on her heels.

• • •

Caulin wasn't enjoying himself. He used to have fun as a klepto, wandering about the city, going wherever he wanted. He'd had status among the kids who met at the pawnshops—he'd been the kid who had all the information and he'd had lots of friends.

But that was before he'd made the stupid mistake of letting Eryyn know that he'd told Otto's gang about Aimee. Eryyn refused to forgive him for being a part, even if it wasn't his fault, of Aimee's death. She wouldn't talk to him now, and, as far as he could tell, he was the only kid in the city that she had refused to let join her gang.

That hurt, considering he'd helped her get it started.

He scuffed down the street, hands jammed into his pockets, staring at the sidewalk and thinking about the look on Eryyn's face when he'd asked her if he could join up. And the look on the rest of her gangs' faces, on Squirt's face, when she told him to go away, that she'd have to think about it.

So much for friends. It's not like he'd *wanted* Aimee to die.

He bumped into someone, who swore at him to watch where the hell he was going. Caulin sighed and looked up. No use getting into more trouble just for taking a walk. Then he noticed the kid leaning against a storefront a few dozen feet away and he gasped. He knew that kid!

"Hey! Hey you!" he called, breaking into a run and quickly closing the distance between himself and the shop. The boy turned to him, startled, but didn't move. Instead, his large brown eyes flicked around for a moment before focusing directly at Caulin.

"What do you want?" he asked coolly.

"I know you," Caulin stated. "You were Aimee's friend. You were with her when she came to talk to me."

The boy's eyes flickered again, looking towards the street. Caulin glanced behind him, trying to see what he was looking for. He didn't see anything out of the ordinary and shrugged. The boy spoke, nodding as he recognized him. "You're the kid with the hat. You're the one who got me and Aimee in trouble by talking to Sasha. What do you want?"

"I-I don't know…" said Caulin truthfully. He didn't really know why he had wanted to talk to the boy. If he were smart, he would have avoided the kid at all costs.

"Then you'd better just get out of here really fast," the boy said quickly, his eyes widening at something he had spotted behind Caulin. "Because…"

"Hey, Rane! Looks like you've got yourself a new friend! Mind introducing us?"

Caulin whipped around to see Otto, a towering hulk of a sixteen-year old, standing right behind him. Otto grinned, showing off lots of teeth.

"I'd tell you, Otto," Rane was saying. "If I knew."

"What's your name, kid?" Otto asked, giving Caulin a playful punch on the arm. Caulin winced and rubbed at the spot. It would most certainly become a bruise.

"I'm Caulin," he murmured.

"Caulin, hey? Anything wrong, Caulin? You look kinda scared."

"No, no I'm not!" Caulin said quickly. "I just wanted to talk to him." He cocked a thumb at Rane. "That's all."

Otto glanced curiously at Rane, who, in turn, gave Caulin a look of pure malice.

"And why is that?" Otto asked. "You have something you've been keeping from me, Raney boy?"

"Not at all," Rane said, narrowing his brown eyes even more at Caulin. "He just walked up and started talking about Aimee."

"Aimee?" Otto said sharply, turning back to look at Caulin shrewdly. "What do you know about Aimee?"

Before Caulin could answer, someone called out to Otto. An instant later, they were joined by a girl wearing a red and gold band similar to the ones adorning the arms of Otto and Rane. Caulin recognized the girl at once. She was the one who had questioned him and taken his hat. He began to step back, suddenly feeling nervous and outnumbered, but Otto reached out and gripped his arm, holding him in place as he turned to the girl.

"I thought I told you to stay in the stronghold and watch the others?"

Sasha ducked her head, looking terribly pale and uncomfortable. "The Foreman's at the stronghold, Otto! He knows about the green bands and he's *mad. Really* mad! He wants to talk to you right away." Suddenly, she noticed Caulin. "Hey! You're that little drip who told me about Aimee and her dumb plan!" The fear on her face was eclipsed by a smug smirk. "Thanks for the hat."

Now Otto was looking at him with new interest. "Oh, so *you* were Aimee's friend. You knew how she was planning to escape?"

"No," Caulin said defensively, painfully aware of the burly teen's hand on his arm. "She just asked me to get a message to her friend, Eryyn. She didn't tell me anything else."

Otto's brows rose and he glanced at Rane, who was frowning. "Eryyn? Aimee was counting on Eryyn to help her escape?"

Caulin shrugged. "Yeah, I guess. That's why Eryyn was so mad when she found out Aimee was dead. And it's because of you," he pointed a finger at Sasha, "that she's mad at me now."

"Erryn's mad at you?" Otto glanced slyly at Sasha. "Why is that?"

"Because she found out that I'm the one who told on Aimee. Now she won't talk to me, no matter what I do, and she won't let me join up with the new…" Caulin slapped a hand over his lips, suddenly aware that his big mouth was about to get him into trouble again.

But the damage had been done. Otto's interest turned to outright glee. From his spot next to the wall, Rane could almost read the thoughts flicking around on the gang leader's face. He sighed heavily and shoved his hands into his pockets. This could not lead to anything good.

"That's Eryyn," Otto said at length. "I know her from a long time ago. She used to be my partner when she first started working as a klepto. She always did have a temper, and she would never forgive anyone for simple, honest mistakes. Like she was perfect and the rest of the world wasn't. You know what I mean?"

Caulin's nervousness disappeared, replaced by wonder and understanding. He nodded, and Rane shook his head sadly. Otto sure knew what he was doing. This battle was as good as won.

"So, she blames you for Aimee's death, even though it wasn't your fault?" Otto leaned towards Caulin slightly, his voice lowered conspiratorially. "I'm *sure* you didn't run up to Sasha here to tell her everything. I'm sure you were...persuaded to talk, right?"

Another nod. Caulin was beginning to look indignant.

"And now, because *her* plans were ruined, Eryyn's taking it out on you. Making you feel bad, stopping you from joining...what did you say it was?"

"Her gang. The gang *I* helped her start."

"Seems kinda cruel to me. Doesn't sound like any gang *I'd* want to belong to. How about you guys?" He looked at Rane and Sasha, his head cocked questioningly. Sasha immediately shook her head, smirking. Rane hesitated for a second, then shook his head when Otto surreptitiously flexed a fist in his direction. Grinning, Otto winked at him, then went back to working on Caulin. "I think she's an idiot. You obviously know your way around the city. *I* think you'd be useful in a gang."

Caulin thought that over. Otto was right, he *would* be useful. He knew the city better than anyone, even Eryyn, and he knew more kids. And it really wasn't his fault about what happened to Aimee. Aimee had chosen *him* to carry the message—she'd made him a target. So it wasn't fair that Eryyn was blaming him. It wasn't fair!

Caulin felt himself getting mad. He'd helped Eryyn get her gang started, he'd tried to make up for Aimee's death, and Eryyn was *still* holding a grudge. Eryyn didn't care about anything but *her* revenge, and she didn't care about who she stepped on in order to get it. But Caulin could get back at her. He could get revenge of his own. And he deserved it, right?

He lifted his eyes to meet Otto's. "You really think I'd be useful in a gang?"

Otto nodded immediately. "You bet."

"Will you let me in *your* gang?" Caulin pointed to the red and gold band around Otto's upper arm.

The gang leader laughed and slapped him on the back. "I thought you'd never ask. Sure, Caulin. If you want in, then you're in. Come on, I'll bring you back and show you around." He draped his arm around Caulin's shoulders and started to lead him out of the market.

Sighing again, Rane turned his head slightly and rested his cheek against the cool surface of the storefront. He closed his eyes wearily. Either this Caulin was *really* mad at this Eryyn, or Caulin was just *really* stupid.

A nudge from Sasha made him move and he hurried to catch up with Otto and the new boy. As he fell into step just behind the gang leader, he muttered sarcastically, "Gee, and I thought we came out here to do some 'pocketing."

Otto turned his head to look back at him and his grin reminded Rane of the expression that had come over Otto's face just before he'd started beating on him. "Don't worry, Raney boy," he said joyfully. "I got just the loot I was looking for."

• • •

Comfortably curled up on his pallet against the wall, Sawyer felt Eryyn's eyes on him from across the room and glanced up from the book he'd been reading. The nest was nearly empty—most of the kids were out working—but Cinder and Shawn were sprawled out on the floor, playing some game Sawyer didn't understand, and Deb was sitting by one of the windows, braiding strips of cloth together to make more bands for their new members. Those three didn't see Eryyn tilt her head meaningfully towards the spare room, and paid no notice to Sawyer as he stood up. Eryyn followed him into the smaller room, then closed the door, throwing them into abrupt dimness.

"Problems?" Sawyer asked.

"No, not really. Just curiosity."

"About what?" The question was useless—Sawyer already knew the answer. But he sat down against a wall and, as his eyes adjusted to the change in light, looked up at her, waiting.

"About your walks."

Sawyer nodded: he'd been right. "My walks? I go to the park. I thought you didn't care anymore."

"I care when you disappear one day for more than two hours and come back carrying a soda."

Sawyer flinched. Dumb mistake. He'd forgotten about the soda Liz had given him. He wondered briefly how he'd been able to climb through the window while holding it.

Eryyn knelt down in front of him, meeting his gaze with hers, and asked softly, "Would you please tell me where you got it? I know you and you'd never waste credits on a soda. Someone must have given it to you."

Sawyer averted his eyes to the closed door while he thought quickly. Liz had finished the Agency house—at least, all the basics were finished. She still needed to stock it with stuff for the school-room and such, but the house itself was fully repaired. Now would probably be an ideal time to tell Eryyn about the Agency. But it was also the worst possible time.

Eryyn's gang was still growing, in both members and status. The reason the kids liked it so much was because Eryyn made sure they were taken care of. If they had someone else, like Liz, or Greg, or Carmen to take care of them, then the gang would break up. Eryyn needed the gang—it was her entire plan for revenge against the Foreman. She wouldn't be happy if everyone suddenly deserted her.

"Squirt?" Eryyn was looking at him, waiting. Sawyer sighed and hid his face in his hands. *It's now or never*, he thought silently, and looked up.

"Somebody did give it to me," he murmured, "A friend."

Eryyn sat down beside him. "A friend?"

"A grown-up. Her name is Liz. We meet in the park every morning and talk."

Eryyn was very quiet, staring at her fingers. Finally, she said, "It's that woman you saw after the rainstorm, right? The day Caulin told us about Aimee being in Otto's gang?"

Sawyer gaped at her and she grinned. "I got it on the first try, didn't I?"

Sawyer nodded, still shocked. "Yeah."

"What do you talk about?"

"Stuff. She...she asks a lot about kids like you and me, you know, street kids. She's got this idea..." Taking a deep breath, Sawyer told Eryyn the entire story of the Agency house and the talks he and Liz had each morning in the park. He mentioned the questions Liz asked and his visit to the house and meeting Greg, and sitting on the stairs, listening in. Through his entire explanation, Eryyn stayed silent, looking at a crack in the floor. Only when he finally paused for breath did she speak.

"And you think this Agency is a good idea?"

Sawyer hesitated, then continued carefully, "I really don't think it's a bad one."

"Why not?"

"Because Liz wants to help. I know she does. She's not the kind of person to trick kids so she can sell them to factories or gangs. She likes kids. And if she got the chance to help them, she would do a good job, and lots of kids would be safe."

"You really think so?"

Sawyer caught the sneer in Eryyn's voice and swallowed hard, hating that she was going to make things difficult. "Yes, I do. Why don't you?"

"I just find it hard to believe that this woman would waste her money just to help out kids who don't belong to her. What does she possibly have to gain from the Agency?"

"I've asked her that, and she told me that all she wants is to make sure all the street kids like us are safe."

Eryyn laughed nastily. "How can you trust her, Squirt? She's a grown-up. Grown-ups cause nothing but trouble."

"At least all the grown-ups *you've* known," Sawyer pointed out. "I always thought all the Enforcers wanted nothing else but to nab kids and throw them into factories, but then I ran into Officer Connel. He was different, really nice, and he helped me."

"A lucky strike."

"Liz could be one too. How do you know she's not?"

"How do you know she is?" Eryyn countered.

Sawyer sighed. "We could go back and forth like that all day. I just trust her, like I trust you. Like the rest of the gang trusts you. The greenbands know you wanna help them and, well, Liz wants to help too. She doesn't want to hurt us."

Eryyn's eyes softened and she plopped her hand on his head, ruffling his hair in a way she had done since the day they'd first met, when Sawyer was still new to the streets and had woken up each night, terrified by nightmares and the noises of the city. "She's like the woman in your stories, isn't she?" Eryyn asked, her voice actually gentle. "The one who lives in the house up at the Sky-End."

"Mm hmm." Sawyer leaned against Eryyn, resting his head on her arm. "She's like a dream."

"Can I meet her?"

Sawyer sat up, looking worried and hopeful. "I-I think Liz would like that. I've told her a bit about you and she says she'd love to meet you."

"When?"

Sawyer shrugged. "Don't know."

"Talk to her, figure it out, then tell me, 'kay?"

"Mm hmm."

Eryyn stood up and started to leave the room, but Sawyer halted her.

"Eryyn?"

"Yeah?" She turned back to look at him. He was still sitting by the wall, his knees drawn up to his chest, his book held in one hand. He smiled at her.

"Thank you for not being mad."

Eryyn smiled back. "Hey, any friend of yours has to be a friend of mine, right?"

Sawyer nodded and Eryyn left. But, once the door was closed, Sawyer dropped his head into his hands again and moaned with relief. Liz was no longer his special secret, but he was no longer holding anything back from his best friend either. It felt like an enormous weight was lifted off his shoulders. Now, he just had to figure out a way for Liz and Eryyn to meet. *That* was bound to be interesting.

• • •

A day of confessions. While Sawyer was spilling his story to Eryyn, Caulin was sitting on a chair in the meeting room, telling *his* story to Otto, Rane, Sasha, and the shadow they all knew as the Foreman. Caulin was shy at first, nervous of the presence in the alcove, but Otto was friendly and encouraged him until all the information of Eryyn's gang, that Caulin knew, had been told.

"So, *Eryyn* is the leader of the green bands," Otto mused. "Who would have thought…little Eryyn. She *hated* the gang we were in together, and now she's gone and started one."

"It's amazing what one will do, when they have a reason," the Foreman's dry voice spoke up from his dim alcove. Both Rane and Caulin jumped at the voice, glancing apprehensively towards the shadow, but Otto merely nodded.

"And she's doing this only to try to break up the gang systems? To make all the kids desert and escape? And that little kid she calls a partner, he thought the whole thing up?" Otto cocked his head and Caulin nodded rapidly. "Yeah, Squirt. He's pretty smart, knows how to read and all. He had this book that he got the idea from and he's helping her every bit of the way."

The silence that followed was tense, mainly because of the man glowering in the shadows. Finally, the dry voice spoke again, "They'll have to be stopped."

Rane shivered in his spot beside Caulin. The man was so simple about it, so matter of fact. It didn't bother him at all to talk about killing kids.

"I know," Otto answered. "But, unfortunately, we can't attack her the way she attacked us. If Caulin's telling the truth about the way she runs her gang, none of those kids are going to leave her and join up with us."

"That wasn't what I meant. You keep working like you always do. Watch your group carefully, don't lose anymore members, or you'll regret it. *I'll* take care of the girl and her partner. I have my means. All I'll need is a little more information."

Otto looked pointedly at Caulin, who nervously wriggled in his seat. His face pale, he turned to Rane, who pointedly looked away.

"This may cause a little flux in my system, but it won't last for long. I'll make sure of that. Those two brats will wish they'd never heard of me." The Foreman shifted, and one hand emerged from the shadows, pointing at the door.

"You three get out of here and go about your own business. I have a few questions I would like to ask our new friend here."

As they stood up and headed for the door, Rane shot a glance back at Caulin. The new boy was watching them leave, his gray eyes wide with terror. Shaking his head, Rane turned to Otto.

"Caulin sure looks likes he's having second thoughts about all this. Will he really be allowed into the gang?"

Otto shrugged. "If the Foreman thinks he's worth it. If you ask me, Caulin's a flipping idiot. *I* don't want him."

"Then what…?" Rane paused, not sure if he wanted to know the answer to the question. He shivered, hugging his arms around his chest, and asked, "Can I go?"

"Not far, in case I decide to call on you."

From the tone of his voice, Rane suspected that Otto *would* call him, just to get on his nerves. He shook his head again, and walked down the hall, away from the direction that Otto and Sasha were taking. As he made his way through the stronghold to the sleeping room, he thought over Caulin's story and decided that Eryyn's idea was the most wonderful plan he ever could have imagined. And, as he entered the sleeping room and sank down on the thin pallet that was his, he began to cry. Because now the Foreman was after Eryyn, and, against him, she didn't stand a chance.

Oh, Eryyn, he thought bitterly, hiding his face in his arms as the tears flowed down his cheeks, *I don't even know you, but good luck. You're going to need it now. You just shouldn't have made him angry.*

TEN

Flint

"Eryyn wants to meet you."

Liz looked up from the blankets she was folding, startled by the sudden announcement. Sawyer was sitting on the bunk closest to her, his feet dangling off the side, helping her with the bed sheets and blankets that had been among the latest of the donations. In his hands he held a pillowcase, which he was folding awkwardly, and he shrugged helplessly when she caught his eyes.

"So, you finally broke down and told her about me, eh? The secret is out?"

"She tortured it out of me."

Liz laughed. "Held you down and tickled you until you confessed?"

"Nah, wouldn't work. *She's* more ticklish than I am. I just goofed and she finally decided that I should tell her. It's not bad, right? You *want* me to tell my friends," He swept his arm back, gesturing around the room, "about this place? Eryyn would want to know first, 'cuz she's the leader and everybody follows what she does."

Liz got up from the floor and joined the boy on the bunk, taking one of his hands in hers. "Of course it's not bad," she said, giving his hand a gentle squeeze. "I've been wanting to meet Eryyn since the first time you told me about her. Anyone who's a friend of yours has to be a friend of mine."

Sawyer stared at her, his mouth hanging open. Then he laughed.

Liz frowned. "What's so funny?"

"That," Sawyer gasped between chuckles, "is exactly what Eryyn said when she told me she wanted to meet you."

Liz smiled. "You're just very likable."

"I try to be." Sawyer batted his eyelashes coyly.

"When does she want to meet?"

"She told me to figure it out. When do *you* want to meet?"

"Anytime, kiddo. Bring her to me."

"Tomorrow? I can bring her in the morning."

"Perfect. I'll remember to get breakfast for two."

• • •

The man was silent and perfectly still in his chair. His back was stiff, his arms held crossed in his lap. His eyes, dark blue, gazed disinterestedly at the wall, but he listened very, very carefully.

"It has to be done quickly, before they can steal any other kids from my gangs, and I want it done well. Find them and bring them to me. I have plans to deal with them in my own way. If you do this…"

The man looked into the hand that was stretched out to him. There was a slip of paper on the palm, with a figure written upon it. He read the figure, showing no emotion, then nodded.

"Two kids, right. Easy. What do they look like?"

"The girl is the older one, about twelve or thirteen. Tall, thin. Shoulder-length hair, brownish-blonde, brown eyes, pointed nose. Answers to the name of Eryyn. The boy is about nine or ten, small, skinny. Short, brown hair, and green eyes. The kids on the street call him Squirt, but my source says his real name is Sawyer."

"Except for the names, you just described about half of the kids in this city. I need more specific information."

"They'll be wearing green bands on their arms—dark green. And the boy has a legal I.D. bracelet. That's all I know."

"A legal street kid?" The man's brows raised, the first change in his expression since he had settled into the chair. "Mmm, a rare catch."

"Get them both, and you get this." The paper was waved in the air. "I believe that you'll be able to handle this little project."

"That's nice to know." The man stood up to his full height. "This will be an enjoyable challenge." He ignored the hand that was offered to him—the deal, in his mind, was already sealed. Formalities were useless. He nodded once to his employer, then left the room, shutting the door quietly behind him.

At his desk, the Foreman returned the nod. He had no doubt that Flint would succeed. The man was a genius at his trade, the best, completely worth the extravagant price he charged. The Foreman had needed his services only once before, but he had not been disappointed. If anyone could find and catch the two brats that had dared jeopardize the Foreman's gangs, it was Flint, the bounty hunter.

• • •

"You'll like Liz, Eryyn. She's really nice. Stop being so worried."

"I'm not worried about meeting your friend, Squirt." Eryyn ran her hands roughly through her hair. "I'm not worried about anything."

"Then why do you keep playing with your hair? You're making it messy."

Eryyn's fingers were making another pass through her mane. She stopped and pulled her hands to her side as she kept step with Sawyer.

"Where is this Agency place anyway?" she asked, looking around distractedly.

"Past the park. Through the Blue plaza, and down a few blocks. It's not in one of the best neighborhoods, but..." Sawyer shrugged. "It's still nice. Liz and Greg and Carmen and Olivia have really worked hard on it." His face broke into a proud grin. "And I've helped a bit."

Eryyn looked perplexed. "I thought I was meeting Liz. Who're the other people?"

"Umm, Greg is Liz's husband. He's okay. I don't know Olivia, but I've already met Carmen a few times. They're both friends of Liz. They helped a lot too."

"So who will I be meeting?" Eryyn looked away again, chewing on her lip as she began running her fingers through her hair.

"Liz!" Sawyer sounded exasperated. "I told you. I talked to Liz yesterday and she wants to meet you, so I told her we'd meet her in the park today."

"Thanks for talking to me about it." Eryyn sounded annoyed and would not meet her friend's eyes.

"You told me to pick a time."

"I didn't know that time would be so soon."

"Ha! You *are* worried!"

"Shut up."

Sawyer obediently fell silent, though a shadow of a smile stayed on his lips even as they entered the park and he led her to the bench where he had been meeting Liz for the last weeks.

Liz was already there, watching them come towards her. She, too, was smiling.

"That her?" Eryyn asked.

"Yup." Sawyer grabbed her elbow and dragged her to the bench. Eryyn's legs felt wooden, but they moved as Sawyer filled in the gap between them and the young woman.

"Morning, Sawyer," Liz said, standing up. She kept her hands to her sides and smiled warmly at Eryyn. "Is this the friend you've been telling me so much about?"

"This is Eryyn, Liz. My blood sister," Sawyer answered, his voice full of pride. He placed his hand against Eryyn's back and gave her a shove forward. She stumbled a bit and Liz reached out, catching her hand to steady her. Eryyn looked up at the grown-up, snatched her hand back with a little hiss and swallowed hard.

Liz frowned to find her hand suddenly empty, but made an effort to smile as she said, "I'm pleased to meet you, Eryyn. Sawyer's so full of stories about you."

Eryyn found her tongue. "Good ones, I hope," she said, sending a look behind her shoulder at her small friend. Sawyer playfully made a point of shrugging.

"Great ones," Liz assured her. "He told me that he would never have survived if it weren't for you."

Sawyer blushed and Eryyn allowed herself a small, satisfied smile. "Well, at least he knows to tell the truth." She sat on the bench, Liz beside her, and Sawyer took a place at their feet, sitting cross-legged on the ground.

"I brought some breakfast," Liz stated, hoping to further break the ice. She held up a paper bag. The aroma of eggs and pastry wafted from it. "I don't know what you like, Eryyn, but Sawyer didn't seem to mind this, so I thought I'd try it again." She handed the bag to the girl, who tore it open and eagerly lifted out a pastry. Her eyes sparkled as she took an enormous bite.

"Another success," Liz said triumphantly, looking greatly relieved. She smiled down at Sawyer, who seemed mildly apprehensive. Of the three, this meeting was most important to him. He desperately wanted his two friends to get along, and, while he knew that Liz would make an effort, he couldn't really count on Eryyn to do the same thing. In fact, she'd been acting rather weird since he'd announced the meeting time.

So he and Liz waited until Eryyn had finished the pastry and had licked all the oil off her fingers before trying to talk again.

"Not bad," Eryyn said, folding the greasy paper that had contained the food. "You've been getting this every morning, Squirt?" She raised her eyebrows at her small partner.

"Not *that*, but Liz brings something, yeah."

Eryyn nodded and turned to Liz. "You really know how to make a friend out of a street kid. Food'll do it every time."

"Well, it took more than food to make friends with Sawyer, Eryyn. It took a lot more."

"I doubt it. Squirt *wanted* to be friends with you. He's always making up these stories about a house on the Sky-End and the people who live there with their..." she glanced at the wide-eyed boy sitting at her feet, "...son. In his stories, the people love their kid and take care of him and make sure he has food and a nice bed to sleep in and lots of toys to play with."

"There's nothing wrong with that," Liz said, noticing that Sawyer was getting embarrassed and indignant. "It sounds like a wonderful dream."

"Doesn't it? Except that's all it is. A *dream*. A fantasy. And dumb fantasies are dangerous to kids like us, aren't they, Squirt?"

"What are you getting at, Eryyn?" Sawyer was staring up at his friend, his eyes wide and hurt. "Stop it. Liz knows already. That's why she's trying to help us."

Eryyn looked down at him, and Sawyer saw something flicker in her eyes, a quick flash of regret, before they hardened and Eryyn's lips turned up in a sneer. "That's the part that I'm still finding hard to believe, Squirt. You keep saying that she wants to help us, but you never say why." Eryyn turned to Liz, her eyes suddenly dark and cold. "Why would she wanna help dirty little street kids like us?"

Stunned by the animosity in Eryyn's eyes, Liz held out her hand to the girl. "I want to help because I can't stand the thought of children having to fend for themselves in this city. It's dangerous, and too many children needlessly get hurt."

"That sounds like a load of bull to me."

"Eryyn! Shut up!" Sawyer cried.

Liz watched the two children glare at each other and spoke quickly to avoid more harsh words.

"It's alright, Sawyer," she said soothingly. "It's understandable that Eryyn has her doubts. You did too. We just have to prove to her that I'm telling the truth."

Eryyn snorted and Sawyer turned back to her, his eyes wounded by her sudden betrayal. "You're doing this on purpose!" he accused. "You never thought the Agency was a good idea, and now you're trying to ruin everything!"

"I think it's a great idea," Eryyn said, bristling defensively. "It's super! But *how* do we know it's gonna be safe?"

"You can trust me, Eryyn," Liz insisted. "Honestly you can. I wouldn't try to hurt you and I would *never* do anything to hurt Sawyer."

Eryyn's look was cold. "And how can you prove that? You're a grown-up! Grown-ups cause nothing but trouble for kids like us. Don't you think I've learned that in all the years I've had to spend avoiding them? I've never met a grown-up I could trust. I doubt there even are any!"

Liz felt her own anger rising. "That's not true. What is it about me that you find so untrustworthy?"

Sensing more trouble coming, Sawyer reached out a quick hand and grabbed at Eryyn's sleeve. "Eryyn? Please, don't," he pleaded.

Eryyn ignored him and spoke plainly. "Pretty much everything. Why would a woman from a Mid-End life want to help a bunch of Dead-End street kids and thieves? What could she possibly have to gain from us?"

"Life isn't only about gain, Eryyn."

"It is if you're street kid and a klepto, and you want to survive in this city. After Squirt told me about you, I had to sit down and think about that question for a minute. What could a Mid-Ender possibly want with a home that would help street kids? I couldn't figure out any good reason for it, except one."

"And that would be?" Liz asked, unable to keep the wrath from her voice.

"Money," Eryyn said simply.

Liz laughed mirthlessly. "Money? That's foolish! In case Sawyer didn't explain it all to you, money was not an issue here, Eryyn. If anything, we've had plenty of trouble because there was so little money to get this project started."

"But how about the money that you could make by getting a bunch of illegals into one place so that the Enforcers could have an easy time picking them up?"

Liz gasped just as Sawyer clapped a hand over his mouth. He looked stunned. The idea had obviously never occurred to him. Pleadingly, he gazed up at Liz, begging her with his eyes to prove that it wasn't true. Eryyn didn't give the woman a chance to defend herself.

"Just in case you didn't notice a missing piece of jewelry on my wrist," she started caustically, "*I'm* an illegal. Everyday I risk my life when I go out, because everyday, an Enforcer might notice me. I've known lots of kids who were my friends and who have just disappeared, never seen again. All of them were illegals, so it was pretty easy to figure out what happened. Someone nabbed them and sold them. Probably to the factories. And that *someone* had to be a *grown-up*. Because street kids stay as far from the factories as they can."

"I would never…" Liz started.

Eryyn plunged on as though she hadn't heard her, "You know, I thought I had done pretty good for myself, staying alive and out of sight of the Enforcers. And I did it while helping Squirt along too. But then, the other day, he tells me about you, and I couldn't believe how well you'd duped him."

"She didn't dupe me!" Sawyer was outraged and stood up, his hands clenched to fists at his sides. "How can you say that when you don't even know her?"

"How much do *you* know her, Squirt? You think she's perfectly safe because she looks like the woman in your dreams. But lots of jerks look safe, even that woman in the market who tried to drag you off. Remember her? I thought that had taught you a lesson, but now I find that you've been meeting with this woman for a couple of months and she's managed to completely turn your head. Bringing you food every morning, telling you nice stories about the Agency. I thought you were a lot smarter than that, Squirt. Don't you realize how easily she's *bought* you?"

That stung. Sawyer's eyes immediately brimmed with tears and he was unable to speak.

"It won't work," Eryyn said, turning her glare back to Liz. She stood up and grabbed Sawyer's hand, pulling the boy closer to her. "Your Agency will never work. Because none of *my* gang will trust you and neither will any of the other kids. You won't be able to gather them all up for the Enforcers. And you're not getting Squirt either. He's *my* blood brother, not yours!"

Liz was at a loss, unable to believe the hatred and distrust Eryyn was showing her. Desperately, she tried to reach out for the girl. "Eryyn. Please, sit down and listen to me for a minute. You're wrong. What you're saying, it's not true. I don't want to do anything to hurt you or your friends."

"I'll be the judge of that. I'm outta here. Come on, Squirt." She started to leave, dragging Sawyer behind her. The little boy didn't resist. Despite his feelings for Liz, Eryyn had been his friend first and he still loved her more than anything. He followed her away from the bench, but looked back when Liz, still stunned by Eryyn's accusations, called his name.

"I'm sorry!" he yelled back to her. "Liz, I'm so sorry!"

"Tomorrow, Sawyer! I'll be here tomorrow. I promise!"

Eryyn continued to pull on the boy's arm, leading him out of the park. But, just before they moved out of sight, Liz saw Sawyer pause, and, to her relief, he nodded.

• • •

No one knew the city better than Flint. It was his home, his life, his entire world. He knew every street and alley, every broken, rusted car or truck, every building from Dead-End crumbling to Sky-End new. He knew the businesses and the factories. He knew the little stores and the park, and the marketplace and plazas. The city was his domain.

So when the Foreman came to him with the job of finding two street kids, Flint knew it would be easy money. Normally, the people he was hired to track and find were criminals or idiots who had made the mistake of angering one of the crime lords of the city. A few of his marks had even been certain crime lords themselves. Never had he been called upon to find mere children. It could quite possibly be a more challenging job, given how well the street kids took to hiding, but he enjoyed challenges. He enjoyed the hunt.

He started by heading directly to the neighborhoods that bordered both the Mid–End and the Dead-End. Most street kids stayed there, where they were close to the empty housing of the Dead-End and to the possible working areas of the Mid-End. Almost instantly he noticed kids hanging around on the sidewalks, kids whose clothes were badly fitted or did not match, who were thin and scrawny, with wary, suspicious eyes. It was two children like these who he would soon be hunting. But first, he needed information.

The Foreman had had a source, a kid probably, who had told him what to look for, but it wasn't much. Two young kids, a girl and a boy, one a brownish-blonde, the other with brown hair. That wouldn't get him far. The fact that they would be wearing green armbands was better. At least he could use that to start.

He walked along the street, heedless of the trash piled up where he stepped. The Dead-End was filthy and ugly, but he was used to that. That didn't bother him.

Two kids, both girls, noticed his approach and slid back against a wall, letting him pass. He gave them a cursory glance, noting that neither wore an armband, green or any other color, then moved on. He made his way down the long main road of the neighborhood, taking his time, acting like he was out for the air. He navigated carefully, walking by the sporadic groups of kids, listening closely as they chatted. Most street kids were timid about being too obvious on the streets. They hung around near alleys where people were less likely to pay any attention to them. However, if one knew where to look, the kids were numerous, and they were always talking and gossiping.

Three hours of walking through the Dead-End and he learned what he needed to know; a gang, run by a girl named Eryyn, had stationed itself in the center Mid-End. It was a fairly new gang, but had quickly risen in status to be one of the strongest on the streets. The girl, Eryyn, was spoken about a lot among the street kids, mostly because they were planning on joining her gang. Unfortunately, the boy wasn't mentioned at all.

Not that it mattered. If he found the girl, he would surely find the boy. All he had to do was bide his time. Already he had learned enough to keep him in the right place, and, with the way the kids talked and the high status of this new gang, it would not take him long to locate them.

With a chuckle, he turned and retraced his steps out of the Dead-End, heading north towards the center of the city.

"Here I come, kiddies," he said in his low voice, still chuckling. "Ready or not."

• • •

"You didn't have to treat her like that. She's a nice person and she isn't doing anything wrong."

"We don't know that, Squirt."

"She's my friend, Eryyn! It's not fair that you did that. You wouldn't be too happy if I went up to Rick or Cinder and treated them the same way, would you?"

"That's not the same thing, Squirt. We know that we can trust Rick and Cinder. It's not that way with Liz."

Sawyer threw his hands up in exasperation. "Why do you keep saying that!" he cried. "We *can* trust her. She's a *friend!* How can you say that we can trust Rick and Cinder more than Liz? You didn't even *know* Rick or Cinder before we started the gang so what makes you trust them so much? And don't say its 'cuz they're kleptos like us because that's stupid! Otto's a klepto too and you wouldn't trust him as far as you could pitch a factory." He paused and wiped at his eyes, ashamed that they had filled with tears again. Eryyn noticed and reached out to ruffle his hair. He jerked back from her hand, shaking his head quickly.

"I'm sorry, Squirt. I didn't mean to hurt you, really I didn't."

Sawyer, his eyes shiny with tears, looked up at her. "So why'd you do it? Why did you talk to Liz like that? Why did you try to make her seem so evil? And why would you say that about *me?* How could you *ever* think that she had *bought* me?"

"I-I didn't," Eryyn lowered her eyes. "I shouldn't have said that to you. It was mean, but I…I was trying to see if Liz was telling the truth or not, and I guess I got carried away."

"You guess?" Sawyer's voice was laden with sarcasm. "You have no idea how much that *hurt*, Eryyn. It wasn't fair, and it *isn't* true!" He paused to wipe at his eyes again, then asked, "And what do you mean 'telling the truth'?"

"I thought…I thought that if I said that stuff to Liz, and it was true, she would say something, or do something that would prove it. I thought maybe I could get her to mess up."

Sawyer frowned. "Did she?"

Eryyn sighed and shook her head. "No. I'd hoped she would get shocked and try to babble her way out of it, but…"

Sawyer smiled as he realized what conclusion Eryyn had been forced to come to. "She got mad at you! You insulted her, because she's telling the truth and she *really* does want to help us, and *I've* been right the *whole* time."

"Rub it in," Eryyn muttered bitterly, finding it extremely difficult to meet her partner's triumphant gaze.

"I *plan* to. Sheesh, Eryyn, didn't you see her? You made her so upset!"

"So? She still wants to keep seeing you. She's not mad at *you*— she loves you. So there was no harm done. I wouldn't want to live in her stupid Agency house anyway."

Banging his fists against his thighs, Sawyer yelled, "*Why not!* It's the best thing that ever happened to this stupid city. It's just what we all need!"

"I can't, Squirt!" Eryyn said desperately. "I can't! I can't give up my gang! Not now! Not when I'm so close."

"So close?"

"To really getting to the Foreman. I'm taking kids away from *his* gangs now! That has to bother him, and there's nothing he can do about it. His own gangs are turning against him, and even if

Otto and his thugs came after us, we have enough kids now to fight them off. We're so close to winning, Squirt! To getting back at him for what he did to Aimee."

Sawyer's eyes narrowed until all their green color was lost. "Is that all you care about? Your gang and getting back at the stupid Foreman?"

Eryyn felt her own exasperation getting the better of her. She struggled not to get mad. "No. You too, Squirt. I care about you too. A lot. I don't want you to be angry with me. But I don't want you to leave me for Liz either, and I can't live in the Agency. Not now. Besides, after today, I doubt she'd take me in."

"You're wrong, Eryyn. She would! I know she would! The Agency is almost done. She can let kids move in now, but none of the kids know about it. Please, Eryyn, if your gang…"

Eryyn cut him off before he could finish voicing the thought. "No. Squirt, if my gang moves into that house, then I lose them. They won't care about being a gang anymore, they won't need me as their leader, and we won't have a chance of beating the Foreman."

"But the *Agency* could help beat the Foreman. If all the kids knew they'd be safe there, then they'd leave the Foreman's gangs, just like they're doing for your gang. We'd still be stealing kids from him and we'd still be winning!"

Shaking her head, Eryyn murmured, "No, it wouldn't be the same."

"But…"

"I'm not going to tell them, Squirt. I'm not gonna tell the others about Liz. Not until I've paid the Foreman back for Aimee. And *you* can't tell them either."

Sawyer's eyes narrowed again and his jaw clenched angrily. "What's to stop me?" he spat.

The stubbornness in his voice was not promising. Eryyn sighed again. "I thought you were going to help me. You came up with the idea for the gang; don't you wanna see it finished? Don't you wanna help me finish this? As my friend, and my little brother?" She caught Sawyer's left hand and lifted it to run her fingers over the pale scar on his thumb.

"That's not fair." Sawyer's voice was softer now; his eyes fixed on the scar and he tried to pull his hand from his friend's grip.

"Eryyn, I *want* to help you. I do! But I don't want to be a street kid forever. Not when Liz is trying to help change that."

"It won't be forever. I promise you. It won't be forever. And *then* we'll tell the others and we'll *all* move into your Agency house. Just a little longer, Squirt…" Eryyn grabbed his other hand, gripping them both tightly as she looked at him pleadingly. "And *I'll* go to Liz and tell her I'm sorry. I'll even help her get more kids for the house…but just give me a little more time. Please. Just stay with me and be my friend and my partner through this. Help me and then I *swear* I'll help you."

Sawyer tried to refuse, tried to look away from her pleading face, but he couldn't. Eryyn was his best friend—his blood sister. She'd helped him more times than he could remember. She'd *saved* him when he would have died of starvation in the dump.

He gave up, sighed just as heavily as Eryyn had a moment before and lowered his head. "Alright," he whispered.

Eryyn shouted with delight and flung her arms around his chest, squeezing him tightly. "Oh, I *knew* I could count on you, Squirt! I knew you'd help me! You're my best friend in the whole world!"

Sawyer was silent and very still for a moment, then returned the hug. "You promised," he whispered. "Remember that. You promised." He carefully blinked back tears and let his head fall against her arm. Eryyn *had* promised, but she had lied to him before, when it suited her to. He knew it, and she knew it. But all he could do now was wait, and hope that she had not lied to him again.

•   •   •

Flint's first course of action upon reaching the Mid-End was to search out and visit a number of small pawnshops. If the Foreman was right, and this Eryyn and her friend were thieves, then the pawnshops would be places they were likely to frequent, and the owners of those shops, though they pretended differently, watched and knew almost as much as Flint did about the goings-on of the city.

The first shop he stopped at was no help. Too close to the Dead-End. The owner had never heard of a girl named Eryyn, even when Flint had flashed an unpersonalized credit tab. The second one, a block away, had the same results. Flint decided to move farther north—apparently the kids had better tastes in where they sold their loot.

And they also didn't migrate much from shop to shop. Flint had to visit five shops before he finally found one man who had heard of the girl.

"Eryyn? Yeah, I knew her," the fat man said absently as he mopped at his dirty counter with an even dirtier rag. "Cheeky little brat."

Flint pulled the credit tab from his pocket and held it up for the fat man to see. "What do you know about her?"

The man's squinty eyes widened at the tab and he licked his lips wetly. Scratching at a red patch of skin on his neck, he mumbled, "Well, what do you wanna know? Like I said, she was a cheeky little brat, always wanted more than her stuff was worth. I would have kicked her out a long time ago if she and her little friend hadn't always brought in some of the best junk."

"Little friend?"

"Yeah, the boy. Everyone called him Squirt, 'cuz he was so small. Timid kid, never much for talking when they came in here. Used to follow Eryyn around like he was her shadow." The man finished scratching and wiped at his nose before pointing a finger at Flint. "But you shouldn't let that fool you. *He's* the one who was the talent in the pair. He had real skill when it came to getting loot. Good kleptos, the two of 'em. Hated going Dead-End, always worked the Mid houses and markets. Always brought in nice stuff."

"Where are they now?"

"Don't rightly know. The little bastards ran off after I tried to give them some help. I have connections, you know? I watch the kids, see what they bring in and sometimes set the better ones up with a friend of mine. The kids end up in his gangs and ply their trades for him and I get a little something for my troubles." He grinned slyly and stuck his thumbs in the waistband of his pants. "After Eryyn and Squirt sold to me for awhile I figured I'd set them up too. I knew it'd be worth my while. But the ungrateful little jerks didn't wanna cooperate. They ran out and ain't been back since. No gratitude for someone just trying to do them a favor."

Flint ground his teeth together impatiently. "So you have no idea where they would be now?"

"No. Why, they in trouble for something? I'm sure I could find them. I have connections." His eyes twinkled with greed. "Eryyn and Squirt taking a hike cost me a few kleptos, but I still have a bunch of kids who can come up with answers if the price is right."

"That won't be necessary. I doubt you'd be of any more help to me." Flint let go of the credit tab and watched it drop towards the counter. It was snatched up before it landed and the broker stuffed it into his shirt pocket.

"You're sure there's nothing else you wanna know?" he asked, wiping his hand under his nose again and looking at Flint with his piggy little eyes.

"Unless you can tell me where they are now, no." The bounty hunter turned to leave and the broker called out to him.

"If you change your mind, you know where I am. And lots of the kids know me by name, just ask for Master John and it'll get back to me!"

Flint kept walking, and slammed the door behind him.

• • •

"Okay, five minutes in…ready?"

Sawyer stared across the street, watching a small sparrow as it pecked at a large chunk of dry bread. As he looked on, a larger bird, this one with black, oily feathers, swooped down from a lamppost and attacked the little sparrow, driving it away with its sharp beak. Then it grabbed the bread and flew off, disappearing.

"Hey! Sawyer! Wake up!" A hand slapped Sawyer's shoulder and he jumped, blinking.

"What?" he asked Jay as he rubbed his smarting shoulder. "What was that for?"

"Did you even hear a word I just said to you?"

Sawyer frowned. "Yeah, you told me to wake up."

"Good, I'm glad it worked. Are we going to hit this house now, or are you gonna keep bird watching?"

Sawyer thought back a few moments, remembering that he and Jay had planned to hit a house on Fifty-Third Street, and then… He blushed. "Sorry, Jay. I didn't mean to zone off. No more bird watching."

Jay nodded. "Okay." He glanced at the crow across the street and shook his head. "Besides, the big one always kicks the little one's butt anyway. Come on…" They both turned to Rick, who bent at the waist and looped his hands together. Sawyer stepped up onto his palms and let the larger boy boost him up through an open window. Once inside, he turned and leaned back out so Jay could catch his wrists and pull himself up. A second later, Jay whistled out the window, signaling to Rick who went to hide in some bushes until they were finished.

"I'll go down the hall that way," Jay said, pointing out the direction, "and you start here, 'kay?"

"Uh huh." Sawyer slipped into the nearest room and surveyed the goods. An office. He loved offices. Lots of little machines and equipment that the brokers went mad over. The first thing he saw was a mini organizing computer. He nipped it, then looked at the big computer on the desk. Sometimes computers had pieces that could be stolen and sold as parts, but Sawyer didn't know which ones were useful. Instead, he found more interesting little gadgets, like a handheld game and a silver letter opener. He took all the little things he could find, then moved across the hall to a family room. The TV, he knew, was out of the question. He could never hope to get his arms around it, let alone lift it. But the little statues and knickknacks speckled around on the shelves were a different story and several of them went into his bag, along with a portable music player with earphones. He nodded with satisfaction. Already the hit had been successful and would cash in well, and he hadn't even seen what Jay was getting.

By then, the five minutes were nearly up, so Sawyer made his way to the hall to wait for Jay. A few minutes went by and the boy didn't show. Curious, Sawyer headed down the hall in the direction his friend had gone, looking into each room as he went. He finally found him in a bedroom, sitting on the floor, staring at a picture.

"Jay?" he asked, stepping across the room to crouch down beside the boy.

Jay glanced up and his blue eyes were troubled. "A kid our age lives here, did you know that?"

Sawyer shook his head. "How do you know?"

Jay held out the picture. It was of a family standing by a big pool of water—a lake. A young woman with frizzy brown hair, a tall man with black hair, and a small girl, all smiling and waving happily.

"Don't you wish, sometimes, that it was you in the picture?" Jay asked. "Don't you wish that you were the one with the family and you were out having fun, having your picture taken, seeing stuff outside the city?"

"All the time," Sawyer mumbled.

"It'd be great, wouldn't it? To have a mom and dad and to live in a house and sleep in a bed. No more gangs, no more Enforcers, no more stealing."

"No more fighting."

"Huh?" Jay glanced up, puzzled for a second. Then he understood and nodded. "Yeah."

"We have to go, Jay. It's been more than five minutes, Rick'll be mad."

Jay heaved a sigh. "'Kay." He climbed to his feet and dropped the picture onto the bed. "What did you get?"

"Bunch of stuff from an office. Eryyn'll like it. You?"

"The parents' bedroom was through there." Jay pointed across the hall. "Some jewelry and clothes."

"Let's go." Sawyer took the boy's hand and pulled him back to the window where they had entered. Jay scrambled through first, using Sawyer's hand to lower himself to the ground, then reached up to help the smaller boy. Once out, they hurried to the bushes, where Rick, looking nervous, was waiting.

"I told you five minutes," he said, tweaking Sawyer's ear for disobedience. "What took you so long?"

"Stopped to look at a picture," Jay replied truthfully.

Rick looked confused for a moment, then decided against asking anymore questions. "Come on, let's get back to the nest so Eryyn can sort through the stuff."

As they sneaked out of the bushes and crossed the street to the other sidewalk, Sawyer noticed that a crow—the same one?—had returned to the place where the bread had been. It started pecking at another bit of food on the ground, but was interrupted by a flock of sparrows, which flew out of a nearby tree and attacked the crow with many loud chirps and vicious stabs of small beaks. The crow was easily outnumbered and took to the air, cawing loudly as it escaped.

Intrigued, Sawyer pointed the scene out to Jay, who watched with a small grin, his brows raised.

"Sometimes," Sawyer said brightly, "the little ones can kick back!"

• • •

Flint took his time walking though the marketplace to his recent apartment. He considered his day well spent. Already he had learned where the two kids normally worked and where they would possibly have their nests. He would head to those particular neighborhoods in the morning and continue his search. Once he found kids with green armbands he would be set, for no one would know where the girl and boy were better than their own gang.

Green armbands. After all these years, the kids were still stupid enough to display their friendships and alliances. It just made it easier to track them and gather information. He'd learned that lesson during his own childhood, when he'd been one of the kids he was now hunting. Back then, even though he'd been in a gang, he'd worked only for himself. Gangs were dangerous—most kids thought they were protected by them, but, in fact, they just made a person vulnerable.

Kids in the gang came to depend on one another. They made friends and shared stories and started to trust. The major thing Flint had learned in his own time on the street was that, to survive, there could be no trust. Because if you trusted someone they held your life in their hands.

So Flint had taken care of himself, had done his duty for the gang, gotten his status, and had stayed alive. The only time he had ever volunteered help for his gang was when a rival had started pressing into their territory and they'd had to fight back. He'd killed for the first time then, and he'd killed intelligently.

While the other kids had been fighting their battles in the alleys, Flint had watched and waited, studying the leader of the rival gang from afar. He had learned that the boy was the planner, the brain of the group. He came up with all the ideas, made all the decisions, ruled supreme over all his kids. That had been his mistake.

Flint had followed him one day, tracked him from his strong-hold, shadowing him all day as he went about his routine. The kid, a fifteen-year-old as Flint remembered, had gone to work, 'pocket-ing with two other kids from his gang, joking and laughing and talking about the losers that made up Flint's gang. Half the day had passed before the kid made another mistake. A mistake which turned out to be fatal.

The boy had left his friends and gone off on his own, deciding to take a short cut through an alley to get back to his stronghold. He had never noticed twelve-year-old Flint following him off the streets. Never heard the smaller boy walking quietly behind him.

Flint hadn't hesitated to bring the brick down on the teen's head and, after collecting something for proof, hadn't even waited to see if the rival boy would stir again. He'd gone back to his own gang's stronghold and told them what he had done. And the next day, the rival gang broke apart. Without a leader to direct them, they didn't know how to continue with their territory war. They were a body that had lost the heart and the head.

The victory had raised Flint in status again and many of the kids called for him to lead them—to break away and start his own gang. He did leave the gang, but he went on his own, realizing that none of the kids had learned anything from the victory. They wanted a leader, someone to follow, but Flint would not let himself fall into a position that would leave him like the other boy, struck from behind in an alley. He became independent.

Dependence had cost that long ago gang their victory, and their leader his life. Dependence could possibly work again now. He could probably count on the green band gang to hover around their leader, seeking her advice, making her noticeable after a time. Then, as he had done long ago, he would set his trap and he would strike.

Flint smiled grimly at the thought and reached into his pocket where he always carried the token he had stolen from his victim in the alley. It had been the symbol of the gang, the item that had distinguished them from all the other gangs. Just a plain strip of cloth, it had been tied around the boy's upper arm in a band. The color of the cloth, curiously, was dark green.

ELEVEN

The trap is set

After the disastrous meeting with Liz, Sawyer and Eryyn avoided each other for several days. It wasn't difficult anymore, given how large the gang had managed to grow—they simply went off each day with different kids, instead of with each other. As the days passed, Sawyer noticed that he was spending more and more time with Jay and Dillan, while Eryyn's clique included Cinder, Rick, and Foxy.

It hurt, once he realized it, but Sawyer didn't say anything. And if she had noticed, Eryyn said nothing either.

So the days went by and they continued their plan against the Foreman, and it seemed to be working. More kids joined until the nest became overcrowded at night and Eryyn decided to move to a different location. Kids who had originally turned down the idea of Eryyn's gang started to think better about it and came back for another try, while kids from rival gangs ditched their leaders so they could join up with the green bands.

Their new nest was an apartment that had been damaged in a fire and abandoned. Three stories high, it had plenty of room for the number of kids who sought shelter there each night. The old nest was gutted of anything useful and left alone.

And each day, the kids went out to scour the streets for loot. They had to be more careful now—with thirty kids wearing green bands on their arms, people could begin to make connections. But

Eryyn solved that problem by assigning shifts to the kids, keeping half in the nest one day, resting while the other half went out, and then switching. It worked well, and Rogers, the pawnbroker, and his wife, Delle quit complaining each time Eryyn dropped by with stuff to sell. Their business had never been better.

And still, Sawyer managed to meet with Liz at the park. The Agency house was finished—stocked with blankets and clothes, toys and books, school supplies and food. Liz wanted to get children to move in, and she wanted Sawyer's help with that, but each day he refused. Finally, her impatience got the better of her.

"Why not!" she snapped, slamming her fists onto the arms of the bench. A flock of pigeons nearby cooed with alarm and took off, flying away clumsily. Sawyer, looking equally shocked, slid slightly away from Liz on the seat and lowered his eyes miserably.

"I can't," he whispered. "Not yet. Soon, but not yet."

"That's not a good answer, Sawyer."

"I know it's not!" Sawyer cried. "I know! But I can't help it, Liz. I promised her!"

"Promised her what?"

Sawyer took a deep breath and mumbled, "That I wouldn't talk to any of the other kids about the Agency until Eryyn wants me too." He sank lower onto the bench, wishing he could disappear, hating the incredulous look Liz was giving him.

"Why…why would Eryyn make you promise that? And more importantly, why would you agree to such a promise?"

"You wouldn't understand," Sawyer whispered miserably.

"Would you at least try me before you decide that?"

Dropping his face into his hands, Sawyer explained the promise he and Eryyn had made days before, right after Eryyn had met Liz for the first time. Then he fell into a depressed silence while Liz mulled over his words. After several minutes, she reached out and took his hand. Sawyer flinched a little but didn't pull away. Instead, he lifted his eyes to look at her.

"You're mad at me now, aren't you?"

Liz paused, then shook her head. "No. I'm frustrated, but I'm not mad. I want to open the Agency *now*, but at least Eryyn said she would help soon."

Sawyer shook his head sadly. "You just don't know Eryyn like I do."

"You think she lied, don't you? You think she'll break her promise?"

"She's done it before." Sawyer shrugged. "She lied when she thought it would help her. And she doesn't really like the idea of the Agency because she thinks it'll make her lose her gang. She likes being a leader."

"Maybe if I had another chance to talk to her…"

"What good would that do? After the way she acted before…"

"I could try to convince her that the Agency is the best thing— that it's better than any gang she could form."

"It wouldn't work. Eryyn's head is like a rock when she's stuck to an idea. She won't budge."

"I still want to try. I want to talk to her again. Maybe…" Liz glanced at the paper bag that sat on the bench beside Sawyer. It was the breakfast she had brought him, forgotten and uneaten. "What if I invited you both to my house for dinner? Eryyn could meet Greg and we could all talk and Eryyn might realize that I'm not a bad person."

Sawyer squirmed on the bench, uncertain. "I-I don't think she'd want to go."

Liz reached around the boy and picked up the bag. "What if I promised to make a *big* dinner and gave her all the leftovers for your gang?"

Sawyer thought that over. "She *might* go for that, if she thought it would be good for the gang."

"Would you ask her?"

The boy nodded emphatically. "I can try. All she'll do is yell at me. And half the time she finds some reason to do that anyway."

Liz chuckled. "Can you make it, let's say, day after tomorrow? That'll give you time to talk to Eryyn and then tomorrow I can make some directions to show you how to reach my home. It'll also make it harder for her to change her mind, after she says yes."

Before he left to head back to the nest, Sawyer leaned over and hugged Liz tightly. "It just might work," he whispered. "I'll see you tomorrow."

• • •

"This stinks."

Startled out of a pleasant daydream in which he was an independent klepto, Rane glanced up from the bracelets he was sorting and focused on Caulin, "What does?" he asked.

"This!" Caulin indicated the small pile of loot in front of them. "Why should we have to sit here doing this?"

Rane shook his head wearily and looked back down at the bracelets. Otto just seemed bent on making his life as miserable as possible. Not only was he expected to wait on the gang leader hand and foot, as Dillan had once pointed out, but now he had to train the new kid in the rules and methods of the gang. And he was quickly finding out that Caulin was not just a blabbermouth...he was a whiner too.

"Just do the work," he said after a moment. "It doesn't go away if you sit and complain about it."

Caulin muttered some insult about taking orders from kids who were younger than him, but he went back to sorting.

Ten minutes later they were finished and had packed the loot into the box that would be handed over to the Foreman later on. As they stood up, Rane looked into the box nervously. It was a pitiful amount and the Foreman would not be pleased. In fact, the last two payments had been pitiful as well. They had lost several more members to the green bands, despite Otto's precautions and threats, and the kids that still remained seemed to have lost most of their fear of Otto and didn't work as much as they used to.

That left Otto and Sasha, still loyal to the Foreman, to do most of the work, along with Rane and Caulin, who were too scared of Otto to disobey. But the four of them had trouble maintaining the quota that the Foreman expected each payment day and Otto's temper, never too steady to begin with, was beginning to truly wear thin. The gang was falling apart around them.

"Will you two hurry it up! You don't have to take all day with that junk!" Sasha suddenly appeared in the doorway, looking anxious and annoyed. Rane handed her the box.

"We're done. But sorting didn't make it any better."

Sasha glanced into the box and paled slightly. Normally the box, and another like it, would have been full.

"This isn't good," she murmured, looking up at Rane. "We need more."

Rane held up his hands helplessly. "There isn't anymore," he said, and gestured towards Caulin and the empty floor. "That's all we collected."

"The Foreman's gonna be mad."

Caulin pulled in a sharp breath and Rane glanced at him. "Glad you joined up?" he asked sarcastically. Caulin gaped at him, wringing his hands. Then he lowered his eyes. Rane knew he was regretting his decision.

Sasha noticed the tension between the two boys, but said nothing about it. Instead, she pressed her hand against Rane's back and gave him a push towards the door. "Go find Otto and tell him about this."

Rane stumbled under the shove and scowled darkly at the girl. "Yeah, that's right, send me. That way he won't be mad at *you*."

"Get going!"

Rane rolled his eyes and left the room, dreading the wrath that would be directed at him when Otto got the message. When he reached the door of Otto's room, he knocked timidly. There was no answer. He knocked again, louder.

"Come in."

Rane pushed open the door and stepped into the room. It was dark inside—Otto hadn't turned on any lights and the only illumination came from the now open door. After a moment of letting his eyes adjust, Rane spotted Otto lying on the sofa.

"This better be good, Raney boy. I'm not in the mood to be annoyed."

Stepping away from the door, allowing more light to enter the dim room, Rane shrugged. "It's not good."

"What is it?"

"The payment box isn't full. Not even by half. We don't have enough to make quota."

Otto sat up slowly and rubbed at his eyes. Gesturing towards the chair behind his desk, he told Rane to sit.

"We did what we could." the twelve-year-old said as he pulled the chair closer to the sofa and sat down. "But we just don't have as many kids as we used to and a lot of the ones who are left don't bother bringing in good stuff anymore. They figure if you threaten them, they can always…"

"I know what they figure, *Raney boy*. I don't need a shrimpie little klepto to tell me."

Rane stared at him, holding his tongue, and eventually Otto sighed.

"What do you expect me to do?" he asked angrily. "Do you think I should march out there and tell the Foreman that we can't make the quota and he shouldn't be mad at us?"

"I don't know," Rane muttered, playing with the loose plastic covering on the arm of his chair. "It's not *my* gang. I never asked to be a part of this."

"No, you just got lucky."

"Bad luck."

Otto laughed bitterly. "Yeah, bad luck all around, thanks to Eryyn."

Rane looked at his hands for a long time before getting up the courage to murmur, "I wish I were in *her* gang. Not the Foreman's."

This time, Otto's laugh was light, full of humor. "Right now, Raney boy, I'm thinking the same thing."

"Really?" Rane glanced around apprehensively, as if saying such a thing would get them in trouble. "But I thought…"

"You thought nothing. Just because I'm a gang leader doesn't mean I have to like taking orders from the Foreman. The guy scares the crud out of me."

"S-so what are you gonna do?" Rane asked, trying to hide his shock at this admission.

Otto shrugged his shoulders. "Don't know. Blame it on you?"

"I wouldn't be surprised." Now it was Rane's turn to be bitter. "I've kinda missed being in the closet; maybe this is my chance to go back there."

"Don't go getting all hackled. The Foreman wouldn't believe me anyway." Otto stood up and stretched, groaning loudly as he raised his arms over his head. "I'll go check out the box. If anything, we can try to fit in a fast hit before payment is due. I doubt it, but it's worth a try. In the meantime, go get me something to eat."

Rane also stood. "There isn't anything. Sasha made us put all the loot in the box; we didn't save anything to get food."

Otto swore under his breath and Rane instantly took a step back. "Then make yourself useful and get me something to drink. We have *water*, don't we?"

Rane bobbed his head.

"Then get me some water, bring it to the meeting room."

Still nodding, Rane left the room.

By the time he brought the water to the meeting room, Otto had already had a chance to survey the box of loot. He didn't look happy. Rane handed him the cup, which he took absently.

"We have a problem," he finally said. "There's no way we can make quota with this, even if we *did* do another hit."

"So what do we do?" Sasha asked.

For once, Otto had no answer. Instead, the four of them sat in the room silently as the hours ticked by, until the time came when the Foreman stepped through the door. Even then, as the man took his customary place in the shadowed alcove, Rane, Sasha, and Caulin didn't move. Only Otto stepped forward to push the box within the man's reach.

"This is all?" the Foreman asked in his low, dry voice.

"It's all we could get in time," Otto replied. "I know it doesn't make quota, but we had no choice, there just aren't enough of us to..."

A hand raised itself out of the shadows, silencing him. "It doesn't matter...this time. The trouble with the other gang will soon be settled and then business will resume as normal."

"Settled?" Sasha asked. "How?"

"I have taken care of it. In a few more days, the green bands will be only a memory in this city. Be assured of that."

"What are you gonna do?" Rane blurted, forgetting for a moment that he was speaking to the Foreman. He leaned back when he felt the gaze center on him. "My methods are not of your concern, *boy*," the Foreman growled. "All you need to think about is how you will fill this box once I have gotten rid of the problem."

Beside him, Rane felt Caulin tense and start to tremble. He knew what the older boy was thinking. The Foreman sounded so *sure* of himself. He felt that his method was foolproof. And if it was, it didn't mean any good for Eryyn. Swallowing past a lump in his throat, Rane risked a quick glance at Caulin. There were tears in the boy's eyes and he didn't bother to wipe them away, even when he realized Rane was looking at him and returned the gaze.

Feeling sorry for what you did? Rane thought bitterly. *You should. Hope you don't expect any pity from me.*

As if sensing what Rane was thinking, Caulin tore his gaze away and focused it on his hands. For the rest of the Foreman's visit, he stayed in that position, refusing to lift his eyes, or dry them of the tears that kept trickling down to drip off his nose. Only when the Foreman left, taking the box of loot with him, did he look up and drag a wrist over his eyes.

"He's gonna kill her, isn't he?" he asked, looking desperately at the three other children in the room. "He's got it all planned. He's gonna kill Eryyn, and probably Squirt too, and it's all my fault."

Otto and Sasha merely shrugged, then stood up and left the room. Just as he walked through the door, Otto called back for Rane to come with them. Rane jumped up quickly, glad to avoid Caulin's pleading, unhappy gaze.

This is *all your fault, Caulin,* his thoughts raced through his head as he followed Otto into the hall. *If you hadn't told the Foreman everything, then he wouldn't have a chance at catching Eryyn.*

But even as they left the boy sitting in the room, and Otto called out for one of the other kleptos to go and keep an eye on Caulin, Rane realized that he did feel sorry for him. It really wasn't *all* Caulin's fault. It was Otto's too, for convincing Caulin that the Foreman could be trusted. And possibly it was his *own* fault as well, for being such a wimp and standing by Otto, even as the gang leader spouted off all his lies.

Sighing heavily, Rane squeezed his eyes closed and rubbed at them with his fists. What he wouldn't give for things to go back to the way they were a few months ago. Now, everything was losing control.

"Hurry up, Rane! Let's go!"

Startled, Rane looked up to see Otto and Sasha standing by the door that led outside. Both were looking back, waiting for him to catch up.

Why are we going out? he wondered, as he hopped forward and moved a little faster. *Collecting? Doubt it. There's no way we can get enough for the next quota with just the three of us.*

"Where are we going?" he asked, reaching the two. Otto and Sasha turned together and stepped outside. Rane followed, just a step behind. "What's the use of going out collecting now? There's no way we could get enough to reach the quota, and the Foreman is gone now, he isn't expecting…"

"We're not going collecting," Otto answered over his shoulder. "We're going to find Eryyn."

Rane stopped in his tracks and gaped at them. "What?"

"Come on!" Sasha backtracked a couple of steps and grabbed Rane by the arm, pulling him into motion again. "We don't have a lot of time."

"But…but…" Rane found he could only stammer, but Otto seemed to have guessed his question.

"It's like I said back in the room, Raney boy, I don't like taking orders from that jerk, the Foreman. This business with Eryyn is probably the best thing that happened to us. Finally that guy is scared, he thinks he's gonna lose everything."

"And he will too," said Sasha, picking up on Otto's train of thought. "Eryyn's kids are good. Just the other day, Denny tried to nab one of the smaller green bands and suddenly two bigger ones showed up and scared him off. Those kids are *safe*. Safer than *anyone* in one of the Foreman's gangs."

"So, it's better for us if Eryyn's gang keeps working, and the only way it'll do that is if Eryyn is their leader. Which means that we have to find her and warn her about the Foreman's plan, even though we don't know exactly what it is. That way, Eryyn can go into hiding or something."

Rane looked at Otto with wide eyes. "How will you know how to find Eryyn?"

"Not sure. But Eryyn and I used to be real close. If we find a green band, we may be able to get to her."

Rane almost scoffed at the idea, it seemed so impossible. "What makes you think they'll believe you? You're the leader of a *rival* gang, remember?"

Otto looked at him witheringly. "I'm aware of that, Rane. But she'll believe me. I know she will."

Skipping forward a step until he was side by side with Otto, Rane looked the sixteen-year-old in the eye. "Why? And why is it better for us if she stays in business?"

Otto paused for a moment, his face straight, thoughtful, and very serious. "Because, after I find her, I'm going to tell her all the Foreman's plans, and warn her to keep low for awhile. And after that, I'm going to ask if I can join the remainder of my gang with hers and leave the Foreman for good."

• • •

The Foreman had gone away in good spirits after Flint had given his report. It wouldn't be long now. Thanks to some of the street kids and local brokers he had questioned, apparently there were some in the city beside the Foreman who didn't care about what Eryyn and her gang were accomplishing, he had been able to pinpoint the area where Eryyn and Sawyer frequently worked and wandered. While stalking through that area, he had found and followed several kids wearing green bands, walking carefully behind them as they went about their daily business. He watched them as they scoured the marketplace and the plazas, saw them 'pocket from unknowing passersby. He trailed them into the upper Mid-End, where he stood at a safe distance while they did hits on houses, carrying away small machines, clothing, and in some cases, food. Only when they were loaded down with loot did they take another route, heading back to the center of the Mid-End, through it, and into a small neighborhood. From their furtive glances while they walked, he guessed that they were finished with their jobs for the day and were going home. Usually a gang kid would report to their leader when they were finished collecting, which meant that he only had to follow them for a few more minutes and they would lead him straight to Eryyn and the boy. Patience now would pay off better than anything else. Patience, and stealth.

The kids were unaware that he was shadowing them. They hadn't noticed the man in the green t-shirt and baseball cap standing a few feet away while they were lifting wallets in the plaza. They hadn't seen the man, minus the cap and with the addition of a new coat, leaning against the tree across the street from the house they'd broken into. And they didn't see the man, minus the coat but wearing a gray sweatshirt now, walking ten yards behind them as they entered the alley that led up to the side-door that served for the entrance of the new nest.

Standing by a trash can, half hidden, Flint's eyes glittered slightly in the dim light as he observed the kids through a window, watching them gather in the large room that served as their meeting area. Only when they were completely out of sight did he move forward again, slinking along the wall until he was directly across from the window and could see almost all that occurred within.

Six or seven kids sat or stood about, talking, laughing, enjoying themselves. The two he'd followed were both kneeling, cleaning out their bags of all their loot. Another kid was with them—a girl, tall, thin, with shoulder length brownish-blonde hair. Eryyn? He couldn't be sure yet.

Still moving silently and cautiously, he stepped away from the alley wall and crossed over until he was pressed up against the building that housed the children. Now he could easily see into the room and counted more than ten young kleptos hanging around. And now, close as he was, he was able to hear what was being said inside the room.

"The watch is worth something, I'm sure of that. The casing is gold, I know by the color. Not plating. But I'm not sure about the ring," one boy was saying.

The girl beside him, his partner and one of the kids Flint had tailed, glanced at him, her eyes narrowing. "You're only saying that, Andy, because *I* got the rings and *you* got the watch. They're both worth a lot! I know it! Aren't they, Eryyn?"

Flint perked up at the name and his lips formed a smirk as the girl kneeling on the floor beside the two, the one with the brown hair, looked up.

"It doesn't really matter what we think they're worth. It's what the brokers think. I know brokers who refused to take prime stuff, just 'cuz they thought it would get them in trouble. Sometimes lower quality loot is easier to sell, even if it does bring a lower price." She stood and dusted off her pants. "But it's a good haul, whichever way you look at it."

While the two kids beamed at her words, Eryyn sidled off to one of the walls where two boys were arguing. She spent a few minutes with them, talking softly, until their argument seemed cleared up, then she moved on, heading this time towards a girl and a boy who were working near a small stove.

Such a good little leader, Flint thought amusedly. *Takes care of everyone.*

A sudden noise at the end of the alley, just where the small pathway met the street, alerted Flint and he hastily backed away from the window and ducked behind a pile of crates.

And none too soon either, as a boy pelted past him, breathing hard and fast as if he had been running for a long distance, and launched himself up the stairs to the door. Flint peeked out from his hiding place as the boy scrambled into the apartment and noted, just before the child vanished from sight, that the boy wasn't wearing a green band on his arm. Stepping away from the crates, Flint again took up a position by the window and began his watch.

The boy burst into the meeting room, stopping before the window, and would have been blocking the view if he hadn't been bent over, clutching his knees as he tried to catch his breath. For a few minutes nothing special happened. Then the boy crossed the room to Eryyn and grabbed her by the arm, pulling her into a corner where he began to speak in hushed tones. The girl listened to him carefully, her arms crossed over her chest, her head cocked to one side. She shook her head a few times, narrowed her eyes and started to speak, but the boy cut her off, clapping a hand over her mouth as he began to talk faster, possibly trying to get out all he wanted to say before she could refuse something. Finally, he fell silent, and the girl stood still, staring at him for a long moment before finally nodding.

Whatever she had agreed too, it made the boy ecstatic, for he threw his arms around her neck and hugged her tight, nearly throwing her off balance. After a long moment of what Flint figured were sincere, babbled thanks, the boy moved away across the room, heading for a small pallet nestled in a corner. He had almost reached it, and was just passing close to the window, when another boy, this one much larger and better muscled, suddenly stood up from lounging on the floor. Not looking where he was going, he bumped into the younger boy and almost knocked him off his feet.

"Rick!" the smaller boy yelped as he struggled to stay upright. "Watch where you're going, you big lump!"

The larger kid, Rick, laughed and slapped his friend on the back.

"Sorry, Squirt," he said between chuckles. "Didn't see you."

Flint's grin widened. The boy's nickname was supposed to be Squirt. Eryyn's friend, and partner in the making of the green band gang. Small kid, not one Flint would expect as a leader. The name Squirt fit him well, and now Flint knew exactly who he was hunting. The rest of the job would be simple.

Leaving the window, the bounty hunter picked his way through the alley until he found a spot nestled between two trash cans that would allow him to remain hidden, yet still gave him full view of the window and who went in and out. He settled himself down into the narrow place and resigned himself to wait. All he had to do was watch carefully now for the boy and Eryyn to leave and he could follow them without the trouble of the rest of their group. Sooner or later the opportunity to attack would come, and when it did, he would be there to take full advantage.

• • •

Jay and Cinder were working the marketplace, 'pocketing during the afternoon break when most people left their businesses and jobs to walk around in the air and do a little window-shopping. Having a successful day so far, the two had decided to take a break of their own and were leaning against the front of a hat shop, sharing a large sandwich bought at a stand, talking and joking about the adults walking by. Cinder was just pointing out a young couple dressed in matching, brightly colored, checkered shirts—a perfect target for a few well placed insults and jokes—when three strange kids approached them.

Two of the kids were older—the larger boy was about sixteen or seventeen, the girl maybe a year or two younger. The smaller boy looked about Jay's age. All three wore bands of red and gold on their arms.

"C'mon, let's get out of here. I don't like the company," Cinder muttered once she had recognized the gang insignia. Not liking the three-to-two odds, she nudged Jay's shoulder and they both climbed to their feet to walk away.

"Hey, hold up a minute. We need to talk to you," the older boy's voice called out.

Cinder paused for a moment, looking back, while Jay glanced through the crowd, spotting two more green bands several shops away. He gave Cinder a slight, meaningful nod. If the Foreman's kids wanted to cause trouble, then Jay could whistle for reinforcements in a heartbeat.

Nodding back, Cinder turned her attention to the three strangers. Placing her hands on her hips, she demanded, "What do *you* want?"

The older boy held out his hands disarmingly. "You don't have to get all prickly, we're not gonna hurt you or anything. We just need to talk."

Cinder caught his use of the word *need* instead of *want*. Her interest was piqued. Was it possible that more red/gold kids wanted to join up with the green bands? Facing the tall boy, she asked, "About what?"

"About Eryyn. She's in trouble."

Jay swallowed and caught Cinder's eye in a silent question. She shook her head, telling him not to whistle for help, not just yet.

"And what do you know about Eryyn?" she asked, turning a shrewd eye back to the teenage boy and his two followers. "You're one of the Foreman's kids."

"Yes, I happen to be aware of that, thank you. My name is Otto and I'm the leader of the red and gold gang. This," he indicated the girl at his side, "is Sasha, my second. And the short one is Rane. I used to be a good friend of Eryyn's and I want to help her now."

"I've heard of you," Jay piped up, crossing his arms over his chest. "You're not Eryyn's friend now. She wants nothing to do with you."

"I need to find her."

Cinder and Jay laughed loudly, drawing looks from some of the people passing by. "Yeah right," Cinder scoffed. "Like we'd be dumb enough to let you anywhere near Eryyn. All you want to do is nab kids so your own gang gets bigger."

"You won't get any green bands," Jay added vehemently. "We can tell you that right now."

Otto was beginning to get impatient. "I don't *want* to nab any of your stupid green bands, just listen to me for a moment, alright!"

"He's telling the truth! Eryyn really *is* in trouble. The Foreman's after her," the boy called Rane spoke up, looking at them both with wide, serious eyes. "You have to listen to him, please! He can help her!"

"And why should we trust you?" Cinder looked scathingly at the red/gold band that Rane had wound around his right wrist, where his I.D. bracelet would have been if he'd been legal.

"Because we know more about the Foreman than you ever will," Otto replied.

"Not true," Jay retorted. "Dillan and Kit were part of your gang. They were the first red and golds to join up with us, and we've had more since. *They've* told us lots about the Foreman and what he does to the kids in his gangs."

"Then you should know that if the Foreman wants to go after Eryyn, she's in a lot of trouble," Rane shot back.

Cinder and Jay fell silent at that. They glanced at each other, suddenly uncertain.

Otto sighed and held up his hands in a gesture of helplessness. "Look, Eryyn was my friend. I have nothing against her and, right now, I like her a lot more than I like the Foreman. If you'll just bring her the message that I want to see her, it would save us all a lot of trouble. Tell her that I want to help…and that I'm willing to join my gang with hers and let her be the leader of everyone."

Jay and Cinder gaped at him.

"Are you serious?" Jay asked, a look of absolute awe on his young face. "You'll really give up being a leader and take orders from Eryyn?"

"If it gets me out from under the Foreman's thumb, yeah. My whole gang."

For a moment, Cinder looked troubled. She unconsciously scratched the scar over her eye, then said, "We can't take you back to the nest. We're not dumb. But we'll talk to Eryyn and let her figure everything out for herself."

"Tell her that I need to see her. That I don't want to hurt her or nab her or anything. She can bring as many of her gang as she wants and I'll meet her anywhere—the market, the plazas… her choice."

Cinder nodded. "Fair enough. And she will bring her gang with her, and, from my reckoning, we're bigger than the red/golds now, so if you're lying and try anything stupid…"

"We're not lying. I just wish you'd take me to see her now, when you're sure there's only three of us, that way there won't be any time wasted."

"Can't do that," Jay said, shaking his head stubbornly.

Otto sighed again, but nodded, resigned. "Then tell her. As soon as you can. Now."

"We're busy," Cinder said haughtily, not appreciating the orders from a kid who wasn't even a member of her own gang.

"Oh, yeah, you both looked real busy when we walked up and you were leaning against the wall, laughing," Sasha snapped. "This is no joke, can't you understand that? This Eryyn girl is in trouble, and if Otto thinks joining the gangs is the best idea, you should listen to him."

Cinder was about to say something back, but Jay put a hand on her shoulder, stopping her. "Maybe we should listen to them and head back now, Cin. If the Foreman really *is* after Eryyn, and I wouldn't doubt it, then she's gonna need the warning."

"Fine," Cinder replied shortly, pulling away from the smaller boy. "But how do we make sure these three aren't just lying and waiting for us to go back to the nest so they can follow us?"

Jay answered that question by whistling shrilly for the two kids he'd seen across the market. They joined them immediately and Jay explained what was going on. The two kids looked at Otto with large, amazed eyes.

"We're gonna head back and try to warn Eryyn. We need you two to stay here and make sure Otto and his friends don't try and follow us."

"Can do," said Foxy, giving Otto another careful look. "Better hurry, I think Eryyn was planning to go out somewhere. With Squirt. He seemed pretty excited about it."

"Right," Cinder turned back to Otto, resting a hand briefly on his arm. "I hope you're telling the truth. And if you are, thanks. We'll see you soon with an answer. C'mon, Jay!"

Jay flashed Otto, Sasha, and Rane a quick smile, then took off behind Cinder, running through the marketplace, heading back to the nest.

"Think she'll believe you?" Rane asked, watching them disappear into the crowd.

"For her own good, she'd better," Otto replied. "It's not smart to play around when the Foreman is involved."

• • •

"And just how are we going to get to this place, Squirt? Do you even know where her house is?" Eryyn was tracing a pattern in the dust covering a rarely used corner of the nest floor. She blew lightly on the drawing, scattering the fine silt, then glanced up at the boy kneeling beside her, her brows raised questioningly.

Sawyer was already nodding. "Um, yeah. After you said yes, I went to the Agency house and…"

"You went there?"

"I've been there a lot. I've been helping Liz with some of the stuff. Anyway, I found her there and told her and she gave me this." Sawyer held up a piece of paper with writing on it. "Directions to her house in the Mid-End."

"Where exactly?"

Sawyer read off the directions to her and Eryyn nodded. "I haven't been there a lot, but I *think* I know where it is. It's not the best neighborhood in the Mid-End, but it's far from the worst." She smiled suddenly. "Guess she's not your Sky-End lady, is she?"

Sawyer scowled darkly. "She's better!"

Laughing, Eryyn punched the boy's arm. "I'm just teasing you, Squirt. Sheesh, you have no sense of humor anymore. Come on, let's go then." She started to climb to her feet.

"Now? It's early." Sawyer scrambled up beside her, his face confused.

"I don't really know exactly where her house is. I haven't been in that area much, so we have to take our time looking for it. Come on, I doubt she'll be mad if we get there a little early. She'll probably just ask us to help out."

"Kay." Sawyer shrugged, following her over to the door.

Just before she left the room, Eryyn turned back to Dillan, who was sitting in the middle of the floor with Kit and another girl named Lecia, plying a needle and thread to a badly torn blanket. "Dillan, Squirt and I are going out for awhile. I'm gonna leave you in charge until Rick or Cinder comes back, alright?"

Dillan looked up from his sewing and nodded. "Where are you

going?"

"There's a house up past the marketplace that I wanna check out. We'll bring back some food, okay?"

"Kay. See you later." Dillan turned back to his work, a grin on his lips at having been left in charge, even for a short time.

"Ready to go, Squirt?" Eryyn asked, turning to her partner, who was hopping from one foot to the other by the door.

"All set." Sawyer was grinning broadly as they stepped out onto the stairs. He hopped over the second step, which was broken, and landed lightly on the pavement

"I wonder what she's cooking for dinner," Eryyn mused as she nimbly stepped over the broken stair and they started walking up the alley. "I hope it's something good."

"Aw, you'd eat it even if it weren't. You'll eat anything," Sawyer joked. Eryyn laughed.

They wound their way through the trashcans and crates that filled the alley on their way to the street. In their preoccupation with what Liz had planned for the menu, they didn't notice the tall shadow that slipped out from between two cans, silently following them.

• • •

"I think this is it," Sawyer murmured, looking at the piece of paper in his hand and then at the number emblazoned on the outer wall of the house. "Unless we took a wrong turn somewhere."

"We didn't, this has to be it," Eryyn looked up at the house, her eyes wide and suddenly nervous. Sawyer, glancing at her, smiled wanly.

"She's not mad at you or anything. You don't have to be afraid of her. And Greg's nice too. He won't bite your head off."

"I'm not afraid!" Eryyn protested. "I'm just wondering if we are actually a little too early."

Sawyer rolled his eyes. "You said that she wouldn't mind."

"Well, you know her better than I do…"

"Right. She won't mind. Believe me."

"I do." But she didn't make any move to go up the stairs and knock on the door. Instead, she continued to stare at the house.

Sawyer could almost see her trembling.

"It'll be okay, Eryyn. Honestly."

"I know."

"Then why don't you move?"

"I'm working on it."

Sawyer groaned, grabbed her hand, and marched up the stairs, dragging her behind him. When they reached the door, he let her go, then knocked. Beside him, Eryyn chewed on her lip.

"She's really nice, Eryyn. She really is."

Eryyn was about to reply, but the door opened in a flood of yellowish light and Liz was looking down at them, smiling warmly.

• • •

Flint had followed the two through the city, wondering where they were going. It was obvious that they weren't out collecting—they didn't have the watchful look of kids who are afraid of getting caught doing something wrong, and they also kept consulting a piece of paper, as if they didn't know where their destination was. The place they finally stopped at wasn't the best house in the neighborhood. In fact, it was downright small. And to make matters more confusing, they stood outside for a moment, then walked up to the door, knocked, and were invited in by a young woman.

Very confusing. But it wasn't Flint's job to find out what the kids were doing in the woman's house. All he was being paid to do was sit and watch and wait for the perfect opportunity to grab them and bring them to the Foreman. He would have done it already, since they had gone off on their own with none of their gang tagging along, but it was still too light, too early, and too many people were around.

But that didn't mean he couldn't just sit outside the house and wait. They'd come out eventually. Hopefully at night. And then he'd have his chance.

The front steps of a building slightly down and across the street became his perch for the wait. It was ideal, away from immediate notice and in a shadow, thanks to a nearby street lamp. Flint lowered himself onto the fourth step and leaned back, staring at the door that had closed behind his prey. He hadn't slept in three days, but he didn't feel any fatigue. If anything, he was fully awake. Soon, very soon, he'd be able to make the catch. He could just feel it, and that instinct lent him energy. Very soon, the kids would be his.

• • •

"You know, Eryyn, from the way Sawyer described your friend-ship, I was always surprised that you never came with him when-ever he showed up at the Agency house." Liz's husband, Greg, was leaning on one elbow on the table, looking across at Eryyn while she moved a game piece along the board.

Eryyn glanced up from her piece and grinned. "I'm really busy, I have a lot of responsibility, so I don't go wandering around much anymore." She turned to Liz and her grin widened. "And you owe me five hundred credits." She pointed to the board and her piece on a certain colored square.

Dinner had been finished for more than an hour, but neither child was showing any inclination of wanting to leave, especially since Liz had suggested they play a few games. Board games un-known to them, Sawyer and Eryyn had agreed, mainly out of curi-osity but also because they were enjoying themselves.

Upon first entering the house, Liz had taken them on a tour of all the rooms, showing them the living room with the sofa and TV equipment; the kitchen, where dinner had been cooking; and the small, windowless room that the couple used as a storage and study. They also saw the bedroom with the neatly made bed, a chest of drawers, and a second, tiny TV set. Also on the chest was a small wooden box, which had drawn Eryyn's attention immediately. Liz, glad to have something to talk about, had shown her the few pieces of jewelry that she owned, including the necklace that had been passed down to her from her grandmother. At one point, she had even taken the delicate golden chain with the small purple stone pendant and had fastened it around Eryyn's neck, letting her look in a small mirror to see the faceted stone twinkle in the light.

Greg had returned from work soon after that and had been in-troduced to Eryyn. To Sawyer's relief and delight, his friend had gotten along with the man immediately and had spent much of the dinner chatting animatedly with him. The night had gone very well and, though nervous at first, eventually Sawyer had relaxed, deciding that Eryyn was not going to repeat the morning in the park and cause trouble. In fact, she was having such a good time that her eyes were glowing as she collected her brightly colored, fake, plastic credits from Liz and added them to her own pile.

"Your turn, Squirt," Eryyn said brightly, running her fingers through her money. Sawyer looked glumly at his own small stack of plastic credits. "Yippee, I can probably lose it all this time."

"But at least you lose with grace, Sawyer," Liz said, placing a hand on his shoulder and smiling sympathetically. Sawyer frowned. Next to Eryyn, Liz had much more money than he or Greg did.

Picking up the die, he rolled it around in his hand, then threw it on the board. It spun several times, then fell to a rest, the number four sticking up. Counting ahead at the colored spaces, he moved his piece up, sighing with relief as he landed on a safe spot.

"Lucky," Greg muttered, taking the die. Sawyer glanced up and grinned broadly. Greg was losing even more than he was and Greg did not take it so gracefully.

Then, as Greg was rolling the die through his hands, he popped an unexpected question that had been itching at him all night. "So, Eryyn, have you and Sawyer always been thieves? Or did you do something more legal when you were smaller?"

Eryyn, who'd still been ruffling happily through her stack of credits, looked up, shocked by the sudden blow. At the same time, Sawyer and Liz glanced at each other and Liz reached out a hand to her husband's arm. "Greg, I don't think we need to discuss that right now. We're having a good time…"

"It's okay, Liz," Eryyn interrupted. "I don't mind answering. Squirt and I *are* thieves and it's dumb to lie about it." She faced Greg squarely and drew a deep breath, "Yeah, Greg, I'm pretty sure I always worked as a thief. At least that's the job my friend Otto and I did as far back as I can remember. And as for Squirt, well, he's been a thief since *I've* known him, and that's been a lot of years. It's what we know."

Greg was frowning. "But how can you do something like that? How can you steal from hard working people who need their money to live?"

Sawyer felt his cheeks start to burn. When put into Greg's words, factory work seemed much more honorable than being a klepto. He looked quickly to Eryyn, who continued to stare at Greg. When the girl finally answered, her voice was light and cool.

"There are worse things. And I told you, it's what we do. What we're good at. Would you rather that we starve to death, or go slave in some factory? That's *my* only other option." She glanced pointedly at Greg's bracelet, and then at her own naked wrist. "Besides, we don't steal from people who can't afford it. All we take is extra stuff, things people will hardly ever miss. I know it's wrong. But we gotta survive, don't we?"

"There are better ways to survive."

"Like the Agency? Yeah, I know. I like the idea now, and I'm gonna get my gang to join it just as soon as I can. Until then, though, we have to keep being kleptos. But I make sure we don't take more than we need."

Sawyer and Liz were looking back and forth as the conversation continued, each nervous that one wrong word would cause either Eryyn or Greg to get angry. But, finally, Greg smiled and murmured, "I think you would make a fine addition to the Agency, Eryyn. You have a good, smart head on your shoulders, if you'd just use it for the right things."

Eryyn smiled back. "Thanks. Are you gonna roll soon? I wanna win."

She did win and wore her victory smile for the rest of the evening until she and Sawyer claimed that they had to leave, or they would get lost trying to get home.

"Where *is* home?" Greg asked as he held the door open.

Both kids hesitated. "I can't say exactly," Eryyn murmured after a moment. "Most of the kids in my gang aren't legal, and if anyone found out about them the Enforcers would attack the nest and drag them off. I couldn't let that happen to my friends."

"But you will tell us eventually, right, Eryyn? Once you join the Agency?" Liz asked, her hands resting on Sawyer's shoulders as if she didn't want to let him leave. The boy, perfectly comfortable in the embrace, had leaned back against her and was blinking against the sleepiness that had crept up during the last half-hour of the visit.

"Oh, sure, yeah, I'll tell you then. It won't matter anymore anyway, 'cuz all the kids'll be living in your Agency house. They won't have to worry about someone storming the nest." Eryyn reached out and grasped Sawyer's wrist, giving a gentle tug to pull him away from the woman. Walking down the steps, she turned and gave the couple a small wave. Sawyer, hating the thought of leaving the warm, comfortable house and returning to the nest, did the same and called out, "Thank you! I'll see you tomorrow, Liz."

Liz and Greg watched them vanish into the darkness that had come with the late hour.

"I wish she would join the Agency now," Liz sighed. "Just to get them both off the streets."

Greg wrapped his arm around Liz's waist and hugged her. "Me too. But it seems to me that she can take care of herself and Sawyer. She's got real guts."

Laughing, Liz turned her face up to look at her husband. "I swear, you really like her, don't you?"

"Yeah, I like her. Like I said, she's got guts. She's a tough kid, there's a lot to admire."

"Except that she's a thief."

"So is your sweet, little Sawyer, and it's obvious he's a good kid," Greg pointed out. "Eryyn'll come around, once she realizes that the streets aren't the only way to live."

"I hope so. Well, I'm exhausted. Having a thirteen-year-old beat you in a board game really wears a person out. I'm ready for bed, how about you?"

"Sounds great to me." Greg turned and stepped back into the house, closing the door behind him. Outside, the street became darker as the light from their hallway was cut off completely.

• • •

Darkness had already taken claim of the street when the door finally opened and the kids stepped out and started to make their way back to the nest. Flint, after waiting a moment for the couple to go back into their house, followed. Now was the time to make his move, when it was dark, the streets were nearly empty, and the kids were by themselves. Quickly, he checked the bag that he always carried on his back, counting and sorting his supplies. Everything was in order. He began to walk faster.

•   •   •

"That wasn't bad," Eryyn mused as she and Sawyer walked along the sidewalk. In her hand, she swung the huge bag that contained the leftovers Liz had given them. "Dinner was great. I know everyone at the nest is gonna like what we're bringing back."

Sawyer smiled, but didn't say anything. He hated walking around the streets at night and stayed close to Eryyn, gripping tightly to her free hand.

"That game was fun," Eryyn continued cheerfully. "I've never played a game like that before. We didn't have them at my house. At least, I don't remember having them. I sure did kick tail, didn't I?"

Another smile. Eryyn pulled her hand from the boy's and pinched him lightly.

"You're quiet. I thought you'd be jabbering non-stop about what a great night it was, and how nice Liz and Greg are, and how great the Agency idea is, and…"

"I'm tired," Sawyer answered. "Besides, you already know what I think. You just said it. It was a great night. I really, *really* like Liz and Greg, and I think we finally lucked out on something."

"Sky-End dreamer," Eryyn murmured.

Sawyer chuckled. "It's better than Dead-End."

"Hey, I happen to have known someone who was very happy to have lived in the Dead-End."

"Your pet rat three years ago doesn't count, Eryyn." Sawyer gave his friend a playful shove. Eryyn, whose hand was in her pocket, stumbled and nearly crashed into a wall. Startled, Sawyer reached out and caught her arm before she fell. "You okay?" he asked, as Eryyn regained her balance. "It's not like I pushed you hard. All that extra weight from dinner making you wobbly?"

"Oh, shut up," Eryyn laughed, brushing down her clothes self-consciously. As she did so, Sawyer heard a small metallic click and, in the dim light of the street lamps, noticed something shining near Eryyn's foot.

"What's that?" he asked, bending over to pick it up.

Eryyn glanced down and paled. "That? That's nothing! Wait,

I'll get it, it's nothing!" She swooped down, trying to grab at the object, but Sawyer was already closer to the ground and reached it first. He picked it up and held it to the light so he could see the thin golden chain and the small, faceted stone pendant. It shone faintly purple in the light.

"Eryyn?" he asked, frowning. "This looks like Liz's necklace. The one she let you wear at the house. Where did you get it?"

Eryyn looked ashamed and tried to mumble an answer. She failed miserably. Realizing the truth, Sawyer's frown deepened and the color drained from his cheeks.

"You took it, didn't you?" he whispered, not wanting to believe his own accusations. "You took Liz's necklace? You stole from them!"

"It's just a necklace, Squirt. I went and got it when I said I had to go to the bathroom. She had four of them, and she said that she never wears this one, so she'll never miss it."

Sawyer shook his head, stunned. "But it was hers! Eryyn, you can't steal from her! You can't take stuff from Liz—she's my friend!"

"She probably won't even notice that's its gone," Eryyn murmured, kicking at a rock near her toe, unable to meet Sawyer's accusing eyes. "And the gang could use the credits from something like this."

Sawyer's eyes widened incredulously. "The gang! That *is* all you care about: the stupid gang! And it's not even about Aimee anymore—it's just about you being leader! It's your gang, and you don't even care if you get revenge for Aimee or not. You don't care about all the promises you made! You don't care that I like Liz, and that I like having her trust me. It doesn't bother you that you just ruined everything *I* cared about! 'Cuz the only thing you care about is yourself!" Sawyer was finally forced to stop for breath, allowing Eryyn a chance to jump in.

"That's not true! I'm still working on getting revenge for Aimee. I'm still working on the gang. I do care, Squirt. Sheesh, it's not that big of a deal. It's just a dumb necklace. You don't have to get so upset about it."

"Then why were you trying to hide it from me? If it's not a big deal, why didn't you want me to see it? Because you know! You know that Greg and Liz don't like us being kleptos. You know that they won't trust you anymore because you stole from them. And you know that they won't trust me anymore either, 'cuz I'm your friend and you taught me every trick I know! It's not fair, Eryyn! It's not *fair*! Why did you have to do it?"

"The gang needs it, Squirt…"

"The gang doesn't need it! I hate that stupid gang! I wish I'd never come up with the idea! You're not the same anymore since we started it! And you lied to Greg! You said we never take stuff unless we need it. We *don't* need that necklace, Eryyn. We have plenty of stuff! You *wanted* to take it. *You wanted to ruin everything!* You never liked Liz or the Agency from the start, and you didn't like that for once *I* had something that you didn't." Sawyer was crying now and hated himself for it. Angrily, he dashed at his wet eyes, and winced as the clasp of the necklace scraped a long line down one cheek. Stamping his foot, he shouted, "So you had to go and mess it up! You had to ruin everything that *I* wanted!"

Eryyn was dumbfounded. She'd never seen Sawyer so angry and upset before. Not even when he'd burst into tears back at Nest Two so long ago, or when he'd figured out that the house he was hitting belonged to the woman who'd attacked him in the market. Eryyn suddenly knew that she had just made a *very* big mistake.

"I-I'm sorry, Squirt," she said, stumbling over her words. "I didn't know it would bother you so much. It's just a necklace. We'll return it, okay? You don't have to be so mad. We'll go back and give it to them."

"It's *not* that easy! Don't you get it, Eryyn? Liz won't trust us anymore! She won't trust me! Even if we do bring the necklace back, it won't be the same."

Sawyer's angry shouting had woken up several people in the surrounding buildings. One man opened his window and leaned out, glaring down at them. "Be quiet! Do you have any idea what time it is? If you don't leave right now, I'm going to call for the Enforcers!"

Enraged, Sawyer ducked down, scooped up a handful of dirt and pebbles and flung it at the window. "Shut up!" he screamed, before wheeling around to run off down the street.

Startled, Eryyn called out, "Squirt, where are you going! Come back, please! I'm sorry!"

For a moment, Sawyer paused and looked back. His eyes were

hurt, betrayed. He shook his head slowly. "It's not good enough, Eryyn. Not this time." He turned a corner and disappeared.

"Squirt!" Eryyn was fully alarmed now. Sawyer didn't know this part of the city. It would be very easy for him to get lost. "Squirt, come back! Sawyer! I'm sorry! I didn't know! I didn't think! Please don't be mad! Please, Sawyer, come back!"

There was no answer except for the man above her, who shouted, "The Enforcers are on their way. You'd better clear out of here!"

Eryyn looked up at him, then back to the street where Sawyer had vanished. She wanted to go after him, but couldn't risk getting caught by the Enforcers. Sawyer had a bracelet—that was some protection for him—but she had nothing. She had to leave and go back to the nest. The gang would be worried by now anyway, and Sawyer would come back once he had let off a little steam. He always did.

Shaking her head, cursing herself for being so stupid and making such a huge mistake, she turned away from the building with its angry occupant and started retracing the steps back to the nest and her gang.

• • •

Now that *was interesting,* Flint thought to himself, having just observed the fight between Eryyn and Sawyer. So, the two weren't very happy with one another. Interesting, but it would make his job a little harder. He'd been prepared to grab them both, but now the boy had run off in one direction, and the girl in another.

He paused at the junction where the two had split and looked in both directions. The girl had headed back towards their nest and the rest of the gang. She could wait. The boy, on the other hand, had run off south, towards the Dead-End. And, considering that they'd used directions to find the neighborhood, Flint guessed that the boy had no idea where he was going, and could quite possibly get lost.

His decision made, Flint checked his supplies once more, pulling out a knife, which he slipped into a sheath on his leg, and a coil of rope. Then he took to walking again, following the path that Sawyer had taken.

• • •

"Damn it!" Sawyer tripped over a loose chunk of pavement, dropping on his knees and scraping skin off his hands as he flung them out to break the fall. Wincing, more tears stinging his eyes, he sat back on his heels and looked at his wounded palms. He couldn't see very well—the alley was much darker than the street had been— but he knew his hands were pretty scraped up, even bleeding. They stung badly and he cursed again, quieter this time.

He didn't really know where he was. The alley and the neighborhood were strange to him, but he wasn't about to turn around and go back. He couldn't face Eryyn again. Not yet. Not for awhile. He needed to think about what he had to do, what he had to say to Liz.

He glanced down at the necklace that had fallen from his hand when he'd tripped. Picking it up, he thrust it into his pocket. The last thing he wanted to do was lose the necklace that had caused the fight. The necklace he knew he had to return to Liz, despite the look she would give him, and the sadness that would be in her eyes.

Sighing, he sniffed back more threatening tears and climbed to his feet. He was exhausted and needed to find someplace to stay for the night. The streets weren't safe in any case, but they were downright deadly to a kid on his own at night. If he could find his way to a street that he knew, then he'd try to make his way to one of the old nests. Then he could relax and try to get over feeling so stupid and betrayed.

The necklace felt like a lead weight in his pocket as he walked along the alley, picking his way carefully around trash and debris. It smelled bad here, the trash hadn't been cleared away for a long time, and it was so dark that he could hardly see where he was going, let alone what obstacles lay near his feet, ready to trip him yet again. After many minutes of slow walking, he came to the other end of the alley and stepped out onto another street. Looking around, he realized that he didn't know this place either.

He walked near the buildings, swallowing back fear and glad for the street lamps again, even though they didn't do much to cast back the shadows. Hopefully, if he kept going in one direction, he'd reach a main street and be able to figure his way from there. Also, if the street sign was still up at the corner at the end of the block, that would be a big help. All he had to do was get there.

Putting on speed, Sawyer headed for the end of the street and the line of buildings he could just see through the darkness. He had almost reached this destination when a tall, shadowy figure stepped out of an alley right in front of him. With a gasp, Sawyer stopped in his tracks and looked up at the stranger, feeling a knot of nervousness begin to work its way into his throat. The person blocking his way was far taller than he was, and *much* better muscled. The figure stepped forward a small pace until he was in the light. An ugly, pimple scarred face leered down at the boy.

"Well, what have we here? It's a little kid, all alone on the streets at night." The teenager made a sorrowful sound by clacking his tongue. "Isn't he cute?"

Suddenly, Sawyer was surrounded by five more teens, all tall and strong and looking at him wickedly. One reached out and poked his arm.

"Shouldn't you be at home in bed, shortie?"

"Yeah, with a teddy bear to cuddle?" another joked.

"Your mommy's gonna be worried. She wants to kiss you goodnight."

"And sing you a little lullaby."

Sawyer turned as each one spoke, unable to keep them all in sight at once. The one who had poked him did it again and when he spun around to face the bigger boy, another pulled on his hair. A third shoved him so hard he stumbled into a fourth. That one grabbed him by the arms and propelled him around and into the nearby alley.

It was as dark as the last alley he'd been in, and choked with just as much junk. Sawyer lost his balance when the bully pushed him and fell over a box, landing hard on his knees and hands. Again, he felt the sting of scrapes on his palms, but this time the pain of a skinned knee joined that of his hands. He gasped and struggled to sit up, taking a deep breath to scream for help.

A hand clamped over his mouth just as he was grabbed roughly by the arms again and dragged to his feet. He was shoved against the damp, filthy wall of the alley and the pimply boy looked down at him with a sneer.

"What are you doing out here so late, baby face? Don't you know that this is our territory? No brats allowed. You're in a *load* of trouble."

Sawyer twisted his head enough to free his mouth from the hand and gasped, "Leave me alone, please...I-I didn't know it was your place. I'm trying to get out anyway."

"Didn't know? I don't care, brat. You're trespassing on private turf." A callused finger reached out and cruelly poked at the scratch that ran down the smaller boy's cheek. "And now you gotta pay the price. "

Sawyer struggled against the kids holding him to the wall. "Let me go!" he cried. "If you don't, you're going to be..."

"Gonna be what?" The pimply kid grabbed Sawyer's chin and forced his head up until they were staring into each other's eyes. "What are you gonna do, baby, cry to mommy that the big, bad kids hurt you? You better shut up right now, or there won't be enough left of you to cry."

"Make him pay a toll, Brad," one boy suggested. "For trespassing where he don't belong."

Brad's eyes lit up. "Yeah, a toll! How much you got on ya, baby?"

Sawyer was so terrified he had trouble breathing. Insanely, he kept thinking about the story Jay had told him back in the nest. It was certainly possible that he could end up just as the other boy had, beaten and left in the alley to die. No one would find him back here, hidden in the trash.

"N-nothing." he stammered. "I-I d-don't ha-have anything. H-hon-honest."

"He's lying! Check his pockets! He's holding out, I know it!"

Brad's sneer widened. "Are you lying, baby?" He used his free hand to check through the pocket on the front of Sawyer's shirt.

Liz's necklace! Sawyer dreaded the thought of the heirloom falling into the hands of these street thugs. He began struggling again, leaning back against the wall so he could kick out with his feet. One heel connected with a knee and the bully collapsed, yowling in pain. Brad paused, looking back, and Sawyer took the opportunity to twist his head again, this time biting down hard on the hand that had gripped his chin.

Brad's scream was louder than the one of the kid Sawyer had kicked, and the bully jumped back, gripping his hand, which now sported a bleeding thumb. Stunned, the other kids released Sawyer, who stumbled slightly, then took off for the mouth of the alley.

"*Get him!* Don't let that little snot get away!" Brad screamed, holding his hand between his knees and grimacing with pain. "I'm gonna kill him!"

Sawyer hadn't even made it close to the alley's opening when he was caught, spun around, and dragged back by his arms and hair. He screamed for help, but another hand covered his mouth, cupping over it so he couldn't bite. He was pulled back to Brad, who was still favoring his bleeding hand. The teen's eyes blazed with hatred and anger. At a gesture, the other boys pushed Sawyer back up against the wall and held him tight, keeping his arms and legs pinioned. Brad, grinning now, stepped forward again and brandished a dirty steel blade before Sawyer's eyes. The sight of the knife put an instant stop to Sawyer's struggling. The little boy was paralyzed, staring in horror at the sharp bit of steel.

"Stupid move, baby. Really stupid. *No one* bites me and lives to tell about it."

Frantically, Sawyer shook his head, pleading behind the hand over his mouth. His words were muffled, but Brad seemed to understand their meaning. He grinned wickedly, showing broken and yellow teeth.

"No second chances, brat. You crossed the line. Stupid. 'Cuz once I'm done here, we're just gonna take whatever you've got anyway." He leaned forward, twisting the knife in his fist for a better grip. Sawyer fought against the arms holding him, then squeezed his eyes shut, waiting for the pain.

"That would be a mistake."

The soft voice, and the startled gasps and muttered oaths that followed it, reached Sawyer's ears and he opened his eyes, realizing that Brad hadn't hurt him. He soon saw the reason.

A man was standing behind the bully, pressing a much longer, cleaner, and sharper blade against the teen's throat. Brad's eyes were stretched wide with terror and he was frozen in place, stuttering under his breath.

"I don't believe the boy did anything to you. So why don't you just let him go and I'll do the same to you," the man whispered just loud enough for them all to hear.

Stunned, Sawyer watched Brad nod, and the dirty knife that had been hovering in front of his face dropped to the ground. The man stepped back and Brad went with him to keep the knife from pressing into his skin. Speaking to the other bullies, the man said, "I suggest you all get lost before there's even more trouble. I fight a lot better than a frightened little boy. And I have a knife of my own, as you can plainly see."

The bullies, showing their true cowardice when faced with someone their own size, scattered, running as fast as they could to the street, where they disappeared, leaving their leader with the strange man and the boy.

"Alright, man, you got what you wanted. Now lay off, will ya?" Brad demanded.

"Gladly." The knife slid off Brad's skin, leaving a thin trail of blood behind it. Brad yelped in pain and reached up frantically to claw at his throat. The man pushed him away disdainfully. "I'll cut deeper if you aren't out of this alley in five seconds."

Brad ran even faster than his friends, screaming all the way to the street about crazy murderers and swearing ultimate revenge if he ever saw either of them again. Once he was gone, the man turned to Sawyer, who was wiping tears out of his eyes.

"You alright, son?" the man asked in a flat voice. Sawyer looked up at him—he was even taller than Brad had been—and gave him a weak nod. Sniffing back more tears, he thanked the man for his help.

"The-they wanted money," he explained. "B-but I don't have any. So they were gonna…" He broke off. The man already knew what the bullies had intended; he'd gotten there just in time to prevent it. "I-I don't really know where I am. Could you tell me where Eighteenth Street is?" He had a feeling that Eighteenth Street wasn't all that far, and if he could find Eighteenth Street, he would be only two blocks from Nest Three and safety.

The stranger stared at him for a moment, then slowly nodded. "Yeah, I know where it is. But I have a bad time with directions. How about I take you there? That way you wouldn't have to worry about getting ganged up on again."

There was something about the way the man was looking at him that made Sawyer nervous, but he realized the man had a point. Brad and his gang wouldn't think to attack him again as long as this stranger with the knife was with him. Still, even as he nodded, accepting the invitation, he couldn't shake the feeling of apprehension.

It's probably 'cuz some jerk just had a knife in front of your face, he reasoned silently with himself. *That's enough to make* anyone *nervous.*

"This way," the man said, turning and heading deeper into the alley.

"That way?" Sawyer was confused. "I don't think that side comes out on a street. I think it's a dead end."

"I know my way around, boy. Let's go!"

Sawyer didn't move. It wasn't the previous attack that had him nervous—it was *this* man that scared him. He suddenly realized that he didn't want to follow him.

"I-I changed my mind," he called to the retreating figure. "I'll find my own way. I don't think it's far. Th-thanks again for helping me." Without waiting for a reply, he turned and headed for the mouth of the alley, wanting desperately to get onto the street where there was light.

He had just reached the road and the soothing glow of the street lamps when he felt a hand clamp down on his shoulder. Before he could react, he was pulled back, away from the light, into the darkness.

"I said that we're going *this* way," a low voice said near his ear. Sawyer cried out and fought, but the man held him easily, wrapping the boy's arm in a vise-like grip. Without a sound, he pulled Sawyer deeper into the alley, back to where Brad and his friends had held him pressed against the wall. When they were so far from the street that Sawyer could hardly see the light, the man spun him around and let him go.

Backing away until he bumped into the wall, Sawyer looked up at the violent stranger. "I told you, I don't have anything," he said, his voice shaking.

The man began fiddling with his coat, pulling something from a loop sewn to the inner lining. He glanced up briefly as Sawyer spoke and flashed the boy a grin. "Oh, I don't want your *money*, son. You could never have enough to make it worth my while anyway. What I want…is you." He finished working with his coat and pulled free a length of thin, coiled rope. He held it out, letting it unwind until it was nearly six feet long.

Sawyer, eyes wide with terror, rushed to the left, trying to dart around the man. An arm casually shot out, blocking his escape and pushing him back towards the wall.

"Naughty, naughty!" the man said, shaking a finger at the trembling boy. "And don't think of running the other way. You were right. This alley *is* a dead end. There's no where to go back there."

"What do you want!" Sawyer cried, feeling more afraid now than he had in the gang's clutches. He was trapped here, blocked by this stranger who was now using his knife to cut the rope into smaller pieces. Desperately, Sawyer stuck out his wrist, hoping the man could see the bracelet. "I'm legal! If you think you can sell me to the factories then you're wasting your time. Let me go! Please!"

The stranger chuckled. "I don't plan on selling you to the factories, boy. They couldn't pay enough for what you are worth. I plan on selling you to a friend of mine who has taken a very special interest in you." He stepped forward, holding out the ropes. Face pale, Sawyer stepped back. But there was no where to escape to. He was soon backed up against a large crate, unable to retreat any further. The stranger grinned, reaching out to grab him again. "I think you've heard of him too. Goes by the name…the Foreman."

Terrified, Sawyer acted before he'd fully thought about what he was going to do. Like he had with the bully, he leaned back against the crate and kicked out as the stranger came closer. The man hadn't expected the attack and the flats of both of Sawyer's feet struck him squarely in the gut.

The man groaned, bending over in pain, while Sawyer dropped to the ground. Not pausing for a second, he jumped to his feet again, shoved an empty wooden crate between himself and the dangerous man, and ran to the left, passing the stranger and sprinting for the mouth of the alley.

The Foreman! The man worked for the Foreman, and he'd been sent to catch him! And probably Eryyn too. That meant that the Foreman knew about the green bands, and knew who was in charge!

His heart was pounding in his chest. If ever there was a reason to make a truce with Eryyn, then this was it! He had to get back to the nest so he could warn her and the rest of the gang!

"That was not a bright thing to do."

Sawyer heard the voice, but he didn't turn around. The man would never catch him this time. He was nearly out of the alley. Just a few more steps and he'd be safe.

He heard the low *pop* just before he felt the sharp pain in the back of his neck. Faltering to a stop, he groped back to feel the injury. Something was there! It hurt when he pulled at it, but came loose easily. He brought it around to look at. A dart. Even as he figured this out, Sawyer grew dizzy and his vision blurred. One hand reached up to rub at his eyes as he staggered against a wall.

"Not bright at all."

Turning his head, Sawyer saw the stranger walking towards him, holding the ropes. Scared, the boy tried to run again, but whatever had been in the dart was too strong and made his arms and legs feel weak, as if they were made of jelly. He collapsed, his vision darkening rapidly. Just as he fully lost consciousness, the stranger reached him and knelt down. He was laughing.

"One down, one to go."

• • •

"Eryyn! Where have you been? We need to talk to you!"

Cinder and Jay rushed Eryyn even as she was walking into the nest. They both grabbed her arms, dragging her away from the door, both talking loudly, excitedly, and at the same time.

"Give her a break, you two. She can't hear you if you're both talking at once." Rick came to Eryyn's rescue, pushing Jay to one side and pulling Cinder's hand off her arm.

"Thanks," Eryyn said gratefully. She was in no mood to be attacked by her own gang members. All she wanted to do was go to her pallet, lie down and wait until Sawyer came to his senses and returned. She started to do just that, but Cinder grabbed her again.

"Eryyn, this is important. We need to talk. Now!"

"What?" Eryyn looked at the girl blankly for a moment, then shook her head to clear it. "Oh, okay. What's wrong?"

"We met your friend Otto today," Jay said, returning to her side and rubbing at his shoulder where Rick had shoved him. "He came up to us in the marketplace."

"Otto?" Eryyn groaned. She didn't want to deal with anything that had to do with Otto. Not tonight. "What did he do, try to nab one of you? You got away. Do we have to talk about it now?"

Cinder looked at Eryyn as if she had gone insane. "What are you talking about? No, he didn't try to nab us. He didn't try to do anything bad. All he wanted was to talk to us. To talk to you. We wouldn't bring him back here though; we made him tell us what he wanted."

"And what did Otto want?" Eryyn asked, sighing.

"To warn you," Jay said.

Eryyn looked at him with barely feigned interest. "Warn me?"

"The Foreman. You've made the Foreman mad, Eryyn, and he's got a plan to get you and Sawyer. Otto knows about it, and he wanted to warn you to be careful. To maybe hide out for a little while, just in case."

"And you believed him? You do realize that Otto is the leader of a rival gang, don't you? The very gang that Dillan and Kit belonged to…and *hated*."

Cinder rolled her eyes. "Of course we know. But he was really believable, Eryyn. He looked scared, like he was doing something he wasn't supposed to do. And then he told us that he wanted to see you, on your terms, and he'd tell you everything himself. And…"

"He wants to join the gang," Jay blurted. "He wants to join the rest of the red and gold gang with yours, and he'll let you stay on as leader."

"Nice of him." Eryyn sounded cool and uninterested, but her mind was racing. It sounded like a trap to her. She said this to Cinder and Jay, who shook their heads.

"You didn't see him, Eryyn. He had these two other kids with him, and both of them looked really scared too. And he promised that if you met with him, you could bring the whole gang along, and he'd come alone. Even if that was a lie, you still have more kids than he does. So what's the harm in meeting with him?"

"I…I don't know. Cinder, Jay, I don't want to talk about this right now, okay? I've had a bad night."

For the first time, Jay noticed that Eryyn had returned to the nest alone. "Where's Sawyer?" he asked, looking back to the door, as if expecting to see his friend walking into the room. "Didn't he come back with you?"

Eryyn sighed and rubbed two fingers against her temples. "That's the reason I've had a bad night."

"You two had a fight?"

Eryyn looked at him fiercely and Jay took his answer from that. He frowned deeply.

"Where is he now?" Cinder asked.

"I don't have a clue. He went for a walk on his own."

"At night?" Jay was incredulous.

"Eryyn, that's bad. After what Otto said...none of us should be out alone, especially not you or Squirt—especially not at night. You may not believe Otto, but Jay and I do. He's telling the truth, he wants to join, he wants to get away from the Foreman. And he's worried about you. You should meet with him and listen to him. Then you'll understand."

"Whatever." Eryyn's reply was dull, submissive. "Fine, I'll meet with him. In the Red plaza. I don't care what time. Fix it up for me if you want. Now can I go and get some sleep?"

"What about Sawyer?" Jay was worried. He and Sawyer had become very good friends in the time since the gang had been formed. "He shouldn't be out at night. It's not safe." The boy glanced towards the window at the black square of the night. He looked ready to leave the nest and go searching.

Eryyn shook her head and put a hand on his shoulder, pulling him a step closer to the center of the room, away from the door. "I don't know about Squirt. I want him to be here as much as you do. I don't like him being out at night. But he ran off, and I couldn't find him. We'll just have to wait until he comes back on his own— it'd be dumb sending everyone out into the dark to search the entire city. I-I think he'll be okay. Squirt does this sometimes when he gets really mad. He just needs time to be alone. Don't worry, he always comes back."

• • •

His head hurt. It had been hurting since he'd awakened and found himself in a dark room, tied to a chair. The ropes around his wrists and ankles were uncomfortable, especially when he struggled against them, and the place on his neck where the dart had hit him itched and stung maddeningly, but his head took most of his attention.

Not that there was much of anything else to hold his attention. The room was completely dark—everything in front of his eyes was lost in blackness. All he had was the painful throbbing of his temples, and his thoughts.

Sawyer was scared. He didn't know where he was, or how long he had been there, but he knew that it was somewhere in the Foreman's power. He'd been kidnapped, and it was because the Foreman had wanted him. Had sent someone out to hunt for him. The man was probably out searching for Eryyn right now, and there was no way he could get a warning to her.

Resting his head against the high back of the chair, Sawyer let out a sob of frustration and began pulling on the ropes that held his wrists down. The bonds were tight. He had no chance of breaking them and only succeeded in hurting himself. Terrified, he squeezed his eyes shut and began to cry.

"Oh, tears. How sad. It gnaws at my heart to see such a sweet young face covered in tears."

Sawyer jerked in his bonds, gasping as pain flared through his wrists and head. Bright spots of color flashed before his eyes as he desperately looked around the pitch-black room, trying to find the source of the soft, low voice.

"Wh-who are you?" he asked, turning his head, wondering where the man was standing. "Where are you?"

"Nearby. And I believe you already know who I am."

"The Foreman," Sawyer said in a whisper.

"Smart boy. *Very* smart, from what I've heard. Smart enough to organize a gang when you're hardly old enough to cross the street on your own. And your gang is quite successful too. Successful enough to cause me trouble with my own gangs. But that, my boy, is not very smart at all."

Sawyer shuddered and bit his lip, trying to keep himself from crying more. "What do you want?" he asked, feeling helpless and terribly scared. "What are you gonna do to me?"

"You sound afraid of me? Are you afraid, Sawyer?"

Sawyer gasped again. "How do you know my name?"

"We have a friend in common. A boy. Named Caulin."

"C-Caulin? How can you know Caulin?"

"I have my ways, boy. They're not of your concern. I asked you a question."

Sawyer shook his head, confused. "I-I don't..."

"Are you afraid of me?"

"Y-yes."

"Why?"

Sawyer sniffed back more tears and wished vainly that he could lift a hand to wipe at his eyes. "What do you care?" he asked, trembling. "You've got me here. You can do what you want now. It doesn't matter whether I'm scared of you or not."

There was a slight movement in the left side of the room. Sawyer heard the rustling of clothes and turned his head in that direction. Faintly, he noticed a slightly darker outline of a man. He stared at it until it moved beyond his line of vision, disappearing behind him. A moment later, two hands rested themselves on his shoulders. Sawyer started at the touch, pulling in a sharp breath.

"Weren't you ever taught that children should always use respect when they answer adults?" the man asked, his voice soft and dry by Sawyer's right ear.

Sawyer didn't reply. He felt it safer to hold his tongue. Instead, he closed his eyes and pictured Eryyn, wondering if she missed him yet. It was possible. He didn't know what time it was, or how long the drug had kept him unconscious—it could possibly be a different day. If that was the case, Eryyn would be worried about him, despite the fight, and she would be looking for him. The thought was comforting, until the Foreman spoke again, giving his shoulders a quick, hard shake.

"Very rude. The children I train know not to ignore their betters. They follow orders precisely and when they are asked a question, they answer promptly."

"Or they end up beaten and strangled in a trash bin the next morning," Sawyer said bitterly, speaking before he could stop himself.

The man behind him was still for a long moment; the hands on his shoulders grew heavy, like weights. Then, "They learn to be obedient, or they pay the price. It's the best way to stay in power."

"I-it's murder," Sawyer whispered. "You kill them. You killed Aimee."

"Obedience," the man repeated. "Complete obedience." His hands tightened painfully. Sawyer winced and shifted on the hard chair. "But would you like to know a little secret, Sawyer? The obedience is breaking up. Those kids don't seem to fear me anymore. They won't take my orders. They won't show me the respect I deserve. Do you know why?"

Sawyer knew. But this time he was smart enough to keep his words to himself. Instead, he drew in a deep breath and let it out slowly, trying to stay calm. The pressure on his shoulders was almost as painful as the throbbing in his head now. Shifting didn't help. His wrists and ankles were latched tightly to the arms and legs of the chair and another rope was fastened around his chest. It was nearly impossible to move anything but his head, and it hurt too much to move *that*. Closing his eyes again, Sawyer listened to the sound of his own breathing, and waited.

Eventually, the Foreman spoke again, continuing his explanation. "They don't listen to me because they think they have an alternative, a better deal. Someplace they can escape to and be safe. You know what I'm talking about...right?"

Sawyer's eyes flashed open and he clamped his teeth into his lip, holding back a cry as the Foreman's fingers tightened even more. The sound emerged as a pitiful whimper and he nodded, willing to answer if it just would make the man loosen his grip. "The gang," he murmured. "Eryyn's gang. They were supposed to be named after Sherwood Forest, but everyone calls them the green bands."

"Good boy. You're right. The green bands. The gang where all the kids are equal, where everyone gets a share of the spoils, and everyone protects their friends. The gang *you* invented and that your friend, Eryyn, is running."

"Kids from your gang have joined us. They know Eryyn'll help them. So they run away from you and the jerks you have for leaders and they come to us."

"They're breaking up my system. I'm losing money. I don't like that, Sawyer. I don't like that at all."

"Why should I care?"

The Foreman laughed. Sawyer heard him move from his position behind the chair, and, a second later, the scraping of metal across stone. "You should care very much, boy. Because *you* are the cause of my problems. You and your friend." The man's voice came from Sawyer's right and was lower now, like he was sitting. "And the best way to get rid of the problem is to beat it at the source."

The boy shivered again and swallowed hard. "So you plan to get rid of me like you got rid of Aimee?" It scared him just to say the words. His mouth went dry and his eyes stung with new tears.

Another laugh. "Aimee was useless. Average talent, average wit, a big mouth, and no sense of obedience. Killing her was no loss. But you? Oh no, I have something much better planned for you and your friend."

Sawyer didn't like the sound of that. "Like what?"

"I'm going to make you an offer, boy. You have to listen closely, because I never repeat myself, not to street brats. I want my gang back, as strong as ever. But it seems that the only way I can do that is to get rid of the green band gang that you created. Or…take over the green bands as my own."

The thought struck Sawyer funny, but he didn't laugh. He was too scared to laugh. Instead, he released another long breath in a sigh. "How would you do that? None of the kids trust you. The reason they're *in* the green bands in the first place is because they wanted to avoid working for *you* or the *other* gangs."

"But that's what *you* are for, my boy. You are the creator of the gang and your partner is the leader. The gang will follow the two of you and do as you say. They'll work for me if Eryyn tells them too."

"They won't!" Sawyer said desperately, shaking his head even though it hurt him to do so. "They won't! They'll leave! They won't stay in the gang if…" He fell silent as the Foreman suddenly gripped his chin, forcibly turning his head to face to the right. Again he could see the dim outline of a man. Then tears blurred the form and Sawyer dropped his eyes, looking away. "And *I* won't do it," he said sullenly. "And neither will Eryyn."

"Oh, she will, Sawyer. She will if she wants her little partner and best friend to stay healthy."

A sob escaped the boy tied to the chair.

"And my plan is simple enough. The gang won't even know that they're working for me. They'll think that they're free to do what they please and Eryyn will continue to be their good little leader. The only change is that her little friend Sawyer will have sadly disappeared, and, without any of the other kids knowing it, Eryyn will make weekly payments to me from the spoils brought in."

Sawyer continued to avoid looking at the Foreman and two tears slid off his nose to land on his arm. "It won't work," he said in a shaky whisper. "It'll never work."

"Oh, I think it will. It's quite perfect really. No one will be the wiser. You and Eryyn had a fight earlier, didn't you? Isn't that why you went off on your own, making yourself all the easier for my hunter to catch you? All the kids in the gang will think that is why you never came back. They won't question it for long. Only Eryyn will know the truth, once I have her here as well. And she'll keep the secret." The fingers gripping Sawyer's chin squeezed mercilessly and Sawyer was helpless to hold back another painful whimper. "Her best friend's welfare will depend on it. I'll have my gang and my weekly payments, the kleptos will continue to think that they're independent and safe, and everyone will be happy." He paused thoughtfully. "Well, not everyone, I guess. But you were the cause of all this trouble to begin with."

"You're crazy!"

"No, boy. I'm smart. Very, very smart. You should have thought about that before you decided to fight me. I always win in some way, no matter what it takes."

The unseen hand finally released his chin and the presence beside him moved again. Sawyer heard the scraping sound, which he assumed was a chair being pushed across the stone floor. When the Foreman spoke again, his voice was softer, more distant, coming from across the room.

"I'll leave you here for awhile to think about what I said. If you're as smart as I think you are you'll realize that it's better for you to cooperate. A few days in the dark, alone, always helps my kids come to that conclusion. After that, we'll see what we can do to get your friend Eryyn here. I'm sure it will be quite easy, considering the bait I plan to use. Goodnight, Sawyer."

Sawyer threw himself against his bonds, terrified at the thought of being locked up in the dark again, "No! Please! Let me go! You can't do this! It won't work! It'll never work! You're crazy to think that Eryyn will listen to you! Let me go!" He hadn't heard the door open, and didn't see any change in the light, but Sawyer did hear the door close, and knew that he was suddenly alone again. Overcome with fear and grief, he dropped his aching chin to his chest and cried. Tears poured down his cheeks to drip onto his clothes. His head screamed with pain, but he didn't care. Because he knew the Foreman was right. The plan was a good one. And if it worked, which it probably would, then soon, very soon, they would *all* be the Foreman's slaves.

• • •

Jay and Cinder had finally left her alone, and Eryyn felt immensely grateful as she curled up in her corner of the floor. But, despite the peace Rick tried to enforce for her, sleep at her pallet was difficult. She was used to having Sawyer beside her. She missed him and, as the night wore on, every noise woke her, and she would sit up, looking at the window, hoping to see her young partner climbing over the sill. Each time she was disappointed, seeing only one of the kids turning in his sleep, or passing the time playing a game. Sawyer never came home.

Even by morning he hadn't returned, and then, Eryyn really got worried. She knew that Sawyer was mad and that, this time, he would probably stay mad for a long time. But he was too smart to let his anger put him into danger. He threatened things, but he never pulled them off. This was the first time he'd stayed away from her for an entire night.

When he hadn't shown up by noon, Eryyn decided it was time to go out and look for him. She was in a bad mood, snapping at any kid who dared approach her with a question and refusing to give out work assignments for the day. Finally, her temper and nerves stretched thin by worry, she passed control over to Rick, and jumped out the window, running down to the street.

"Okay, Squirt. Where are you? I'm *sorry* already." She looked up and down the roadway, hoping to see her friend.

"Eryyn! Hey, Eryyn, wait up!"

Eryyn turned and saw Jay running towards her, waving his hand for her to wait.

"What?" she asked shortly, when he stopped beside her. "I'm not in the mood to hear anymore stupid stories about Otto."

Jay gave her a wounded look. "I wasn't going to talk about Otto," he retorted. "I-I wanted to know if you're gonna look for Sawyer now?"

Eryyn nodded, looking back at the street. Trying to keep her attention, Jay reached out and grabbed her arm.

"You're worried about him, aren't you? That's why you were so upset. You think something happened to him?"

"I don't know!" Eryyn exclaimed, exasperated. "I doubt anything happened to him, but he's never stayed out all night, no matter how bad our fight was. I just want to find him so I can..."

"Apologize?"

Eryyn hesitated, but, when Jay raised his eyebrows at her, she nodded. "Yeah."

"Can I come?"

Eryyn turned and started walking away. "I want to be alone for awhile, Jay, alright? Go find something else to do."

But Jay wasn't easily put off. He followed her, matching her stride. "He's *my* friend too, you know? You're not the only one who's worried about him."

"I don't need your help, Jay."

"Four eyes see a lot more than two. You may be the gang leader, but you can't stop me from trying to help my friend, Eryyn."

Eryyn turned to the younger boy and, seeing that he really wanted to help her find Sawyer, nodded again. Jay was right. Two people could cover a lot more ground than one. And Jay had a knack for finding things. He could be useful.

"Okay, you can come. I'm heading towards the south Mid-End, near the Orange plaza."

Jay frowned. "Orange plaza? What would you want there? It's only apartments, and none of them are very good. Not even worth hitting."

"You know the area?"

"Yup. I lived around there for a few nests. Then I decided to leave."

"Why?"

The boy shrugged. "Nothing good there. Not for hitting. And 'pocketing is hard too, 'cuz people don't walk around so much. There are gangs that hang around there. They go after people. If they catch someone, they make them pay a toll, or…well, I found out what happens if you can't pay. Nearly killed me."

Eryyn smiled sympathetically. "Sorry. But it's great that you know the area. You can show me around. It's where Squirt and I went last night, but we had a paper with directions and when Squirt got mad he ran off with the page."

"I couldn't read it anyway," Jay said, blushing slightly.

"Me neither. But I remember one of the streets we were on. Ninety-Fourth. Can you find that?"

Jay nodded vigorously and led her through the streets she and Sawyer had walked the night before. True to his word, he did know his way around, and they easily reached the street where Liz and Greg had their apartment. Eryyn, after a few minutes of searching, located the street where Sawyer had run.

"He went down *there*?" Jay stared down the street, his brows furrowed. "Why?"

"I don't wanna talk about that."

Jay chewed on a fingernail, still frowning. "Eryyn, he shouldn't have gone down there. This isn't the best neighborhood in the Mid-End, but this street is safe enough. But over there, that's south, closer to the Dead-End. The Enforcers don't patrol much and there are a lot of gangs. Sawyer's little…easy to mug. If one of the gangs caught up with him…"

Eryyn felt a lump work its way into her throat. How could she have been so dumb, letting Sawyer run off and not trying to follow him? If they'd been together, there would have been a little safety in walking around. But alone…he didn't stand a chance.

Jay seemed to read her thoughts on her face. He clasped his hands behind him, looking uncomfortable. "He's probably okay, right? Sawyer *is* little. But he's smart."

"Maybe he went to one of our old nests and decided to sleep there," Eryyn murmured. "That's a possibility."

"Where are your old nests?"

"Not around here. Not near the Dead-End. We stayed away from the Dead-End whenever we could."

Jay looked glum, but tried to stay hopeful. "We can go check your nests first. Then come back here and look around?"

"I suppose." Eryyn glanced up the street to the house where she and Sawyer had eaten dinner with Liz and her husband. She considered the possibility of going over there and asking Liz if she'd seen Sawyer. Maybe he'd waited, watched her leave, and then gone back to the apartment to return the necklace.

The thought of the necklace crushed all thoughts of talking to Liz. The woman might not have discovered the absence of her heirloom yet, but if Eryyn went to her she'd have to explain why she and Sawyer had had the fight, why he'd run off on his own. Then Liz would know, and she'd be mad. She probably wouldn't help her find Sawyer; instead, she'd call the Enforcers.

"Eryyn?" Jay was tapping her arm, looking at her expectantly.

"Huh? Oh, yeah, right. The nests. C'mon, show me back to the market and I'll show you them all."

Jay walked away, leaving her to follow, which she did automatically. But as she walked, she looked around carefully, memorizing the trail they took. If, for some reason, she needed to make her way back here by herself, then she would know the way. It wasn't much, but Liz and Greg *were* adults. If she found out that there was trouble, and Sawyer was involved, it was good to know that there was possible help. That is, if Liz could ever forgive her for what she'd done.

• • •

Rane was pacing around the meeting room, tense and bored. An annoyed grunt stopped him for a moment and he looked over at Otto and Sasha, who were lounging on the sofa. "You told them this was important. Why are we just hanging around here? If you want to talk to Eryyn, don't you think you should be outside, so her gang can find you?"

Otto pulled in his breath sharply. "Will you shut up about Eryyn? Sheesh, Rane, don't be an idiot. Do you want to get caught?"

"Caught?" Rane frowned.

"Do you have any idea what the Foreman would do if he found

out about what we did yesterday? If he knew what I plan to do?"

Rane nodded weakly. "Probably about the same thing you did to me because of Aimee."

"Worse. About a hundred times worse."

Hard to believe, Rane thought. To Otto, he said, "How would he find out? We were the only three who went yesterday. You wouldn't tell him. Sasha won't tell him. And you could bet your life that *I* won't tell him."

Otto cocked his head and grinned at the younger boy. "Aww, Raney boy, are you saying that you like me so much you wouldn't take the chance to get me in deep crud with the Foreman?" he asked jokingly.

Rane made a face. "*That* would be the greatest thrill of my life. But I wouldn't face the Foreman to get it. No way."

"How sweet of you. And here I'd thought we'd been getting along so well. Like brothers. But if you want to know why we can't talk about yesterday, I'll tell you. The Foreman was here last night."

Sasha and Rane stared at him, mouths hanging open in shock.

"Why?" Sasha asked, her voice tight and small. "Payment's not due."

Otto shrugged. "Don't know. Didn't ask. He didn't try to find me or anything. All I know is that he was here, I heard him in the halls, and he didn't leave for a few hours."

Rane felt his cheeks go pale. "You think he knows? You think he had someone follow us or something?"

Another shrug.

"Damn," Sasha whispered, her own face draining of color. She leaned back against the sofa, closing her eyes. Rane could see her shivering. Nervously, he cast his glance to Otto, who shook his head wearily.

"Things are falling apart, aren't they, Raney boy?"

Instead of answering, Rane turned on his heel and left the room, walking quickly down the halls to the exit. The stronghold felt different now—colder, less safe. In all the years he'd been living there, Rane had never thought that the Foreman would come at night and walk around while all the kids were sleeping. The Foreman, in his mind, had always belonged in the meeting room, in his dark alcove. To know that he went elsewhere was a scary thought. Rane wrapped his arms around his chest and shivered. He needed to get out, to take a walk in a place that wasn't corrupted by that man's touch.

He continued down the hall, almost to the door that would take him to the street. Then he heard the voice and stopped, cocking his head. It had been faint, almost like someone was shouting outside, but he was almost positive that it had come from *inside* the stronghold. And that it was from someplace nearby.

"Hello?" he called. "Somebody there? Otto? Sasha?" He listened, but there was nothing but silence. Wondering if he'd imagined it, he turned to open the door. And then he heard it again. A voice calling out. Calling for help. And it *was* inside the building, coming from somewhere to his right. He looked, but the only door nearby was the one that led to the room where Otto locked the new kids before they were added to the gang. He remembered the last time he'd been in there, when Otto had told him to convince Aimee to cooperate.

But no new kids were being added to the gang. There wouldn't be anyone in there. Not now. And none of the gang members ever went into that room if they could help it. It was too full of bad memories. But he was sure that was where the voice had called from.

Stepping up to the door, he knocked timidly. "Is there someone in there? Hello?"

No answer. Confused, Rane tested the knob. The door wouldn't open. He glanced up and immediately saw why. A deadbolt was fastened to the wood of the door above his head, the bar slid into the locked position. Standing on tiptoe, he reached up for it, but he was too short. He jumped, and just managed to brush it with his fingertips. That wouldn't do. He turned around and ducked into one of the nearby rooms—the kitchen—and grabbed a chair that stood beside the grime-caked window. He dragged it out into the hall, painfully aware of the scraping sound it made on the floor, and positioned it in front of the locked door. By climbing up on the chair, he was able to reach the lock and, though it was stiff with rust, he managed to pop it open with a few hard slaps.

Jumping down from the chair, he tested the door again. It still wouldn't open. Confused, Rane looked closely at the knob, then back up at the defeated deadbolt. He couldn't understand why the door still refused to open. Then he lowered his eyes, and groaned when he saw the second deadbolt close to the floor. Kneeling, he slid that one open too, then stood up and gave the knob a third try.

This time the door swung open, revealing the small, dim room. Swallowing hard, he stepped inside, leaving the door open behind him to let in light. He looked around. There was no one there. The room was completely empty.

The voice cried out again, startling him with it's closeness. And then it dawned on him that the voice was not coming from *this* room, but the room *beyond*. The room where all the kids spent their first days after being caught for the gang. The room where they were tied to the chair…alone…in the dark.

The only way into that room was a short door in the corner. It was small, barely three feet high, and heavy. Rane walked over to it and knocked on its surface.

"Help!" someone screamed from inside. "Help me! Please!"

This was wrong. If a new kid had been nabbed for the gang, Otto would have told him about it. Would have told them all about it. New kids weren't kept secret and Otto liked to brag every time he managed to catch one. For a moment, Rane debated between opening the door to see inside or running back to get Otto, just in case.

"Is someone there? Please!" The voice was shrill, terrified. Even through the thick door, Rane heard the distinct sound of a sob, and then, much lower, "Please, someone help me."

That decided it. Glancing back towards the room he'd just left, making sure no one had followed him, Rane took a deep breath and grabbed the metal handle of the door. He pressed down, half expecting it to be locked like the other one. It wasn't. There was no need to lock it. The kids inside were usually tied up, and none of the kids in the gang would ever choose to go in there, not after their first time. And if any of the new kids happened to escape from the chair, then the deadbolts on the outside door would keep them from running away. Rane heard another clicking sound and the door cracked open slightly. He pulled, swinging it wide, and looked inside.

Faint light from the hall illuminated the tiny room…and the small boy who was strapped tightly to the chair in its center. The boy's eyes were squeezed shut, his head ducked low as the sudden light washed over him.

"Oh wow," Rane murmured breathlessly.

The boy risked a glance up, squinting. He looked terrified. "Who're you?" he asked. "Can you help me? Please? He kidnapped me, and I have to get out of here! I have to get out now."

Kneeling down, Rane crawled through the tiny door and squatted just inside the room. The boy watched him apprehensively.

"You have to let me go. Please! Before he comes back."

"Who?" Rane asked, thinking he already knew the answer.

The boy confirmed his suspicions. "The Foreman! He kidnapped me, and he's gonna go after my friend! I have to get to her first. I have to warn her. Please, help me."

"Who are you? How long have you been here?" Rane was still stunned by his discovery. And finding it hard to comprehend the boy's desperate pleas.

"M-My name is Sawyer. I don't know how long I've been here. It's been really dark. It feels like it's been hours though. I have to get out of here."

Sawyer? Rane groaned. "Oh no. You-you're that kid from the green bands, aren't you? You're Eryyn's friend."

Sawyer stared at him, amazed at how many strangers seemed to know who he was. "How do you know that?" he asked cautiously. He glanced at the band on Rane's wrist and trembled slightly.

"Everybody here knows," Rane said, and pointed a finger at him. "You've caused a lot of trouble for us. The Foreman has been really mad these last few weeks 'cuz we keep losing kids to the green bands and can't make the right payments."

It was Sawyer's turn to groan. He leaned back against the chair, shutting his eyes. Rane noticed that his cheeks were wet from crying.

"What happened?" he asked. "How did he get you? I thought all the green bands protected each other."

"I did something *really* stupid," Sawyer mumbled, not looking at him. "I didn't know. I didn't know he'd sent someone out to find us."

Rane moved closer to the chair. "The Foreman?"

"Yeah. He had someone looking for me and Eryyn. I didn't know, and I ran off. I ran away from Eryyn, and he caught me." Sawyer was crying again. Tears squeezed out from under his closed eyelids and trickled down his cheeks.

Rane didn't know what to say. The boy in front of him was even younger than he was. He wanted to comfort him, but he knew from experience that it was hard to feel comforted when tied to the chair, and this kid was different. He was not here just to be a new member for the gang—the Foreman had purposely hunted him out.

"He's crazy, you know?" Sawyer said before Rane could think of anything to say. "He told me what he plans to do. He wants to *own* the green bands. But he's not going to let anyone know. Instead, he's going to make Eryyn pay him from the loot they collect. That way the kids'll stay in the gang, 'cuz they'll think they're free."

So *that* was the Foreman's plan. He didn't want to destroy the green band gang—he wanted to run them in secret. Rane wanted to rush out of the room, back down the hall, so he could tell Otto. But Sawyer had opened his eyes again and was looking at him.

"What's your name?" he asked softly.

"Me? I-I'm Rane."

Sawyer frowned. He'd heard that name before, somewhere. But he couldn't remember where.

"Will you help me get out of here?" He flexed his wrists against their tight bindings. "If you cut these ropes, I can run and warn Eryyn. Please?" Now that there was light in the room, Sawyer could see how it was made. The only way out was through the room from which Rane had appeared, and the only way out of *that* room was through a door that led to a hall. Now he could see how the Foreman had come in before without his noticing. The first room had no windows, just like his prison. So when the door was closed, it was completely dark, and provided no light for the next room. But both rooms were little—he could see the hall from where he was tied, and could escape if he could just get loose from the chair. He looked back to Rane, still trying to remember how he knew his name. "I won't get you in trouble. I promise. I'll just run."

Torn, Rane let his eyes flit between the captive and the hall. He shook his head. "I'd get in trouble anyway. We all would. The Foreman would blame all of us who haven't joined your gang yet."

Sawyer lowered his eyes. "I have to get out of here," he whispered. "It's my fault. I shouldn't have run away. And if he gets

Eryyn..."

"I'm sorry," Rane said lamely. "It...it's just that I don't want to make him mad. I don't wanna end up like Pammy and Aimee."

Sawyer's head whipped up at the name. "You knew Aimee?" His eyes widened. "That's it!" he cried. "Rane. You were her partner. Caulin said so. I remember."

Rane nodded. "That's right. Caulin's here, you know?" he said.

Sawyer frowned. "Here? The Foreman kidnapped him too?"

Rane found it hard not to laugh bitterly. "No. Caulin volunteered. I was with Otto when he decided to join. He said that he was mad at Eryyn, 'cuz she was holding a grudge and keeping him out of the gang; he wanted to get even. So he joined up with us, and the Foreman used him to get info on you, Eryyn, and the green bands. I-I guess that's how he figured out how to..."

The younger boy looked stunned. Stunned, and hurt. Angrily, he pulled on the ropes holding his wrists to the arms of the chair. Rane could see, by the red marks on his skin, that he had done it before with the same results. He reached out and grabbed Sawyer's shoulder, stilling him.

"What good will it do if you hurt yourself?" he asked.

"Get lost!" Sawyer cried, twisting frantically to get free of Rane's hand. "What do you care? I have to get out of here! I need to get to Eryyn. And if you won't help me...!"

Rane looked again towards the door, wishing that Otto, or even Sasha, was around to make the decisions. They would probably be able to come up with a plan. Then it dawned on him. He grabbed Sawyer's hand and gave it a quick squeeze.

"Listen, I can't let you go. Not now. I don't know when the Foreman's gonna come back, and if he found out that you were gone, then all the kids here would end up dead. But I *can* do *something.*"

Sawyer calmed down immediately and fixed his damp eyes on the older boy. "What?" he asked desperately. "Please..."

"I can get someone to go and warn Eryyn. They can tell her what happened, where you are, and what the Foreman plans to do."

Sawyer nodded vigorously. "Yes! Will you?"

"I can try. But I don't know if she'll believe it. Any kid I get to go will have a red and gold band on their arm. She may think it's a trap."

The smaller boy slumped in the chair, gnawing on his lip. Then he brightened and pointed his chin towards his chest. "My pocket." he exclaimed. "Look in my pocket."

Rane obeyed, reaching into the front pocket of Sawyer's shirt. His fingers closed around a metal chain and he pulled it out, peering at it curiously. A tiny purple stone glittered as it hung from the gold necklace.

"Eryyn'll know that," Sawyer said. "She'll know who you got it from, and then she'll believe you."

Wrapping the necklace around his wrist, Rane nodded and smiled. "Excellent." He turned to go.

"Wait!" Sawyer's voice sounded worried. Rane paused and looked back.

"You have to tell her that the Foreman's gonna set a trap for her. He wants to catch her too. And he said he's gonna use me to do it. Tell her not to trust him. No matter what he says. And…and tell her that I'm sorry I got so mad. And I'm sorry that I ran off. This is all my fault."

"No." Rane murmured, finally finding a way to comfort the other boy. "This is all the Foreman's fault. Blame him."

The smile Sawyer gave him was weak, but the boy nodded. "I'm scared," he admitted. "I really want to get out of here."

"You're not the only one." Rane was also scared. Terrified actually. If he were caught he wouldn't have to worry about being locked up in the closet anymore. The Foreman would treat him worse than he'd treated Aimee. Quietly, he made his way back to the door. "I'm really sorry I can't untie you. I hate having to lock you up again."

Sawyer closed his eyes and didn't answer. Rane could see him trembling at the thought of being left alone in the dark. He sighed and crawled back into the other room. Just as he was about to shut the small door, Sawyer spoke again.

"Where is this?" he asked. "I-I never got to see where they took me."

"The stronghold. Otto's. We're low Mid-End. I'll let Eryyn know." Rane pulled his head away from the door and closed it slowly, shutting Sawyer in the darkness once again.

• • •

Caulin was miserable. No, not just miserable, *absolutely* miserable. Nothing was going right; ever since he'd joined Otto's gang, things had gotten steadily worse. Otto wasn't nice like he'd been on the street. The jobs were boring, and he wasn't allowed to make any decisions of his own. He wasn't even allowed out of the stronghold. One of the other kids, usually Denny or Philip, was always assigned to stay with him in case he tried to escape. He wasn't a member. He was a prisoner.

When Rane found him after leaving the dark room and Sawyer, Caulin was lying on his pallet, curled up on one side and staring dully at the wall. He didn't look up as Rane talked to Denny, telling him that Otto had ordered a change of the watch, or when Denny left, glad to be free for awhile. Rane sat down on his own pallet, which was nearby, but Caulin ignored him and only sighed when the younger boy cleared his throat, trying to get his attention.

"Can I talk with you for a minute, Caulin?" Rane asked, sounding impatient. "It's really important."

"What does Otto want me to sort now?" Caulin turned over, burying his head in the bundle of rags that served for his pillow.

Rane stuck out a foot and prodded the prone boy with his toe. "Not Otto. Me. I need a favor."

"Joy." Caulin's voice was muffled and flat. Rane rolled his eyes.

"You have to find Eryyn and give her a message from Sawyer."

Caulin sat up, blinking. "What?"

"Down the hall there's a room where Otto keeps new kids for a few days just after they're caught. You know, until they're tame enough to work for the gang. You never went in there 'cuz you were dumb enough to join up voluntarily. Anyway, it's really dark in there, and the kids are always tied up and...and I just met Sawyer there. The Foreman caught him, locked him up. And he's gonna go after Eryyn next."

Dropping his head into his hands, Caulin moaned. "I wish I'd never come here."

"Big surprise." Rane started to stand up. It was a mistake to think Caulin could do anything. The boy was useless. All he cared about was how miserable he was. Rane would have to try and find

Eryyn by himself—he couldn't really trust any of the other gang kids to help him. It would be a lot harder now. The only good thing about Caulin was that he knew practically every kid in the city and was a master of all the roads and alleyways. That could have been a big help finding the elusive leader of the green bands.

"Hey! Where are you going?" Caulin sounded startled. He reached up and dug his fingernails into Rane's arm. He dragged the smaller boy back down. "What happened? How'd the Foreman get Squirt? What's he trying to do to Eryyn?"

Rane sat back down, but Caulin didn't loosen his grip. "I think the Foreman's gonna try to take over the green bands, and he's gonna use Eryyn and Sawyer to do it," he explained.

Caulin sighed heavily and Rane continued without a pause.

"If we want to stop it, we have to warn Eryyn. Otto could do it, but Eryyn doesn't trust him, so I thought…"

"She doesn't trust me either," Caulin interrupted, his voice glum. "Not after what I did to Aimee."

"More than Otto," Rane replied.

"So what's the favor? As if I couldn't guess on my own…"

Rane looked down. "I hate it here. Just as much as you do. But it's next to impossible to escape from the Foreman. Aimee tried, and look what happened to her. But Eryyn…she made a plan that works."

"If she can keep out of the Foreman's hands," Caulin concluded dully.

"Can you find her and tell her? Sawyer said she would believe you. Here." He tore the necklace from his wrist and tossed it on Caulin's pallet. The older boy picked it up and looked at it critically. "Sawyer said she'd know it, and she'd let you get closer to her than me or any of the other gang kids 'cuz she knows you. Please, Caulin…please do it. Don't let the Foreman ruin everything."

Caulin glanced towards the door. "I-I'm not supposed to go out."

"Denny's not here to stop you," the younger boy pointed out. "This is your chance to escape."

"What if Otto catches me?"

"He won't," Rane stated emphatically. "Even if I have to set him on fire to keep him from noticing you."

"Why can't you go?"

Rane shrugged. "For some strange reason, Otto seems to like having me around now. I'm his little slave. He'd notice in a heartbeat if I ran away. You...? Well, I don't really think anyone would care if you disappeared. You're the best chance we've got."

"Gee, thanks."

Rane ignored his heavy sarcasm. "And I don't know the streets like you do. Or as many people. You could find Eryyn quicker than I could."

Caulin stood up, wrapping the necklace around his wrist like Rane had. "I hope you're right," he muttered.

"Me too." Rane climbed to his feet and rushed out the door, checking the halls. They were empty, and, judging by the noise from the meeting room, he could guess that Otto and Sasha were still in there. He nodded to Caulin and tilted his head towards the exit. "Get going."

Caulin slipped past him and walked down the hall towards the door. Rane went the other way, walking quickly to the meeting room. He got there just in time. Otto was coming into the hall. Rane hurriedly jumped in front of him.

"Get out of my way," Otto snarled.

"Where you going?" Rane countered. He knew he was asking for it. Otto was in a bad mood—Rane could tell from the look in his eyes. The smart thing would be to back away. Instead, he stood his ground, waiting for an answer.

The gang leader's eyes widened in anger when the small boy didn't move. "None of your business." Otto shoved him roughly to one side. Rane, thrown off balance, bumped into the wall, hitting his forehead against the molding. It hurt, but as he was rubbing it, he looked down the hall to see the exit door hanging slightly open. Caulin was gone and Otto hadn't seen a thing. He nodded and allowed himself a weak smile. Otto frowned at him, muttered something about kids going crazy, and walked away.

Rane slid down to sit against the wall, his fingers pressed tightly to a welt that was forming above his left eyebrow. "Good luck, Caulin," he whispered.

• • •

"Good morning, Sawyer. Or afternoon. Or evening. I doubt you can tell the difference in here."

Sawyer clenched his teeth as the voice of the Foreman drifted through the darkness. Exhausted, he had fallen into a doze after Rane had left and hadn't heard the man enter the room. Now he looked around uselessly, trying to find the source of the words.

"What do you want?" he asked, hearing the fear in his own voice. His throat was very dry from crying and screaming. He desperately wanted a drink. And some light.

"Just to talk. Have you thought about what I said last time?"

"There was nothing else to do," Sawyer replied, then figured it would do him no harm to add, "I'm thirsty."

"Are you? Well, maybe we'll take care of that in awhile. After we finish with business."

"What business?" Sawyer peered through the darkness, straining his eyes, trying to find the vague outline he had seen the first time the Foreman had spoken to him. He couldn't see it anywhere. "I'm not gonna do anything for you, I already told you that."

"Oh, you don't have to do anything. All that I expect from you is an appearance at the meeting I have arranged with your young friend this evening."

Sawyer gasped, but held back on the tears that immediately surged to his eyes. Crying did no good, he had decided, and only made him feel worse. Thinking back to the last conversation with his captor, he murmured, "I thought you said you'd keep me here longer. Why change your plans now?"

"Who said I was changing my plans? I said I would keep you locked up in here for awhile and I have. Don't you know you've been here for two days already?"

It was impossible. Sawyer couldn't believe that so much time had passed since he'd been taken captive. But then he remembered that he had fallen asleep several times, and how he had awakened each time, feeling more and more hungry and more uncomfortable in the hard chair. It wasn't impossible. It was true.

Sawyer lost control of his tears and started to cry again.

"The darkness here really does foul up the sense of time, doesn't it?" the Foreman mused. "You thought it had only been a few hours, didn't you?"

"I *hate* you!" Sawyer screamed into the dark.

"You wouldn't be the first child to say that. And I sincerely doubt that you'll be the last. Now listen closely, Sawyer. Here is what will happen. You and I are going to go for a little walk to a certain place I have chosen. I had my friend, the one you met not too long ago, send a note to Eryyn, telling her that someone very special to her will be waiting in this meeting place. Of course she will come, and when she gets there she will see you." A hand touched Sawyer's hair from behind. The boy jumped violently, a gasp tearing itself from his dry throat. "I'm guessing there will be a tearful reunion. She'll have missed you these past couple of days. She'll be too preoccupied to realize that I, and my friend, will be lying in wait."

"I'll tell her! The second I see her I'll tell her that it's a trap!"

"No, you won't. I have that planned as well. She won't have any idea until it's too late. And then my problems will be over. It's perfect. Don't you think?"

Sawyer didn't answer—his throat felt like it had been clamped shut. The Foreman laughed at his silence. "I knew you'd agree." The sound of clothing rustling signaled the man moving away. When he spoke again, Sawyer heard him from across the room. "Oh yes, by the way, Sawyer, who was in here with you earlier?"

Sawyer's heart skipped a beat. "I-I don't know what you mean," he stammered. "N-no one's been here except you."

"You're lying. The locks outside were tampered with, and I have sensors on this room that tell me another person was in here. I'll find out soon enough, and whoever it was will be severely punished. You'd do better to tell me now and save yourself the same fate."

Sawyer muttered a low curse, somehow fitting in every foul word he had learned through life on the streets. The Foreman sniffed. "Suit yourself. You have a few hours until we have to leave. You might want to spend the time thinking about what I'll do when I figure out who you were talking to."

"You're not gonna get away with this."

A dry laugh floated through the darkness. "I already have." The door closed.

• • •

Eryyn looked glumly at the piece of paper in her hand. It had been nailed to the door of the nest when she and Jay returned, empty handed, from their second day of searching for Sawyer. Jay had noticed the paper first, tearing it down to hand to her.

"What is it?" Jay asked, hopping from one foot to the other. "Wh-who would know about where our nest is?"

Eryyn wished bitterly that Sawyer were with her. He was the only one in her gang who could read what was on the page.

"Eryyn?" Jay touched her arm. She glanced up into the younger boy's blue eyes, seeing the worry in them. He was chewing on his fingernails again, looking over her hand at the paper he couldn't read any better than she could. "What is it?"

Eryyn shook her head. "I don't know. I don't know what this says."

"Do you think it's from Sawyer? What are we gonna do?"

"Umm..." Eryyn glanced back the way they'd come, seeing the street and the people walking along it. She swallowed. "You're gonna go back in the nest and tell everybody to start packing up the stuff. We're moving, just as soon as I get back, okay?"

"Moving?" Jay was stunned. But he nodded. "Okay. Where are *you* going?"

Eryyn was already running away. She called back over her shoulder, "To find someone to read this to me!"

The first person she tried to stop brushed past her as if she were nothing more than a fly. The second glanced at her and muttered something about being late and not having the time. The third, a young woman, jumped back at Eryyn's approach, holding her hands over her neatly starched dress.

"Get lost!" she snarled, "If you get me dirty..."

Eryyn turned and walked away before she could finish. Grownups! If it were up to her, she'd never have anything to do with the losers. She looked around, trying to find a friendly face, then marched up to a young man in a suit.

"Excuse me?" she asked, stepping in front of him. "I need some help. Will you help me?"

The man looked down at her, frowning. Eryyn smiled sweetly.

"Please?"

He sighed, checking his watch. "Okay, kiddo, if it's quick. What do you need?"

Eryyn held out the piece of paper with her left hand, taking care to keep her right hidden deep in her pocket. "Can you read? Will you read this to me?"

The man took the page. "You look old enough to know how to read for yourself," he mentioned.

Eryyn didn't answer, just looked expectantly at the page.

"Alright. It says, 'Someone who loves and misses you will be waiting behind the bank at the Blue plaza. Please meet me at sundown, alone. And, Eryyn, I'm sorry.'" The man handed the paper back to her, a grin playing around the corners of his lips. "Sounds like your boyfriend did something to make you mad at him and wants to be forgiven. If you're Eryyn, that is." His grin widened and Eryyn returned it weakly.

"Yeah, I am. Thanks a lot."

"Not a problem."

Eryyn left, heading for the park instead of the nest. She needed time to think, and for that, she needed to be alone. Picking a bench across from a small pond full of mud and weeds, she held the paper in both hands, staring at it seriously.

It would be just like Sawyer to write her something when he was mad at her. He knew she couldn't read, and would be embarrassed about asking someone for help. It was a good way to get revenge. But *why* would he want to get revenge when *he* was apologizing.

Because he's Squirt, she thought, *and he doesn't want to admit that he was wrong about running off.* That was certainly possible. Of course, it was her own fault for making him run off. But if he wanted to apologize, she was willing to give him the chance. And then she'd do the same. At least she'd finally get to see him and could stop worrying.

"Sundown," she murmured, remembering the note. She looked up at the sky. The sun was hidden behind clouds, but she could still see that it was early. She had a few hours to wait before she could go meet Sawyer.

Standing up, she returned to the nest, where Jay had already instructed the kids who were there to pack up all their stuff. The boy was working with Cinder and Kit, rolling blankets, but, upon seeing Eryyn walk through the door, he dropped what he was doing and immediately ran over.

"Did somebody read the note? What did it say? Was it from Sawyer?"

Eryyn nodded. "Yeah, it's from Squirt. How's it going here? Almost ready to leave?"

Jay scowled, annoyed that she wouldn't tell him more. "Eryyn...?" he started. Eryyn held up a hand, cutting him off. "It's fine, Jay. Don't worry. Squirt's coming back soon." She wanted to tell the boy about the note, but she was afraid Jay would want to come with her and she wanted to spend some time with Sawyer alone. Plus, the note had asked her not to bring anyone along and, right now, she didn't want to do anything that would upset Sawyer even more. So, to take Jay's mind off the note, she started organizing the move, setting all the kids to chores necessary before they could leave and head for a new nest. As a precaution, she asked Jay to go with Cinder and scout around for possible new nests.

"But..." Jay immediately started to protest, knowing that she was sending him out so she wouldn't have to answer any of his questions.

"Now, Jay."

"Right." Still scowling, Jay joined Cinder again, spoke briefly to her, then headed for the door. Just as he was leaving, he looked back at her, his brow creased in a frown. Eryyn gave him an encouraging smile, and he stomped out of sight.

"Okay. The rest of you keep packing. The note was from Squirt, but I think it's time to move on anyway, especially with all that Otto business. I want to be ready to go by the time Jay and Cinder find us a place. Got it?"

The group nodded as one and returned to their packing. Eryyn watched them for a few minutes, then pitched in. By the time they were finished—Eryyn was amazed at how much stuff they had collected since the gang had been formed—three hours had passed. Close to meeting time.

"Good work," Eryyn said, rolling up the last of the blankets and shoving them into a box. "Anyone who's hungry, there's food in the second room from yesterday. It'd be smart to eat it before we go—less to have to carry with us—so have a blast. I'll be back in a little while. Try to save me some."

"Where are you going *now*?" Rick, who'd returned from 'pocketing an hour ago, asked. "You're getting really flighty, Eryyn."

"I have to go and meet someone."

"Otto?" Foxy asked. "Don't you want us to come along then? And why go at night?"

"No! Not Otto. Not yet. I'm meeting Squirt, if you *must* know."

"Oh, he's finally decided to come back, eh?" Rick laughed.

"I think so. I'll know in a bit. See you all later." Eryyn left before they could ask her anymore questions or protest her going out without protection. Outside, the air was chilly, but she hadn't thought to bring a sweater, and she wasn't going to go back. She wrapped her arms around her chest, hugging herself for warmth as she made her way along the streets to the plaza mentioned in the note. Though she wished he had decided to meet during the day, she was glad that Sawyer had picked a spot they had frequented often: it made it easier to find the place in the dark. But she didn't know what bank he'd been talking about.

When she reached the plaza, she had to walk around slowly, looking at each of the darkened shops. Though it wasn't really late, the stores had closed and there were few people around. She was nearly alone as she padded back and forth along the sidewalks, staring at the signs, trying to recognize one as a bank. After a quarter of an hour went by with no luck, she switched plans and started looking for alleys instead. Unfortunately, there were small alleys between almost every building. It took some time to peer into each one and no one was answering her calls.

Just as she was about to give up, figuring that Sawyer had played a joke on her, she came upon an alley that was slightly larger than any of the others. A working street lamp was situated at its mouth, illuminating a good half of the tiny street, and windows in the surrounding buildings lit up the rest.

Eryyn paused on the street and looked down into its depths. It was easier to see into this alley than any of the others, which was the only reason she had noticed the box that rested in a shaft of window light…and the little boy who sat upon it.

• • •

Most kids were scared of the dark in the city. They didn't like walking along the streets or in the parks and plazas at night. There was always the danger of older gangs and low-end adults who lurked around, looking for easy prey. And among the littler kids, there were rumors about monsters that lived in the sewer systems and only came out at night, looking for people to grab and devour.

As he walked through the city in the dark, looking for Eryyn, Caulin thought about each and every rumor and story he'd ever heard. The stories no longer bothered him. He didn't mind the dark all that much and he had learned long ago that if there were any monsters lurking around in the city, they were only kids and grown-ups, and if a klepto knew what he was doing, most trouble could be avoided. At least, in the years he'd been a klepto, Caulin had been able to avoid most of it.

Now, having met the Foreman, Caulin started to believe in the monsters in the shadows again. Every slight noise caused him to jump and spin around. Every movement made his heart race. And every change in the light and shadows drove a cry from his lips.

He couldn't find Eryyn anywhere, even though he'd checked all her normal places. The market had been full of people headed home from work, and kleptos helping them by making their load slightly lighter, but Eryyn hadn't been among them. Nor had she been in the park, or around the houses on the central Mid-End streets. And none of the kids he'd asked had seen her, though most had asked him where *he'd* been for so long.

The very thought made Caulin shudder. He knew that, once he'd found Eryyn and warned her, he wouldn't go back to the stronghold. He was out, and he was going to stay out. Even if he had to get down on his hands and knees and beg Eryyn to allow him into the green bands.

Of course, the down side to running was that he had left Rane and Sawyer back in the stronghold. Rane hadn't exactly been friendly to him, but he hadn't been outright cruel either, and Caulin had always liked Sawyer. Those two didn't deserve such a fate—they deserved to be free too—but he couldn't do anything about that.

Possibly Eryyn could. He'd have to see. Right now, the most important thing was to keep *her* out of the Foreman's hands.

He kept looking, running down the streets instead of walking, dodging around late night walkers, peeking into shops and alleys, ducking quickly into certain buildings. Nothing. Not a sign of a green band anywhere. And the city was *huge*. He had a lot more ground to cover.

The plazas were next, all five of them, arranged in a wide circle around the main market, some branching off into the other ends. The closest, by his calculation, was the Blue plaza. Twelve blocks away. Even that distance made him groan, but he took off towards it, running harder, continuing his quick searches of the shops he passed.

The plaza was empty when he finally reached it, the shops all dark and closed. Caulin pulled to a halt, breathing heavily, his chest burning from lack of air. He'd never find her at this pace. It seemed impossible. Like a needle in a haystack, so he'd once heard someone say.

Then, like a bolt of lightning during a summer storm, luck struck.

"Sawyer! Hey, Squirt, are you there? Talk to me, I can't find the place! Sawyer?"

At first, Caulin nearly bolted at the sudden voice. Then he recognized the name called. There was only one person in the city, as far as he knew, who answered to both Sawyer *and* Squirt.

"Hello needle!" he said, brightening considerably. Eryyn was somewhere close up ahead. Dragging a long breath into his tired lungs, he started running again.

• • •

"Sawyer? Is that you?" Eryyn stood at the mouth of the wide alley, looking back to where a dead end was created by a building on the next street. There were a lot of crates and trash bins blocking her view, but she was sure that there was a boy down there. A boy who was just Sawyer's size.

"Hey! Squirt? Answer me!"

The boy on the crate started to turn around, but stopped suddenly and looked back at the blank, brick wall. Eryyn stepped a few paces off the street. The figure had his back to her—she couldn't see the face—but she was sure it was Sawyer. Who else could it be?

Her voice seeming weak in the empty dimness of the street, she called, "I'm really sorry, Squirt. I made a big mistake the other day. I never should have taken the necklace from Liz. You were right."

No response. Eryyn tensed. Why wouldn't he answer her? Was he still that mad? Then why had he sent her the note? Something felt definitely odd here—it almost felt like someone was watching her. But she couldn't see anyone besides the silent boy. The small hairs on the back of her neck started to tingle as she took another tentative step into the alley.

"I-I miss you. I really do. Please forgive me and come back to the nest. If you give me the necklace, I'll bring it back to Liz and tell her everything. I'll apologize to her." She held out her hands, clasping them in front of her, and stepped further off the street.

"Eryyn! Wait! Stop for a second!"

Eryyn paused and looked back. To her surprise, Caulin was racing towards her, waving his arms madly.

"Stop! I need to talk to you! Eryyn, Squirt's in trouble!"

Caulin knew about Sawyer? Eryyn hadn't seen Caulin for weeks. What could he possibly know? Perplexed, and immediately worried, she hurried back to the street, reaching the sidewalk just as Caulin pulled to a stop, panting and wheezing from lack of breath.

"Caulin? What's going on?"

Caulin shook his head, doubled over at the waist, gripping his knees as he gasped for air. "Saw...yer's...in...t-tr-trou...ble," he managed. Eryyn grabbed his arms and forced him up straight until they were nose to nose.

"What are you talking about! Where is he! How do you know?"

"F-Fore...man. Got...Sawyer. Foreman!"

Eryyn frowned, feeling that odd tingle on her neck again. What in the world was he talking about? "The Foreman's got him? What do you mean? How? Will you stop that and talk to me!" She shook him roughly.

Getting his breath, Caulin struggled to push her away. "There's gonna be a trap! The Foreman's got Squirt and he's gonna use him in a trap for you."

Eryyn's frown deepened. "But Squirt wrote me a letter, he wanted me to meet him here and…"

Caulin shook his head, still finding it hard to breath after his long run. He fumbled with the chain around his wrist, pulling it free, and thrust the necklace into Eryyn's hands. "It was a trick. Sawyer's in Otto's stronghold. I know—I was just there and Rane saw him. *Talked* to him. He said the Foreman's after you."

Eryyn looked at the small, purple pendant, stunned, then turned to gaze down the alley. "But…?" Caulin followed her eyes and paled. Grabbing her arm, he attempted to pull her away.

"We gotta get out of here, Eryyn. Now!"

"*No!* That's Squirt down there! He told me to meet him! Let go, Caulin!" Eryyn fought him, desperately trying to run down the alley to her best friend. She couldn't leave him now, not when she was so close to having him back.

"Eryyn! Come on! It's a trap, you idiot! Why would Squirt have you meet him here, of all places? It's the Foreman! He's trying to trick you!" Caulin managed to drag her a few steps away from the alley, but Eryyn was strong, and she was desperate. In a few seconds she would break free and go running into the alley. Tightening his sweaty grip on her arm, he pulled hard, almost slipping off his feet as he forced her to take another step back onto the street. Eryyn slapped at his hands, squirming and twisting like a snake to escape his grasp. She managed to get one arm free and turned around to run back to her best friend.

Then, much to Caulin's relief, luck struck again as a large, dark shadow stepped away from the wall ten feet down the alley and started towards them. Caulin had just enough time to see a knife glittering in the figure's hand before Eryyn spotted it and screamed like a factory whistle. Her concentration on getting to Sawyer broken, Caulin was able to renew his grip and ran again, dragging the girl behind him.

"No!" He heard Eryyn shriek as the distance between them and the alley lengthened. "No! Caulin, please! Sawyer's back there! I have to get Sawyer!"

"Don't be stupid! You'll only get caught! Later! We'll get Sawyer later!" Caulin glanced back and saw a tall man standing where he and Eryyn had been just a few seconds before. He swallowed hard against a burning lump that had found its way into his throat. It had been close. Too close. If he'd been only been one minute later...

Eryyn was crying behind him, but she had stopped struggling to break loose and was matching his stride. "He's got Sawyer!" she wailed, covering her wet eyes with a hand and nearly tripping them both. "I saw him! He'll hurt him now! I have to help him. It's all my fault!"

Caulin couldn't answer her—he didn't have enough breath—and it was too important that he keep Eryyn moving to a place of safety. He put all his strength into running and they quickly left the plaza area and entered the park.

"No! Not that way!" Eryyn stopped suddenly, jerking painfully on his arm and almost pulling him off his feet. *Sheesh*, she was *strong!* Caulin's shoulder immediately began to throb as the punished muscles protested the abuse. "This way." Eryyn turned, running in a new direction, pulling Caulin along with her.

"Why?" Caulin gasped, following her without complaint.

"The nest. My gang. They'll help us. They'll help me save Sawyer."

Caulin nodded and let her lead the way. He desperately hoped she knew what she was talking about.

• • •

"Damn it! Damn it, you stupid fool!" The Foreman slammed his fist into a crate, splintering the weather-weakened planking. "What the *hell* were you thinking! I almost had her! Just another few seconds and she would have broken loose and *you* had to move too soon!"

Flint scowled. "It was the other boy. He knew what was going on. I heard them. And she was already spooked—she would have run anyway. I decided it was better to grab her before she got the chance."

"And it worked very well, didn't it?" The enraged man crushed another box with another hard blow. "They're both gone."

"You still have the boy. She'll be back for the boy." The bounty hunter gestured towards Sawyer, who sat on a crate at the back of the alley not two feet from where the Foreman stood. The boy's wrists were bound tightly to his knees with thick, silvery tape. More pieces strapped his ankles together and a double strip covered his mouth, effectively muting him. "As long as you have that little one, the girl will be putty in your hands. Didn't you hear her screaming for him?"

"I heard her running away and escaping. That's what I heard." The Foreman glared at the boy, who was looking at him with wide, frightened eyes. Sawyer flinched away when the Foreman, angry over the lost opportunity, threatened him with a raised fist. He looked down at his bound hands, his chest hitching as he struggled not to sob. Satisfied that the boy was suitably afraid of him, the Foreman turned back to Flint, who spoke quickly to calm the dangerously frustrated man.

"Give it a little more time," the bounty hunter reasoned, though he still burned with anger at the failure. "The next time we won't miss, because she'll know the consequences. She'll do whatever you want in order to keep her little friend safe. In fact, now she'll be waiting to hear from you, because she knows where the brat is."

The Foreman allowed his wrath to subside a bit and drew in a deep breath. Then he smiled and rested his hand on Sawyer's head, toying with the boy's disheveled hair. "Right. As long as I have this one, I have the girl too. It's no use fuming over lost opportunities. Right now, our best bet would be to get the boy back to the strong-hold and plan for the next move. Isn't that correct, my little trouble-maker?" He leaned down to look into Sawyer's face, his grin widening. Sawyer turned his eyes away, blinking rapidly. Tears flowed down his cheeks.

"What will be the next move?" Flint asked. "Another note?"

"Possibly. I'll have to think it over. For now, just get this little brat back to his room. It's past his bedtime. I have some kids I want to talk to."

Flint nodded and lifted Sawyer off the crate. The boy thrashed in his arms but quickly stilled when the bounty hunter threatened to drop him to the cement. They left the alley and the botched trap, returning to the stronghold. As he walked, the Foreman inwardly fumed. The trap should not have failed. It had been fool proof. But then that boy had shown up and ruined it all by warning Eryyn. He knew the boy too. It was Caulin, the self-pitying brat who had given him all the information he had on the green bands and their leader. *That* boy was supposed to be confined to the stronghold, to avoid problems just like this, but, somehow, the brat had gotten out. He'd have to make sure Otto received a reprimand for that. And he still had to figure out who had gotten into the dark room to talk to Sawyer. It couldn't have been Caulin—despite his show of courage at warning Eryyn about the trap, the boy was still too cowardly to have sneaked into the dark room. No, someone else was the sneak, and he had to find out who that someone was. He'd deal with that first, then plan another trap to get the girl. And, the next time, he would make sure that he couldn't possibly fail.

• • •

"What are you going to do now?" Caulin stood in the center of the main room in Eryyn's nest, surrounded by her gang members, who were all looking at her, confused and apprehensive, wondering what was going on.

Eryyn had collapsed upon stumbling through the door and was leaning against the wall, her knees drawn to her chest, her face buried in her arms. She was crying.

"What's going on?" A boy, younger than Caulin, touched his arm to get his attention. He glanced at the sobbing Eryyn, worried. "What happened?"

"I can't leave him there!" Eryyn wailed into her folded arms. "It's all my fault he got caught, I just can't leave him."

"Leave who?" The boy, Caulin suddenly remembered that his name was Jay, turned to him again. "It's Sawyer, isn't it? Did something happen to Sawyer?"

Caulin was surprised for a second, but then realized how the boy had come to that conclusion—Sawyer was the only kid who could get such a reaction out of Eryyn. If she was *this* upset, then something had to have happened to her small partner. He nodded.

"What?" A girl Caulin immediately recognized as Cinder shoved her way closer. "What happened?"

"The Foreman," Caulin said. It was explanation enough. Most of the kids gasped and some paled visibly. Near the far wall, a little girl began to cry. A red-haired boy standing beside her put his arm around her shoulders, but he, too, had tears in his eyes.

Ignoring the gasps, Cinder hurried over to Eryyn, dropping to her knees so she could hug her. "I'm sorry," she whispered. "Eryyn, I'm so sorry."

"We'll get him back, Eryyn," a tall boy, one Caulin couldn't put a name to, stated. "No matter what we have to do. No green band is going to be prisoner of that jerk."

His words were answered with a chorus of agreements from the other kids. Eryyn finally looked up, her face streaked with wetness and puffy red from crying. "Get him back?" she repeated, her voice dazed.

"Yeah, we'll get him back," Cinder said, squeezing Eryyn harder.

"How?"

That silenced them. None of the kids knew how they could rescue Sawyer. Not from the Foreman. Eryyn stared at them as they grew silent. She nodded.

"Right. The Foreman's got him, and he wants me too. He set a trap for me tonight, and I would've been caught if Caulin hadn't shown up. But now the Foreman's gonna keep a good hold on Squirt, 'cuz he's the bait. There's nothing *we* can do." She paused for a moment, chewing on her lip and staring at the floor. Two tears dripped from her nose to splash onto the floorboards. "But..." Another long silence.

"But..." Jay prompted. "But what?"

"But there *is* someone who could help."

"Who?" That came from a thin blonde girl. "Another gang?"

Eryyn shook her head. "No. Not a kid. A grown-up. A friend of Sawyer's. She'll help us. At least, I *think* she'll help us. I kinda made a big mistake and she might be mad at me."

"But she's *Sawyer's* friend, right?" Caulin asked, confused by Eryyn's mumbling. "She's not mad at Sawyer, is she?"

"No."

"Then she'll probably help, 'cuz Squirt's the one in trouble."

"But you said she's a grown-up, how would Squirt know a grown-up?" the tall boy asked.

"It's a long story. It has to wait." Eryyn was climbing to her feet, wiping away the tears that still clung to her cheeks and lashes. "I think you're right, Caulin. It's worth a try." She turned and hurried to the door.

"Where are you going?" Caulin called after her.

"To get help."

"I'm coming with you." Caulin hurried to follow and was joined by Jay and Cinder. Eryyn looked at the three of them and shook her head.

"You guys have to stay here and move the nest. The Foreman knows where we are now, and none of us are safe here anymore. Cinder, you and Jay found a new place, didn't you?"

Cinder nodded. "Yeah, a warehouse down near the Red plaza. Across from a little playground. There's plenty of room for everybody."

"Then you should all work to take the stuff there."

"Not a chance," said Jay, his jaw setting stubbornly. "They can find it themselves." He glanced back at the other kids, who all nodded. "You need protection. We're not gonna let you go out alone, not if the Foreman's after you."

"That's what I was thinking," Caulin added, not about to let Eryyn out of his sight now that they were back on speaking terms.

"Let them go, Eryyn," the tall boy, Rick, spoke up. "I'll make sure the moving goes okay."

Eryyn stared at them, her eyes tearing up again at their loyalty, then nodded. "Alright." She hurried out the door with the three kids following her. Then she explained where she was headed.

"We were there the other day. That's where you said Sawyer ran off," Jay supplied.

"Right. We were visiting Squirt's friend. Come on." Eryyn led them to the neighborhood where Liz and Greg lived, needing only a small bit of help from Jay and Caulin. When she found the house where she and Sawyer had had dinner and played games with the couple, she paused, suddenly uncertain.

"Go on," Cinder urged from behind. Eryyn looked back at the girl, seeing that her eyes were wide with fear. Jay and Caulin wore similar expressions, their cheeks so pale that the gray and blue of their eyes stood out in startling contrast. It had been a long time since any of them had had any contact with adults that didn't require stealing from them. This was a new, frightening experience. Then Jay glanced away from the house and caught her stare. He tried to give her an encouraging smile. Eryyn smiled back, then took a deep breath and timidly walked up the steps and rapped on the door.

There was no answer for a long moment. Eryyn knocked again, wondering fearfully if either of the adults were home. Then the door cracked open and revealed Liz, standing in the front hall. The woman looked down at her, confused for a second. Then she scowled.

"Come back for more?" she asked acidly. "Well, we don't have much left, but you might want to try the people next door, they're even poorer than…" She faltered to a stop as Eryyn burst into tears and flung herself forward, straight into Liz's arms. "Eryyn? Eryyn, what's wrong?" All of Liz's anger melted away in the face of the girl's misery. She stepped back, pulling the girl into the hall with her, then noticed the three kids standing on the sidewalk, looking up at her apprehensively. On her shoulder, Eryyn continued to sob loudly.

"Liz?" Greg's voice drifted from the kitchen. "Who is it?"

"Greg! Come here, please! I think I'm going to need your help."

Greg appeared in an instant and looked confusedly at the strange scene. Seeing Eryyn, his lips tightened into a frown. "What's going on here?" he demanded.

Liz shook her head confusedly and patted Eryyn's hair, then pointed at the door. "I don't know—that's what I'm trying to figure out. Please, find out who those kids are. I'll talk to Eryyn."

"You sure you want *her* in the house again? You don't have much jewelry left."

His words made Eryyn cry even harder. She pressed her face into Liz's arm, sobbing repeatedly, "I'm sorry, I'm so sorry. It was a mistake. I'm sorry!"

Liz tried to shush her, then looked up at her husband. "Please, Greg. Just do it." Without waiting for a reply, she led the distraught Eryyn into the living room and sat on the small sofa, pulling the girl down beside her.

"I know you're sorry," she whispered, when Eryyn continued her monotonous wailing. "I know. It's alright. I'm not mad anymore. Calm down. Tell me what's wrong."

Eryyn's cries started to subside until she was left with only whimpers and a bad case of the hiccups. Liz rubbed her back, still whispering soothingly, trying to coax some sort of explanation out of her. Then Greg walked into the room, followed by the three children Liz had seen outside. Her husband was pale and ringing his hands in front of him.

"This is some bad news, Liz," he said in a low voice. "These are all friends of Sawyer's."

Hearing the name of her small friend, the boy she hadn't seen since the night of the dinner, Liz felt her own face drain of color. "What happened to him? Is he alright?" she asked.

Greg shook his head. "He's in trouble. Bad trouble."

In her arms, Eryyn began to cry again. Greg continued, "He needs our help."

• • •

Half an hour later, Liz had heard the entire story. All four of the children, once Eryyn had calmed down again, had chipped in, telling her and Greg about a man called the Foreman, and his gangs, about a girl named Aimee and a plan for revenge. Liz now knew how Eryyn and Sawyer had formed the green bands to break up the Foreman's system, and how their plan had worked very well for awhile. But it seemed the Foreman had come up with a plan of his own. The older of the two boys, Caulin, had told her about the trap that Eryyn had almost fallen into, and how Sawyer had been the bait.

"He's got Squirt now," Eryyn said dully, after Caulin fell silent. "He knows I'll do *anything* to protect Squirt. He's gonna win. I don't know what to do."

Liz patted her arm comfortingly and looked up at Greg, her eyes questioning. Greg knelt in front of the girl and took her hands in his.

"Do you know where Sawyer is now?" he asked gently.

"I do!" Caulin piped up. "At least, I think I do. The Foreman had him at Otto's stronghold before. In the dark room. I know where the stronghold is. I was there."

"You can find it again?" Liz asked.

"Easily."

Greg nodded. "Then it's simple. We'll call the Enforcers and get them to help. If this Foreman is what you say he is, then the Enforcers will be glad to get him under wraps. Crime lords are one of the biggest problems of this city."

"We can't go to the Enforcers," Eryyn protested, looking horrified. "None of us are legal! None of us! The Enforcers will take *us* too."

"The Foreman is more important to them. You'll be fine." He reached out and took Eryyn's chin gently in his hand, forcing her to look in his eyes. "But, if we do this to help you, you have to bring all your gang to the Agency, alright? A favor for a favor. No more gangs, no more stealing, no more street life. You know that the Agency will protect you. It would have protected you before, and none of this would have even happened."

Eryyn wiped away a stray tear and nodded. Caulin, Jay, and Cinder looked at her, confused. Knowing that Eryyn had made Sawyer keep the Agency a secret from the rest of the gang, Liz explained about the charity house and the plan to take in the homeless children of the city.

Cinder's cheeks blazed with sudden color, causing the scar across her eye to stand out in startling white contrast. "You're kidding!" she exclaimed. "You knew about this, Eryyn, and you never told anyone? All this time there was a place that wanted to help us and you never told us?"

Eryyn ducked her head under the accusing words and muttered, "I-I needed to get even first. I was *going* to tell everyone. I was going to bring the whole gang to the Agency…after I'd won."

"Won what?" Jay had joined Cinder in being angry. It didn't seem fair that Eryyn hadn't even given them the choice between the gang and this new Agency house. His eyes flashed as he glared at Eryyn, who sighed miserably and said, "Won my fight with the Foreman. For killing my sister, Aimee. That's what I wanted the gang for." She hung her head, ashamed that the kids knew how she'd been using them and unable to face their angry eyes.

"I think, before anyone starts making accusations, we should remember that Sawyer is the important one here," Liz said, coming to Eryyn's rescue. "He's a friend to all of us, and he's the one being held prisoner by a man you all agree is cruel and dangerous."

Eryyn looked at her gratefully as the other three nodded. Greg stood up and walked into the kitchen to make the call to the nearest

Enforcer station.

"They will help, right?" Eryyn asked, watching him go. "They'll get Squirt back for me? They'll keep the Foreman from hurting him?"

"I can't give you any guarantees, Eryyn. But I hope so. I know they'll do their best. You just have to tell them everything you told Greg and me."

"Everything?" Eryyn sounded ill.

Liz nodded. "*Everything*. Everything that led to Sawyer's kidnapping."

"They'll know what we are!" Eryyn swept her hand back to indicate Caulin, Jay, and Cinder, using them to suggest her entire gang. "They'll know what we do! The Agency can't protect thieves."

Liz ran a hand through her hair, unconsciously messing up the blonde strands. "We'll have to see what happens. I don't know what they'll think, Eryyn. I'm sorry, but I don't."

Eryyn nodded meekly and leaned back on the sofa, dejectedly crossing her arms over her chest. Caulin reached over and took her hand, offering some comfort from the angry glares of Jay and Cinder.

Officers Connel and Pritchard arrived at the door twenty minutes later. The two men looked surprised to see four ragged, unkempt children sitting on the sofa and floor of the living room, but did their best to hide it as Greg filled them in on the immediate situation. Eryyn and the others looked at the officers warily, feeling immediate fear at being so close to the very people they had worked so hard to avoid. Jay, his naked wrist shoved deep into his pocket, even moved closer to Liz. He sat beside her on the sofa, obviously thinking her the best form of protection in the room. Smiling comfortingly, Liz wrapped her arm around his shoulders, doing the same for Eryyn on her other side, and listened as her husband tried to piece the story together again from the many different bits he'd been told.

After a time, one of the officers stepped away from Greg and turned to the sofa. He kneeled down before Eryyn and asked her name. She gave it and he nodded. "So you're the one who started all this?" he asked.

"I-I guess so. Yeah. It's my fault."

"I didn't say anything was your fault, young lady. I just asked if you had started all this. There's only one man at fault here and we've been after him for years."

Jay gaped at the Enforcer, his blue eyes wide. "You know about the Foreman?" he asked, his mouth hanging open.

The man nodded. "Well, that's the name he goes by among the kids of the city. He's got a few others. But yes, we've known about him for a long time, and we're very eager to get any information on him that we can. He's proven very hard to catch."

Jay looked stunned—he'd never believed that anyone in the city could outsmart the Enforcers. The Enforcers were the law. They were above everyone and everything. Nobody beat the Enforcers.

The officer read these thoughts on the boy's face and had to suppress a smile. He held out his hand to Liz. "I'm Officer Arnold Pritchard. I have to ask these children a few questions. Would you please step over to my friend? I believe you know Officer Connel, right?"

"I do. I've worked for him for years." Liz shifted a bit, pulling her arms out from under Jay and Eryyn, and stood up. "But first, I think I'll make us all something to drink. It's been a long night." She raised her eyebrows at Pritchard and cocked her head in Eryyn's direction. "And I have an inkling it's going to feel a lot longer before it's over." It was her way of asking the man to go easy on the children, who were obviously scared and very upset.

The Enforcer nodded, understanding. Liz walked away, vanishing into the kitchen. Pritchard turned his attention back to Eryyn and her friends.

"Okay, I know you're all nervous and have been through this once before, but I want to hear the entire story from you. Starting at the beginning. Alright."

Eryyn, with a glance at the others, nodded and sat up straighter. "Okay. It pretty much started when my friend, Squirt...I mean, Sawyer, and I stopped at Master John's pawnshop to sell some of our loot. Um, that's when we met up with an old friend of mine, a kid named Otto..."

TWELVE

The crow and the sparrows

Rane was doing his best to sit perfectly still. It was safer not to draw attention to himself right now. Not when the Foreman was so obviously angry at something. And not when Otto was receiving the brunt of his anger. The gang leader wasn't going to be a very pleasant companion after this. He and Sasha could perfectly hear the Foreman's shouting, even though they were down the hall from the meeting room. Otto was getting torn apart over Caulin's disappearance.

"I wonder how he got away," Sasha mused. "I mean, he was always watched, all the time. He never had a chance to escape."

Rane didn't say anything. He stood up and walked to one of the boarded up windows, looking through a hole out at the darkness. There would be trouble if Otto questioned Denny and found out that it was Rane who'd been with Caulin just before he'd gotten away. Nothing Rane could say would make Otto disbelieve Denny's words. He had a bad feeling that the closet wouldn't be the worst of his punishments.

But if the Foreman was yelling about Caulin, it probably meant that the boy had managed to warn Eryyn. So there was some good news, though it was hard to feel happy when Otto's wrath seemed imminent.

He sighed and crossed the room again, leaning against the wall for only a minute before restlessness sent him back to the window.

Soon, he was pacing.

Sasha watched him briefly, then demanded, "Will you sit down and stop that! You're making me sick."

"Then we're even," Rane muttered, still walking back and forth.

"You want a black eye?"

Rane sat down again. Sasha didn't sound like she was joking. He crossed his arms over his chest and scowled at the floor.

"Sheesh, the way you look, it could be you in there getting yelled at," Sasha pointed out. Rane looked at her coldly and she went back to the pattern she was carving into a floorboard with a nail. The entire area around her pallet was covered in little scrawlings and doodles, even the walls.

Unable to sit still for long, Rane stood up again, drawing another angry look from the girl, and walked out of the room. The halls were empty—all the other kids were back in the sleeping room with Sasha. They were oblivious to the shouting that echoed through the house. Besides Rane and Sasha, only Denny was still awake, keeping watch in one of the upstairs rooms. Taking advantage of being alone, Rane slipped down to the room across from the kitchen. The deadbolts were still in place—he'd relocked them after leaving the room the last time. However, they easily gave way once he dragged the chair over again to reach them.

Knowing that he was tempting fate with the Foreman so close, he entered the small front room, leaving the door open a crack for light, and crossed to the tiny entrance of the dark room. Sawyer was still bound to the chair, but Rane immediately noticed that there was now a piece of tape over his mouth. He appeared to be sleeping. His eyes were closed and his head was leaned forward against his chest. The room was very quiet.

Tiptoeing, Rane walked to the chair and tapped the boy's hand. Sawyer jumped, his eyes popping open, a muffled scream issuing from behind the gag. Startled, Rane clamped his hand over the tape, whispering loudly. "Hey, it's only me! Don't do that!"

Sawyer seemed to recognize his voice and quit struggling, but squeezed his eyes closed tightly. Rane frowned. It took him a moment to remember that when the doors were closed the room was in complete darkness. The sudden illumination had to have been painful for Sawyer.

"Sorry." Rane shifted, standing in front of the door and blocking a lot of the light. After a few seconds, Sawyer risked a glance up, then sighed and opened his eyes completely. He tried to speak, but the gag made it impossible to understand what he was saying.

"Hold on a second." Rane reached out and gripped a loose corner of the tape. He pulled hard, tearing it from Sawyer's lips. The boy yelped at the sting and looked at him reproachfully.

"There must have been a nicer way to do that," he said angrily.

Rane shrugged. "I don't have time. I just wanted to tell you that I sent Caulin out and he managed to warn Eryyn. She's okay, I think."

"I know," Sawyer said, his voice tinged with bitterness. "I was there."

Rane looked at him with confusion.

"I was the bait," Sawyer whispered, his voice breaking with a sob. "To lure her into the trap. She almost fell for it, but Caulin stopped her just in time. I-I heard her crying out. She was saying that she's sorry, and-and…" Tears welled up in the boy's eyes, overflowing onto his cheeks.

"But she got away, didn't she?"

"Yeah." Sawyer sniffled. "This time. But the Foreman's not done yet." Pleading green eyes looked up at Rane. "Not as long as he has me. He's gonna try again soon, I know it."

Rane caught the meaning of Sawyer's look and glanced back towards the doorway. It *would* be easy to untie the boy and run away now, while Otto and the Foreman were preoccupied with each other. Then *he'd* have a chance to escape too. And if Eryyn knew that he'd helped her friend…well, she couldn't refuse to let him into her gang, then, could she? Sawyer would probably vouch for him. Besides, once the Foreman was finished with Otto, and Otto questioned Denny…

There's my answer right there, he thought, and to Sawyer he said, "Right, but if the Foreman doesn't have his hostage…"

Sawyer's eyes brightened with hope. "Please?"

Rane nodded and turned to the arms of the chair, where Sawyer's wrists were bound tightly. His heart sank. The last time he'd been in the room the boy had been tied with ropes. Now there were energy binders. There was no way he could unlock one of those without the right key.

"You can't unlock them, can you?" Sawyer had seen the look of despair in Rane's eyes. He knew that he hadn't been tied with ropes again—the nearly invisible beam of the energy binders caused an annoying tingle when activated—but he'd hoped…

"I'm sorry," Rane murmured, covering his eyes with a hand.

Sawyer let out a long breath and didn't reply.

Rane glanced up. "May-maybe he'll go back to the ropes again. Then I can do something."

Sawyer looked bleak. "It might be too late by then. Isn't there something you can do now? Someway to block the beam, or…"

"Block the beam?" Rane hadn't thought of that. If something were lowered through the beam, cutting it off from the other projector…? It could work. "Hold on, maybe I can do that. Let me find something to use." He left the room, closing the doors behind him, and crossed to the kitchen. It was mostly empty, the kleptos had no use for the ancient refrigerator or stove, but he knew that there were still some implements in the drawers—knives and spoons and such. He started searching through the drawers, sending up shafts of dust and startling hidden nests of mice, but found nothing useful. It looked like they'd all been emptied. Frustrated, he peered around, trying to find *anything* that would be of use.

A cupboard over the counter still had some stuff in it. It was a possibility. He clambered up onto the tiled shelf and opened the glass-fronted door. It was full of discolored, cracked, and dusty plates and bowls. He didn't think any of those would do any good, but at the back, tucked slightly behind a large, flat dish with a pattern on the front, he saw an odd-looking knife with dull edges and a wide, triangular blade. Perfect!

He leaned forward, reaching for it, and accidentally knocked the platter from its spot. It fell onto a pile of plates, knocking the top one off. It toppled out of the cupboard and landed, with a crash, on the floor. To Rane, the noise was horrendous.

Wincing, he grabbed the pie-server and jumped down, slipping on shards of shattered porcelain.

"What the hell was that!"

Rane winced again. Of all the times for Otto to come out into the hall. Anxiously, he thrust the server into a drawer, slamming it shut, then peeped around the doorway to see the gang leader glaring down the hall.

"Sorry. Some stuff fell. I'll clean it up."

"Later!" Otto snarled. "Thanks for saving me the trouble of looking for you. The Foreman wants to talk to all the kids. He has a few questions he wants to ask. You first, Raney boy."

"Why? What did I do?"

"How should I know? I'm not about to go asking *him* why. Just get your skinny butt up here now."

Rane sighed, but knew it was useless to argue. He trotted up the hall and stepped into the meeting room where the Foreman waited. His sudden apprehension at having to talk with the dreaded man completely wiped away the thought of Sawyer. He forgot that the chair he'd used to reach the top deadbolt was still pushed up against the wall. Both locks were still open, and, in the dark room, Sawyer sat waiting, the tape once used to cover his mouth now lying in a crumpled ball on the floor.

• • •

"Rane, is it?"

Rane nodded and slid into the seat indicated by the hand that thrust out of the dim alcove. His eyes stared into the small room, trying to see the man who was hidden there, but all he could make out was an outline. Behind him there was the sound of the door closing as Otto left him alone with the man. Rane turned as the latch clicked shut, his breath quickening.

"You look nervous, boy."

Rane wriggled a bit in his chair. "Umm, yeah, a little."

"Why? Do you think you're in trouble? Did you do something that would warrant you being in trouble?"

Rane didn't know what warrant meant, but he had an idea. Lying, he shook his head. "Am I?" he asked.

"I'm not sure. Someone in this stronghold is, but I don't know who just yet. That is what I'm trying to find out. Now, you've been in this gang for three years, isn't that right?"

So, the Foreman kept track of the kids in his gang. That was a surprise. Rane repeated his nod.

"You know all the rules then. All that you must do in order to be happy here."

Happy? That was stretching it. Rane nodded yet again. If the questions were all going to be this simple, then he didn't have much to worry about. That was what made him nervous.

"Rane, do you know the door down the hall, the one with the two locks on it?"

There it was. Still simple, but now dangerous. Rane answered carefully, "Yes, sir. It leads to the room where the new kids stay. Sometimes gang members go there to talk the new kids into cooperating."

"Very good. But there's a rule that no children are allowed in that room unless they are told to go there by their leader. Or by me."

"I didn't know that," Rane lied. "But none of the kids would want to go there anyway, right? There's nothing in there, and most of them probably remember when they were locked up in there...I do."

"That didn't stop one kid."

Rane didn't speak. He didn't know what to say. How had the man figured out that someone had gone into the room to see Sawyer? He'd been careful to replace the locks and move the chair back to its original...

Rane tensed. *The chair!* He'd forgotten about the chair! And the locks, they were all open! He'd left them open, because he'd been planning to go back into the room to...Oh, sheesh! He'd even taken the tape off of Sawyer's mouth. How dumb could a kid get?

"Rane? I asked you a question."

Rane snapped back to attention. "What? I-I guess I d-didn't hear it. S-s-sorry."

There was a silence from the alcove. Rane felt eyes on him and wanted to shrivel into his seat. *Did I just make a big mistake?* he wondered. *Wouldn't be the first.*

Finally, "I asked, have you, for any reason, gone into that room? Or have you seen any of the other kids go into or come out of there?"

"No," Rane answered quickly. Too quickly? Well, let the mistakes just pile up, they couldn't possibly get him into *more* trouble.

"Sir, I haven't gone in there. And I don't think any of the other kids have. At least, I haven't seen them. Why?"

"Not your business." The eyes, hidden in the dark, continued to stare piercingly at the boy. "But someone has been in there. I know for a fact. And when I find out who, that person is going to be very, very sorry. Disobedience doesn't go over well with me. But you know that, don't you?"

Rane bit down hard on his lower lip. And nodded.

• • •

This was the one. He was sure of it. Guilt and fear were simply covering the child's face. He knew he'd done something wrong, and he knew he would get in trouble if he were caught.

You're caught, the Foreman thought joyfully. *It's all over for you, boy. But let's see what a little more fear can make you confess.*

To the boy, he said, "Rane, do you know what I do?"

Rane stared into the darkness that cloaked him. "Do? What do you mean? Y-you run the gangs, right?"

"More than that, boy. I run the city. I own it."

The thought made Rane want to laugh. But you didn't laugh at the Foreman. Not if you wanted to live to see the morning. Instead, he continued to peer into the darkness and shifted uncomfortably on the chair. "How can you own the city? It belongs to everyone. All the people who live in it."

A cruel laugh filled the room. "*You* live in the city, boy, and you don't own *anything*. Not even your own freedom. The city belongs to whoever has the power to possess it."

"And you do?"

"I do. I made myself the power and I take everything that I want. Because I can. I can kill if it suits me. Not just street kids either." Across the room, the Foreman could see Rane's eyes. They were wide and very dark, their color lost to worry and fear. "Most of the factories in this city work under my rules. The people who make them function pay heed to my orders. But if someone needs to be…disposed of…well, that's a job that I've never done with my own hands. Do you know why?"

Rane shook his head. He looked like he wanted to run—like a

small, terrified animal caught in a trap.

"Because then I can never be caught. And a large part of having power is being able to easily dispose of what doesn't suit your needs and start off clean again. That's why, in all my buildings throughout the city, I have little surprises waiting, just in case."

"Surprises?" The boy cocked his head to one side, confusion joining the other emotions visible in his eyes.

"If any problems arise in one of my buildings all I have to do is push a little button and they all disappear. Simple as that."

"H-how?"

The Foreman ignored the question. "Don't you understand, boy? Power is the ability to take care of all the problems and still come out on top. I always stay in power. Even if it means cleaning the slate and starting again. The lives of one little boy and his friends don't matter to me at all. It makes no difference to me whether they wake up the next morning or not. As long as I come away unscathed."

He's talking about Sawyer! Rane thought, horrified. *He's talking about killing Sawyer!* Without knowing it, he gasped slightly, tensing again. In the darkness, the Foreman smiled.

"Just a simple push of a button, my boy, and everything will just…"

"*Foreman!*"

The voice was weak, coming from a distance. But they both heard the sound of feet on the stairs, heard Denny as he ran down to the first floor, screaming.

"Foreman, they're here! The Enforcers, they're right outside! They're surrounding the stronghold!"

Denny was one of the few kids in the gang who was still loyal to the Foreman. His warnings would be true. And he sounded frantic.

The conversation was over. Rane jumped up from his chair and ran to the door, flinging it open to look out one of the hall windows. He was stunned to see that it was light already. The night was over and the street outside was filled with people, most in the uniform of the Enforcers. Suddenly, Otto was beside him, looking out the same window, swearing softly under his breath.

"How?" Rane asked, glancing quickly at Otto, then back to the window. Otto didn't need to answer—Rane had just spotted Caulin, nearly hidden in the crowd, and knew how.

Denny kept screaming his warning, and kids started coming out of the sleeping room, wiping bleary eyes and asking what all the noise was about. In answer, the Foreman spoke up from the meeting room, his angry voice ordering them all in. Puzzled and frightened, the kids immediately obeyed, and Rane found himself pushed along with them. In the confusion, he never stopped to wonder if the stronghold could have been one of those problem places the Foreman had been talking about. The places with the push button surprises.

• • •

"He's got Sawyer in there." Eryyn stared at the large building, straining against Liz's hands as the woman tried to keep her from running forward to find her partner. "Squirt's locked up in there, I have to get to him."

"That's what the Enforcers are here to do. Give them a chance, Eryyn. You can't go in there. Not now."

"But Sawyer…"

"They'll get him. You just have to give them a chance to…"

"No, they won't. I have to get him. I have to help him."

"Eryyn, no!" Liz wrapped her arms around the girl. "You have to wait."

Across the street, Officer Pritchard was raising a bullhorn to his lips, preparing to call out a warning to the Foreman, telling him to surrender without a fight, so that nobody had to be hurt.

"Why don't they just go in there and get him?" Eryyn asked impatiently, stamping her feet and clinging to Liz's encircling arms. "They're the Enforcers, they can do that. Why don't they?"

"There are kids in there, Eryyn. Sawyer and lots of others. Nobody wants them hurt."

"But…" Eryyn didn't finish as a loud, high-pitched voice began to scream from a second floor room, calling warnings to the crime lord below. All around, the Enforcers began to get into the positions for a fight. The siege was on.

• • •

"Those are the Enforcers out there. They know we're here. They know what you kids have been doing." The Foreman spoke from his alcove, addressing the stunned, confused, and terrified children before him.

Rane, standing beside Otto, could hear the sounds of a man calling to them from outside. He demanded a surrender. Demanded that all the kids come out, along with the Foreman, that nobody had to get hurt. Rane trembled.

"What are we going to do?" Sasha asked, squeezing her hands together in terror.

"You're going to stay here for now. I'm going to leave, out the back door. After ten minutes you will start to do the same, two at a time. You will leave the building and make your way to the house on Sixth. If you go quietly, then those idiots outside will be none the wiser."

There was a collective nod and many fearful eyes glanced towards the windows.

"If you don't follow my directions exactly, then you will be caught. And none of you…are legal. You won't stand a chance."

The warning was very clear. The fear increased and the kids nodded again, showing their eagerness to obey and stay safe.

"Good. Remember, ten minutes, then come out two at a time." A man stepped out of the alcove, coming into full view as he crossed the room to the door. Gasps and cries arose from the kids. The Foreman had never allowed himself to be seen before! He had left the shadows; now they all knew what he looked like.

Rane was terrified. Something here wasn't right. Why would the Foreman show himself now? Why would he let them all know his face? And where had this plan come from? He'd never heard about any escape plan before.

Just a simple push of a button, my boy, and everything will just…

The words came back to Rane in a rush. He gasped, and looked at the man who was stepping out into the hall. In the Foreman's hand was a small contraption that looked familiar, like the remote thing that made TVs work. He held it up, and Rane saw a dozen small green buttons on its surface.

Little surprises waiting, just in case…If problems should arise in one of my buildings, all I have to do is push a little button, and they all disappear…cleaning the slate…

He couldn't mean…? Sirens went off in Rane's mind and he grabbed Otto's arm, a scream tearing itself from his throat.

"Otto! He's got a bomb! Explosives! *He's gonna set off explosives! He's escaping and he's gonna kill us all!*

Otto jumped, and looked down at the younger boy, trying to understand. Rane's eyes were frantic and he was clawing at his arm, nearly drawing blood. The boy pointed to the retreating Foreman.

"That thing in his hand! He's gonna use it to set off a bomb! *Otto, there's a bomb in the stronghold!*

Something clicked in Otto's brain. The Foreman had shown everyone his face! They all knew what he looked like now! But he couldn't do that, not if he wanted to keep his identity secret. Unless…

"No!" He shoved Rane away and jumped forward, running out of the room. The Foreman was nearly gone, had just ducked into the hall that would take him to the back door and his escape. Otto ran faster, trying to catch up. He did, just as the Foreman was lifting the small remote, his finger poised to push the button. "Don't!" he yelled.

The Foreman looked up, startled at having been followed. Then he grinned and moved his finger closer to the button.

Otto barreled into him, using all his sixteen-year-old muscle to knock the man off his feet.

"I won't let you do it. I won't let you kill us all!" he screamed. "You're not getting away from this." A furious fight ensued, during which Otto learned that the Foreman was very strong. It took all his strength to hold the man down, trying to keep his hands pinned, while he struggled to grab at the remote. Several times he nearly had it, only to lose his grip on the sweaty wrist. And all the time he had to hold the other hand down, to keep it from the button it strove to push.

The Foreman punched Otto several times and had to thrust a knee into his gut before he finally managed to push the boy away. Then he struggled to his feet, wiping blood off his lip and spitting on the teenager writhing on the floor.

"Go back and say goodbye to all your friends, little boy. You don't have much time." He raised the remote again. And pushed a button.

"No!" Otto screamed, struggling to his feet. But it was too late. The button was glowing. The bomb was set. And the Foreman was smiling at him.

"I'll get some new kids in the next city. Hopefully I'll find one like you, Otto. You were wonderful, too stupid to realize what was really going on. Just in it for the power trip."

He turned, heading down the hall for the door.

Furious, Otto lurched to his feet and looked around. He grabbed the first weapon he could find, lifted it over his head, then charged down the hall, screaming at the top of his lungs. He swung the metal chair with surprising accuracy, bringing it down in a long arch that connected squarely with the Foreman's right leg. There was a loud *snap* as the limb splintered under the blow, and the Foreman went down with an agonized cry.

"You're not going anywhere," Otto sneered. "I want you to see your bomb work. Close up." He grabbed the man's ankle and dragged him away from the door, down the hall to the center of the house. The Foreman howled in pain and thrashed out, trying to kick the boy with his good leg. Otto, skipping nimbly away from each attempt, pulled the man into an old bathroom and closed the door on him. "It didn't work this time, Foreman!" he yelled, running back to the room where his eight remaining gang kids still waited, terrified and confused, questioning a frantic Rane about a bomb.

"Everybody out, now!" Otto screamed, waving his arms from the door. "Get out, hurry! Before it goes off!"

Shrieks of fear filled the halls and the kids stampeded for the door, colliding with one another in their desperation to get out of the doomed house. The hall was full of screaming, terrified kids, all heading for the door. It burst open under their onslaught, and they streamed out into the streets, directly into the waiting arms of the Enforcers, who, hearing the terrified babbling about a bomb, quickly moved everyone back.

Rane was one of the last to leave the room. He fell in beside Otto, who was struggling to help Sasha. The girl had been pushed by Denny during the rush and had fallen, twisting her ankle. She could hardly walk and had to lean on the gang leader for support.

Rane grabbed Otto's sleeve, trying to hurry him along.

"What happened?" he asked frantically. "What did you do? There's a bomb, right? He started it!"

"He pressed a button," Otto replied through gritted teeth, half dragging, half carrying Sasha down the hall. "The bomb's gonna go off. We have to get out."

"Where's the Foreman?"

Otto didn't answer, he just kept running. Rane went with him, one hand on the gang leader's sleeve. They had just reached the exit when he happened to glance back and saw the chair standing in front of the door to the darkroom. He'd forgotten Sawyer! Had left him tied and helpless in the chair! *The boy would be killed!*

Swiftly, Rane whirled around, running back. A hand clamped on his shoulder.

"Where the *hell* are you going, idiot?" Otto asked. "*There's a bomb! We have to get out now!*"

Rane shook his head. "There's a kid in there!" he shouted. "He'll be blown up if I don't get him out!" Rane shoved at the hand, pushing it away. Otto lurched for him again and missed. The smaller boy rushed away, running back down the hall. Otto screamed for him to stop, to come back, not to be stupid. But Rane didn't listen. All Otto could do was stumble out of the house, still helping Sasha, and nearly fall down the stairs as he tried to get away. He glanced back through the door, hoping that Rane had come to his senses and was following him out, but there was nothing. Rane was gone, vanished deep into a house that was set to blow up at any minute.

• • •

Eryyn watched as the terrified, screaming kids streamed out of the building. She listened as the words *bomb* and *explosives* were shouted over and over. But she paid no attention. She was searching the crowd, trying to find a face. Looking desperately for someone, but not finding him.

Then she spotted Otto, stumbling out of the house, supporting a girl who seemed to have somehow hurt her foot. She screamed for him, and, after a moment of fierce struggling, broke loose from Liz's grasp, running over to the gang leader.

"Otto! Otto! It's me, Eryyn!"

Otto was already surrounded by people, some were helping him with the injured girl, others were asking him questions as they pulled him further away from the stronghold. It took Eryyn another minute before she managed to shove her way through them, squeezing her wiry body between the crowd until she was face to face with the gang leader. She grabbed him by the shirt collar.

"Where is he!" she screamed. "Where's Sawyer!"

Otto looked at her blankly. "Sawyer?" Someone was dabbing at a cut on his face, which was bleeding. He looked like he'd just fought a losing fight. Eryyn didn't care—he could bleed to death for all it mattered to her, but first he had to answer her question. She pushed off all the hands that tried to move her away from her former friend and continued to question him.

"Squirt. My partner! Where is he? Why didn't he come out of the house?"

Otto shook his head dazedly. "What are you talking about, Eryyn? I don't know where Squirt is."

"But he was in there!" Eryyn screeched. "He was in the house! The Foreman had him! He's in there! I know he is!"

Understanding dawned in Otto's eyes and he groaned, remembering Rane's words before he had run back down the hall.

There's a kid in there...he'll be blown up...

"Oh no. No. He didn't!" Otto collapsed, pressing both hands to his face. Eryyn continued to shake him. "What?" she demanded. "Otto, where is he?"

"Inside," Otto said dully, starting to cry. "He must still be inside. Rane went to get him. But there's no time, Eryyn. There's no time. There's a bomb! It's gonna kill them both."

By then, Liz had caught up with Eryyn and grabbed her by the arms. She was just in time to hear Otto's last statement and Eryyn's scream of anguish. The girl whirled around, fighting her grip, as she struggled to get to the house.

"I have to get in there!" she yelled. "He'll be killed! I have to help him. Liz, there's a bomb in the house and Squirt's inside! He's going to be killed!"

Fighting back a cry of her own, Liz lost her grip on Eryyn and ran to follow her to the house. Two Enforcers jumped forward to stop them, but Liz slapped away their hands, demanding to be let through.

"There are two other children in there!" she cried. "They're both going to die if we don't get them out. Somebody has to go in there and…" Her sentence was cut short as an enormous blast shook the street, and the house exploded, blowing them all to the ground. Liz hit the pavement hard, scraping her knees and elbows, her face and chest. For a long moment she could do nothing but lie prone, trying to draw air back into her starved lungs as debris rained down. Then she weakly tried to struggle to her knees, feeling blood trickle down her forehead. Her ears were ringing from the sound of the blast, a loud, high-pitched tone that was instantly maddening, but not loud enough to drown out the keening, anguished wails of Eryyn as she crawled towards the rubble that was all that remained of the building.

"Sawyer! *No, Sawyer! No! Please! No! No! No!*"

Liz looked up at the girl, and then at the house. Her heart sank. There was nothing left but a pile of stones and two far walls that were near crumbling. A cloud of dust was rising from the wreckage. Neither child had gotten out.

• • •

The screaming in the halls was so loud that Sawyer heard it in the little room where he was imprisoned. Wondering what was going on outside, he began to feel a knot of fear clench his stomach.

Then the door opened and Rane stepped through, his face pale with panic, his eyes wide.

"Where have you been?" Sawyer asked. "I was beginning to think you were never coming back." He pointed his chin at the binders. "These things burn."

Rane laughed dully and hurried across the room. "Sawyer, right now, that's the very least of our troubles. We have to get out of here, and *now!*"

"What's going on?" Sawyer was suddenly filled with alarm. "What was all the screaming about?" He watched as Rane, holding a long, triangular metal object, started working on the energy binders. "Is there trouble out there?"

Rane laughed again and stuck the metal thing into the beam. "More than you can imagine, Sawyer," he said, grasping Sawyer's wrist and trying to pull it through the binder. The beam, a faint shimmer of light normally, flared brightly. Sawyer gasped in pain and looked down at his hand. The beam hadn't been broken by the obstacle—he was still trapped. Realizing this, Rane cursed loudly, then muttered, "There's a bomb in the building. Set by the Foreman. It's gonna go off…real soon."

It took a moment, after the disappointment with the binders, for his words to dawn on Sawyer, but then the boy pulled in a whistling breath and his eyes flooded with tears. "No! Get them off!" he pleaded. "Please! Rane, please, hurry!"

Rane swallowed hard and looked at the mechanism that worked the beams. It was nothing but a small black box with gears bolted to the arm of the chair. Out of ideas, he struck at it with the pie-server, splintering the plastic and shattering the inner workings. To his astonishment, and great relief, it worked. The beam fluttered, spat a few sparks, then stopped altogether. Sawyer lifted his burned wrist, staring at it in shock as Rane attacked the box on the other side. In a heartbeat, his second wrist was free and Rane was pulling him up from the chair, supporting him on legs that were shaky from having been sitting too long.

"Come on," Rane urged, "we don't have a lot of time. We have to get out of here now."

"Not so fast, my boys."

Both children turned to find their way blocked by a tall man. He stood in the doorway, his weight supported by one leg, scowling down at them ferociously.

The Foreman.

"I knew it was you, Rane. I just knew it. I could see it all over your face. You've been a very bad boy."

"Leave us alone!" Rane demanded, putting himself between the man and Sawyer. "Just leave us…" He gasped and his heart started to pound hard against his chest as the man lifted a pistol out of his shirt and pointed it at them.

The Foreman clacked his tongue disapprovingly. "A *very* bad boy," he repeated. "And now you're going to have to pay. Both of you." His sneer was terrifying. Sawyer couldn't hold back a sob and grabbed Rane's hand in a tight squeeze. Rane squeezed back and forced himself to face the man.

"It doesn't matter if you kill us," he said, his voice trembling. "Your power's nothing now! *Nothing!* They *all* got out! They saw your face! They know who you are. You'll never get away this time!"

The Foreman's aim wavered slightly as he looked from one frightened boy to the other, then he slipped the gun back into his shirt. "You're right, boy—I'm finished here—but that doesn't mean I can't start over again somewhere else." He suddenly rushed forward, limping awkwardly on a broken leg. He grabbed the two boys, pulling them apart as he held each one with a hand. "And you two will be coming with me. I'll need a few kleptos to start off with." His fingers closing tightly on Rane's upper arm and Sawyer's wrist, he dragged them out of the room, heedless of their kicking and struggling.

"Let me go!" Sawyer screamed as they entered the hall. "Stop! Please, let go!" Rane echoed his cries and beat furiously on the man's chest with his free hand. It didn't work. The Foreman might have been made of stone for all his efforts worked. The man continued to hold them, pulling them down the hall. Rane watched in despair as the exit door grew further and further away.

"You know, Rane, I'm surprised you managed to figure it out. It's my fault, really. I told you too much. I should have realized that you'd be bright enough to figure it out. Not that it will matter now." The Foreman hauled them along, slowed only slightly by his injured leg and both boys, who fought madly, screaming and pleading to be let go.

They passed a window and Sawyer grabbed madly at the sill, digging his nails into the wood. Through the smudged glass he saw the crowd, all gathered in front of the house, excited and tending to the kids who had managed to escape. Then, surprisingly, he caught sight of Eryyn, running through the people, pushing her way around as she headed for Otto.

"*Eryyn!*" he shrieked, pulling hard on the hand that captured his wrist and banging his fist against the windowpane. "*Eryyn, help!*"

The Foreman chuckled, even though his face was tight and drawn with agony. "It'll do you no good. No one could get here in time."

He continued to drag the two boys down the hall, pulling Sawyer away from the window, and shoved them both into the meeting room. Limping across the floor, oblivious of the struggling children in his grasp, he kicked aside a small rug that lay in a corner, revealing a door built into the floorboards.

Rane stared at it, amazed. In the three years he had been living in the stronghold, he had never noticed the rug, and had never thought to wonder if there was any way out of the building other than the front and back doors.

"Open that!" The Foreman shoved him closer to the door, pushing down on his arm until he was bent over the handle. Rane grasped it in his hands and tugged hard. The door came open with a loud groan of badly oiled hinges and Rane stared down into a midnight black hole that obviously led to a tunnel under the floor.

"Get going. We don't have much time left!" The Foreman gave Rane another shove, forcing him down the first of the stairs, and hurriedly followed, dragging Sawyer behind him.

By now, Rane had stopped struggling. The Foreman was right—there wasn't enough time left to escape. The bomb was set to go off at any minute and they were too far away from the exit doors. The only way out was through this tunnel, as a prisoner of the Foreman. As he was pushed down another step, a sob rose in his throat and he glanced up at Sawyer, who was crying and still fighting to break his wrist free of the Foreman's grip. Then, as his gaze drifted past the smaller boy, Rane caught sight of the darkened area that was the Foreman's alcove. The area that was separated from the rest of the room. An extra addition to the house. There was no second floor above it. And it was sheltered, at least partly! Maybe there was a chance after all! If they could just reach it in time...!

"Sawyer! *Bite him!*"

Surprised by the sudden order, Sawyer stopped struggling and immediately obeyed, grabbing the Foreman's hand and clamping his teeth into the skin of his knuckles. At the same time, Rane lifted his foot and brought it crashing down onto the man's broken knee.

Pain overwhelming him from two places, the Foreman screamed in agony and let them go, reaching down to grab his knee as his legs began to buckle underneath him.

Knowing that time was short, and that they would only get one chance, Rane grabbed Sawyer's hand, leapt out of the hole and raced across the room, yanking the frightened, confused ten-year-old with him.

"*The alcove!*" he cried. "*We have to get to the alcove! There might just be a chance!*" He tugged on Sawyer's hand, pulling the boy in front of him, then gave him a hard push. Sawyer jumped ahead, springing for the depression in the wall. Rane followed. They were close. So close. Just a few more feet and…

Something caught against his foot, tripping him. He crashed to the ground just two yards from safety. Glancing back, he saw that he had tripped over one of the boxes they had used to give the Foreman his collection quota. The old, dry wood had broken under his feet and was now lying in pieces around his legs.

"*Rane! Hurry!*" Sawyer yelled.

Desperate, knowing that time was running out, Rane scrambled to his feet, tripping again as the broken pieces of wood tangled against his legs. With a cry of terror, he kicked his feet frantically, knocking all the wood away. He was free! Jumping to his feet, he saw that Sawyer had paused just short of the alcove and was looking back at him, bouncing on his feet, urging him to hurry.

"*Don't stop!*" Rane screamed. "Keep going!" He sprinted forward, arms outstretched, and covered the last bit of distance, striking Sawyer full force with his hands and shoving the small boy into the alcove. He followed, just as the walls seemed to burst around him. A deafening roar filled his ears and he screamed in pain, falling to his knees. Noise was all around and debris started to fall. The walls were collapsing! Rane struggled to get up again, crawling towards the alcove where Sawyer was crouched, his face a small white oval in the cloud of smoke that was rising up everywhere. One hand reached out towards Rane, even as chunks of ceiling started to topple between them. Rane reached out too, stretching for the hand that wanted to drag him to safety. Their fingers touched, the tips hooking together…and then a chunk of plaster fell, striking Rane on the side of the head. He collapsed, half inside the alcove, half out, and everything went black.

• • •

"No! No, please, please, please, please, no, no, no!" Eryyn continued to breathe the same words over and over as she crawled frantically towards the rubble that had once been Otto's stronghold. She had twisted her ankle when the blast had sent her sprawling to the ground, and had cut her cheek pretty badly on the concrete, but she didn't feel any of *that* pain. What she felt was a lump in her chest, a lump that burned and scalded her. A lump that no amount of screaming would release.

She crawled forward, cutting her hands on shards of glass and pieces of sharp rubble and debris that littered the sidewalk, intent only on getting into that house. She didn't hear the screams around her, the cries of horror, the wails of pain, or the shouts for help. She kept moving. Even when she felt two hands on her shoulders, lifting her to her feet.

"Eryyn! Eryyn, wait a minute, let me help you!" Liz's voice was faint, like she was far away. Then Eryyn realized that it was caused by the buzzing in her ears. She couldn't hear very well—the blast had been so loud.

"I have to get inside! I have to find him!" Eryyn said, her own voice sounding just as low and distant. "He may still be alive! I have to know!"

"I know, Eryyn, I know. I'll help you. We'll look together." Liz's pretty face was tired and very anxious. She held the girl carefully, supporting her since Eryyn could only put weight onto one foot. Together they limped towards the house.

"Hold up, you two, you can't go in there! The rest of it may collapse at any second." An Enforcer, wearing a dust covered uniform, stepped in front of them, holding out his hands to keep them from going any further. Liz recognized him as Officer Connel. She walked past, pushing him aside.

"There was a boy in there, Officer," she said dully. "A boy you should remember. We have to get to him, if he's still…" She couldn't bring herself to finish. Eryyn's eyes, turned to look up at her, were too painful. "Come on," she said to the girl. "Let's go find him."

They picked their way through the debris, stepping over chunks of wall and plaster, taking care to avoid broken glass, ducking under leaning rafters and pushing aside battered doors. The rooms were destroyed—it was hard to tell where one stopped and the other started. Their feet crunched on broken bits of wall, and slipped on pebbles and splinters of wood, but they kept looking, searching all the rubble, checking under all the debris. They couldn't find anything. Eryyn began to sob and buried her face in Liz's shirt. Liz held her closely, tears of her own pouring down her cheeks as she tried uselessly to comfort the girl. Her cries were so pitiful, so heartbreaking and sad. And then, with a start, Liz realized that the cries did not all belong to Eryyn. Someone else was crying, somewhere in the house!

"Eryyn! Eryyn, listen! Listen, do you hear that?" Liz pushed the girl away from her, holding her at arms length as she tried vainly to listen to the faint sound. Eryyn, confused, managed to slow her sobs to sniffles and cocked her head. Then she heard it—someone weeping loudly nearby.

"It's him!" she exclaimed, her eyes suddenly flashing with new life. "He's alive!" She whirled around, limping through the mess, her ankle threatening to give way beneath her as she screamed out her friend's name.

"Sawyer! Sawyer! Answer me! It's Eryyn! Sawyer, where are you?"

There was no reply, but the cries grew louder as she moved deeper into the demolished building. Liz followed behind, her ringing ears straining to hear. She looked carefully through all the debris, tears filling her eyes as she imagined Sawyer, the sweet little boy she had learned to love, stuck inside the house as it exploded around him. She held back the sudden urge to get sick, then heard Eryyn calling for her.

"*He's here!*" she was screaming. "*Liz, I found him! He's alright!*"

Liz rushed forward, tripping through the ruins. She found Eryyn leaning on a chunk of wall that was larger than a car, looking down into a small depression, her face awash with glee.

"Sawyer!" she called. "Are you okay? Sawyer, it's me! I'm so sorry! Up here, Squirt, look up."

Liz reached the girl and looked over the block of plaster. There was Sawyer, kneeling on the ground amid the piles of rubble, alive and crying, his pale face streaked with tears and blood from many scratches. He was hugging his right arm to his chest tightly and leaning over a fallen rafter, staring at something on the ground. Then Liz realized that his cries weren't just cries. They were words.

"Wake up! Please, wake up! You have to get up. You can't be

dead! Please, don't be dead, please, please, don't be…you saved me. You have to be alive. You have to!"

"Sawyer?" Liz called down. "Sweetie. Are you alright? Stay there, we're coming down to you. You're going to be fine. We'll get you out of here." She started to climb down to him, accidentally knocking loose a chunk of white plaster.

As the powdery, white rubble dropped around him, Sawyer glanced up, noticing them for the first time. His eyes, sparkling with tears, widened. "Liz?" he asked, "Eryyn?"

"Yes, sweetie, it's us. You're going to be alright."

Sawyer shook his head, confused, then pointed to the rafter. "I can't get him to wake up. He won't open his eyes, Liz. He saved me. He saved me from the bomb and now he won't wake up. Please…help me wake him up…we have to get him up."

Liz turned around and called for the other people who had started investigating the remains of the building. She shouted that she had found a survivor who needed help immediately. A man's voice answered her, telling her they were on their way. Liz climbed over the chunk of wall, and lowered herself down into the depression. A second later, Eryyn dropped beside her, wincing as she landed on her ankle. Then she was on her knees, grabbing Sawyer in her arms, hugging him tightly even as he screamed from the pain in his arm. Liz bent down beside him, looking him over, unable to stop herself from stroking his cheek lovingly. She could hardly believe that he was alive. Tears welled up in her eyes as she gazed at him. He was badly hurt—scratches on the face, his arm possibly broken, a cut on his neck bleeding profusely—but he was alive!

"Oh, thank heavens," she murmured. "Thank heavens."

Clasped in Eryyn's arms, Sawyer looked at Liz briefly, then locked his eyes behind her, beneath the rafter. He was still crying and repeating, "He won't wake up, Liz. Why won't he wake up?"

Liz turned to look, and gasped when she saw another young boy lying prone beneath the rafter, his face and arms covered in blood, his eyes closed. Stunned, she crawled over to him, mindless of the plaster that tore at her knees and the palms of her hands. She touched the child's face, her fingers coming away bloody, and winced. Then she moved her hand to his mouth, feeling for breath. There wasn't any. She glanced back at Sawyer, who was watching her anxiously. Her fears must have shown on her face, for his weeping increased and he turned to bury his face in Eryyn's chest. The girl held him tightly, whispering to him, as he sobbed, "It's not fair! It's not fair! He saved me! He pushed me and he saved me!"

Feeling tremendously sorry for the boy, for *both* boys, Liz reached out and took the still child's hand, cradling it in her own. She patted the soft palm gently, stroking the fingers up to the tips, then absently traced the line along the thumb down to the wrist. Then she felt a soft pounding beneath the skin. A pulse. This boy was alive too!

But he wouldn't be for long. The rafter was across his chest, stopping him from breathing. She had to move it. Standing up, Liz saw what had saved his life. One end of the rafter had landed on the arm of a large, overturned chair. Only this had kept the heavy wooden beam from crushing the child.

Pressing her hands against the rafter, Liz pushed hard. It rocked slightly, and the boy beneath it moaned in pain. She stopped immediately, stooping down to touch his face. He was breathing again—she'd moved the rafter enough to allow him to get air. But he was still trapped. Looking around, Liz found a long pipe, probably from the plumbing, and a piece of rock that had once been part of the wall. She set the rock down beside the rafter, using it as a fulcrum, while she pressed the pipe beneath the wood, levering it up and over. It worked. The rafter moved, toppling over behind the chair. The boy was free.

Liz dropped to her knees beside him, checking his chest again and his pulse. Using the hem of her blouse, she carefully wiped away the blood from his face, glad to see that most of it came from small scratches and scrapes. There was a large, bloody bump on the side of his head, but she couldn't do much for that. Not until help arrived. So she busied herself with cleaning him up, relieved, at least, for the sound of his breathing and the occasional moan.

Behind her, Eryyn was whispering to Sawyer. When he didn't seem to hear her, she tapped on his shoulder. "It's okay, Squirt. Look! Look what Liz did! He's okay. He's not dead. Look! He's breathing now."

Liz turned around just as Sawyer looked up. The boy's face was still covered in tears. He stared at the unconscious child, his chin trembling, then gasped with relief when he saw the boy's chest move up and then down.

"Rane?" he asked, glancing up at Liz. She nodded and smiled, reaching out a hand to him. He took it, squeezing it hard, his eyes fixed on the other boy.

"They're coming," Eryyn said, hearing footsteps through the rubble, moving towards them. Sure enough, two men dropped into the alcove an instant later, each carrying bags with medical emblems on them. Sawyer yelped, startled, as one knelt beside him, taking his hand. Liz realized the boy hadn't heard the man—hadn't heard either of them approaching—just as he hadn't noticed her or Eryyn until she had dropped the plaster down to attract his attention. Liz's felt her heart sink slightly—her *own* ears were still ringing from the blast, and Sawyer had been a *lot* closer to it than she had. She wondered what had happened to him because of that.

The boy was clinging to Eryyn at the moment, refusing to allow the man to pick him up. He continued to cry brokenly and hid his face against her shoulder. But the man was persistent, though gentle. He pulled Sawyer away from the girl, speaking to him soothingly, even though he, like Liz, seemed to have realized that Sawyer couldn't hear anything. Shaking his head sadly, he started to clean and dress the boy's wounds. The arm Sawyer had been clutching was checked over carefully, then splinted, even though the boy screamed in pain at the slightest touch of the limb.

Meanwhile, the other man had kneeled beside Liz and was working on the unconscious boy, checking him over for more damage than was apparent, wrapping an ankle and his left wrist, and fastening a plaster ring around his neck.

"Is he going to be okay?" Liz asked, looking into the boy's still, pale face. "Will he live?"

"Hard to say. He's pretty banged up. And that bump on the head could turn out to be worse than it looks. We won't know until we get him to the hospital. But the fact that he's still breathing is a good sign."

Liz sighed, relieved, then noticed the man looking her over. "You could do with a trip to the hospital yourself." He jerked his head back towards the street. "Most of the people out there needed some medical attention. I think you should come with us."

"I wouldn't have it any other way," Liz announced. She turned towards Sawyer, who was being strapped onto a long stretcher that had been brought by another pair of doctors. The boy was fighting them, resisting the straps that they were trying to fasten over his chest and legs. Standing up, Liz hurried over and grabbed Sawyer's hand.

"It's okay, sweetie," she said, when the boy turned his tearful eyes to her. "These men are trying to help—they aren't going to hurt you." She smiled reassuringly at him then glanced at the doctor who was about to administer a shot that would help Sawyer with the pain. The man nodded and patted Sawyer's hand gently.

"You're going to be just fine," he said, giving the boy the shot. Sawyer's green eyes widened at the sting of the needle, then slowly drifted closed. Liz sighed and stroked his hair lovingly.

"I'm coming with him to the hospital," she announced, as the doctors finished strapping the boy to the stretcher. "I won't let him out of my sight. Not again."

One man bobbed his head, then turned to help lift and strap the older boy onto a stretcher of his own.

A few minutes later, both boys had been carried out of what remained of the house. Liz was left behind with Eryyn, who needed her help climbing out of the depression and making her way back to the street. The girl clung tightly to her, one arm around her shoulders, the other around her waist, stepping carefully through the rubble. It wasn't until they had gone several yards that Liz suddenly realized Eryyn wasn't holding her so tight for stability. The girl was hugging her. She smiled, and hugged her back as they passed by three Enforcers who were carefully shifting the rubble, looking for signs of the Foreman.

"Do you think he's dead?" Eryyn asked.

Liz shook her head. "I don't know. I definitely hope so."

"Me too. But Sawyer's still alive. And that other boy. That's what matters. They weren't the bad ones."

Liz nodded. "That's right. They weren't. They'll be okay."

Eryyn stopped and hugged her hard. "Liz, I'm so sorry. I never should have taken the necklace from you. It was stupid. I'm really sorry. I know you won't want to be my friend anymore, but please don't be mad at Squirt. He had nothing to do with it, and he loves you. It would break his heart if…"

Liz took Eryyn by the arms and held her out so she could look her in the face, "You stop that right now," she ordered. "What happened with the necklace is forgotten! Of course I still want to be your friend! And Sawyer's too! The necklace is just a stupid thing. It's worthless. You two are important to me. I love you both, and don't you forget that."

Eryyn stared at her for a moment, her lips trembling. Then she burst into tears and flung herself into Liz's arms, sobbing as though her heart would break. Liz held her tightly, hugging her and stroking her hair.

A voice called her name and she looked up to see Greg running towards her, frantically tripping and sliding over the rubble. When he reached her, he threw his arms around her neck in a tight embrace.

"I just saw Sawyer! He's alive, but it looked like he was really hurt. They're taking him to the hospital right now."

Liz nodded. "I know. We found him. Eryyn and I." She ran her fingers through Eryyn's hair, and the girl looked up, smiling.

"Squirt's going to be okay," she said to the man. "I've got him back now, and he'll be just fine."

Greg smiled at her and touched her cheek fondly. "But how about you? That ankle looks broken. We'd better get you to the hospital too." Without waiting for her answer, Greg bent down and swept the girl up into his arms. Eryyn gasped and quickly wrapped her arms around his neck. Her grin widened.

"We'll join the Agency now," she said, resting her cheek against his shoulder. "I don't need the gang anymore. I'll make them all join the Agency, and I'll join to. With Sawyer."

"Oh, I don't think you two will have to join," Greg replied, winking at Liz. The young woman felt her heart soar at the expression on his face and tears filled her eyes as she mouthed the words, "Thank you," to her husband.

Eryyn looked confused. "What do you mean?" she asked. "I thought you wanted us in the Agency."

"You'll see," Greg said. He started carrying her through the rubble, out to the street, where the doctors where waiting to transport all the people who had been injured in the blast to the hospitals.

Liz stood quietly for a minute, watching the two before moving to follow. She clasped her hands tightly against her chest, feeling amazingly happy despite all that had happened. She wondered if Eryyn, as Greg carried her towards one of the ambulances, had guessed what the man had meant. Had guessed that she was not just a young street girl that Greg was carrying out of the demolished building, but his new daughter.

• • •

The Foreman had him! Was holding his wrist and refusing to let him go as he dragged him through the house towards the yawing hole in the floor. Sawyer struggled desperately against the man, but he couldn't get away! The Foreman was hauling him to the tunnel, down the stairs, into the darkness…

With a gasp of horror, Sawyer awoke and sat up in the bed, his heart pounding furiously against his chest. Sweat poured down his forehead as he continued to breathe harshly. His eyes wide, he looked around the room, searching frantically for the evil face of the man who had held him prisoner.

There was nothing. The Foreman was nowhere to be seen. The room was dim, but Sawyer could see that there was no one around. He was alone. Slowly, as his breathing calmed, he studied the room around him. It was strange—this wasn't the main room of the nest, nor was it the dark room where he had been held captive, tied to the chair. Even though there wasn't much light, Sawyer could see that the walls were painted yellow, and were very clean. The floor was tiled, and almost completely covered in large machines. Machines with glowing words and numbers on their screens and lots of tubes and wires, most of which ran across the floor, up the side of the bed—bed?—and were attached…to him!

Dumb-struck, he lifted his hands and looked at them. One, the right one, was completely encased in a solid white sleeve all the way up to his elbow and hurt badly when he moved it, while the left was festooned with little wires and tubes that were taped on—and *into!*— his skin! Plastic bags of liquid hung from a rack next to the bed, and Sawyer could see, from following the tubes, that the bags were dripping their contents into him.

The movement of looking up caused his head to hurt terribly and he reached up, gingerly touching his forehead and finding little pads stuck to him there. More pads were stuck to his arms and chest.

Where was he? What was going on? What were all these weird things?

Without warning, bright light flooded the room and Sawyer squeezed his stinging eyes shut with a hiss of pain. Then hands were touching him, patting his head and his arms, running through his hair. Feeling surrounded, he wriggled away and would have fallen off the bed if not for the thick plastic fence that surrounded the sides. Warily, a bit at a time, he opened his eyes to see faces before him. Slowly, those faces became familiar and he recognized them as Liz, Eryyn, and Greg. All were smiling, looking at him anxiously, and Liz was saying something. At least, her lips were *moving* like she was saying something, but no words were coming out. Confused, Sawyer shook his head. Eryyn leaned closer and spoke, but nothing came out of *her* mouth either!

What was going on? Why weren't they talking to him, telling him where he was, and what had happened? His head began to hurt more and tears formed at the corners of his eyes, stinging them as badly as the light.

Then, like a sudden flash of lightning, it all came back to him. The stronghold...Rane helping him...something about a bomb in the house...the Foreman catching them. There had been a gaping hole in the middle of the floor...an explosion...it was all coming back, every horrible detail. The destroyed house...the pain of his broken arm...Rane's pale, bloody face. Rane had saved his life, but had been badly hurt.

"Rane!" Sawyer cried suddenly, though no sound reached his ears. "Where's Rane!"

Beside the bed, Liz, Greg, and Eryyn were looking at him worriedly. Liz started to speak again, but Sawyer didn't hear her. That's when he realized that he couldn't hear *anything*. Not Liz, or Greg, or Eryyn, not even himself! He couldn't even hear his own breathing!

"No!" he screamed, seeing his friends flinch although the room around him stayed silent. No, this wasn't right! Why couldn't he hear them? Where was Rane? Why did they all look so worried?

Whimpering, Sawyer curled up under the thin blanket that covered him to his chest. The tubes and wires pulled and stretched against his skin and his arm throbbed madly. But his head hurt the most. Pain screamed behind his eyes and he squeezed them shut, blocking out the pain, blocking out the room and the people he couldn't hear. He felt hands touching him, trying to turn him over again, but he fought back, wriggling and curling up tighter until they left him alone. Tears squeezed out from beneath his closed eyelids, soaking his cheeks and dripping onto the blankets. And, in the darkness, Sawyer began to cry. He cried because of the pain, and the strangeness of the room, and for not being able to hear. He cried for the terror he had felt in the house, when the Foreman had had him, and when the bomb went off. And he cried for Rane, because the boy had saved his life, and because he didn't know if Rane was alive or not. He cried until another set of hands started to touch him, and he felt a stinging pain on his arm, and then, mercifully, he fell back to sleep.

• • •

"It was too much for him," Greg said, watching the nurse as she recapped the needle that had been used to administer the sedative to Sawyer. "He couldn't take it, not so much, so soon."

"He couldn't hear us!" Eryyn said, staring at the sleeping form of her best friend. "Didn't you see him? He couldn't hear us, and he was so scared!" Grabbing onto Greg's arm, Eryyn leaned closer to him and started to cry.

Liz immediately knelt down beside her, reaching up to stroke the girl's face. "He'll be alright, Eryyn. He was overwhelmed, that's all. A lot of horrible things happened to him yesterday, and he just couldn't stand to remember them yet. Plus, he's in a strange place, and in a lot of pain, too. He just needs a little time to be able to understand everything."

Eryyn turned her face to look at the young woman, tears shimmering on her cheeks. "But he looked so scared! How can he *ever* get over what happened to him?"

Greg hugged her close. "Sawyer's a tough little guy, Eryyn. It's surprising what kids can live through. He's made it this far, hasn't he?"

Eryyn nodded and sniffed back her tears. "But it's going to be so hard for him, I know it."

"*We're* here, Eryyn," Liz comforted. "He has us to help him, and to protect him. He was scared today, but he'll soon find out that no one is going to hurt him anymore. That he's safe now."

Eryyn nodded again and allowed the nurse to lead her out of the room so Sawyer could rest. Liz and Greg stayed a little longer, watching the small boy as he slept soundly on the hospital bed.

Suddenly, Liz turned away and started dabbing at her eyes with a handkerchief. Greg put an arm around her shoulders, holding her close as he whispered, "It's going to be alright now. You don't have to cry."

"I know," Liz said brokenly, wiping at her damp cheeks. "I know. But I can't help it. I feel so helpless when I think about how frightened he looked when he saw us. He was terrified, Greg, absolutely terrified. And despite what we told Eryyn, I can't help but wonder if he *will* be okay—if he'll ever be able to feel safe again, once he finds out that they never found the Foreman."

• • •

Sawyer awoke slowly, drifting upward from a warm, comfortable haze, and realized that, for the first time in days, he didn't have a headache. That thrilled him, and he quickly turned to the chair beside his bed where Liz was dozing.

Eight days had passed since the stronghold had exploded and Eryyn and Liz had found him in the ruined remains of the alcove. Since then, he'd been in the hospital, as one of the star patients. He had a room of his own, with a large bed, clean sheets, and *lots* of expensive machines that monitored every part of his body and let the doctors know how he was doing.

Seeing that Liz was still asleep, not wanting to wake her, he glanced at the nearest machine, which recorded the beating of his heart. For a few minutes he lay there, watching the jagged green lines move across the dark screen, coupled with the gentle *bip beep bip beep* that was his heartbeat. That occupied him for a time, but soon grew boring. He turned to the IV lines, looking at the tubes that ran liquid medicines down from the bags on the stand and into his hand. The needles that had inserted the tubes had been uncomfortable, but the pain had passed now, and Sawyer was merely fascinated by what the doctors were using to make him well. In fact, the *whole* process of the hospital, now that everything had been explained to him, was fascinating.

He felt eyes on him then and looked again to Liz. She was awake, just barely, and smiling at him.

"Morning," he said brightly, trying to sit up so he could see her better. Liz was on her feet in an instant, helping him and fluffing the pillow under his head so it would support him. "You don't have to do that," Sawyer complained. "I'm fine. Really."

"I want to," Liz replied, laughing. "Just humor me."

Sawyer returned her smile—it was good to be able to hear her voice again. For the first few days after the explosion, he hadn't been able to hear *anything* except a harsh, annoying hissing in his ears. It had terrified him, being deaf and seeing lips moving without making a sound, and he'd been immensely relieved when he'd finally recovered some of his hearing. It wasn't much—sometimes he still had to strain to hear what people were saying—but the doctors said that, in time, his ears would work again properly. Good to know. Reading lips wasn't any fun.

"Where's Eryyn?" he asked, after giving Liz a quick hug.

"Right here." Eryyn hobbled into the room on crutches, smiling widely. She was clean, her hair combed neatly, and wearing nice clothes. After the doctors had put a cast on her broken ankle, she had gone home, under protest, with Greg, but she came to the hospital everyday to see him. Liz stayed at the hospital all the time, leaving Greg to take care of the Agency house with Carmen. It was full now, so Liz and Eryyn had told him, with all the members of the green bands, and all the kids from the red and gold gang too. Caulin was there, helping out a lot, and so were Cinder and Jay. None of them had been seriously hurt in the blast and had only spent a few hours in the hospital before being released into the care of the Agency workers.

"How are you feeling, Squirt?" Eryyn asked, using her crutches to limp up to the bed.

"Better," Sawyer answered. "No headache."

"That's good," Liz said, raising her eyebrows approvingly. The on-going headache had worried her.

"How about the arm?"

Sawyer lifted his broken arm, which was wrapped in a snow-white sheet of hard plaster. It itched like a fleabite, but hardly hurt anymore. He told them this and received two laughs.

"I think you're really on your way to recovering," Liz said, laying a hand on his forehead. "You may be able to come home soon."

Sawyer's smile brightened. Home was not going to be the Agency house, but with Liz and Greg. That's what had been explained to him, written on a pad of paper, when he'd woken up the third time. Liz and Greg were adopting both him *and* Eryyn, filling their two kid quota with one paper signing. They were planning on buying, with the new, larger, credit allowance they were getting for running the Agency, the apartment next to theirs and tearing out a few walls to make it large enough for a family of four. It was to be complete with two bedrooms for the kids, and lots of shelf space for toys and books. The thought really appealed to Sawyer and he gave Liz a pleading look. "Can't I go home now? I'm better, aren't I?"

"That's not for me to decide," Liz said, tapping him on the nose. There was a small scrape there that was healing over nicely and Liz kept telling him that the mark looked like a little heart. She'd even shown it to him in a mirror, and he'd had to admit she was right. He was going to have a tiny heart-shaped scar on the bridge of his nose. "You have to wait until the doctors say so. I think they still want to run a few more tests and wait until your ears are better. Probably just a few more days."

Sawyer groaned and dropped back on the bed, staring at the ceiling. The hospital may have been fascinating, but it was incredibly annoying when you wanted to be someplace else even more. Then he sat up again. "What about Rane? Can't I at least go and see Rane?"

Liz looked at Eryyn, then back at the little boy. Sawyer had been asking about Rane since the first time he'd awakened in the hospital and every other time since. He wanted to know how the other boy was doing, and had become very depressed and angry when they wouldn't tell him anymore than that Rane was alive.

Now, seeing their look, he frowned deeply. "Why won't you let me see him?" he asked, making a fist with his good hand and slamming it onto the sheets. "He saved my life! I want to see him. I want to know how he's doing."

Liz nodded. "I know you do, sweetie, I know. But Rane's in a different part of the hospital. He was hurt worse than you were, and he's going to be here for a lot longer. The doctors are watching over him very closely and you have to have their permission to see him."

"Can't you get it? Can't you ask? Or if you could bring one of them in here, *I* could ask them. They all like me."

Liz laughed at the confidence in his voice. "Who doesn't? You have a heart on your nose. That makes you very likeable."

Sawyer wasn't going to be distracted, though he did favor the young woman with another smile. "Please?" he begged.

"Oh, alright. I'll ask them." Liz stood up, hesitated for a second, then left the room. Once she was gone, Sawyer turned to Eryyn, wanting to talk to her about something he hadn't yet had a chance to.

"I heard you that night," he said. "In the alley."

Eryyn nodded. "I saw you. You started to turn around. Then you stopped."

Sawyer blinked. "The Foreman wouldn't let me. He kept yelling at me and threatening to hit me. I-I was too scared."

"I don't blame you. I would have been too."

"You're not mad at me for running off like an idiot and getting myself caught?" Sawyer ducked his chin a little, looking sad and upset. "It's all my fault that we got into this trouble in the first place."

"No, it's not." Eryyn sat down on the edge of his bed to rest her ankle. She folded her crutches up beside her. "It was an *accident*, that's all. We *both* made mistakes that night, and we had to pay for them. But things worked out okay anyway."

"You sound like Greg," Sawyer quipped.

Eryyn laughed. "He's the one who told me that. Exact words, actually."

"I thought so." Sawyer fell silent, looking at the bedspread that covered him to his waist. "I heard some of the nurses talking—they didn't know I was awake at the time—and they were saying that the Foreman isn't dead, and that no one knows where he is. Is that true?"

Eryyn winced, not wanting to be the one to give her friend this news. "Yeah, Squirt, it's true. They're thinking that he's still alive—they found this door in the stronghold that led to a tunnel underground. They think he escaped through there."

Sawyer nodded slowly, shuddering. "He was trying to take me and Rane down there before the bomb went off. He said he was gonna go somewhere else, start over again, and that he was gonna take us with him."

Eryyn couldn't think of anything to say to that. Instead, she reached out and grasped Sawyer's hand, thinking about how close she had come to losing the boy for good. She blinked away a few tears that started to sting her eyes, not wanting Sawyer to see her crying, then took a deep breath and said, "You don't have to worry, though. The Enforcers are looking really hard for him, 'cuz now they have a description from all of Otto's kids. They'll catch him soon. And besides, Greg and Liz aren't gonna let anyone try to hurt us again, they said so."

Sawyer chewed on his lip for a minute, staring at one of the tubes that ran into his hand. "What about all his gangs?" he finally asked. "They're free now, right?"

Eryyn breathed a sigh of relief and instantly launched into the more promising subject. "Yup. And the Enforcers are checking all the factories he owned, taking the underage kids out of them and putting them into the Agency. They've come up with this new rule that any homeless kid, legal or not, can live in the Agency until they're adopted, or they turn sixteen and can apply for a job and maybe earn their citizenship. The Enforcers have even come up with a payment for families who adopt an illegal kid and make him or her legal. You should see how many kids are showing up now! Greg and Carmen are really going to have their hands full."

Sawyer grinned brightly at this news, then quickly sobered again. "Did they ever find the other guy?"

"Other guy?"

"The one who kidnapped me. The one who was working for the Foreman."

Eryyn hadn't heard anything about Flint the bounty hunter, though the Enforcers were searching for him now, following Sawyer's hazy description. It was possible that he had gotten wind of the search and moved on to another city. They might never catch him. Eryyn mentioned this and Sawyer nodded, though he didn't look happy.

"He scared me almost as much as the Foreman," he murmured. "It's really bad if they *both* got away."

Eryyn was about to reply, but was interrupted by Liz, who returned, pushing a wheelchair in front of her.

"Guess what?" Liz said, smiling radiantly. "You get to go on a visiting tour, as long as you make it a ride."

"Fine with me!" Sawyer exclaimed. He smiled just as brightly as Liz and Eryyn helped him off the bed and onto the chair, wrapping him securely in a small blanket.

"Here we go," Liz said, turning the chair by tilting it back and whirling it around.

They wheeled Sawyer slowly through the hospital corridors, answering all the questions he had to ask about certain equipment they passed, or certain jobs the doctors performed, or certain medicines they gave to the patients. He never seemed to run out of questions.

"Sheesh, you're learning so much you could grow up to be a doctor," Eryyn noted. Neither Sawyer nor Liz seemed displeased with the idea.

Then, as they approached the area of the hospital where Rane was being kept, Sawyer fell quiet and thoughtful. He continued to look around curiously, but the machines here seemed more important, the doctors busier. The people in this wing of the hospital needed more care than the patients in his own brightly-colored, pediatric hall. It was sad to think that Rane had to be here.

Liz continued to push the chair through the corridors, smiling and returning greetings from doctors they passed, asking directions every now and then. Finally, they came to a room that was mainly windows. Pink curtains had been drawn closed over the glass, making it impossible to see in, but when Liz spoke to one of the nurses, the woman obligingly pulled one curtain back, allowing a view into the small chamber.

Sawyer stood up from the chair and put his hands against the window, looking in. It was a sad sight.

Rane was lying on the bed, covered to the chest in a blue blanket, his eyes closed. He seemed dwarfed by all the machinery around him and had more tubes hooked up than Sawyer believed possible. One even ran into his nose.

Sawyer frowned and turned to Liz, who read his questions off his face.

"He's doing a lot better, sweetie. It looks much worse than it really is. Rane's going to be just fine. He's even woken up a few times and doesn't seem to have forgotten anything."

"Why would he forget anything?" Sawyer asked, returning his gaze to the boy behind the glass.

"Rane was unconscious because he got a bad knock on the head when the building collapsed. Sometimes, when a person gets hit on the head, they start to forget things. Because their brain is injured. The doctors have figured that that hasn't happened to Rane. But he does have three broken ribs, and he had some trouble breathing when they first brought him in here, which is why they had to put an aspirator in his nose—it helps him breathe easier. He also has a broken ankle, a broken wrist, lots of bruises and cuts, and a condition called whiplash from the explosion. That's something that hurt his back. The doctors were surprised that you didn't have it too."

"I was protected," Sawyer replied solemnly. He continued to stare at the boy who had risked his life to save him. Rane had run back into the stronghold to free him, even though he had known there was a bomb. Sawyer was never going to forget that.

"There's something else, Sawyer," Liz said, touching his shoulder gently and interrupting his thoughts. Sawyer didn't turn away from the glass, just asked, "What else?"

"Remember how you couldn't hear anything after the explosion, and how it took a few days to get even some of your hearing back?"

Sawyer turned to look at her and nodded, suddenly worried.

"Well, the same thing happened to Rane. Only...only the doctors don't think he'll get his hearing back as soon as you did. In fact, he may not get it back at all."

Sawyer was horrified. "He's deaf?" he asked. "He can't hear *any-*

thing?"

"Well, a little bit after the first few days. But it hasn't gotten any better since then. Yes, sweetie, they have a bad feeling that Rane is going to be mostly deaf."

Sawyer bit down hard on his lip. "It's all because of me. Because he came back to save me." He looked through the glass again. "He didn't even know me very well and he still saved me."

"He's gonna get better," Eryyn murmured reassuringly.

Something else caught Sawyer's attention. Rane's unbandaged right wrist was lying out on the sheet, exposed to full view. It had a flimsy, plastic hospital I.D. bracelet on it, but not the silver bracelet of a legal citizen. Sawyer glanced down at his own wrist, and his own I.D., then whirled around to Liz again.

"What's going to happen to him after he leaves the hospital?" he demanded. "Rane's not legal. He doesn't have a bracelet. Eryyn's gonna have a bracelet once you and Greg adopt us, so she'll be legal. But you can't adopt Rane too. What are they going to do with him? Are they gonna send him to the Agency, even if he can't hear anything?"

This gave Liz a chance to smile—she had a happy answer to this question.

"Don't worry, sweetie," she said, "Nothing bad is ever going to happen to Rane again. You remember Carmen?"

Sawyer nodded—Carmen was the chubby woman who worked with Liz and was helping out with the Agency. He'd met her several times and thought she was really nice, very energetic and bubbly.

"Well, a few days ago, Carmen came in to see how you were doing. She was worried because she'd heard that you'd been hurt. You were asleep at the time and she didn't want me to wake you up. So I told her everything that had happened, including what Rane did for you. She demanded to see Rane after that, and the doctors actually let her come down here and she got to meet him during one of the times when he was awake, and guess what?"

Sawyer shook his head.

"Carmen said that a hero like Rane deserved a good home as soon as possible. She's going to adopt Rane herself and take him home once he's ready. He'll get a bracelet of his own and he'll never have to worry about being in a gang again."

"She doesn't care that he's going to be deaf?" Eryyn asked, her eyes on the boy behind the window.

"Carmen loves a challenge. Rane's going to be just fine. He'll have a good family now."

Sawyer smiled wanly, turning back to peer through the glass. Suddenly, he began to cry and his legs gave out on him. He slid to the floor, covering his eyes with both hands.

Liz and Eryyn both jumped forward to pick him up and help him back into the chair. Several doctors and nurses walking by glanced over, curious. Liz told them that everything was fine, then bent over so she could talk with the sobbing child.

"What is it, sweetie? Are you okay? Does something hurt?"

"No," Sawyer cried. "Yes! I don't know. It's just...he looks so *sad* lying there. He was so badly hurt, and none of it was his fault! Why did it have to happen, Liz? Why did the Foreman have to do that? Why would he want to kill so many kids? None of them had ever hurt him before!" Sawyer broke down, sobbing helplessly. When Liz hugged him he turned to her, hiding his face against her shirt. Liz lifted him into her arms and started walking away down the hall, leaving the wheelchair where it was. Eryyn followed on her crutches.

"I probably shouldn't have brought you here. Not yet. It was too soon," she whispered. On her shoulder, Sawyer shook his head, but couldn't stop crying. Through his tears, he managed to gasp, "I had to see him. I just didn't know..."

Eryyn put her hand on her friend's arm, squeezing it gently until Sawyer offered a hand to hold. She took it and squeezed it instead, smiling encouragingly.

Liz brought Sawyer back to his room, put him in his bed, and covered him with the blanket. Sawyer looked up at her and gave her a tiny smile, which quickly wavered, then disappeared. She smiled back and patted his arm. Ten minutes later, he had fallen asleep, and she was sitting in her chair by his bed, staring out the window thoughtfully.

She knew that their problems weren't over yet—that, even though the physical wounds were already fading, the emotional healing was going to take a lot of time for all of them. Rane included. And it wouldn't be easy in the hospital, seeing so many people in pain and being reminded of all that had happened to them. Really, they couldn't begin to soothe the scars inside until they were at home, where they'd have lots of love and plenty of quiet time for rest. Then things would get better.

Eryyn, sitting on the edge of the bed, suddenly reached out and touched Liz's hand, gesturing towards Sawyer.

"He looks better now," she said quietly.

Liz looked down into his face, peaceful now in sleep, then smiled at Eryyn. The girl seemed much happier now that her gang life was behind her and she was settling into the house.

Yes. That's when the true healing would really begin. When they were all home, safe and sound. Liz felt her smile widen at the thought. She couldn't wait to get her new children home, so they could finally be a family.

Eryyn seemed to be thinking the same thing. She leaned forward and gave Sawyer a gentle kiss on the cheek. "You were right, Squirt," she whispered, lifting his hand and pressing the scar on his thumb to the matching one on her own. "All this time, you were right. Dreams really do come true."

In his sleep, Sawyer murmured softly and smiled.

The End

Printed in the United States
19089LVS00002BA/190-195